The Capricious Nature of Being

The Capricious Nature of Being

A Collection
of Stories

Richard Plinke

Internet addresses given in this book were accurate at the time it went to press.

This book is a work of fiction. All of the names, characters, events and incidents in this book are a product of the author's imagination. Any resemblance to actual persons or events is purely coincidental and not intentional. If long-standing institutions, agencies, public buildings and geographical locations are mentioned, the characters and events surrounding them are wholly imaginary.

Printed in the United States of America
Published in Hellertown, PA
Cover design by Dina Hall
Library of Congress Control Number 2025902496
ISBN 979-8-89420-042-2
For more information or to place bulk orders, contact the author or the publisher at Jennifer@BrightCommunications.net.

In Memory of
Jonathan Bortz
1991-2014

CONTENTS

The Capricious Nature of Being

Have you ever noticed that the only thing in life you can count on, the only thing you can be sure of, the only thing you can really expect is the unexpected?

> *But Mousie, thou art no thy-lane,*
> *In proving foresight may be vain:*
> *The best laid schemes o' Mice an' Men*
> *Gang aft agley,*
> *An' lea'e us nought but grief an' pain,*
> *For promis'd joy!*

In his famous poem, "To a Mouse," Robert Burns may have been ostensibly writing about a mouse whose life gets turned upside-down when a farmer plows over his carefully planned world, but he may very well have been writing about all of us and the folly we deceive ourselves with that we have control over our existence.

We do not.

Most literature basically boils down to that simple premise, that life is a Secret Santa, and despite your hopeful expectations, you never know what you're getting until you open the propitiously decorated package. Good writing should balance that intrigue, taking the reader through the twists and turns of dark passages, narrow roadways and promisingly consequential journeys, leaving one in an unexpected and provocative place. And that unexpected and provocative place can be the beginning or the end, a treasure of new opportunities and possibilities, or the unintended entanglement of imminent demise.

Whichever outcome attends us is usually a matter of perspective—how do we perceive the world around us and how do we process unexpected and transformative change; how do we navigate through those unforeseen and often unwelcomed twist and turns that seem to befall us mortals by the whim of some apathetic hand?

As flies to wanton boys are we to the gods; they kill us for their sport.

Life's a box of chocolates and all that. In this collection of stories, I have endeavored to illustrate a bit of that capricious nature of being.

I hope you enjoy it.

The Safe

She sat cross-legged on the floor in front of the anachronistic monstrosity, trying to decide what to do. Should she open it and chance the release of who-knows-what dramas—what new sufferings—or let the auction company haul it away, unopened and safe, along with the other well-worn, barely salvageable furniture in her father's home office?

The black, ponderous box at one time had boasted rather impertinently on its door "Alpine Safe & Lock Co., Cincinnati, O. U.S.A." in gold, 19th-century script spread symmetrically around the handle and dial, but the letters had practically faded away to oblivion, emblematic of her own life. The safe had been in the corner of her father's office since before she could remember, sitting like an inscrutable Buddha, collecting dust and lives.

What was it Hal, her father's young law partner, had told her in one of their conversations about settling her father's affairs? "There are some things people aren't meant to see."

"You mean that I'm not meant to see, don't you?" Hope had asked, more of an accusation than a question because she already knew the answer.

Here I sit, she thought, *the virtuous daughter of good Presbyterians—played it by the rules, assiduously, earnestly, wholly devoted, and for what? No drink or smoke has touched these lips, no drugs, gambling, or cloaked skeletons looming precariously in the closet next to my prom dress. What you see is what you get, a virgo intacta, technically but still principally intact at the ripe old age of 61, like a vintage car that somebody's grandmother only drove to church on Sundays, virtually unblemished and still looking for that elusive something, that promise to bring it all into focus, to make sense of it—no, not closure, more a glue to put it all together, to make things stick.*

Or maybe to make them unstick?

Can I find that in my father's secret life locked behind the thick steel door? Not hardly, she told herself as a wry smile crossed her face. Some secrets are better left secret.

Hope's mother had died from colorectal cancer more than 20 years ago, leaving her father alone … and terrified. Hope had stepped in to fill the void, acting as his companion and caretaker until his death two days after his 86th birthday. Of course, that meant giving up her precious career and perfectly pristine home with little observable life within and moving back into the snow globe of her youth, as imaginary and fictitious as the delicate, decorative displays her mother arrayed at Christmas. But this ostensibly transparent sphere was never shaken, and the one time it was, mistakenly, it never stopped snowing.

There was a time when Hope was engaged to a young man in med school, but that relationship couldn't withstand the snowstorm, a storm she could have weathered if only she'd been able to break out of her cocoon of God-fearing-construction, surrounding her in the guise of protection, but instead, stifling and belying promise, leaving an unfulfilled life of synthetic incrimination. But that was a long time ago, before she'd become an old maid, a prochronism in term and substance she hoped, because she didn't want to believe it—not yet. She hadn't planned it this way; it's just what happened on its own volition, like a runaway train, careening down the tracks, out of control, on course to … where? Despair? Disillusionment? No, that can't be it; that's already familiar ground. Maybe it's a journey with no discernable conclusion, as vacant and worthless as snow falling on little plastic people in little plastic worlds where nothing ever changes.

Hope had graduated college with a degree in English literature and obtained a job as a proofreader with a large book-publishing company. Growing up, she had dreamed of becoming a writer, but a couple of creative writing courses had convinced her that she was better at critiquing than creating, so she chose to pursue a career in editing. Before she had succumbed to her obsessive need to correct not just verbiage, but thoughts and consequences as well, before she heard the siren's call to fix the unfixable and moved back in with her dispirited father, her job had been her safe haven—a respite, a place to hide once the fear set in, the agoraphobia she wouldn't treat, wouldn't even allow herself to identify, hidden safely in her attained position as senior editor where she controlled not only the printed words in front of her but the lives of the people writing those words. *If only I could control my own life as effectively,* she contemplated as she sat on the cold, wooden floor, staring at the safe.

Her father had continued to work at his downtown law offices a couple of days a week until he was in his late 70s, but he still kept the files of many clients locked in his safe at home. Hal told Hope that her father sedulously kept duplicate files so he could work at home, and Hal wanted those files. There were also personal papers, insurance policies and other documents in the safe Hal would need to settle her father's estate. Her father had given the combination to Hal, along with instructions—according to Hal—that only Hal was allowed to open it.

Hope was having none of it. As executrix to her father's estate, she overruled Hal and told him she would deliver the files and papers he needed to his office, much to Hal's consternation and objections.

"Your father was quite explicit in his instructions," Hal protested.

"Well, I'm in charge now," Hope said with the confidence of someone who had spent years confronting temperamental writers.

"But I have the combination," Hal countered.

"So do I."

Hal took a palpable breath. "Your father told me that nobody else had the combination. And there are some things in there that I had the impression he didn't want you to see."

"We won't worry about that now, will we? Thank you, Hal. I'll be by tomorrow," Hope said to decisively conclude the conversation.

She now held the combination, handwritten on a slip of paper, in her left hand and inspected it with contrition and foreboding.

I should never have seen this, she told herself.

It had been her parents' 25th wedding anniversary, and Hope and her brother planned a surprise celebration. Hope had the idea of getting their marriage license blown up and hanging it on a wall in the banquet room, and she was sure the license was kept in the safe. How to get in the safe was a dilemma, though—a seemingly insurmountable obstacle. Hope's brother had suggested they instead blow up a picture of the colorful plate hanging in the dining room. Some years earlier, their mother had taken a ceramics class and made an overelaborate plate to commemorate her marriage. On it, she had prominently placed the date of the wedding: April 16, 1960.

They decided to make that the backup plan; first Hope wanted to try to get into the safe. She called a locksmith, who told her that he could open it but that it would be messy and costly. That solution was out of the question, so Hope asked if he could pick the lock. The locksmith laughed and told her she'd been watching too much television. He advised she first try to find the combination.

"Most people write down the combination and hide it," he told her. "They do things like tape it to the bottom of a desk drawer or write it on the back of a picture in their wallet. Look in places like that."

Hope had no luck with the desk drawers, but struck gold—fool's gold—when she snuck her father's wallet out of his bedroom one morning while he showered and her mother was making breakfast. The combination was written on the back of a picture of her parents, holding each other and smiling. *What a sweet, sentimental man,* she thought—a thought that didn't last long. When she opened the safe and found the marriage certificate, she was confused at first, then horrified. The date on the license was June 11, 1960, and Hope's birthday was January 21, 1961, dates that were just seven months apart.

Sitting in the dining room all those Sundays, birthdays, Easters, Christmases and other family celebrations, the formal center of our family, hanging there on the wall, a blasphemous lie, a scandalous misrepresentation of all that was held to be righteous and sanctified, a constant reminder of the fraud perpetrated against everything I'd been taught to believe, she thought.

My own parents!

Hope wrestled with the implausible concept. *De-ceivers! Liars! Sinners! A lifetime of inherited reproach, my burden and legacy. And what other secrets lie within those indifferent, unforgiving walls of merciless iron? Open that door and people's lives come tumbling out, spilling onto the floor, never to be swept away, like my story, all waiting to be told, some inconsequential, some momentous, some arbitrary, some impetuous, but all here for the taking.*

Still holding the slip of paper containing the combination to the old safe, an artifact written many years earlier in her youthfully concise handwriting and contemplating the capricious nature of being, Hope reached out with her other hand and turned the dial.

The Door

1

It was the great post-midday-meal-meltdown, as predictable and regular as Mussolini's trains.

And it was hard on Winton, but a circadian rhythm ruled his will.

He had an endless supply of energy and creative juices in the morning, but after lunch, his imagination and vigor dissipated into a dull haze, sending him into a stupor-like trance where his brain couldn't jam it into gear. He tried to fight through it with coffee, Red Bull, 5-hour Energy and other caffeinated, stomach-lining disruptors, but it was useless—he just wasn't an afternoon guy. Much like the character Turkey in Herman Melville's *Bartleby, the Scrivener*, who, too, was useless in the afternoon. Unfortunately, Winton had no counterpart like Nippers, who was no good in the morning, but productive in the afternoon. Like the draft and draw gears in the coupling of railroad cars, Turkey, the morning guy and Nippers, the afternoon guy, fit together to make a whole: one good employee.

Winton hated the idea that he was like that—half an employee—but comforted himself with the knowledge that he revved up again after his noontide torpor wore off, and he finished the day strong.

But in the middle of the day, he was a vagrant. That was easier to deal with when he'd been in sales, out on the road with the freedom to pull into parking lots or a rest area and take a short power nap, quickly restoring his high-level octane. It all changed when he accepted the position of sales manager, a much less mobile job that kept him chained to a desk for most of the day. The exception to that dull routine came when he was spending time with one of his salespeople out in the field—which was even more torturous because he had to muster up a massive effort to stay focused and "in the moment," a cliché he'd come to hate. At least in the office he could bury his head in his computer and look like he was accomplishing something.

Which is what our hero was doing on this fine day: perusing sites of a lascivious nature and, even more insidious, Facebook.

In truth, Winton, like many people who are compulsively drawn to the ubiquitous social media platform (like taking another shot of morphine), hated Facebook, but the site was addictive. And Winton Fine was definitely a user. With much condemnation, he religiously read the hateful posts about haters, the judgmental rantings against judgmental cretins, the myopic opinions about narrow-minded Neanderthals, and especially the sanctimonious posts from the PC police who seemed rather flexible relative to their current attitudinal adjustment.

He was especially mystified by people and their cats. Why did they need to post pictures of their cats every day, many ridiculous, some disturbingly inappropriate? He thought cats were more secure in themselves, but apparently, their owners didn't share that same self-confidence. Maybe this was some kind of group sublimation for overcoming feelings of inadequacy to dog owners?

And where were those dog people? Where were the pictures of dogs wearing cute bonnets or rolling in fields of dandelions? Were the dog people's relationships with their pets so serene that they felt little need to broadcast them all over the world? Did they not have to remind everyone all the time that they loved their animals more than anyone else loved their animal, ever?

As was the case with people compelled to proclaim undying love and enduring gratitude to their partner, describing the relationship as strong and endurable as the Great Wall of China, in language straight out of a Hallmark greeting card. *What the hell was that all about?* he wondered. *What are they covering up? Or wishing for? Or praying that lots of pretty words can change reality. Like throwing perfume on a skunk's stink.*

Winton knew better—from experience. *That didn't work.*

And maybe that's why he was drawn to this cyber land of broken toys. He knew the territory and could spot all the trail signs.

Like the meme with the blue-and-red doors that popped up in his news feed.

2

Winton loved being in sales. He didn't know he loved being in sales until he was no longer in sales. What he didn't love, and what he knew he didn't love, was being a sales manager. Accepting the job was a mistake, one he regretted every day for the past two years, ever since stepping into the shoes of his adored old boss who had died prematurely. But Winton's wife, Yayla, wanted the security and stability of the management position.

He had a degree in chemical engineering from Lehigh University, and chemical engineering was where he always saw himself. Upon graduation, he had planned to pursue his doctorate and eventually work on the leading edge of scientific development and discovery. He wanted to change the world, to make it a better, safer place. Winton Fine had high hopes and aspirations. He wanted to be an important man.

Instead, he became a salesman.

That's because he was saddled with so much student loan debt that he had no choice but to go to work paying it off. His parents were working class and didn't have the resources to contribute much to an education at an expensive private college, but they made enough to disqualify him for any need-based grants. In Winton's keen sense of irony, he knew that ridiculous catch-22 existed primarily because those affected couldn't be easily defined as a voting bloc. He was a good student and had secured a partial scholarship, but even with some other small assistance, he received along the way, like work-study programs, 20-plus grand a year was daunting, and most of the heavy lifting fell on Winton.

It took him over 15 years to free himself from that albatross.

He did that by being the top producer at Biochemical Lubricants Incorporated, selling metalworking fluids and industrial lubricants to light and heavy industry throughout the Northeastern United States. He traveled a great deal peddling his wares, and that absenteeism was one of the things Yayla wanted to stop.

And one of the things Winton missed most. He loved driving from town to town, meeting new people, sampling the local flavor and simply enjoying the freedom he found in being his own boss and making his own schedule. But being tied to an office day in and day out was killing him. He was sure that after another few years on the job, he'd be flatlining in the back of an ambulance pulling out of BLI's parking lot.

Regrettably, that was only part of Winton's misery, although he supposed it was all tied together somehow.

3

They'd seen a marriage counselor, but that only made things worse. *As if that were possible,* Winton thought as he pedaled his expensive bicycle along the Delaware and Lehigh rail trail that paralleled the Lehigh River, cutting diagonally through the Lehigh Valley and dumping into the Delaware River and on out to sea.

His daily rides were his salvation. Most days (weather permitting—and sometimes, when he was overly stressed and confused, when the weather wasn't so permitting) around 4 p.m., after the first shift of the plant shut down and all the secretaries and support staff had gone home, he would practically run to the men's locker room in the production facility to change into his riding gear. In the winter months when the sun went down earlier (because Winton rode year-round, heartily enjoying his smug feeling of superiority as the thermometer dipped into the teens), he might leave at 3, but because he was in the office every morning at 7—and on those days he would eat lunch at his desk while working—he had no remorse over cheating the company out of its time during the workday. And, at this point, the powers-that-be wouldn't have cared anyway.

Once attired in his eclectic, highly functional riding outfit, he'd grab his sturdy bicycle from the storage room and mount it to the back of his Lexus SUV Sport model, part of his employment package. At his request (more like a demand), the expensive vehicle came equipped with a state-of-the-art rack that held multiple bikes (like he needed the extra rack space since Yayla had long ago quit sharing his life). Locked and loaded, he'd jump into his snazzy vehicle and take off for the peace and quiet of the wooded pathways.

His rides were not just his downtime—they were *his* time, a time when nothing in the world mattered but climbing the next hill and pushing through the invigorating exhilaration of muscle pain and oxygen deprivation. No monthly sales quotas or malingering salespeople to worry about, no backups in production, no distractions from his kids' myriad dramas that incessantly bombarded him like piloting the Millennium Falcon through a meteor storm, no disengaged, disapproving scowls or snide remarks from his wife of 20 years, only the amity and harmony of nature.

But today he couldn't shake it—that troubling meme with the inviting blue-and-red doors that popped up during his comatose afternoon respite, the one that had the whole jumble percolating in his head and tormenting him with the road not taken, the one that made all the difference.

What if he had taken the other road? What if he still could?

Ridiculous concept and extremely unproductive use of his time, but still …

4

Winton sat at his desk a week earlier, listening to the indigenous language of sales-speak, the persistent wallowing of self-serving self-pity that salespeople every-where practice to an art form. At that, Luanne Schickle was a master. She was one of his top producers, work-ing the Southwest territory, including the entire state of Texas, where Luanne lived. Dallas, that is, and when she said Dallas, it sounded bigger than Texas, bigger than the United States. She had that kind of Dallas arrogance that stood her well in the male-dominated world of industrial oils and chemical compounds. And she was his biggest bitcher. Not that there was much bitching at BLI, where everybody loved his or her job. Well, maybe not everybody.

Maybe all but one.

BLI was a family-owned company that had been around for three generations, and the present-day Clarence Alderfer was the president and CEO. He had inherited the position from his father, who had inher-ited it from his father, and they were all named Clar-ence. Clarence-the-First went to work for Bethlehem Steel when he was 16. By the time he was 30, he was Bethlehem Steel's largest supplier of industrial lubri-cants, having taken advantage of an opportunity when it presented itself and using his Pennsylvania Dutch instincts to turn it into a profitable business—a very profitable business.

As long as Bethlehem Steel was around.

For years, Bethlehem Steel was his only customer. Even when his business grew and prospered, Bethle-hem Steel continued to command the lion's share of his production facility's output. Present-Day-Clar-ence's father, who had earned a double major at Le-high—chemical engineering and business—saw the inherent danger of BLI's dependency on Bethlehem Steel, and when he came home from World War II, went to work marketing BLI's products not only in the United States, but all over the world. The company grew, especially internationally, and by the time Bethlehem Steel shuttered its plants, it accounted for less than 5 percent of BLI's billings, a hiccup swallowed up faster than a cookie discovered at an obesity camp.

Present-Day-Clarence took over the company after his father had a massive heart attack on the fourth green of the Old Course at the Saucon Valley Country Club. (Which is how Clarence-the-Second's death was always described: a massive heart attack. Winton found that humorous, like it would have to be a MASSIVE heart attack to fell a Clarence Alderfer. *Really, Winton thought, is it necessary to say "massive" if the heart attack kills you? Isn't the fact that you're dead a good indicator it was a fairly substantial event?*)

Present-Day-Clarence was educated at private schools and then, naturally, at Lehigh, where he mostly learned to drink and hate Lafayette. He was a bit of a dilettante and not overly involved in the actual operations of the inner workings of the business, but loved being the boss. He was basically a nice guy, a bit frivolous and limited, but easy to work for.

And he loved Winton. That's because Winton had played football at Lehigh, even though he never started and didn't play much except on special teams. That was before the Patriot League allowed athletic scholarships, and even if they had, Winton wouldn't have earned one. He was a good athlete, an all-league linebacker in high school, but he was a step too slow and 25 pounds too light to be an impact player at the collegiate level, even at the level where Lehigh played. However, in his senior year, he made a crushing tackle on a kickoff, causing the Lafayette ballcarrier to fumble—a fumble that led to the deciding touchdown for a Lehigh win. And on South Mountain, it doesn't get any bigger than beating Lafayette in the last game of the season, the only game of any real consequence to many Mountain Hawks and Leopards supporters.

Oh yeah, and Winton was BLI's top salesman for years, too, but come on, man, we're talking Lafayette here, as Present-Day-Clarence liked to joke when discussing Winton's attributes.

Fortunately for Present-Day-Clarence, he had smart, hardworking kids. His oldest son, Clarence-the-Fourth, whom they called Young Clarence even though he was in his 40s, was Vice President of Operations; his second son, Robert, whom they called Robert, was Vice President of Finance; and his daughter, the youngest, JoAnne, whom they called Jo, was Vice President of Marketing. Winton was Vice President of Sales (because Present-Day-Clarence only had three kids), and together, the four of them made up the management team that met with the entire sales group the first Monday of every month.

Which is why Luanne Schickle was in town and sitting at Winton Fine's desk instead of trying to intimidate plant managers and industrial buyers amidst the tumbleweed and rattlesnakes.

5

Winton pedaled past a dark and forbiddingly beautiful outcropping of limestone and shale, 40 feet high, gnarled and creased by years of runoff from higher elevations farther north. He could smell the deep, sweet scent of damp vegetation growing in and around the ancient rock, a virtual map of time itself, exposed when they built the railroad along the river to carry anthracite down to the blast furnaces in Bethlehem, creating an industry that would someday offer Winton the opportunity to be dissatisfied and melancholy.

On the other side of the trail, he saw an eagle fly-ing above the river, slowly following the swift current, searching for prey, patiently waiting to swoop down in a thunderous arc of sudden death and cleanly snatch an unsuspecting trout out of the only world it had ever known, then soar away in harmony with the eter-nal plan. Winton felt like the trout, unharmoniously snatched away in a misunderstanding and miscon-struction of his life, carried off in the clutches of an unseen and unwelcome force.

What force? And when did I become its victim?

He'd walked through several spurious doors on his journey to disillusionment, so the meme with the choice of the two doors intrigued him and stirred his imagination. Winton often fantasized about what his life would have been like if he had made different choices along the way, so the concept was not com-pletely foreign to him.

The headline on the meme read, "Which door would you choose?" and under it were pictures of a blue door and a red door. Over the blue one was written, "Go 15 years into the future with $50 million," and over the red one, "Start life anew at the age of 10 with all the knowledge that you now have."

What would you do, Winton? he had been asking himself all afternoon.

He was already 48 years old, so the thought of jumping ahead to 63 was not appealing, even with $50 million. Winton liked money as much as the next guy, but he thought time was more valuable.

Maybe.

On the other hand, he didn't want to go back to be-ing 10—no thank you—and have to live in his parents' house again and deal with all that pain and grief. If he could go back, he'd want to go back to the day he met Yayla.

And walk the other way.

But then again, with 50 mil, he could walk away from everything.

Of course, going back to 10 years old and knowing what the future holds could pay off big, probably dwarf $50 million.

What to do, what to do.

Winton was chewing on that stimulating and disturbing conundrum like he really had a choice as he navigated through one of several labyrinthian gates along the trail, designed to keep out dirt bikes and ATVs. And he was thinking about what a sales trainer had said a week earlier at the monthly company sales meeting, the subject Luanne Schickle was grousing about at his desk while emery-boarding her bright-red fingernails.

"All that crap about agendas and the choices we make and all that crap—do you believe that crap?" she asked with a smile and a twinkle in her eye. Luanne always had a twinkle in her eye because she loved life. And she loved her job. And her freedom. And her money. Especially her money. Sales reps at BLI made good money.

Thanks to Winton.

Winton had eight sales reps reporting to him. Two worked out of the office in Bethlehem—the one who took Winton's place in the Northeast territory and the one who worked the Mid-Atlantic territory—while the others worked from their homes spread out around the continental United States. Additionally, he had four sales assistants, each one handling two salespeople, and six customer service reps in the Internet Sales Department, all of whom worked in the office. That department used to be called International Sales and was responsible for the vast, complicated worldwide distribution network Clarence-the-Second had built. That business, along with domestic sales—to some extent—had dissipated after his *massive* heart attack and the company fell into the hands of the Cryin' Scion, as Winton called Present-Day-Clarence because of his insipid whining about the loss of business.

Until Winton took over sales.

Winton's first objective had been to update BLI's web presence and modernize the inventory and distribution systems. The Aldefers had been extremely successful for decades utilizing the procedures and methods Clarence-the-Second had put in place, and although the company was progressive in areas such as employee relations and benefits, it was less than open-minded about the way it produced revenue. Online sales accounted for only about half of its business, almost all of it coming through distributors around the world who sold BLI products via their own proprietary websites, which meant the company was obligated to pay huge commissions on those sales.

With great effort, research and a thorough presentation of logistics, cost analysis and revenue forecasts, Winton persuaded the management team to hire a digital marketing specialist and a supply chain management expert and contract with an outside advertising agency that specialized in internet sales. Working in conjunction with Jo Alderfer, who was the most web-savvy Alderfer and a huge supporter of Winton's initiatives, revenue increased 20 percent his first year on the job and more than 30 percent the second. And because BLI stopped selling through distributors, it was saving on all those commissions. As a result, profits skyrocketed.

The improved systems also helped expand domestic sales, and Winton's salespeople were able to handle a larger base of business by channeling more and more orders through the new network. To help him better manage his team and keep a closer eye on day-to-day activity, Winton introduced a slick customer relations management (CRM) software that the salespeople hated at first but came to tolerate once they saw their inflated paychecks. Thanks to all the innovative changes, projections for the next three years were through the roof, and the Cryin' Scion was now the Much-Fun Dutchman.

Winton may have convinced himself he hated his job, but he was remarkably good at it.

6

On the first Sunday of every month, all the out-of-town sales reps flew into Lehigh Valley International Airport and spent Monday and Tuesday at the office in meetings. Monday mornings were dedicated to the confab with Present-Day-Clarence and the four VPs, and in the afternoon, there would be some kind of training, either on product or sales. On Tuesdays, each sales rep would have an individual, hour-long meeting with Winton, and in between would meet with their assigned sales assistant, production or finance departments to go over their accounts and review and resolve any problems.

The week before Winton's blue/red-door-apocryphal-life-altering-dilemma, present-day-Clarence had hired a sales trainer for the Monday afternoon session, the one Luanne was less than enamored with. The trainer was a sales coach who had written a couple of critically acclaimed books. Present-Day-Clarence, who was always on the lookout for interesting speakers to bring in for the monthly training sessions, had been introduced to him by a friend from the country club. Winton, who had become a devoted student of the art of selling, didn't know anything about the trainer before he met him on that Monday afternoon. As always, he was a bit skeptical about present-day-Clarence's finds, some of them being of the smoke-and-mirrors school of take-the-money-and-run. Winton wasn't a big fan of gimmicks like walking across burning coals or linguistics sleight of hand.

But on this particular Monday, he was pleasantly surprised—the guy was good. He talked about the choices salespeople make every day, whether to protect themselves or take a leap of faith in an effort to help their prospects and customers. He believed most people operated from a platform of fear, the fear of rejection and failure, and until they can overcome those self-imposed limitations, success will be difficult if not impossible. Using attractive and colorful illustrations, he showed how the path to success runs through the prospect's agenda, but most salespeople choose the path that goes through their own agendas, where they feel safe but locked in. He quoted Zig Ziglar, who said you can have everything in life you want, if you will just help other people get what they want.

"Before you can help anybody else, though," he said, "you first need to help yourself—you need to fix yourself. And that takes some hard work. You need to focus on strengths and not weaknesses; learn to take advantage of opportunities and not dwell on threats—a classic SWOT analysis process; Sales 101. Stop playing the victim and take charge of your life."

The speaker talked a lot about the choices we make and why we make them: Mostly, he believed, to protect ourselves from the unknown, and therefore, the uncontrollable. "We're all fighting for control," he added. "But control is an illusion. You can't have it, so forget it. Stop spending your whole life trying to get control. It's taking up all your time and energy, and it doesn't exist. What does exist is your innate ability to harness the opportunity inside you and all around you. So stop living within your own agenda and use a little empathy to get what you want out of life."

The last thing the guy said that day was, "If you want things to change, first change yourself, and the world will follow." Those were the words that the blue-and-red doors had stirred up in Winton as he traversed his bike along the winding pathway. *I can't change myself,* he thought. *I'm too far gone. I'm locked in. For once, why can't the world change for me, like walking through one of those doors?*

But that's not what he told Luanne; that's not how he answered her question.

"No, I don't believe it's a bunch of crap," Winton told her. "And you don't either. You're one of my best reps at taking care of your customers. You care more about them than you do about yourself. You have it figured out, Luanne, and that's why you're so good. No, you believe every word he said. Your problem is: You hate having anybody tell you what to do. You're an old-time, stubborn Texas dame."

Luanne gave him a crooked smile, closed one eye and aimed an index finger at him with her thumb in the air, like a gun. She pressed her thumb down and made a clicking sound with her tongue.

"You nailed me," she said.

I'd like to, Winton thought, as he had a thousand times before, but never would. First, he would never mess around with anybody at work, and second, he would never mess around. Period. He liked to fantasize about Luanne and carefully study the female anatomy on the internet, but the only woman he wanted was Yayla.

The old Yayla—the one he met at The Shack.

7

But she was no longer available; hadn't been for some time. It didn't happen overnight. It took years for her to slowly withdraw into her own world, her personal nightmare. That was after the time bomb went off, as Winton saw it—not in an explosion like the big bang, but more like a chemical weapon that, once released from its carefully constructed casing, safe and manageable, diffuses its viral toxin throughout the system, destroying everything on its deliberate, poisonous journey. What caused the bomb to go off was irrelevant at this point because, in retrospect, he realized it had always been there, patiently waiting—biding its time—and it was going to ignite sooner or later. Winton, the chemical engineer, understood that you could only control dynamite under the most careful conditions, and if you let your guard down for a moment ... pow! Or in this case, more of a slow, silent implosion, taking collateral damage in its path, including Winton.

He didn't know exactly when it started to seep out, but he remembered the first time he was aware of it, frozen in his mind like the brand on a newborn calf, seared into his trusting, callow innocence. It was a night like any other, nothing special or out of the ordinary when he rolled over in bed and touched Yayla's shoulder. She winced and pulled away.

"What's wrong?' Winton asked, surprised by her stiff response.

"Nothing," Yayla replied, coldly. "I'm just not feeling right."

And there it began, soon becoming a quiver, then a quake and finally a noticeable, unconcealed repugnance. Yayla literally seemed to be repulsed by Winton. Along the way, she stopped hugging, kissing, or showing him any signs of affection. Their infrequent lovemaking became simple, perfunctory sex with as little touching as possible, leaving Winton frustrated and dismayed. He fought it, though, and as she continued to distance herself, he tenaciously pursued her in desperation, trying to recapture the magic they once shared. But his persistence only made things worse. In a symbiotic death spiral, the more he pushed, the more she disengaged—the draft and draw coupling coming perilously close to complete separation.

No, it wasn't just her nightmare anymore, assiduously suppressed, neatly tucked away in a hidden part of her subconscious where the door was always locked tight. But you can't keep the monster locked up forever, and it had become a real imbroglio, infecting both their lives.

And Winton wanted nothing to do with it.

Which is why his life now consisted of going to his kids' activities when he wasn't visiting one of the sales territories, riding his bike and working 70 hours a week because Winton worked at home every night and on weekends—better than spending time with Yayla, alternately fighting and ignoring each other. He liked the ignoring much better than the fighting because Yayla, in all her passive-aggressive splendor, no longer participated in the actual fighting, only the instigation thereof. She would artfully antagonize, stir the pot, then withdraw and let Winton simmer to a raging boil.

She had the technique down pat.

When Winton was reaching the end of one of his rides, like today, he would get a queasy feeling in the pit of his stomach at the thought of facing her. When he got home, he would eat quickly and then disappear into his home office and spend the rest of the evening on the computer, checking the CRM, inventory and supply programs to track the day's activities, sending out group and individual emails, calling his West Coast reps and setting up his schedule for the next day.

It hadn't always been like that. He used to look forward to spending time with Yayla. It was the best part of his day. That's when she still smiled, a smile that could light up the world and shoot tingling stabs of delight through Winton, like a shot of good whiskey spreading out from the solar plexus and warming all parts of the body. And she laughed all the time, a laugh that would make the gods jealous and practically bring tears of joy to Winton's eyes.

He had loved her madly.

Where did that all go? he thought as he rode around the last bend in the trail and headed for his car. *Maybe I should take the red door and go back and fix things. Maybe I could change whatever happened. Maybe I could …*

"If you want things to change, first change yourself, and the world will follow," echoed through Winton's mind as he caught the sight of a beautiful blue heron standing by the river's edge. He loved the herons and marveled at their dignity and elegance. The heron looked up and saw Winton moving fast and took off. It bent its spindly legs and snapped them straight like a spring, launching its body upward as it beat its mighty wings and left the ground. Arduously, it continued its powerful efforts, gradually, almost in slow motion, rising above the river and gliding only a few feet above the roiling water, trying to gain altitude; like watching Howard Hughes's Spruce Goose take off on its only flight, its only triumph after years of heartfelt toil. Finally, the magnificent bird pointed its head toward the heavens and soared off in a breathless orchestration of splendor and grace.

8

It was a gorgeous April day, so Winton took the long way home from his bike ride, driving down old country roads alive with bloom, springtime green replacing the dull gray tapestry of winter. He opened his window and listened to the radio. When Winton had been in sales and driving 50,000 miles a year, he listened to satellite radio, but now that he was in the car only a few minutes a day, that expense seemed superfluous. In its place, he had programmed 10 music radio stations: three from the Lehigh Valley, one from Wilkes-Barre/Scranton, one from Reading and five from Philadelphia. The reception came in and out on some of them, plus Winton hated hearing commercials and happy talk, so he changed stations often.

In the golden-olden days of commercial radio, every station had its own format, but in today's world of corporate-owned media where all local flavor and individual creativity are washed clean on Wall Street, they all sounded alike, a mishmash of genres and eras. As a result, on any given channel, you could hear the same song you just heard on another channel.

Like "I Melt with You."

That song, with a Moody Blues etherical-like quality, was written and recorded by a British New Wave band called Modern English, and Winton first heard it in 1983 when it was starting to get airplay in the United States. A nascent teenager at the time and just beginning to get into music, he was a sucker for a hard-driving bassline and loud, pulsating percussions and the song immediately appealed to him—it was the first record Winton ever bought. And for some unfathomable reason, decades later, the tune was still getting enormous amounts of airtime.

On all of Winton's programmed stations.

So it was no surprise that as he drove down the road with the wind blowing through his hair, he heard: "I Melt with You." Winton immediately pushed a button and changed stations. He'd already gone through enough mental gymnastics today and didn't want to have to deal with that painful memory right now.

Or ever.

According to the songwriters (because you'd never get it from the opaque lyrics), "I Melt with You" is about a couple making love during a nuclear attack, the narrator rhapsodizing about his beautiful love while a nuclear bomb is dropping. Appropriately, to Winton's retrospectively acute eye for life's hidden meanings, it was playing when Yayla walked into The Shack on Saturday afternoon, July 2, 1996—a perfect metaphor for their relationship to come.

That summer, Winton had rented a shore house with three friends from Lehigh, a small Cape Cod in Sea Crest, New Jersey, about 30 miles south of Atlantic City. He was four years removed from college and had recently started working for Biochemical Lubricants Inc., and to celebrate his new job, decided to spend weekends lying on the beach and drinking beer with his pals. He was still living with his mother in Bethlehem, so the break from her would be a welcomed change.

On that afternoon, Winton had just returned to the small house from a run on the beach with one of his roommates and was looking forward to a cold beer.

Or four. After a quick shower and changing into the prescribed attire for the evening (for every evening in Sea Crest)—shorts, polo shirt and boat shoes—the four of them headed out to The Shack for happy hour. The Shack was built along the beach half a century earlier, when you could still build things along the beach, and was nothing more than a shack, really. Originally, it was called Mac's Crab Shack, but Mac (whoever he was) sold the place and it became The Crab Shack. A few years later, they added a deck and a covered dance floor, and from then on it was known simply as The Shack.

And it was still a shack; not much more than that, but a magnet for young women and young men looking for summer adventures. The beer was cold, and the seafood fresh and succulent, with loud music and an abundance of seaside ambiance—the perfect place to exercise rambunctious youthful stupidity.

Winton and his friends were standing in a small alcove off to the side of the dance cabana when Yayla walked in. Winton spotted her across the crowded dance floor, honing in on her like a heat-seeking missile. She was tall and thin with dirty-blonde hair that she wore in a short, stylish bob. Swept-over bangs just about covered her creamy hazel-green eyes, and Winton thought she was magnificent.

It wasn't exactly love at first sight, but he was pointedly interested in meeting her. Winton was not a handsome man by Hollywood standards, but he was nice looking—safe looking, with that boy-next-door, all-American look. His hair was light brown, naturally casual and free of manipulative lubricants, and he had deep, dark expressive chocolate eyes. His white and perfectly straight teeth complementing a soft, smooth complexion. His was the kind of face you'd expect to see in an ad for the Army ROTC, the kind of face you trusted.

And Winton had learned to use that trusting look to meet women.

He took a long swig of his beer and walked across the dance floor. In the background, the beat of "I Melt with You" measured the cadence of his stride.

And the beat of his heart.

He was only about two inches taller than Yayla, so when he stood in front of her and smiled, they were almost eye-to-eye.

"I'd like to ask you to dance," Winton offered. "But I can't."

Yayla gave him an exaggerated look of concern. "Why?"

Winton was a natural salesman, drawing in the prospect and inducing her to ask for more information.

"Because I can't dance," he replied.

"Is that a physical or mental condition?"

"It's my left foot."

"Oh, I know that movie," Yayla quipped. "But you look a bit more ambulatory."

They both thought that was much funnier than it was because they laughed in tension-breaking relief, pleased with the first few successful steps of the mating cha-cha-cha. Winton was utterly taken with the sound of her laugh.

"Okay, seriously. What's the problem with your left foot?"

"I have two of them."

"Boo!" Yayla scolded. "That's really bad. I hope it gets better from here."

And it did. They danced and drank and had fun. When Winton asked for her name, she told him it was Yayla.

"Yay…ya…Yayya?" Winton tried.

"No, Yay-la," she tutored. "Y-a-y-l-a. Yayla!"

"Sounds like you spell it a lot."

"I'm well-practiced," she sighed.

"That's an unusual name," Winton said. "I don't think I've ever heard it before."

"You never have. It's very obscure with some heritage from Turkey, I'm told. But that has nothing to do with why it's my name. My father was a big fan of Eric Clapton, and I was supposed to be Layla. But he was drunk and slurring, and the nurse thought he said Yayla. He went nuts when he saw it on my birth certificate and threatened to sue the hospital. But my mom, queen of enablers, said she kind of liked it, that it was different. So here I am, Yayla the Different."

"It's very pretty," Winton offered, although he wasn't sure at this point. It seemed a bit flaky, or maybe the word he was looking for was "familiar." The Clash's "Should I Stay or Should I Go" played in the background, but Winton didn't notice.

"So, what's your name, hot shot," she challenged.

"Win-ton. W-i-n-t-o-n. Winton!"

"Don't you mean Winston?" she asked. "Was your dad drunk, too?"

"As a matter of fact, he was. But no, Winton's an old family name, actually, an old family surname. It was one of the few things my great-great-grandfather brought with him when he graced the shores of the new world, sometime in the middle part of the 19th century. I expect to be the last Winton in the family. At least, I hope so."

"Winton the Different," Yayla giggled. "We're quite a different pair, aren't we?"

If only she had known, Winton reflected.

9

They walked on the beach that night and ended up sitting on a lifeguard stand in the dark, where they exchanged their first kisses between exposition and confessions. They talked about their attenuated family lives, and it became a bit of a competition to outdo the other with painful stories about their fathers and mothers. By the end of the night, Yayla was clearly ahead in the dysfunctional-family sweepstakes, although Winton had put up a good fight.

Indeed, Winton was no slouch when it came to dysfunctional family life. His father was what used to be euphemistically referred to as a functional drunk, and his mother, next in line to the throne if Yayla's mother was the rightful queen of enablers—sweet and obsequious—was self-protectively blind as a bat to reality. His dad was a mailman, and on his route was a bar called McDermott's, where he ate lunch.

Sort of.

He had the same thing every day: two pickled eggs, two Yuengling Lagers and two shots of Jack Daniel's. He didn't drink in the morning, and he didn't drink in the afternoon, only at lunchtime—on his own time—and that's why he qualified as a functional drunk: He could keep a job. All the drinking he didn't do in the morning and didn't do in the afternoon, he made up for in the evening. And like most alcoholics, he could be a mean drunk. Sober, he was a nice man, but come around dinnertime, watch out. Winton never saw him hit his mother, but he saw plenty of emotional abuse, dished out fresh and hot daily.

Unfortunately for Winton and his sister, he was just as tough on them. Winton's sister was two years older and took the brunt of their father's wrath, shielding Winton to some degree. She moved out of the house two weeks after her high school graduation and never looked back until their father died of cancer during Winton's senior year in college, a month before his graduation. It was a mixed blessing—the family had been in total panic over how to keep him sober for the ceremonies and reasonably cognizant during the after-party.

Winton had a more pragmatic disposition than his sister, though, and his father was easier on him. Winton believed his dad had a deep psychological problem with women because of the way he treated his wife and daughter and because he told Winton repeatedly to be wary of women: They can be treacherous. Winton wrote it off as drunk talk and tried to pay it no mind.

Tried to, anyway.

But he couldn't write off the abuse. Winton hated how his father treated his mother and sister and was still mad at his mother for putting up with it, for not trying to stop it. She always put up a good front, and to the world, the Fines looked like an average family trying to get by. She was adept at ignoring the obvious and promoting the nonexistent—a master deceiver. For self-protection against this make-believe world that covered over the constant fear of his reality, Winton learned to stay within himself and focus on his own needs.

And he did that well, to the exclusion of almost everything else, including opening up to other people. That's why that first night with Yayla was so mystifying: He trusted her for reasons he couldn't understand—he simply had never before cared enough about anybody to share his innermost feelings. *Why can I still not do that?* was what that damn song on the radio and those damn doors had him thinking about while tooling down the highway.

Busy castigating himself for obsessing over his problems with Yayla all afternoon and for unmercifully beating up on himself, he was interrupted by a strange sight ahead on the side of the road. A red compact car that looked to be a bit north of a decade old was sitting on the cindered shoulder. It wasn't a junker yet, but sat on the cusp of compactor reincarnation. Next to the back fender was a small, elderly Black woman bending over the gas cap. Upon closer inspection, she appeared to be yelling into the gas filler—no, it looked more like she was blowing, blowing into the gas tank.

What the hell?

Winton had a rule: He didn't stop for anybody along the road. After years of heavy traveling, he had learned that it almost always led to trouble, the least of which was being late for his next appointment. And Winton was always in a hurry. Also, he knew the world was full of do-gooders and buttinskies, and he didn't want to deprive anybody of their self-righteous hour in the sun.

But in this case, he felt compelled to stop. He never before had seen someone try to fellate a Ford Focus.

10

Winton pulled over behind the small car, put on his flashers and turned off the engine. He walked around the geriatric Ford, surveying the situation, stopping in front of the small woman, who looked up at him with a helpless smile. Winton was not a big man—5-foot-10 and 180 pounds—but he towered over her. She couldn't have been much more than 5 feet tall, frail, probably in her late 60s or early 70s. She was wearing a loose-fitting, brightly patterned housedress that danced in the breeze, looking like it might catch the wind—like a sail—and blow her off to points unknown—a tiny balloon caught in an updraft, heading for Oz. Her hair was salt-and-pepper, neatly tucked and pinned tightly around her head. She wore glasses, and her eyes appeared to sparkle, but Winton couldn't tell if they were tears catching the sunlight.

"What's the problem?" he asked.

"I'm out of gas," she answered.

"How do you know you're out of gas?"

"Because there's no gas in the tank," she answered, accompanied by an expression that asked, "Do I look stupid?"

"Why were you blowing in the gas filler?" Winton asked.

"Because my grandson told me that if you run out of gas, blow into the gas tank and your CO_2 will mix with the remnant gas fumes and produce enough combustible liquid to get you a few miles."

Winton chuckled and said, "You're kidding, right?"

"No, I'm not. That's what he told me."

"Well, I'm a trained chemical engineer, and I can tell you that's pure nonsense. You can blow into that gas tank until the Model T makes a comeback, and you're still going to be stuck along this deserted country road. I'm guessing your grandson isn't the freshest lettuce in the crisper."

"He's pre-med at Penn, smart as a whip. And he's always playing tricks on me, that little devil. It looks like he was having some fun at his grandma's expense. Again!"

"Let me have the keys, please. I want to try it," Winton offered.

"You don't believe me? They're in the car."

Winton gave the key a couple of turns, and the starter and ignition switch sounded strong, but the gas needle was below empty.

Winton walked back to the old woman. "Do you have a gas can?" he asked.

"No."

"Neither do I. Do you belong to an auto club?"

"No."

"Is there anybody we can call to come get you?"

"No."

"Do you have any ideas?"

"No."

"I can't leave you here. Is there any place I can take you, any place I can drop you off?"

"No."

"Where were you going when you ran out of gas?" Winton questioned.

"Here."

"Here?"

"Yes, here."

"Where's here? You're on the side of a road."

"I'm where I'm supposed to be," she said and defiantly folded her arms in front of her chest.

"Really," Winton said, but thought, *Oh boy!*

"I guess I'll have to call the auto club."

"But I told you I'm not a member."

"I am," Winton said.

"But it's my car," she responded.

"Doesn't matter. I'm the member, not my car. The guy bringing the gas isn't going to care as long as he gets his trip charge."

"That's kind of you. I appreciate it," she said.

"It's the least I can do to help you on your way to the next side of the road you need to get to."

"You're funny," she said. "And kind. My name is Axelle. What's yours?"

"Winton. Winton Fine."

"Nice to meet you, Mr. Fine."

"Nice to meet you, Miss Axelle. While I grab my membership card and make the call, why don't you wait in your car. Perhaps you should hum it a nice lullaby. Maybe that will comfort the car and it might start up for you," Winton said with a big, warm smile, the smile he'd been using to open doors his whole life.

"Ha, ha! You and my grandson would get along just fine."

11

"You say you're a chemical engineer?" Axelle asked. "What does a chemical engineer do?"

Winton had made the call and was told it would be 30 minutes to an hour until they could get to him. They were pretty far out of town, and it was a very busy time of day. Winton climbed into the front passenger's seat of Axelle's car to wait with her. She was in the driver's seat.

"I don't chemical engineer. I went to college to chemical engineer, but I'm a salesman. More accurately, I was a salesman. Now it's worse: I'm a sales manager."

"That doesn't sound so bad. Don't you like your job?"

"Not really ... I don't know. I used to like it; I used to love it, but now ... I don't know."

"Don't you like being in sales?"

"Yeah, I do. I did. I mean, yeah, I really like sales."

"What do you sell?"

"Metalworking fluids and industrial lubricants to manufacturers with any kind of machinery. We grease the wheels of industry," Winton said with a grin.

"Is that chemical compounds and things like that?" Axelle inquired.

"Yeah, chemical compounds and oil-based products."

"Is your company involved in chemical engineering?'

"You could say that."

"And does it help you sell their products and help you help your salespeople because you understand the chemical engineering part?" she continued.

"I suppose so," he replied. "Of course, it does."

"So, you're involved in a business where you benefit from your degree in chemical engineering, and you like selling the company's products. Right?"

"Sure, you could put it that way," Winton conceded.

"Do you like the company?"

"Yeah, I really like the company."

"So why are you so unhappy?" Axelle asked. "Sounds to me like you have a good job."

"Doesn't make much sense, I know. My attitude hasn't been too good lately. I'm dealing with some stuff, and it's poisoning the well," Winton admitted.

"Problems at home?" she asked.

"Yeah, you could say that," he answered. "My wife and I are in a bad place. We barely speak anymore." He gave her a long look. "I can't believe I'm talking to you about these things."

"Sounds like you need to talk to somebody."

Winton thought about that for a moment. She was right—he needed to sort through the issues, to exorcise the demons invading his soul. "I don't know what happened to us. I've spent the past several years blaming my wife for all our problems. We blame each other, actually. I think. I really don't know because she doesn't share her thoughts or feelings with me any longer—only her intense anger. It's been extremely toxic, affecting each of us, the kids, our whole world. We've really made a mess of it."

"Kids?"

"We have two, a boy and a girl. Teenagers."

"You have my sympathy," Axelle consoled.

"They're not what I expected," Winton confessed.

"I know, you wanted the ones in the JCPenney Christmas pictures, the ones who are just like you. At least, the sanitized you in 20/20 retrovison."

"I didn't expect it to be this hard."

"The more things you have to lose, the harder it gets," Axelle offered. "Maybe you'd like to have less? Maybe for you, less would be more. Maybe you need a change in your life. Maybe walk away from it all?"

"That's an intriguing question. And very insightful," Winton offered and examined her more closely. "You're an interesting person, Axelle. Who are you? Are you some kind of sorceress?"

"If I were, I'd have sorcered up some gas instead of standing next to the road blowing into my gas tank, as ridiculous as that must have looked."

"Oh, it looked ridiculous. But maybe that was just a gimmick, a way of trapping me here so you could perform your hocus pocus."

"You nailed me."

Winton sat up in his seat. "Now you're messing with me, aren't you?"

"Somebody's messing with you."

Winton looked away and stared out the windshield. "Look, I've had a really bad day. I've been wrestling with the choices I've made and the choices ahead. I'm confused and perplexed and angry, and I can't seem to find …"

"The door?" he heard in a voice that no longer sounded like Axelle—not exactly like Axelle. Its deep, echoing sound reverberated through the car, like it was coming from all around him.

Winton slowly turned his head to what was no longer Axelle, at least not the Axelle he had just been with. In her place was a … a what? He wasn't sure. Her face had transformed into a kind of changing, pulsating liquid that oscillated in and out of focus, like the stuff in a lava lamp. Her hair was long and snow white and she? he? it? was wearing a luxuriant robe that looked alive with kaleidoscopic patterns of shifting shapes and colors surrounding this incomprehensible presence. Her eyes were gone, and in their place were two bright, sparkling diamond lights that bathed the car in a pervasive white aura. They were transfixed on Winton.

Winton was trembling. "Who are you? What are you? What the hell's going on here?" he gasped.

"What do you think is going on here?" Axelle asked.

"Is this a dream? Am I dreaming?"

"You tell me."

"I'm losing it, aren't I? What are you? Why are you here?"

"I take care of the doors, and I'm here for your decision. What's it going to be, Winton: the blue door or the red door?"

Winton had to call on all his inner strength to pull together some understanding of this discord, this chaotic intrusion into his fears and anxieties. All day it had been haunting him that he was losing himself, who he thought he was, that he didn't really understand what his life had become, and now some apparition appears to throw it in his face, to confront him with these fanciful choices, to entice him to break the bondage of his charade, to confront him with his self-imposed enslavement, to dare him to discard the baggage of years—a lifetime—of pain and suffering, pain and suffering he had never admitted to himself, never allowed to creep into his consciousness, blaming external forces in its stead.

And now, here he was, facing the ultimate external force.

"Run away," he heard a voice inside telling him. "Pick a door and get out of this horrible nightmare you made for yourself."

"This is your chance, Winton," Axelle encouraged, like she was reading his mind. "Pick a door and change your life. Which one's it going to be?"

Winton thought about it. *This isn't real,* he told himself, *so it doesn't matter. This is a dream, or a hallucination, but it's not real, right?* He was almost frantic.

"I want the red door," he blurted out.

And just like that, he and Axelle were standing in front of a red door. Everything around the door was impenetrably black, including the floor they were standing on, if they were standing on anything at all. To Winton, it looked like he, Axelle and the door were suspended in space with no connection to anything else.

"Are you ready?" Axelle asked.

"Wait," Winton gulped. "I don't want to go back to when I was 10. I want to go back to July 2, 1996. Can you do that?"

"The day you met Yayla," Axelle said in a low voice. "Are you sure?"

How does she know that? Winton thought, but it seemed almost silly to try to interject rationality at this point. "Yes, I want to go back to the day I met Yayla."

"Then what are you going to do?" Axelle wondered out loud. "Walk away or try to change things?"

"I don't know. Does that matter? Can you do it or not?"

"Have it your way," Axelle said as she raised her right arm and pointed to the red door. The door slowly opened, revealing a bright white light, so bright it was hard to look at. Winton shielded his eyes.

"Have a great life," Axelle said, then she was gone. She didn't dissolve into a small dot and fade out or disappear in a puff of smoke—she just wasn't there anymore.

Winton stood in front of the open red door and wondered what he would do if he went through it … *when* he went through it because he knew that decision was in the rearview mirror. His heart was pounding, his brow damp with sweat. Excited and scared to death, he took a deep breath and smiled.

"I have nothing to lose," he whispered, then walked through the open door.

12

Winton was naked and dripping wet, standing next to a bathtub he recognized but couldn't put his finger on how he knew it. He grabbed a towel off a rack and started patting himself dry while surveying the room. Someone knocked on the door and a familiar voice said, "Come on, Winton. We're waiting for you."

It was Alan Greene's voice, a friend from Lehigh. And then it hit Winton: He was in the bathroom of the Cape Cod they had rented in Sea Crest for the summer of 1996.

"Holy Mother of God," Winton said softly to himself. "It worked. This is unbelievable."

He went to the sink and took a comb out of his dopp kit. It was an automatic move—he didn't have to think about it. He looked into the dopp kit and examined its contents. *Man, I remember all this stuff,* he thought. *This is wild!* He took a deep breath, tasted the clean salt air and smelled the slightly damp, musty odor of the old house. It brought on a flood of nostalgia, as smells often do.

Winton looked in the mirror to comb his hair and was startled. Staring back at him was 26-year-old Winton Fine. The gray highlights in his hair were gone, and so too were the smile wrinkles on his face. The image in the mirror was fit with a hard, youthful body, not one fighting the ongoing battle of the bulge, laboring to stop the growth of a Stella Artois tumor—a barricade Winton assiduously tried to build with 1,000 crunches a week. He couldn't believe who he was looking at in the vintage, time-scarred mirror, but it brought a grateful smile to his face.

He grabbed his Sea Crest uniform from a hook on the back of the door, dressed and walked out into the small, sun-drenched living room where he was greeted by the youthful incarnations of Alan Greene, Willie Evans and Big Bob Trombour. He was momentarily overcome with joy and sorrow, colliding emotions—the ecstasy of seeing these guys again, and the agony of knowing too much. He was beginning to wonder if he could handle possessing knowledge of the future. It didn't look like it was going to be easy to keep it in perspective and control his emotions.

"It's about time, Mary," Big Bob Trombour bellowed. "Did you have trouble with your tampon?"

Winton couldn't stop smiling and they all gave him quizzical looks.

The four had bonded in college over football—and over not belonging at Lehigh. They all came from humble, working-class backgrounds, and socially speaking, they were not in Lehigh's league. They didn't drive late-model sports cars—preferably convertibles—or dress according to Ralph Lauren and J.Crew, and they didn't live under the presumption of success as a birthright. Just the opposite for Willie, Bob, Alan and Winton. They expected life to be hard and expected to only get out of it what they worked for.

They were the odd men out—not the only ones on campus, for sure, but their quartet stuck out like Gladys Knight & the Pips: a sore thumb and three dancing digits. The sore thumb was Willie Evans, the star running back on the football team and a big man on campus, as long as he scored touchdowns, kept his place and paid proper homage to the patronizing patricians. He came from Harrisburg, and although he was a couple of inches shorter than Winton, he outweighed him by 20 pounds and was built like the proverbial brick shithouse. And he could run.

Willie had gone to law school and became a successful, respected criminal attorney in his hometown. There was talk of him running for a judgeship when, on a rainy, dark winter evening on his way home from work, a drunk driver ran a red light and broadsided his car. He was killed instantly, leaving a grieving wife and two young children.

Alan Greene was a true genius. He didn't have an athletic bone in his body, but he loved football and wanted to be part of the team. So, he became a manager, fetching towels and water bottles, helping players with their uniforms and equipment and being an all-around great guy. He was tall—6-foot-1—but as skinny as the 20-yard line. He had a full ride to Lehigh;

Winton was the only one of the four who didn't. Alan earned his scholarship with his brain, Willie and Big Bob with their bodies. And although Lehigh didn't give athletic scholarships when they were in school, there were alternatives—ways around the rules.

Alan had just completed his doctoral degree in chemical and biomolecular engineering at Georgia Tech that summer and was kicking back before moving to Los Angles in the fall to work for NASA. They didn't see much of each other after that until Winton got his sales manager job. One of the side benefits was that he got to see Alan when he visited his West Coast rep, although Alan had changed. He didn't have a family or much of a life outside of work; work was his life. Whenever they got together, all they had to talk about was their jobs and the past. And Lehigh football, of course. Winton liked seeing Alan, but it was a bit sad.

Big Bob Trombour was Winton's best friend. He stood 6-foot-3 and went 275. He played defensive tackle and excelled at hurting people. He grew up in the woods of New Tripoli—about 25 miles northwest of Bethlehem—where he learned to hunt, fish, dip, chew, smoke and eat lots of red meat—red meat and potatoes. Big Bob received a degree in civil engineering and went to work for PennDOT (Pennsylvania Department of Transportation) after graduation. He rose to the position of district manager and had a good life with a good wife and three good kids, whom he coached in various sports.

He was Winton's best man and stood for Winton's son, Lee, at the baptismal font. They spent a lot of time together over the years until Big Bob, who had swelled up to well over 300 pounds, suffered a fatal heart attack while sitting at his desk at work. To kill Big Bob Trombour, Winton knew, it had to be massive. It certainly left a massive hole in Winton's life, one he fig-ured he could never fill, along with all the other holes left by people gone away ... especially the one left by Yayla.

Winton stood in the middle of the living room knowing that all three of them were out of his life now ... then ... in the future. Thinking about it, his grief was palpable, and he wondered if he could change any of it. With that undeveloped thought in his head, he walked over to Big Bob, who had a cigarette dangling from his mouth, grabbed the butt and stomped it out on the hardwood floor.

"I don't ever want to see you smoke again," he cas-tigated Big Bob.

Big Bob reached down, put his extra-large hands under Winton's armpits and lifted him off the floor. "If you ever do that again," Big Bob threatened somewhat playfully, somewhat piqued, "I'm going to pile-drive you through the floor." Big Bob was a WWF fan, nat-urally.

"Come on, let's get out of here," Willie said. "There's a cold beer with my name on it waiting at The Shack."

As they made their way down the beach, Winton was amused that he didn't think about turning back and changing his history, his life. But he couldn't re-sist—he wanted to see Yayla. He could always walk away the next day or the next day or the next, but he was curious to view his past through the prism of his wizened perspective, and that thought amused him even more: wizened—who was he kidding.

No, the truth was much simpler—and more com-pelling: He had to see her again for the first time.

13

The beach remained fairly crowded for a late after-noon, but that wasn't surprising. The sun still hung hot in the sky, and it was Fourth of July week. A couple of teenage boys were throwing a football back and forth. The one throwing toward Winton and his buddies wound up and let go a long pass. It was obvious that it was going to sail over his friend's head, so Willie took off and made a spectacular one-handed catch in stride, like he was still wearing the brown and white. He tossed the ball back to the other boy, and when he got back to the group, Big Bob said, "Too bad you didn't make catches like that for Lehigh."

That didn't happen last time, Winton thought. *There was no spectacular one-handed catch, no smart-ass remark. Last time we were here a couple of minutes earlier, though, because we didn't have the exchange over Big Bob's cigarette. I'm already changing history,* he considered. *This could be dangerous—I better be careful. I might have already irreparably changed my life.*

Is that a bad thing? he asked himself. *Isn't that why you're here?*

At The Shack, Winton took his mark leaning against a railing in the small alcove next to the dance floor, just like the first time. He was nervously kibitzing with the boys, feeling anxious, apprehensive.

"What the hell's a matter with you?" Big Bob asked. "You look like you have to whiz."

Winton could only manage a weak smile.

The DJ changed records, and when Winton heard the first few pulsating beats of the song that would haunt him through the years, his heart began to thump as hard and fast as the downbeat. He felt like a teenager at his first dance and he warned himself to be cool, to stay in the moment (and that old bromide made him smile).

When Yayla walked in, everything else seemed to stop—it was just him and her, and he literally lost his breath. She was more beautiful than he remembered, and he suddenly forgot all about the past 22 years. He was fully back in 1996, mind, body and soul.

"Are you okay?" Alan asked. "You look … goofy."

"He is goofy, the original Goofy," Big Bob teased. Willie laughed.

"Blow it out your ass," Winton said as he took a long swig of beer. He crossed the dance floor, and when he reached Yayla and their eyes met, he thought he detected a hint of familiarity, a strange sense of recognition coming from her … like they already knew each other, knew of each other, like they were always meant to be together, always were together, even before they met. Of course, they had met before, but she had no way of knowing that. Did the same magic exist the first time, but he'd been so focused on impressing and bedding her that he had missed it completely?

Was he that obtuse? *Of course, I was,* he told himself, and that was only the beginning.

He delivered his clever lines on cue and she repeated hers flawlessly, and the night progressed according to the original script. When they were leaving The Shack, Winton told his friends, just like before, that he was going for a walk on the beach and he'd see them later. Alan gave him a smile, Willie said, "Atta boy," and Big Bob contributed a pretty fair Fat Albert: "Hey, hey, hey!"

14

The newly united/reunited couple sat on the lifeguard stand as preordained by a history only one of them knew and spoke of the same things they had spoken of 22 years earlier. Yayla was talking about her job. She grew up outside of Doylestown, Pennsylvania, a picturesque area with narrow roads and old stone houses, and she attended Temple University in Philadelphia where she graduated with a degree in English and a certificate in secondary education.

"I teach English at Westfield High School," she was saying.

"I know that school," Winton said. "We played them in the playoffs, but they beat the snot out of us."

"Well, it is a football school," Yayla added. "It's so huge and there are so many other activities and options for students. But, you know, football's king."

"As it should be," Winton affirmed.

That made her smile. "I love everything about being there," she continued. "The facilities are the best, and the students, for the most part, are engaged. If it wasn't for …"

"Frank Growers," Winton blurted out before he could catch himself. Frank Growers had harassed Yayla for the past two years, ever since she got her prized job at Westfield. He was a phys-ed teacher and a total lech. The varsity softball coach and a married man, Growers had cornered her in the teacher's lounge on more than one occasion and made inappropriate suggestions and gestures. He was always putting his hands on her arms and back, and one time let his hand slip down her backside. It angered her, but she took it because she didn't want to lose her job. It made her feel dirty and weak, but that's the way it works. *That's the way the world is,* she admonished herself. *Nothing I can do about it.*

She told Winton that story at their first meeting on the lifeguard stand, and it exposed a vulnerability and honesty that captivated him. The thought crossed his mind that he should have been more involved in dealing with her anxieties and fears over Frank Growers, that he should have supported her more conscientiously.

And then maybe it wouldn't have eventually brought the memory back into daylight in so painful and destructive a manner—uncaged the demons of fear of what else might have happened, what else had she repressed for so long, so carefully, so completely, until it could no longer be controlled. With a little more empathy and compassion, maybe he could have …

Yayla stared at Winton in shock, her mouth hanging open. She quickly composed herself and asked, "How do you know about Frank Growers?" But she couldn't hide the incredulity in her voice or the growing dread in her eyes.

Winton didn't know what to do or say. In his excitement, he'd screwed up. He hadn't yet decided what he was going to do, how he was going to play this unusual (to say the least) situation. But now the cat was out of the bag, he supposed, and at this point there was probably no way to handle it but to come clean, make his confessions and let the chips fall where they may. And all those other clunky clichés.

"You told me about him," Winton finally said after a long pause.

"I told you about him?" Yayla asked, taking short, fast breaths. "When? Have we met before?"

"Yes, we have."

"When? Where?"

"Here, 22 years ago today," Winton offered softly.

"What are you talking about?"

"I'm going to tell you something that you're not going to believe, but I'm from the future. Our future. It would be too hard to explain how I got here, but here I am. I'm sure you don't believe me, that you think I'm crazy, but please hear me out."

"You're kidding, right?" Yayla questioned, almost amused. "No, I don't believe any of this hokum. Are you a friend of Doc Brown? Do you have a DeLorean hidden behind a nearby billboard?”

“No DeLorean. It’s really quite complicated. I don’t understand it myself, but like I said, here I am.”

“Yes, here you are. That’s apparent, but from what loony bin did you escape is the question. And another question: How do you know about Frank Growers?”

Winton pointed over her left shoulder to the night sky. “Do you see that group of stars? They make up the Little Dipper. Can you see it?”

“I know the Little Dipper—I’m not a complete rube. Are you going to wave a wand and make them vanish or perform some other mystifying magic?”

“Keep looking in that area,” Winton said calmly. “In a few moments you’re going to see a shooting star.”

“You can do that, too? My, your powers are great,” she mocked.

The next thing Winton heard was her startled gasp as a bright supernova shot across the sky and faded into the ether.

“Oh my God,” she blurted out. “How’d you do that?”

“I told you,” he said with great patience. “I’m from our future. I’ve been here before, with you, on this very night. Now make a wish.”

“Oh yeah? Did we make wishes on this very night, the first time you were here on this very night?”

“As a matter of fact, we did. You wished for world peace, and I wished to get laid that night.”

“Did you?”

“Noooooo!” Winton drew out in exaggerated disappointment. “Seriously, we didn’t tell each other our wishes. We were afraid they wouldn’t come true if we did and debated whether that worked for shooting stars or just birthday cakes.”

“So, what was your wish?” she asked.

"To get laid that night."

Yayla laughed, and a jolt of pleasure shot through Winton's body.

"Your best friend growing up was Marlene McDougal. You were seniors in high school with only a few weeks left before graduation. Neither of you had ever cut a class, and you wanted to try it. You decided to cut calculus, but the two of you were so naïve that you didn't have a clue what to do once you cut. Scared, you went to the auditorium and hid behind the curtain at the back of the stage, shaking and waiting for next period to hurry up. You were very smart in school, but not so much when it came to deviant behavior."

Yayla was mesmerized, biting her lower lip and fidgeting with her hands. "That's interesting. You're a very clever wizard. I'd ask you how you know these things, but I'm sure it'd be like asking Bud Abbott who's on first."

"I'm from our future," Winton repeated.

"First base!" Yayla shouted. "So, what exactly is our future that you hail from?"

"It's really marvelous. We get married, have kids, you quit working and stay home to raise the kids; I become a semi-success and we end up hating each other."

"Fascinating," she responded. "If we hate each other, why did you come back?"

"So that maybe we wouldn't hate each other anymore … in hopes that I could fix things."

"Well, you're not doing too well so far. I can assure you of that. Why didn't you come back and just walk away?"

Good question, thought Winton. "At first, that's what I wanted to do, but when I saw you tonight, I changed my mind. We used to be very much in love—we had a great life together. We made each other happy before the time bomb went off."

"The time bomb?"

"That's what I call it. You don't call it anything. You don't acknowledge the changes; you acknowledge very little about us anymore. You barely speak to me," Winton said, looking noticeably pained.

Yayla squirmed in her seat. "Tell me about when we were in love."

"I proposed to you right here one year to the day after we met. I got down on one knee right in front of this lifeguard stand, the whole bit. You said yes, and we sat here for hours, talking and making plans. We made love in the dunes and got caught in the rain."

"Sounds like a bad song," she said.

"That's what you said that night. We had to run back to The Shack and debated whether to drink champagne or p*iña* coladas, since they're both in the song."

"What did you decide?"

"What did *we* decide? P*iña* coladas and fried clams. It was the best night of my life."

"Really?" she tenderly sighed, a smile crowding out her apprehensions. "Tell me more."

"Your father and uncle run a construction company in Bucks County, a company your grandfather started. Like my dad, your dad's an alcoholic, or in my dad's case, was an alcoholic. It was the main thing we had in common, the subject we bonded over that first night."

"We talked about that all night? No wonder you didn't get laid."

"During your freshman year in college, you spent a long weekend at the home of a sorority sister and were shocked to learn that everybody's father didn't start the day with a beer."

"That's true," she acknowledged.

"Your father told you on more than one occasion that you're kind of pretty but not beautiful and that you were going to have to study hard because there weren't going to be any Prince Charmings in your future. I told you that night I could hear my father saying the same type of thing to my sister. Our fathers were drunks, Yayla, and drunks say mean things, stupid things, things that come out of their alcohol-soaked, demented brains that don't make any sense. And your dad was wrong: You are more than pretty. When you walked down the aisle at our wedding, I almost cried at your beauty."

Yayla leaned her head against Winton's shoulder and took his arm. "This is all very bizarre," she said. "I think you're sincere and you know things about me that nobody else does. I really don't understand what's going on here, but please, tell me about my kids."

15

A breeze was blowing in off the water and Winton put his arm around Yayla to help keep her warm. He needed to be close to her but didn't want to push it, and the slight chill in the air gave him an excuse to make his move. She snuggled up close.

"We have a 17-year-old son named Marley, after Bob Marley, your favorite. We call him Lee, and he's a good kid. He has an entertaining personality and can be quick and witty when he wants to be."

"Sounds familiar," Yayla interjected.

"He gets decent grades and plays drums in a progressive rock band, whatever that means anymore."

"You disapprove?"

"Not really. I just never envisioned my son not playing football," Winton said. "It was a sore spot between us for a long time, and I'm afraid I pushed him pretty hard. He had no interest in sports, especially football, but he tried for a few years just to please me. Finally, you stepped in and saved him from my vicarious ambitions.

"He has a couple of tattoos and piercings, and I should have blamed myself for each one, but instead I blamed you. It was one of our flashpoints, one of the misdirections we used to avoid dealing with the real issues."

"Piercings? You mean like earrings?"

"Okay, let's go with that for now. We have a 15-year-old daughter named Izzy. Her real name is…"

"Isabell!" Yayla exclaimed. "After my Aunt Belle, right?"

"Yes, after your sweet old Aunt Belle, your touchstone of sanity in the otherwise unsettling chaos of your family circus."

"Aunt Belle is so sweet," Yayla said, smiling.

"Sweet, yes. But batty as a loon. Izzy and you are having some problems…"

"Am I a bad mother?" Yayla interrupted.

"No, you're a good mother, but she's 15, and that's the witching hour for mothers and daughters. The problem is, she's just like you."

"What do you mean?"

"Let me see … how can I put this? She can be a real pain in the ass."

"How sensitive of you."

"Seriously, she has her own mind and is resolute in what she wants, just like her mom. I'm having my own problems with her—I can't stand the way she dresses. Her clothes are too tight and skimpy and much too revealing, but that's the way of the world these days, or, I mean, those days to come."

"What are you saying? Our daughter dresses like a slut?"

"That's a bit harsh, but yes, by today's standards. Some girls and women dress very provocatively in the brave new world, and that's applauded as asserting their independence. If men or boys notice or take the bait and react to the provocation, they're labeled sexual perverts and sent to sensitivity training."

"That doesn't sound right," Yayla mused.

"Welcome to the new millennium," Winton announced. "Where there is no right, only wrong."

"Doesn't sound like much fun, but I'm sure you're being glib. So, what happens now? Didn't you change the future by showing up here tonight?"

"Probably," Winton contemplated. "Most likely, yeah. No, definitely. It's called the butterfly effect."

"The butterfly effect? What's that?"

"It's part of the chaos theory that says if you alter the flight of a single butterfly, the repercussions will eventually spread through everything and change the future, or from my present perspective, history."

"If that's true," Yayla observed, "then we might never get married, and we won't have our kids—at least not the ones you say we have."

A sharp pain shot through Winton's heart. He didn't want to erase his kids; he didn't want to change that. He wanted *his* kids. "Maybe we can ... not everything has to change. I don't know. At least I know the important dates."

"Really? You want me to move forward with this freaky scenario and end up hating you? And you hating me? That's quite an offer. I don't think that sounds like a road I want to take."

"But it doesn't have to be that way. I can change it. I know I can," Winton almost implored.

"What happened to us?" Yayla asked. "And what's this about a time bomb?"

"You carried it inside of you for years, and what you needed was a bomb disposal expert, but instead you got stuck with a blasting cap."

"You?"

"Yes, me. I was the worst thing that could have happened to you. You needed room and support, but I was wrapped up in myself. I put constant pressure on you to take care of me when you really needed to take care of yourself. I was a narcissistic black hole that sucked all the life out of our relationship."

"I can't believe it's all your fault. It usually takes two to ruin a relationship. And if you know all this, why couldn't you fix it where you came from?"

"Because I didn't know it then."

"You seem to know it pretty well now. When did this revelation hit you?"

"When I saw you walk into The Shack tonight. It brought everything into focus, crystallized all my confusion and reminded me of how much I love and need you. I guess I always knew it but got lost in my own fortress of self-protection. But I'm sure I can fix it now; I know I can change things."

"What's there to change? We hardly know each other," Yayla observed. "Wouldn't you have to wait until we get to that point to do something about it or prevent it?"

"I can prevent it. Now!" Winton insisted. "We can do something about it now."

"Do something about what?"

"At Thanksgiving dinner, your junior year in high school," Winton started, and Yayla pulled away from him and sat up straight.

"You were at the dining room table with your mother, father, sister, aunt and grandfather ."

Yayla gave Winton a hard look and said, "Okay, that's enough."

"You stood up and reached across the table to get something."

"Stop it," Yayla ordered while climbing down from the lifeguard chair.

Winton continued. "When you reached in front of your grandfather, he grabbed your breast and squeezed it a couple of times."

"That's it," Yayla said. "You're crazy, and I'm not listening to any more of this!" She started walking back toward The Shack.

Winton climbed down and followed her. "Your father laughed while your mom, sister and aunt pretended they hadn't seen anything. You slumped in your chair, humiliated and violated, feeling tremendous guilt—guilt that would eat at you for years to come until the bomb went off."

"Shut up!" Yayla yelled as she started running.

Winton chased after. "It wasn't your fault! You didn't do anything wrong! You were just a kid!" he yelled back.

Yayla stopped and turned around. "Look, you don't know what you're talking about. Leave me alone. If I see you again, I'll call the cops," she seethed and took off down the beach.

Winton was frozen in his tracks. "I can help you!" he shouted. "Please, give me a chance! I can change it all! I can fix it! Please!"

She stopped again and turned on him, getting harder to see in the misty darkness. But Winton could still make out that she was in an aggressive posture, crouched with her arms bent and her fists clenched.

She looked like a madman. "Fuck you!" she screamed, turned and disappeared into the night.

Winton stood there mumbling to himself, "But I could have fixed it, I know I could." A cool wind blew down the beach and sent a shiver up his back. He ran down to the water's edge and splashed in up to his knees, soaking his boat shoes and splattering his shorts. With his arms outstretched in front of him, his suppliant hands opened like a beggar and his eyes raised to the heavens above, he let out a noise that barely sounded human, a frightening howl of complete and utter despair.

The power of his outburst sent him stumbling. He lost his balance and almost fell into the briny seawater.

"I want to fix it!" he screamed to the wind as he tried to gain his equilibrium. "I want my life back! I want to make it better!"

Tears streamed down his cheeks, dripping into the waves as they rolled up on the soft, white sand, salt to salt, agitation to agitation.

"I need to go back. Please!"

Out of nowhere, Axelle, or whatever it was, appeared hovering above the water, fluid and polychromatic, lustrous and modulating, with those two penetrating, sparkling diamonds coming from its unfathomable visage.

"Axelle," he pleaded. "I want to go home, I want another chance."

"But you weren't happy there," she said. "This was your choice."

"I made a terrible mistake. It was all my fault. Please give me another chance. I want to change things."

"If you want things to change, first change yourself and the world will follow," Axelle said in her reverberating voice.

"I can do that. I can change myself. I will change myself. I know I can. I love her and need another chance. Please."

"That's sweet, but completely irrelevant."

Winton let out another unhuman-like sound, this one more like a guttural moan coming from deep inside.

"You want to go back to all that pain and suffering?" she asked. "Why? You can simply turn around and walk away from it all. Start a new life and be better at that one."

"I don't want a new life," he insisted, tears and saltwater stinging his eyes. "I want *my* life. I can do better. I will do better."

Winton's shoulders slumped, and he shook his head in anguish. In a barely audible voice, he sobbed, "I'll die from this unbearable pain if I can't go back."

"This isn't Oz," she said. "There are no ruby slippers to click together. You made the decision of your own free will."

Trembling and beaten, devoid of all hope, an empty shell of a man, Winton Fine made the only decision he thought he had left. He moved into deeper water. His head was bent and his body limp from the overwhelming grief as a wave came out of the darkness and knocked him down. He swallowed a mouthful of water and struggled to get up, but another wave erupted in front of him, pushing him even deeper into the black cauldron. He was losing his strength—and his will—and the last thing he heard before a strong riptide grabbed him from below and carried him out to certain and welcome death was, "Have it your way."

16

He felt something.

Then he felt it again.

The cobwebs started to peel back as a voice came through the tangle, a familiar voice. "Wake up, Winton. You fell asleep. The man from the auto club is here with the gas."

He opened his eyes and saw Axelle, the real Axelle, sitting in the driver's seat with a hand on his shoulder, gently shaking him. Behind her he could see the sun setting over a distant mountain, painting the sky in a brilliant mix of warm pastels that gave him a sense of comfort. He felt safe.

"You okay?" she asked. "You really passed out."

"Yeah, I'm good," Winton said, shaking his head to clear the rest of the fibrous mesh. He sat up straight and looked around. "I guess it was just a dream," he added timidly, almost a question. "Must have pushed too hard on my bike ride. How long was I out?"

"Quite a while," Axelle replied in a quiet, calming voice. "You look … well, different. You don't look the same. I guess you needed that nap."

"I did," he said with a far-off look in his eyes. He turned his head and looked at Axelle with a whimsical smile. "I really did."

After the mechanic from the auto club had finished his business and pulled away, Axelle took Winton's arm in her hand and said, "I can't thank you enough for your kindness. I only hope I can repay you in some way."

"You already have," he said and bent down and gave her a kiss on the cheek.

As Winton was walking back to his SUV, over his shoulder he thought he heard, "Have a great life."

He quickly turned and shouted, "Wait!" but she was already back in her car. He wanted to go after her but stopped and stared, unsure what to do. After a few moments, he figured it out: He jumped into the Lexus, grabbed his cellphone and punched up Facebook. It probably didn't take him all of 15 seconds to deactivate his account. *I'm done with that derivative validation for good,* he thought as he rolled down the windows and hit the accelerator. When he passed Axelle's car, she was still sitting in the driver's seat watching him go by. For the few seconds they made eye contact, he could have sworn he saw two sparkling diamonds.

Winton took off down the road, turned up the radio as loud as it would go and started to laugh. He couldn't believe what he was hearing.

" I Melt with You."

Of course!

The Accident

Holy Matrimony

Dr. Margaret Mary McAllister sat next to her sister, Delores, and her brother-in-law, old what's-his-name, at the wedding ceremony of Margaret Mary's niece and Delores's and old what's-his-name's daughter, Matilda, at the Grand Cathedral of St. Leo's Catholic Church in the heart of the decaying city of their youth. Although Margaret Mary and Delores had never really lived in the decaying city of their youth, it's where they spent much of their time attending various proselytizing events at St. Leo's: weekly services, Sunday school, Easter and Christmas pageants, summer Bible study, youth campaigns, athletic contests against heathen Protestant churches, etc., etc. What Margaret Mary learned at St. Leo's mostly was that she was going to Hell.

On an express train.

Margaret Mary and Delores actually grew up in a swanky suburb of the decaying city of their youth where their father worked full time at being noble, and their mother worked part-time at first but grew it into the full-time job of pickling her liver. Delores was following in her mother's footsteps, and if the degeneration of an inebriate were a baseball game, Delores would be rounding second base heading for third. Before dinner, old what's-his-name liked to have a scotch and soda in the winter and a gin and tonic in the summer, whereas Delores preferred vodka and vodka and keep 'em coming.

Margaret Mary could smell the vodka on Delores's breath as they stood up, sat down, knelt, stood up, crossed themselves, sat down, knelt, stood up, crossed themselves, ad infinitum in the interminable ornate spectacle of receiving the Sacrament of Matrimony at the incensed, bell-ringing, smoke-waving anachronistic pageantry of the Nuptial Mass.

The entire ordeal made Margaret Mary feel guilty, intimidated and angry—all at the same time. The only good part was that both her parents were dead. Thank God she wouldn't have to endure that inquisition.

What a horrible, selfish notion, Margaret Mary thought as she reached into her purse and took hold of a plastic medicine bottle filled with fentanyl—a gift from an unknowing yet enabling colleague prescribed under the guise of back pain. She gave the bottle a squeeze as if to remind herself that relief was merely a swallow away.

Margaret Mary was nursing a broken heart, a broken spirit and a broken sense of self. At 42, she still wasn't sure who she was or where she was going. A lifetime of church, school, parents, sister, friends, lovers, community, the country, the world and the entire collection of cosmos reminding you on a fairly regular basis that you're not Delores (thank God), and rather dissimilar to the other boys and girls, will tend to have a discombobulating effect on your identity. As the saying goes, if enough people say you look like a duck, swim like a duck and quack like a duck, you're probably paddling your webbed tootsies like crazy to keep from becoming tangled up in *l'orange.*

For sure, Delores was the golden goose and Margaret Mary the ugly duckling, although she wasn't ugly, really, just plain. Delores, Margaret Mary's only sibling and senior by four years, was, according to those in the know (which, by Margaret Mary's account, included everybody in this and every parallel universe), better at everything. Delores was tall and thin with blue eyes and dirty blonde hair; Margaret Mary was average height and skinny with eyes she described on applications as colorless and dirty brown hair. Delores was the pretty one; Margaret Mary the smart one. Delores was the athlete; Margaret Mary the klutz. Delores was popular; Margaret Mary eschewed contact with those of the Homo sapiens variety, although she liked spending time with her cat, Miss Chatelaine.

Miss Chatelaine's preferred *modus operandi* was feed me, pet me and leave me alone. Margaret Mary could relate.

It had been made painfully clear to Margaret Mary by almost anyone with a larynx that she was different, and she had recently learned that she wasn't even good at that. Delores had tried to help Margaret Mary through the years, but to no avail, as Delores would lament to old what's-his-name after a couple of vodka and vodkas.

"Stand up straight," Delores would tell Margaret Mary. "You look like you're trying to scrunch yourself into a ball."

She was ... and roll away.

"Get your hair out of your mouth," Delores would admonish. "That's disgusting!"

Margaret Mary had given some thought to legally changing her name to Disgusting Margaret Mary.

"Stop doing that," Delores reproved when Margaret Mary reached puberty and started doing what girls and boys do when they reach puberty. "Nice girls don't diddle themselves."

"Diddle? Really?" Margaret Mary shrieked. "What's the matter, Delores, can't you say, 'play with themselves?' Or how about 'masturbate?' Can you say 'masturbate,' Delores?"

"Stop it, Margie," Delores pleaded, almost in tears. "You're disgusting."

"Come on, Delores, just one time. Be disgusting. Say *masturbate*."

"There's something terribly wrong with you, Margie," Delores said, in full blubbering overdrive.

"Masturbate!" Margaret Mary yelled. "Say masturbate, you diddle-brain."

Their mother came stomping down the hall into their shared bedroom.

"What's all the commotion?" she asked, huffing and wild-eyed.

"We're just playing a game," Margaret Mary said. "It's called Words Delores Can't Say."

"Well, I don't like it," their mother said. "I don't like it one bit. And I certainly don't like what I'm hearing."

"Margie's being disgusting," Delores said, her eyes bleary.

"It's late, Margie. Stop being disgusting."

"Should I wait until morning to be disgusting, Mother?" Margaret Mary asked, smiling a smile of great satisfaction.

Their mother glared at Margaret Mary. "Please behave, Margie," she said and stomped back down the hall.

"Not 'please behave, Delores,' or 'please behave, girls,' but 'please behave, Margie'—the story of my life," Margaret Mary told her soon-to-be former psychiatrist a couple of years ago.

One of the few pleasures in Margaret Mary's life was tormenting Delores, which wasn't easy, her being so perfect and all. But one day they were watching an episode of *Seinfeld,* and the title character, Jerry Seinfeld, couldn't remember his girlfriend's name. He knew her name rhymed with a woman's body part, and throughout the show, he tried to remember what the body part was. After it was too late, he remembered that her name was Delores.

"What body part rhymes with Delores?" Margaret Mary, who was 13 at the time, asked Delores.

"Don't be disgusting," Delores said.

"What did I say? How's that disgusting?"

"You're disgusting," Delores answered.

Margaret Mary pulled out the volume of their *Encyclopedia Britannica* on female anatomy and studied the pictures and text until she discovered the clitoris. Then, she went into her dad's office, found his medical dictionary and looked up clitoris. It read "sensitive organ of the vulva." Next, she looked up vulva and was particularly pleased to learn that it was an "external female sex organ."

Cool, she thought.

That night at dinner, after Delores told Margaret Mary to sit up straight, Margaret Mary looked at Delores with daggers and said, "Delores, Delores, rhymes with clitoris."

Her father put down the evening paper and peered over his reading glasses. Her mother dropped her fork and took a big swig of the clear liquid in her water glass. Delores got up and ran out of the room, crying.

One of Margaret Mary's fondest memories.

Cocktail Hour

Margaret Mary was not seated at the family table in the front of the banquet hall. Not that she wasn't technically family, but "estranged" or "alienated" would be a more appropriate affixment to her familial status. Accordingly, she was affixed to the "close friends of the family" table next to the family table, although she really didn't consider herself a friend of the family, more a superfluous, unwanted appendage, best kept at arm's length. Truth be told, she was much more comfortable at the "close friends of the family" table where she didn't have to feign interest and where she could remain in her familiar state of indifference—her favored mode of social intercourse.

As soon as Margaret Mary arrived at the country club where old what's-his-name spent as much time as possible, she went directly to the bar to get a glass of chardonnay. She wasn't much of a drinker—mostly wine—but certain occasions called for some serious self-medication. She squeezed the bottle of fentanyl in her small, formal purse that barely held enough room for her hand and took a big drink from her glass of wine.

Margaret Mary sat down at her assigned table of purgatory and tried desperately not to make eye contact with anyone, but unfortunately, a robust, very present woman leaned her sequin-garbed bulk halfway across the table and stuck out her hand.

"Hi, I'm Sophie," she said, smiling like a Cheshire cat—not necessarily a disingenuous smile, but an over-the-top smile that came off as trying too hard. "You're Delores's sister, aren't you?"

Margaret Mary gave her a tight-lipped smile and nodded, almost imperceptibly. There was no way to deny it.

"Margie, isn't it?" Sophie continued.

"Margaret Mary," Margaret Mary said, somewhat emphatically.

"Nice to meet you, Margaret Mary. My son, Eric, was Denny's best friend."

Was? That's an odd thing to say at a wedding, Margaret Mary thought. *Denny? He's the groom, right?* Margaret Mary asked herself.

"Well, they were best friends … before … before the accident, but I don't want to talk about that today. This is a festive day, a day to celebrate, a day to rejoice!" Sophie rejoiced and lifted her amber-colored drink as if she were making a toast.

Margaret Mary tipped her glass of wine slightly in a small gesture of acknowledgement.

A young man, probably in his mid-20s, wearing an ill-fitting blue suit, sat down next to Sophie. He was carrying two glasses of beer, and from the red in his eyes, it didn't look like they were his first—or at least not his first ingested mood-adjuster on this day of rejoicing.

"This is my other son, Wesley," Sophie gushed. "Say hello to Margaret Mary, Wes. She's Matilda's aunt."

"Helloooooooo, Aunt Matilda! Uh, I mean Aunt Marga … what was it?" Wesley asked and offered his hand. "How come you're not at the family table? Are you a reprobate like me?"

"Wesley!" Sophie seethed between clenched teeth and grabbed his wrist, as if to rein him in. "Please behave."

Margaret Mary gave him a knowing smile.

A young woman who looked like she'd been crying sat down on the other side of Sophie.

"This is Julie," Sophie said. "She and Eric were going to get married before ... before the accident. But let's not talk about that today, not on this joyous occasion."

"She's a piece of work, isn't she?" asked a voice from Margaret Mary's left side.

She turned and was confronted with a nice-looking boy she hadn't seen sit down. He was wearing the same stylish gray tuxedo as the groom and groomsmen, but he looked to be a few years younger.

"Shouldn't you be with the wedding party for pictures?" Margaret Mary asked.

"The accident, you know," he said and laughed.

"Are you Eric?" Margaret Mary asked.

"At your service," he said. "Or should I say, out of service?" he added and laughed again.

Nobody at the table was paying any attention to Margaret Mary's conversation. They were busy talking to people stopping by the table and joyously celebrating—all but Julie, who hadn't said a word since she sat down and was spending most of her time dabbing her eyes with a tissue.

Sophie was talking to a man and waving her drink around when she stopped in mid-sentence and pointed at Margaret Mary. "This is Margaret Mary, Sonny. She's Delores's sister."

Margaret Mary smiled at Sonny, and he said, "Nice to meet you."

Margaret Mary nodded and turned back to Eric, but he was gone. She surveyed the room but didn't see him anywhere. Meanwhile, the noise around the table became louder as more people ambled by and stopped to chat. Sophie kept introducing Margaret Mary to strangers she had no interest in meeting, Wesley kept swigging beer and slapping people on the back and Julie kept not saying anything and dabbing her eyes with a tissue. The room started to close in on Margaret Mary as her stomach turned over and her palms began to sweat. She thought her head was going to explode. She stood up abruptly. Her chair screeched against the hardwood floor and tipped back, then rocked forward with a bang. All the chatter stopped for a moment.

"Are you all right?" Sophie asked. "You look pale as a ghost."

I wish I were a ghost, Margaret Mary thought. "I'm fine, just a bit tired. I'm going to get some air," she said and walked away. The inharmonious babble resumed immediately, and the vacuum Margaret Mary had created with her histrionic exit quickly closed up as if she'd never been there, like water filling a hole in the ocean.

Introduction of the Wedding Party

"Are we having fun yet?" Eric asked, smiling at Margaret Mary.

"That's not the word I'd use," Margaret Mary said.

"Oh, come on. You have to admit, my family's a hoot. And I can only imagine the dysfunctionally fun dynamics of the McAllister clan."

"You don't want to imagine that, believe me," Margret Mary said and smiled a real smile for the first time all afternoon. There was something about Eric that relaxed her. He wore a friendly, safe aura.

Eric was standing to Margaret Mary's left, leaning against the waist-high, ornate stone wall that enclosed the sturdy balcony off to the side of the banquet room. His arms were folded across his chest, and his legs were crossed at the ankles. He looked casual and comfortable, although Margaret Mary hadn't noticed him at first when she went out to smoke a cigarette. *It was a small balcony, so that was odd,* she thought. "Odd" was becoming the theme of the day.

"My mother has a tendency to overcompensate," Eric said.

Margaret Mary nodded and examined Eric closely, like a doctor triaging a patient. He was a bit thin but seemed in good shape, altogether healthy-looking except for his complexion. His face appeared to be covered with some kind of pancake makeup, giving the impression of smooth, perfect skin—just slightly off-kilter. She assumed he was covering over acne scars, but she couldn't detect any blemishes on his profile, except for a few small irregularities and what looked like a pockmark over his temple.

"Overcompensate for what?" she asked and lit her cigarette.

Eric smiled, or more accurately, smirked. "And my brother, well, he drinks too much. You may have noticed."

"He does seem to be having a very good time," Margaret Mary said, blowing smoke out of the corner of her mouth as she spoke.

"You think so? And then there's Julie—dear, sweet Julie, the love of my life. Unfortunately, she has become functionally challenged. Or, speaking of dysfunction, dysfunctionally affectual," Eric said and laughed loud and hard.

"You don't seem to think much of your family," Margaret Mary baited, hoping to draw out some details to fill in the blanks. She felt like she was trying to put together a 1,000-piece jigsaw puzzle and all the pieces were so small she could barely hold them between her fingers.

"Like you, I love my family, but we've both lost touch, haven't we?" Eric mused.

Margaret Mary stared at him, well beyond intrigued at this point.

"How do you know anything about me and my family?"

"You're sitting with my family, aren't you? You don't have to be Jim Rockford to figure that one out."

"So, Mr. Private Eye, why have you lost touch with your family?"

"The accident. Haven't you heard?" Eric said with a jigger or two of acerbity.

"If it wouldn't be imposing, please tell me about your accident. I'm very curious," Margaret Mary said as she took a draw on her cigarette.

"Curiosity's a killer. Just ask your cat. I thought we weren't talking about my accident on such a joyous occasion," he said and laughed again, but Margaret Mary started to notice an element of cynicism influencing his humor.

"Here's what I can tell you," Eric continued. "My mother's overbearance, my brother's drinking, my girlfriend's near-comatose state of being—all from my accident. They all blame themselves. And throw Denny—you know, the guy who's marrying your niece—into that pool, too. They all blame themselves, which is easier than facing the truth."

"And what's the truth?" Margaret Mary asked as she took the last drag of her cigarette and turned to put it out in the sand-filled ash urn. She heard the door to the balcony open, and when she turned, a young couple was leaning over the side and looking out at the golf course, talking quietly.

Eric was nowhere in sight. Again.

Margaret Mary went back into the ballroom just in time to see Matilda and Kenny-is-it? make their entrance to "Raise Your Glass" by Pink, a song Margaret Mary, to her amazement, recognized. That recognition only heightened her melancholy. *Phil loved modern music, if Pink is still considered modern music,* she wondered. Painfully, she knew she wouldn't be listening to Pink or any other music in the foreseeable future—not since Phil, her longtime lover and roommate, packed up and moved out, taking both Bluetooth speakers they shared.

They had a small stand-up stone plaque they'd purchased for 50 cents at a flea market that read, "Sharing is Caring." *Interesting,* Margaret Mary thought: *Phil didn't take that.*

First Dance

"So raise your glass if you are wrong," Margaret Mary heard blasting from the DJ's huge speakers as she clapped along with the other guests to the introduction of the new Mr. and Mrs. something-or-other. When the song ended, she went to the bar for another drink. As she stood in line waiting for her turn to enhance this joyous occasion, she noticed old what's-his-name standing at the end of the bar talking to a short dumpy woman, or a short dumpy man. It was hard to tell from a distance, but Margaret Mary made the assumption it was a woman. The woman was wearing khaki pants, a red-and-black checkered shirt and clean work boots. Her hair was cut short, and she wore black horn-rimmed glasses. Margaret Mary imagined what Phil would say about the woman: "Why does she have to look so severe? Can't she maintain a little sartorial decorum?"

"One person's sartorial decorum is another person's expression of self-identity," Margaret Mary would counter.

"But like all of us, she has an obligation to make the world a better place—to promote truth and beauty," Phil would say. "There's nothing truthful or beautiful in that get-up. She's at a wedding, for Christ's sake, and she's dressed like a plumber. Very untruthful; very unbeautiful!"

"You're a piece of work," Margaret Mary would say. "You're so judgmental and narrow-minded sometimes. I think your reaction to her style says more about you than it does about her."

"What style? You mean her complete lack of style and total disrespect for her surroundings? Not to mention the people occupying those surroundings. I'm offended. And if that says anything about me, it says that I have a moral compass that's always pointing north."

"It says you have a moral compass that's always pointing up your ass," Margaret Mary would say, and may or may not, at this point, depending on what kind of day she was having, walk away from Phil in a huff.

Phil would think the entire encounter was funny.

As it turned out, Margaret Mary was the one offended, but then, everything old what's-his-name did offended her. He was tall, about 6'2", and towered over the woman dressed like a plumber. His body language and facial expressions screamed "sanctimonious condescension," as if he understood perfectly well why someone would dress like a plumber at a wedding. He was wearing a black-tie tuxedo, not one of the fancy gray ensembles favored by the younger testosteronites because, *let's face it,* Margaret Mary thought. *Old what's-his-name doesn't possess a cool bone in his body.*

What he did possess, however, according to Margaret Mary's keen assessment, was the inexhaustible ability to bore the shit out of anyone at any time and in any place, which is precisely what she presumed he was doing now to the woman dressed like a plumber. The woman dressed like a plumber wasn't saying anything, just nodding her head and occasionally interjecting—what looked to Margaret Mary like—"uh-huh."

Margaret Mary knew well the pain the woman dressed like a plumber must have been feeling. She had learned a long time ago to avoid, at all costs, conversations with old what's-his-name. Once, several years earlier when Margaret Mary had brought Phil home for the first time to meet the family, old what's-his-name had cornered them during Delores's annual Christmas sublimation gala for what seemed like an eternity, going on and on about some big-time deal he was working on for his big-time investment firm. Or perhaps it was his big-time bank—who could keep track? The minutiae and obdurate gesticulations melted together into a miasma of agonizing perpetuity that Margaret Mary had combated by counting to 100, a polite amount of time to endure any consummate dullard. When Margaret Mary reached 100, she excused herself, saying she needed to powder her nose, and went into the bathroom and took a pill.

Phil didn't need a pill, possessing the innate ability to feign interest in almost anything and anybody. On another trip home one summer, Phil was able to brave a tedious recitation by old what's-his-name on old what's-his-name's golf game that morning, stroke by excruciatingly mundane stroke. Phil had never held a golf club and probably didn't understand a word of the meticulously unyielding narrative, but that was

Phil all over, and that's why everybody loved Phil ... including Phil.

As Matilda and Danny-is-it? took the floor for their ceremonial dance, old what's-his-name excused himself and hurried off to accost some other poor soul closer to the dance floor.

The woman dressed like a plumber stood alone for a moment, a confused look on her face.

Margaret Mary ordered two glasses of wine and immediately chugged one.

Bouquet Toss

Dr. Margaret Mary McAllister hated weddings. And funerals. And anything else that took place in a church, for that matter. She and Phil had attended a few wedding ceremonies of their friends in a park, at the beach and one time on a rollercoaster—safe, noncommittal locales that bothered Margaret Mary for their affectation, but not as much as sitting in a church and feeling the stained-glass windows staring down at her in judgment. Jesus arduously carrying the cross. Jesus with a gentle lamb. Jesus breaking bread for the multitudes. Jesus, Jesus everywhere, looking down on Margaret Mary in disapproval, or was it disappointment like her mother used to say? Why didn't Jesus love her, too, Margaret Mary wondered. Even as an adult, that same old feeling of inadequacy and disenchantment haunted her in the claustrophobic confines of a sanctuary, pressing in and choking the breath out of her lungs, a constant reminder of the serpent she'd embraced.

Serpents were her lifelong companions, always there as a reminder of her original sin: being born. No, not simply being born, but being born Margaret Mary McAllister, scandalous sister of Delores, damned daughter of Dr. and Mrs. James McAllister, imposturous interloper of duplicitous darling Phil, devastatingly disturbed denizen of time and space, soulmate of serpents everywhere, like here at the wedding of Matilda, a niece she hardly knew, and Benny-is-it?, whom she had never met before today, chasing a new and different kind of snake than any she had encountered previously in her entangled life of crimes against virtue … or was it the Holy Writ?

And there was that elusive serpent again, leaning on the bridal party table, hands in his pockets and looking detached and amused as the young ladies in floor-length bridesmaid gowns and short cocktail dresses nudged each other on the dance floor for better positions in hopes of catching the promise of the next Prince Charming. But Eric wasn't looking at the scrum—he was watching Margaret Mary as she turned from the bar and made eye contract. He gave her an enigmatic, wry smile with what should have been a twinkle in his eyes, but instead, cast a trenchant scrutiny that seemed to look directly into Margaret Mary's much maligned and weather-beaten soul.

Margaret Mary caught Eric's piercing grin (or was it a hiss?), and for a moment, she could've sworn she saw the quick, deliberate twitch of a scaly tail. That image, and Eric's penetrating scrutiny, sent a chill through her that was both frightening and exhilarating. She started to make a move toward Eric when Wes, Eric's merry brother, bounced up in front of her carrying two empty, foam-stained beer glasses as if they were precious and delicate artifacts, one in each hand, gingerly held by index fingers and thumbs.

"Hi there, Aunt Matilda's...," he mumbled as he blocked her view of the dance floor and wedding-party table. "Got to feast the beast," he bellowed and ambled past her on his way to the bar. Margaret Mary couldn't tell if he was being clever or slurring, but then again, she didn't really care. What she did care about, though, was that after Wes passed, Eric was gone.

That sent an even bigger chill up her spine and overwhelmed her in sudden terror. *Maybe Dr. Pill Meister is right,* she thought. Her mind was racing now: *Does this Eric character even exist? Is he a figment of my imagination? Am I constructing him out of bits and pieces of information I'm picking up here and there? Am I creating a buffer zone to, in some twisted way, protect myself? Is this a* Beautiful Mind *moment; am I a borderline schizophrenic suffering from cognitive perceptual disorder, as Dr. Pill Meister suggested?*

Am I completely fucked up?

No, she told herself. *I'm a trained doctor, and I know I'm only partially fucked up. I'm depressed, anxiety ridden, a sometime insomniac, an erstwhile anorexic, all diagnosed by Dr. Pill Meister with prescription pad in hand, writing enthusiastically, not being able to contain his joy in penning practically unreadable scripts for each disorder he could unearth in his quest to go on every promotional trip to exotic destinations sponsored by the pharmaceutical companies.* But when he began talking about bipolar disorder, Margaret Mary dumped Dr. Pill Meister before he could finish writing out aripiprazole.

Not an Italian dish.

I may be a mess, I may be a lot of fucked up, but I am definitely not psychotic. Neurotic yes, definitely, neurotic as the day is long, she had said to herself at the time. She knew all her moods and all her personalities, and they seemed to coexist, if not harmoniously, then cooperatively within accepted boundaries. Being misdiagnosed and treated like something she wasn't was not new to Margaret Mary. When she was still in junior high, her father wanted her medicated for her bursts of anger, her lugubrious personality and her unsettling propensity for using vulgarities. As she got older, "fuck" became her favorite adjective, adverb, noun, verb and punctuation. Her mother wanted to send Margaret Mary to a phrenologist to read the bumps on her head. They settled on a therapist who specialized in teen angst, until a rather unpleasant incident during her freshman year in high school when they sent her to a psychiatrist who medicated her for depression, which depressed the hell out of Margaret Mary.

Margaret Mary was not able to communicate what was going on with her, even to herself. It was too dangerous … and Jesus was watching.

Joyously Celebrating

Margaret Mary stood beside her chair at the "close friends of the family" table watching her sister dancing with old what's-his-name. Even in their 40s, they still made a youthfully handsome and vivacious couple, gliding around the dance floor with an ease and confidence withheld from Margaret Mary. *By what?* she wondered: *Nature? Nurture? Or a combination of both? Or neither? Just an unlucky draw of the cards, and here I am, all gawky elbows and left feet. Ah, but gifted hands,* she reminded herself—*the hands of a skilled surgeon who can make quick, lifesaving decisions and respond with remarkably expeditious dexterity.*

A troubling thought occurred to Margaret Mary as she watched Delores gracefully flow through her steps, attracting the attention of the room—just as Phil would have—a thought she'd never had before, or never realized before, or worse, never let herself recognize in all its guileless and obvious implications: Phil was very much like Delores; perhaps Phil had replaced Delores in Margaret Mary's ongoing struggle for recognition and acceptance. They were both tall, good-looking, garrulous, charming, self-assured (at least in their public personas) and vibrant—all characteristics never attributed to Margaret Mary and ones she coveted growing up. As an adult, she'd been able to sporadically subjugate her insecurities by focusing on becoming a skilled trauma doctor, one of the best in the city of her choice where she had lived and practiced since her medical residency, a city far away in distance and sensibilities from the decaying city of her youth, far away from the envy and self-loathing attendant to being the sister of a purported goddess that she both revered and abominated.

Jesus! Margaret Mary thought. Had she been living with (chasing, as it were) a carbon copy of her sister? Was she substituting one unattainable relationship for another? Why had she not seen it before? Was she too close to the situation when Phil was still in her life to diagnose a practically palpable preoccupation to win her sister's validation? Her love?

Maybe I am *completely fucked up.* She reached into her purse once again and squeezed the medicine bottle.

As Margaret Mary stood there, chardonnay in one hand, fentanyl in the other, surrounded by Eric's enigmatic family overcompensating for an accident of some undetermined complexity, watching the sister she never really had, the sister she never really let herself have, the sister she thought had denounced her from the start—had rejected Margaret Mary for being Margaret Mary—it occurred to her that Phil could be extremely critical of her at times, much like Delores had always been and still was. Was that part of her need? Phil's criticisms were more idiosyncratic, though. No "sit up straight." Oh no, that would be too easy. Phil would say things like, "Try to look prettier."

"How the fuck do you look prettier? This is what I look like," Margaret Mary would respond with her open hands outstretched in a show of frustration.

"Put on some makeup, wear some jewelry, buy some stylish shoes," Phil would say. "And stop walking around in an apologetic posture all the time."

"For not being fucking prettier?"

"Oh, Margaret Mary, stop being so overly dramatic. Stop feeling sorry for yourself."

Phil and Delores had anodyne, bordering on obsequious, attitudes toward everybody but Margaret Mary, who thought they could and should fix.

Margaret Mary didn't even know she needed fixing; just some support and understanding would do. Was that too much to ask? Apparently so, which is why Margaret Mary spent so much of her time studying and working in the hospital. She may be fucked up, but there was nothing fucked up about her in the operating room, where she was lord and savior and where everything made sense in its order and procedures.

As she pondered this disturbing enlightenment, another insight emerged in her tattered, tired brain. There was one thing Delores and Phil didn't have in common: a work ethic, or more accurately, a directed, productive work ethic. Delores was a prolific doer, Phil an accomplished dilettante.

Delores may not have been the sharpest kid on the block, but she made up for it in her diligent quest to be pure and defectless, always organizing and volunteering and lending a hand. In high school, her grades were decent—not sensational—but together with her slightly above-average SAT scores, she was accepted into the state university where she met old what's-his-name at a fraternity party, of course.

They were married after she graduated with a bachelor's degree in secondary education, and old what's-his-name got a B.S. in b.s., then proceeded to have a girl and a boy, the perfect family, of course: Matilda and what's-his-name junior. Margaret Mary was godmother to neither, of course. Delores taught high school French (she loved French—the language, not the kissing) and sex ed. Margaret Mary could imagine Delores in front of a classroom of young girls: "Diddling yourselves is normal behavior for some girls your age, but don't do it too much or you'll go blind."

Delores quit teaching when she had Matilda and didn't go back to it until old what's-his-name junior started high school. Since then, she had worked her way up the food chain and two years ago had been appointed an assistant principal, a job she loved because it was mostly an advisory position that gave her the opportunity to do for other girls what she had done for Margaret Mary. She continued to volunteer for various charitable organizations, most within the church, and played tennis on weekends while old what's-his-name golfed. Other than that, she pretty much filled her time with vodka, but she did it perfectly, of course.

On the other hand, Phil hadn't finished college and never accomplished any sustained success, other than hooking up with Margaret Mary, who made a shitload of money.

Evidently, Margaret Mary's greatest quality.

They met at a reading by a local poet at an eclectic bookshop in the artsy section of the city of her choice, introduced by the shop owner who presented Phil as an actor and poet. Phil seemed distracted, surveying the room as if looking for somebody while giving Margaret Mary a cursory smile. When the shop owner mentioned that Margaret Mary was one of the leading trauma surgeons in the city, Phil perked up. It was love at first cha-ching.

That was six years ago, not too long after Margaret Mary had decided she would be spending the rest of her life alone, a spinster who couldn't bake cookies or crochet. God, she wasn't even good at being a failure! But Phil changed all that. It was Margaret Mary's first serious relationship. She had experimented a bit in college, had a few trysts in med school and dated occasionally since, but she had never before said "I love you" to anyone. The few times Delores had said it to her, she responded with a snide remark. Her parents never said it, but Phil was good at saying it, and Margaret Mary believed it, completely smitten and swept off her feet …

… until she wasn't.

Toast

Margaret Mary took a sip of wine and watched the young ladies in their fashionable attire swing and sway around the dance floor with their male counterparts. It brought back memories of her senior prom, and that reminiscence made Margaret Mary smile a smile of detached perspective.

Margaret Mary didn't want to go, but Delores had insisted and fixed her up with a friend's brother. He was a year behind Margaret Mary in school, as if Margaret Mary couldn't have been embarrassed enough by having to be "fixed up." Delores came home from college for the weekend to help her sister with the details of being the belle of the ball, although Margaret Mary was sure she'd be more like one of Cinderella's ugly stepsisters. Margaret Mary and her mother had picked out a gown, which Delores rejected at first sight and "helped" Margaret Mary select one more appropriate for a girl not auditioning to enter a nunnery. Delores and their mother had to work for hours on Friday night and Saturday morning altering the dress to fit the skinny, shapeless body of a forlorn yet resigned Margaret Mary.

On Saturday afternoon, Delores took Margaret Mary to a salon, where the stylist sculpted Margaret Mary's short hair into a chic spiked pixie cut with blond highlighted bangs. Delores helped Margaret Mary with her makeup and jewelry (things Margaret Mary had never done before), and when Margaret Mary made her grand entrance, carefully navigating the stairs of her parents' house in high heels (another new experience, one she had been practicing for two days), her mother and father couldn't believe their eyes. Wearing the floor-length, black strapless dress with a slit up the left side and an open back that Delores had picked out (much to Margaret Mary's displeasure), Margaret Mary was hardly recognizable.

She was stunning.

Waiting in the living room in high anxiety, Margaret Mary was expecting a pimply faced nerd and was shocked when Todd showed up at her door wearing a tuxedo with a white dinner jacket and a red boutonniere. He was handsome—very handsome and very improbable. Delores introduced them and told Margaret Mary that Todd played on the football team, as she pinned on Margaret Mary the corsage Todd had brought. That was Margaret Mary's first date—ever—and although she had been apprehensive about the entire enterprise, one look at Todd and she was absolutely terrified. *Delores must have paid him to go out with me,* she thought. He's probably just happy to be going to the senior prom as a junior, even if he has to take a mook, and he probably thinks that with a senior, there might be a little action.

Well, if it's action you're looking for, how about vomit all over your white jacket and red carnation?

Margaret Mary didn't say much during the evening. They ate dinner, danced a little, but mostly hung out with Todd's friends, all of whom existed outside of Margaret Mary's circle of influence, a small circle that included one, and not an influential one at all. Later in the evening, Todd suggested they get some air, so Margaret Mary followed him to a gazebo behind the event center where they usually took wedding pictures. As soon as Margaret Mary had climbed the two steps into the ornate shelter, Todd turned and grabbed her in his arms. He kissed her on the lips while putting a hand on her breast, the one without the corsage (he had obviously practiced the move). Margaret Mary didn't know what to do, so she let him. Then he put his other hand on her ass and squeezed it. Margaret Mary didn't know what to do, so she let him. Then he stuck his tongue in her mouth. Margaret Mary didn't know what to do, so she threw up on him.

Margaret Mary was beside herself with humiliation and white-hot terror. She ran back into the building and locked herself in a ladies' room stall, where she remained for the rest of the evening. Eventually, a teacher, who was there as a chaperone, called her parents, and Delores coaxed her out of the bathroom and drove her home.

Delores was mortified. Without an ounce of empathy for Margaret Mary's fragile emotional state, she said, "You've totally embarrassed me, Margie. I hope you're happy. By Monday morning, everybody in school will know what you've done. Nobody will ever ask you out again."

Good, Margaret Mary thought, but instead said, "Fuck you, you fucking fuck!"

Delores practically hyperventilated and cried the rest of the way home, so the night wasn't a total loss.

The wedding DJ brought Margaret Mary out of her reverie when he introduced the best man and the toast. Wyatt who? stood in the middle of the dance floor holding a glass of champagne and looking at the happy couple seated at the head table. Next to the groom, to Margaret Mary's amusement and wonderment, sat Eric in the best man's seat. He looked over at Margaret Mary and gave her a wink just as what-was-his-name-again? started his speech. Margaret Mary wondered if Eric had a lower-body situation, since every time she saw him he was either sitting down or leaning against something. Was that what the accident was all about, that Eric's legs were incapacitated? No, that couldn't be. She saw no wheelchair or crutches or anyone around to assist him.

What's with this guy? she asked herself as the best man droned on.

"… Denny and I are good friends, have been most of our lives, but let's be honest, I'm really just a stand-in. Everybody knows who should be standing here today…" and with that, Eric lifted his left hand and waved "…but that's not possible. So to all of us, I say, "As you ride the sea of tomorrow, you still wander the land of sorrow." Here's to Matilda and Denny—love you both," and he raised his glass and took a drink.

"What the fuck?" Margaret Mary said out loud, and everybody at the table looked at her.

"Sorry," she said. "But that was a very strange toast, wasn't it?"

As Sophie turned away Wes asked, "Are you going to drink that? If not, I'll take it."

Margaret Mary gave him a flinty smile and downed the champagne.

"Attagirl!" Wes said.

Cutting the Cake

The DJ threw it into high gear, and the revelers were ready to party. Margaret Mary was not. She had eaten only about half of her lemon panko-crusted salmon and was nibbling at a piece of wedding cake, thinking about the last time she'd been in this room— she had felt precluded from the merriment back then, too. That was 24 years ago at Delores's wedding reception. She was in the bridal party for that one, although she had pleaded not to be. Her father sat her down and told her she was hurting her sister's feelings and that if Margaret Mary wasn't in the wedding, it would look bad for the entire family. "Do you really want to put yourself under that kind of judgmental scrutiny?" he'd asked.

Like I get from you and mother every day? she thought.

"Please do it for me," he said. Her father almost never made personal pleas to Margaret Mary, and she almost never refused them.

That's because she respected her father, even though she wasn't sure she liked him. She knew she didn't like her mother, and she had spent the better part of her life trying to figure out if she loved her parents, and if so, why? Her mother's agitated rancor with her second daughter was palpable, but her father was an enigma. As a general practitioner, he had great compassion for his patients, but little at home, where he was, at best, patronizing to Delores and forbearingly disengaged from Margaret Mary.

Margaret Mary blamed her mother for killing any patriarchal predisposition in her father, but what disappointed Margaret Mary most was that out in the world he tried so hard, almost gallantly, to do the right thing, but made little effort with his children. He wasn't cold and standoffish, but rather stoic and resolved.

The only time he ever told Margaret Mary that he was proud of her—the only time Margaret Mary could remember him showing any pleasure in her myriad academic accomplishments, such as making National Honor Society and graduating valedictorian from high school, where she gave a laudable speech on intolerance and prejudicial conceits in spite of running to the bathroom for two days in preparation—was when she received an acceptance letter to a prestigious medical school.

Margaret Mary had been sad when her parents died, not because she'd miss them, but because she would never get the chance to really know her father. She felt she already knew her mother and all her foibles, but still, she was her mother. Phil told her she should take some time to grieve, but Margaret Mary went to work and took time off only to fly home for the funeral. She and Delores met with the county coroner, who told them that their parents had died before the explosion, instantly, with no pain.

Margaret Mary knew that was bullshit. She'd seen enough victims of electrocution to know it's an extremely painful way to go and that many people burst into flames before they die, but she kept her mouth shut for Delores's sake, fighting the urge to tell the coroner he was a stupid fucking son of a bitch.

Her father owned a single-engine Cessna he loved to fly. Margaret Mary's mother would sometimes accompany him on weekend trips, and while returning home from one such trip two years ago, they ran into a storm that threw the small plane into high-voltage lines while trying to land. It hung there for a few moments, hissing and sparking, then burst into flames and blew apart.

After the funeral, Delores begged Margaret Mary to stay for a couple of days, arguing that they needed each other in their time of mourning, but Margaret Mary flew home that night and went back to work the next day.

Phil was right, Margaret Mary thought, as she took the last sip of her fourth glass of wine: *I hadn't let myself grieve,* she castigated herself. *But then, there really was no reason for grieving.* Most people are devastated when they lose a parent, let alone both of them at the same time, but, Margaret Mary reasoned, *You can't lose what you never had, can you?*

Margaret Mary needed a cigarette. She went out to the small balcony to see Eric standing where he had been before, in the same stance, arms folded across his chest, legs crossed at the ankles, wearing a look of nonchalant satisfaction. Margaret Mary wore a look of superable diffidence.

"You look like hell. What's the matter? Didn't you love that toast?" Eric asked sarcastically and slapped his right thigh, chuckling.

"Are you real?" Margaret Mary blurted out. "I mean, are you really here, or am I imagining you?"

"I was just about to ask you the same question," Eric said. "Maybe neither of us is real. Maybe nothing is real," he added and grinned. "Everything here is certainly unreal, isn't it?"

Margaret Mary took out a cigarette and lit it, lifted her head and blew a cloud of smoke toward the heavens. "Very existential, but that doesn't answer anything. And before you say, 'Does anything ever answer anything?' Freddy Nietzsche, tell me about your accident. Please."

"What's there to tell?" Eric asked rhetorically, standing up straight and turning his head toward Margaret Mary, exposing the left side of his face for the first time. "As I'm sure you can surmise, I was right-handed," he added and let out a sinister laugh.

Margaret Mary gasped, which was out of character because she had seen and treated thousands of gruesome wounds during her career. On the left side of Eric's head, just above the hairline, was a hole about the size of a quarter. *An exit wound,* Margaret Mary thought. The hole was blackened around the edges with pieces of white bone, gray brain matter, pink tissue and blood oozing out, mixing with the pancake makeup and creating a grotesque mess. She should have recognized what she had assumed was a pockmark on the right side of Eric's face as an entrance wound. *You're really off your game today,* she told herself.

"Nice, huh?" Eric chided.

"That was no accident," Margaret Mary said.

"No shit! It's the most definitive thing I ever did."

"Why'd you do it?" Margaret Mary asked.

"Why'd you do it?" Eric shot back.

Margaret Mary slid her hand into her purse and squeezed the bottle of fentanyl.

"I didn't do it," she replied, meekly.

"Only because you failed."

Before Margaret Mary went to high school, she never had a close friend. There were girls and boys she grew up with whom, once in a while, she'd spend time doing different activities, but no one she felt close to. Then in ninth grade, she met a girl named Polly who came from the other feeder middle school. They developed an instant rapport. Polly was not exactly geeky, but she wore her hair in an old-fashioned pageboy, sported blue-tinted granny glasses and dressed plainly, in the same vein of sartorial understatement as Margaret Mary. They were both taking a full slate of advanced-placement courses, and they shared a certain erudite cynicism toward conformity.

While other girls their age were talking about boys and clothes, Margaret Mary and Polly would discuss the paradoxical Euclidean geometric concept of π as a mathematical constant and Lady Macbeth's choice of hand cleanser—and silliness.

"What's a snarfer?" Margaret Mary asked Polly.

"I don't know," Polly said. "You made up that word."

"No, I didn't. It's somebody who sniffs bicycle seats."

"Eew, gross!"

"What's a snart?"

"I really don't want to know," Polly insisted.

"That's when you sneeze and fart at the same time."

"You're disgusting, Margaret Mary."

"I know," Margaret Mary said. With so little practice, Margaret Mary was a wee bit behind the learning curve in the area of social development, but in spite of her awkward entrance into amity, Margaret Mary and Polly became inseparable … until a few of the post-pubescent high school boys started to notice that under the strident veneer, Polly was pretty and possessed a nice body. Accordingly, sometime later that fall, Polly was invited to a cool kid's party.

"You're not really thinking about going, are you?" Margaret Mary asked.

"Yeah, I am," Polly replied.

"Why?"

"Simple. There'll be some cute boys there."

"And what about us?" Margaret Mary implored.

"Us? We're friends—that doesn't change."

But it did change everything. Margaret Mary felt like Polly was selling out and abandoning her. And then it got worse.

"Do you think I could go with you?" Margaret Mary asked.

"I think that's a bad idea," Polly said.

"Why?"

Polly looked at Margaret Mary as if she were studying her, then said, "I don't want to hurt your feelings."

"What is that supposed to mean?" Margaret Mary questioned, getting irritated.

"I didn't want to tell you this, but I was specifically told not to bring you. I'm sorry, they just don't get you—it doesn't change anything between us."

But it did change everything.

They were at Polly's house at the time. Margaret Mary made an excuse and left. When she got home, she went into her parents' bedroom and opened the drawer to her mother's nightstand. Buried under the Bible was her mother's diaphragm and a bottle of Seconal. There were 17 pills in the bottle. Margaret Mary went into the bathroom and swallowed them all. When Delores got home a half-hour later, Margaret Mary was lying in her bed unconscious. She was rushed to the hospital where they pumped her stomach.

Margaret Mary survived, but that was the end of her and Polly. They remained acquaintances.

Margaret Mary's father used his influence at the hospital to alter the record to reflect that Margaret Mary had experienced a severe reaction to allergy medication. They sent her to a shrink who treated her for depression, and that was that. It was never again spoken of in the McAllister home.

"Yours was no accident, either," Eric said. "The only accident was that it didn't work."

"Yes, I'm an abject failure at everything," Margaret Mary mumbled.

"Except at saving other people's lives," Eric said. "Did you ever wonder why you chose that field of medicine? Maybe it's because you think if you can save enough lives, you might someday be able to save your own?"

Margaret Mary stared at Eric, believing she was on the verge of going bat-shit crazy, with a one-way ticket. "So, why'd you do it?" she eventually asked.

"To be perfectly honest, I don't know. It's not like I thought about it, planned it or anything. It just came to me. I was having a bad night, frustrated and feeling helpless. I was trying to figure out what to do, then I picked up the gun. The rest is the fractured history of Eric's family and friends," he said and laughed again.

"Were you depressed?" Margaret Mary asked.

"No, I don't think so. At least, I wasn't aware of it, if I was. I had a couple of issues that I thought were insurmountable, but what 20-year-old isn't overwhelmed by life? I made a bad decision. It was impetuous and stupid, the ultimate cowardly act. Oh sure, it ended my life, my pain, but it traumatized everybody around me. In the end, it was selfish and thoughtless. I ran away, quit, and in so doing took all the petty troubles I was having off my shoulders and put them squarely on the shoulders of my friends and family. And they're going to carry that weight for the rest of their lives. I really messed up."

"So, you're sorry you did it?"

"Of course I am. What do you think I'm talking about? I so much want to be here," Eric wailed and took on a look of excruciating pain and despair that made Margaret Mary start to cry. Her tears mixed with the small amounts of eye liner and mascara she wore, creating little black and blue rivulets streaming down her face.

"It's not the answer, believe me," Eric said after a time. "That little bottle of pills you keep grabbing will only create more problems than it will solve. Do you really want to give Delores the opportunity to be even more of a martyr?"

Margaret Mary laughed through her tears. "That's the last thing I want."

"I know, there is no joy in Mudville. But here's what they don't tell you: Sure, the mighty Casey struck out, and the Mudville Nine lost the game, but Casey came back the next day and played another game, took more swings, probably hit a home run or two. One swing, one at bat, one game didn't define who he was. And one narcissistic asshole doesn't define Dr. Margaret Mary McAllister."

Eric gave Margaret Mary a soft smile as she took the last puff of her cigarette and turned to stub it out. When she turned back, Eric was gone, as she expected. What she didn't expect made her cry even more. Sitting on the ledge of the waist-high wall where Eric had been leaning sat a bird looking at Margaret Mary, a type of bird she had never before seen. It was black on top with a large, white mark under its wings and a splotch of crimson red on its breast that made it look like blood was flowing from its head. *It's breathtakingly beautiful,* Margaret Mary thought. The bird cocked his head, fluttered his wings and took off, soaring high into the sky over Margaret Mary's head. She watched the bird until it disappeared into the ether, wiped her tears with a tissue and went to the ladies' room. She locked herself in a stall and sat there for some time holding the bottle of fentanyl, debating whether to take them or flush them down the toilet. She finally put them back in her purse and said out loud, "Another day."

Margaret Mary went to the sink and washed her face, reapplied eye liner and mascara and touched up her very pale pink lipstick. She stood there for a moment, holding the lipstick and staring at herself in the mirror. She smiled at the image and wrote on the mirror in big block letters with her lipstick:

ERIC,

I THINK I'LL TAKE A COUPLE MORE SWINGS.

THANK YOU!

Till Death Us Do Part

Delores was standing next to the close friends of the family table, talking to Sophie and holding a glass filled with ice and clear liquid. When she saw Margaret Mary approaching, Delores said, "Oh, there you are. I've been looking for you."

Sophie turned away and struck up a conversation with someone at a nearby table.

"Are you enjoying yourself?" Delores asked.

Margaret Mary reached across the dirty dessert dish and grabbed her name card. She held it up for Delores to see.

"Really?" Margaret Mary asked.

Delores took the card out of Margaret Mary's hand and inspected it. The card read "Margie McAllister."

"Oh, I suppose we could have put 'Dr. Margie McAllister,'" Delores said. "Does that really bother you?"

"Margie?" Margaret Mary stressed. "You know I hate that name. It makes me sound like I'm 10 years old."

Delores took a sip from her glass and continued looking at the card, ignoring Margaret Mary's comment.

After enough time had passed for Margaret Mary's words to dissipate, Delores looked up and said, "I'm sorry about seating you at this table, but when you called last week to say Phil wouldn't be coming, I had to scramble. We had you seated at our table, but if we kept you there, it would have made an odd number."

"That *is* me, isn't it?" Margaret Mary said, dryly. "An odd number."

"Oh, Margie. Stop being so overly dramatic. Stop feeling sorry for yourself."

Margaret Mary gave Delores a look of consternation.

"Are you all right?" Delores asked. "I'm being told you're acting a little strange."

"I'm acting strange? Are you kidding me?" Margaret Mary exclaimed. "I'm at a wedding where everybody refers to a self-inflicted gunshot wound through the frontal cortex as 'The Accident,' the stand-in best man gave a eulogy instead of a toast, and this whole fucking affair revolves around a dead guy. And you tell me *I'm* acting strange."

"Please Margie, don't be vulgar. Eric's death was very hard on all of us; it's been a huge burden to carry."

Margaret Mary could hear Eric's words in her head: "Do you really want to give Delores the opportunity to be even more of a martyr?" The thought made Margaret Mary smile.

"You know, Margie, we were all so sorry to hear about you and Phil."

So was I, Margaret Mary thought. *Maybe not to hear about it, but to realize that I had been a fool—played like a mark. How could one person steal your entire self-es-*

teem? Because I let Phil do it, that's how. I let myself believe what I wanted to believe, what I needed to believe. Maybe Eric was right: I used Phil to define who I was. Maybe I was using Phil as much as Phil was using me. Let's face it, Phil had been window dressing, a good-looking accessory to bolster my low self-esteem, an external show of worth for the world to see: There goes Margaret Mary: She must be very special to be with somebody like Phil.

Phil put up a good front. They had planned to marry twice, but the first time, four years ago and two weeks before the impetuous small affair was to take place, Phil claimed to have received an offer to work on a television movie screenplay and had to fly to the West Coast for a couple of months. For some unarticulated reason, the show was never produced. The second time, two years later, was well organized in advance by Margaret Mary, but had to be postponed because of the death of Margaret Mary's parents. Every time the subject came up after that, Phil's sophistical deftness conjured excuses until they stopped talking about marriage completely.

And then Phil dumped her.

They had been sitting outside at a small café, drinking sangria that the waiter brought in a carafe.

"I need to talk to you about something," Phil said while pouring more sangria.

"What's that?" Margaret Mary asked innocently.

Phil took a drink and a deep breath, then said, "I don't think this is working for me any longer."

"Pardon me. What's not working?"

"Us. We're not working."

Margaret Mary set down her drink and looked at Phil. "What are you saying?"

"I'm saying that it's over between us," Phil said softly.

"Where the hell did that come from?" Margaret Mary demanded, raising her voice.

"Please, remain calm, Margaret Mary. Can't we be civilized about this?"

"Civilized! Is that why you brought me to this cute little public setting? So I wouldn't make a scene and embarrass you? God forbid I humiliate Miss Delicate."

Phil looked mortified, and Margaret Mary lowered her voice. "Can we talk about this?"

"There's nothing to talk about. I made a decision. It's been a long time coming and you know it. I moved my stuff out of the condo today while you were at work. I tried to figure out what was mine and what was yours the best I could, but if you have a problem with anything, we can work it out. I left Miss Chatelaine. She's always been more your cat than mine."

"So that's it? You just move out behind my back for no reason?"

"This is very difficult, Margaret Mary. What do you want from me?"

"How about some honesty? That might be a good place to start."

"Okay, but you're not going to like it."

"I don't like any of this already."

Phil took a big drink and said, "You're just not lesbian enough for me anymore."

"I'm not lesbian enough for you, Phyllis?" Margaret Mary said, practically yelling. "Is that what you're saying? That's rich coming from the queen of lipstick lesbians."

Phil didn't say anything, just looked down at her hands folded in her lap.

"It seems to me, Phyllis, that I was plenty fucking lesbian enough for you in bed last night!"

Everybody was looking at them. Tears were rolling down Phil's cheeks.

"I just need more," Phil said.

"What does that mean, Phyllis? Do you want me out carrying signs and wearing a pussy hat? Is that it? You know that's not my style."

"The problem is, Margaret Mary, you have no style. No presence, no real identity. I need to continue to grow, and you're rooted in obstinate complacency."

"Complacency! Are you kidding me? Come spend one fucking shift with me—you know, the place where I go to work to make money to support you—and see how fucking complacent I am. See how complacent the people I save are."

"That's not what I meant," Phil said.

Margaret Mary stared down at her glass of sangria. "What can we do?" she almost whispered. "How can I fix this?"

"You can't."

"So, you're going to throw away six years because of some nebulous concept of lesbian identity that I don't even understand?"

"Well, it's more than that."

"What else?"

"There are other things."

"Like what?"

Phil took a breath. "I met somebody else."

Margaret Mary froze as time stood still. A swirl of emotions erupted and spread through her body like a cold chill, quickly replaced by a rage from someplace deep inside, someplace she'd sealed off years ago and assiduously guarded. Her hands were shaking as she picked up her almost-full glass of sangria and threw it in Phil's face.

"I hope your new fuck is dyky enough for you!" she shouted loud enough for the entire trendy bistro to hear.

Which effectively ended any further communication between Margaret Mary and Phil.

"You know, Margie, we always liked Phil," Delores said.

"I know," Margaret Mary responded. "It's me you don't like. Embarrassing Margaret Mary."

"Don't be ridiculous. Of course we like you. And you don't embarrass us. We're proud of the work you do," Delores said and added, "I think it's you who's embarrassed of us. You flew in yesterday, refused to stay with us, got a room at the airport and will be flying out first thing in the morning. It hurts my feelings, Margie."

Margaret Mary was stymied. She wasn't ready for true confessions from her sister, and it made her feel guilty … and very much alone. "I have a couple of weeks' vacation coming up next month," she said. "Phyllis and I were planning a trip to Hawaii, but I guess that's off. Maybe I'll come back and spend a few days with you."

"That would be wonderful!" Delores gushed. "I would like that so much. You know I love you."

"I love you, too," Margaret Mary said, to her own amazement.

A smile crossed Delores's lips. "You've never said that to me before, Margaret Mary."

"And you've never called me Margaret Mary before."

"Well then, I guess there's hope for both of us," Delores said and laughed.

"Maybe there is," Margaret Mary answered.

"Speaking of hope, I hope you find happiness, Margie. I really do. You deserve it," Delores said. "I know there's somebody out there for you, a soulmate, somebody, you know, another one like you."

"Can't say lesbian, can you, Delores?"

"Now don't you start on me."

Margaret Mary took Delores's glass and set it on the table. Then she reached out and clasped her sister's hands, looked at her with a broad smile and said, "Delores, Delores, rhymes with clitoris."

The Train

He felt the train coming before he heard it.

A mosquito buzzed around his left ear. He swatted at it, rubbed the gray stubble on his craggy face, then pulled a cigar out of the chest pocket of his dungarees. With his other hand, he scratched an itch on his right leg that used to be there.

The lightning bugs flashed their bioluminescence against the blackened park across the tracks, the park where he and Bobby spent most of their lives together. He could barely make out the basketball courts from the dim, ambient light of the streetlamps, but he squinted and tried to visualize the two of them shoveling snow off one of the courts on cold, blustery winter days so they could shoot baskets until their fingers bled.

As he slowly unwrapped the cigar, he could taste the thick July heat and smell the sweet, pungent odor from the mud that lined the banks of Turtle Creek, the line of demarcation that separated Riverview and East Riverview and marked the northern boundary of the park. He and Bobby would laugh at the designation "east" since East Riverview was adjacent to the northern end of town, an early lesson on the capricious nature of being—life makes little sense.

He and Bobby lived on the other end of the park at the top of Cedar Street. Their house backed up to the woods that ran along Turtle Creek up past the park, and although they were allowed to play in the woods, they were forbidden to go near the creek. But that old creek had a siren's call, and they were drawn to it like a bullet to the bone. He lit the cigar and took a long, slow draw, chuckling at the memory of the time he and Bobby built a raft and Bobby got caught in a swift current and ended up down past the park and under the Broad Street bridge where the flimsy collection of rotting limbs tied together with their mom's clothesline got caught in the tangle of a fallen tree. He remembered running home and their mom calling the police, who had to call the fire department, who put their rescue boat in the water and fetched a defiant and pleased Bobby.

Dad whupped us good that night, he recalled, smiling.

He didn't know what drew him to the railroad tracks. He couldn't remember if it was the anniversary of that night, but might be. *How long's it been?* he wondered. *Maybe 60 years, maybe more.*

He heard the train whistle from about two-and-a-half miles away, he figured. *Must be crossing Elmer's Pike,* he said to himself. *Be here in two or three minutes.* He shifted his weight, and the prosthesis gave a little on the unstable gravel that lined both sides of the tracks. Bobby and he would lie in bed, listening to that whistle almost every night, Bobby always on the top bunk because he had first choice, being the oldest—by 17 minutes. Bobby would say that someday he'd be on that train taking him away from Riverview forever.

"It's a freight train, you moron," he would say to Bobby. "Sometimes they carry livestock, though, so maybe you could ride with the hogs."

He thought about how different they were for two who were so close. Bobby wanted to see the world; he was content in their small town along the Delaware River. He looked forward to growing up and joining the fire company, like their dad, and marching up Main Street in the Fourth of July parade in one of those sharp, blue uniforms. Bobby thought that was the funniest thing he ever heard.

"Not as funny as you riding with a carload of hogs," he'd reply, weakly, because deep down inside he wanted to be more like Bobby. In many ways, even way back then, Bobby, with his seemingly fearless and indomitable spirit, was his hero. Bobby wasn't afraid of anything, like that train they'd hear rumbling through town every night.

Their nana had warned them about the danger of those railroad tracks and the perils that had befallen many a young man, like the boy who tried to jump an open freight car years ago … and missed. She would go into graphic details about how the boy had tried to time it perfectly so he would be running with the train when he jumped, grabbing the floor beyond the open door and swinging himself into the boxcar. But he mistimed the jump and couldn't grab anything to hold on to. The boy bounced off the side of the car and slid under the big, steel wheels that cut him in half.

"Did he ever try it again?" he recollected Bobby asking while rolling on the floor laughing. Nana would get so angry and tell Bobby he was the devil's helper, for sure!

He blew out a large cloud of cigar smoke and thought about how Bobby had become obsessed with that damn train. *Bobby couldn't let it go,* he told himself. *Bobby just had to push it, always had to be proving something, and there was no way to stop it once it got rolling.*

They felt the train coming before they heard it.

He wobbled a bit on his artificial appendage as the train approached, whistle blaring and the huge head-light temporarily blinding him. *That was the worst night of my life,* he told himself. *That and the night I got my leg blown off in Vietnam.*

Some things you never forget how they felt, he mused. Like his leg: Sometimes it still itched. And like Bobby: Sometimes it felt like he was still standing next to him.

The Snowball Incident

One

He preferred back roads to highways. With noise barriers, endless road construction and unrestrained property development, he thought highways offered little topographical character or scenery of interest. Not that he didn't know well the nuanced constitution of what his young wife called his "longcuts," he still preferred the pastoral tranquility of Pennsylvania's rapidly diminishing natural beauty over man's insatiable need to build more stuff and create cacophonous havoc.

An interesting perspective for a rock 'n' roll dude who specialized in loud, huh?

Calvin was in no hurry as he made his way through the twists and turns of vestal farmlands and forests heavily wooded with oak, maple, pine and ubiquitous hemlock. Familiarity with his myriad alternate routes through the boonies never became routine and was always a pleasant respite, especially in the middle of ski season when the Pennsylvania Turnpike's Northeast Extension would be clogged with folks from Philadelphia and its sprawling suburbs on their merry way to a weekend of schussing, stem christies and hot rum punch. By habit, Calvin was never in a hurry, but since his 40th a couple months earlier, time seemed to be rushing at him in a torrent of harsh reality, and his preferred leisurely pace was being jolted completely out of square.

And in his presently jumbled mind of inconsistencies and incongruities, the prospect of joining the square was messing with his square. *An interesting paradox,* Calvin thought, as he drove around a large bend in the road, winding through an uneven pattern of sheared cornfields, when what to his wondering eyes did appear...

"What the ...?" he mumbled.

The fields on both sides of the road looked like they were covered in snow, a deep layer of snow, but it wasn't snowing—hadn't snowed for weeks, leaving the weekend warriors to cavort in the artificial wonderland of water droplets pumped at high speed through Star Wars-armament-like condensers to cover the slopes in bizarro-world snow and fool Mother Nature. But it wasn't the lack of snow that was on Calvin's mind—he didn't ski and hated snow. He hated snow because it mucked up everything and caused gig cancellations, and here were the overly excitable, blow-dried blond meteorologists in skin-tight dresses and pasteboard smiles, all pearly white teeth and hysterical predictions of massive quantities of snow (or white shit, as residents of snow towns refer to it) arriving later that day: "Better get 'cha to the store and stock up on milk, bread and eggs for that French toast y'all eat when it snows because we got ourselves a rip-roarin' major happening bearing down on us from the Northwest—a real Siberian express on track and headin' straight for us. Woo-ee!"

As it turned out, snow was one of the things on Calvin's mind and how it was screwing up his well-ordered life, but this wasn't snow he was looking at. It couldn't be—not yet, anyway. No, this snow-like matter was moving around with more snow-like matter flying about overhead. It took him a few moments to realize he was looking at some kind of birds, massive quantities of white birds. Calvin finally figured out they were geese, pure white geese. He couldn't remember ever seeing them before—certainly not in the countless gaggles that covered the vintage farmland in a shocking layer of whiteness that permeated the entire countryside.

Must have been tens of thousands of them.

Calvin pulled into a cutout along the road where a couple of cars had stopped to better view this remarkable occurrence. He walked over to an old man who was studying the assembled flocks through binoculars and asked, "What are they?"

"Snow geese," the old man said.

"I've never seen them before," Calvin said.

"That's because you weren't looking."

"It's hard to look for something you don't know exists," Calvin offered somewhat sheepishly.

"Ain't that the truth," the old man snorted.

"Do they come here often?"

"Their migration pattern usually takes them farther south, down around Lancaster County, but they show up around here every once in a while. They like the corn stubble. As abundant as they are, it's my guess most people live their whole lives and never see them. It's really something to behold, isn't it?" the old man asked.

"It's unbelievable," Calvin marveled, and as he said it, a souped-up, lowrider Toyota with a loud, pulsating subwoofer came around the bend, scaring the birds nearest to the road. Hundreds of them lifted off the ground *en masse,* beating their wings in unison, like the ground itself had taken off and ascended toward heaven.

It was an amazing thing to witness, and for a moment Calvin was filled with wonder, momentarily freed from his consternation.

The old man wasn't as impressed. "Asshole!"

Two

The dog chased the rabbit across the dirt and cinder road and into the woods.

"Fagen!" Calvin yelled. "Get back here."

Fagen, a 3-year-old chocolate Lab, stuck his nose out of the brush, looked around, then trotted ahead of his master as they walked down the deserted road nearly wide enough to accommodate two passing cars. It was a few hours before the skiers would arrive, all hyperactive for a weekend of fresh, real snow. It had already started coming down, softly, as Calvin Coffman and his best friend ambled down the well-worn trail in silence, both preoccupied—one with chasing rabbits, one with not. Calvin smiled as Fagen darted into a clump of rhododendron. " If you go chasing rabbits, you ain't no hound dog, ..." Calvin said out loud in a sing-song voice, evoking a quasi-Elvis Presley draw to the bastardized Jefferson Airplane lyric. He loved playing "White Rabbit," a song that Calibration, his band, did occasionally if the crowd was in a more cerebral mood, as opposed to the usual headbangers out to get wild and crazy.

Calvin's life had come down to entertaining numbskulls and imbeciles—alike, yet different forms of stupid. A numbskull was born stupid, would always remain stupid, but never know he was stupid. An imbecile occasionally acted stupid but knew the next day he'd been stupid and vowed never to be stupid again, or at least until the next night out. Both types would get drunk and climb on the stage and try to get funky with Calvin's beautiful 27-year-old wife, Molly, who was the singer in the band. The numbskulls normally had to be physically escorted off the premises, whereas the imbeciles could be removed from the stage without much incident.

Calvin's life had degenerated into a world of incremental stupidity. Unless, of course, it snowed and the gig got canceled.

Molly would drive up later in the day from Bethlehem, where she worked for a large insurance company, utilizing her BS degree in actuarial science from Penn State—a far cry from singing in ski resorts and ersatz biker bars for aging never-weres "but I got me a shitload of horsepower between my legs, momma." Calvin was worried she might have trouble on the roads if the snow started piling up, but Molly didn't need anybody worrying about her. She was highly competent at almost everything, including keeping Calvin in a constant state of anxiety over losing her.

Why would a bombshell with a brain like Molly pick me? Calvin would agonize.

Molly would say she always fell for the guitar player.

And w*hat if I'm no longer the guitar player,* Calvin asked himself as he and his dog kept a sharp lookout: Fagen for rabbits, Calvin for rabbit holes.

Three

Molly took a half-day off from work, not because of traffic or the impending storm, but because she had an early afternoon appointment and wanted to get to their mountain cabin early so she could spend time with Calvin and have a little talk. He was wrestling with some undefined (at least to her) issues relating

to what she suspected was the onset of a midlife cri-
sis (in spite of her knowing little about midlife crises).
Since he'd turned 40 a few months earlier, he'd been in
a funk, which was uncharacteristic for Calvin—he was
always upbeat, forever seeing the glass half full, usually with beer and usually not long enough to ponder the
philosophical implications of point of view.

When Molly had spoken to Calvin mid-morning,
when he had called to tell her the job scheduled for
that night was canceled by The Last Run Inn in Tan-
nersville because of the impending storm, he was perplexed.

And pissed.

"Why would you cancel a band for a Friday night in
a ski bar because it was snowing? Isn't that what skiing
is all about? Snow?" he had asked her.

"It's the lawyers, Cal," she had said. "They're afraid
people will drink too much and drive home in the middle of a blizzard, get in wrecks, mess people up—you
know. They're afraid of being sued. Think of it as a
compliment: They think we'll draw too many people.
We're a hot band, man!"

"Well, this is total bullshit!" he had said.

"What's that you always say, babe? Bullshit makes
the world go 'round."

And the bullshit seemed to be piling up on Calvin,
Molly thought as she inched along the Turnpike with
all the eager snow enthusiasts. "And now I'm about to
add to it," she said to no one.

Molly had met Calvin at a summer festival four years
earlier, three months after graduating from college.
The county fair was complete with rides, sideshows
and lots of artery-clogging food. Calibration was the
featured band that night, playing on an old, wooden
stage, but retrofitted with huge Yamaha speakers and

aluminum scaffolding to hold the multicolored stage lights. The fairground was located on an enervated dirt track where legendary race cars, such as midgets, modifieds and fender benders used to raise the dust on Friday and Saturday nights; the only remnants of those glory days on that hot-as-Hades Saturday night were the lightning bugs and mosquitoes, all part of the old-fashioned ambiance.

Molly was there with two girlfriends, about a half-hour drive from her parents' home (where she was presently domiciled, much to her chagrin) in a small town west of Allentown, and as she sat in her barely moving car on the Northeast Extension trying to get to their cabin on that pending winter-wonderland-Friday afternoon, she was thinking about traveling up the same roadway four eventful years ago and how that trip changed her life. *Was this trip going to change it again?* she fretted.

Molly loved music, all kinds of music. She had sang in her church's youth chorus and moved up to the adult choir when she turned 16. In high school, she was chosen for chorale, a very select touring choir. She loved being on stage and played Cassie Ferguson in *A Chorus Line* her junior year and the lead in *The Unsinkable Molly Brown* when she was a senior, winning a coveted regional award for her performance. She went to Muhlenberg College, where she majored in theater, but after a year of 12-hour days, going to classes, workshops and rehearsals and learning scripts—all while enduring her father browbeating that most actors are starving—she transferred to Penn State and entered the Smeal College of Business, packing away her theatrical dreams.

Until she met Calvin.

She was smitten from the first incredibly loud D chord coming out of Calvin's Fender Stratocaster as the band lunged into a rousing rendition of "Reelin' in the Years." She couldn't take her eyes off the lead guitar player. He wasn't a noticeably good-looking man, rather ordinary, actually, but there was something about him, a stage presence, a charismatic flair, something she couldn't quite put her finger on. Molly and her friends stood for the entire rockin' set, swaying and dancing and clapping their hands, but Molly was much more than simply having a good time like her friends. She was totally mesmerized.

When the band took a break, Molly made a beeline for Calvin, who was walking out from behind the stage. If he had been taking notice of his surroundings instead of fixated on a sloppy bridge on "Old Time Rock and Roll," he would have noticed a tall, stunning girl with long, chestnut brown hair and piercing hazel eyes walking toward him, so he was a bit startled when she stopped directly in front of him blocking his path, stuck out her hand and said, "Hi, I'm Molly, and I'm a singer."

Four

Jake and Jack Teduska were excited about the forecasted 15 inches of white gold. The brothers operated a tow truck out of their father's junkyard in Long Pond, and a good snow always meant plenty of stuck drivers and, better yet, accidents. They would be going all night and all weekend, pulling city drivers out of driveways and roadsides, but their bread and butter was monitoring a police scanner and jumping calls the cops made to other towing companies to pick up wrecks.

Wrecks were their business.

The junkyard their dad operated specialized in cars that faceless insurance companies had totaled, where customers could walk the fields inspecting the hollow corpses of American dreams, picking out salvageable parts. It was a good business, and Jake and Jack had big plans to make it even better.

Named after Biblical characters by their religiously overwrought mother, Jacob was 22 with a wife and two-year-old son, and John was 19 and had a girlfriend he hoped to marry in the not-too-distant future, if only he had a not-too-distant future. They both had graduated from Vo-Tech where they studied automobile mechanics, and where Jack turned out to be some kind of internal combustion savant. He never read a manual or looked for instructions; he would just unceremoniously dive into an engine and fix it. They were saving some of the towing money for a down payment on a building and equipment to open a repair shop, and they probably would have done it—if they hadn't met Calvin and Molly.

Five

The Chevy Camaro made the corner on all four wheels, but just barely. It hardly slowed down to make the turn as the road workers stopped to watch the shiny white blur go by, shaking their heads in disgust and whistling at the hot blonde behind the wheel, all at the same time. Harper Fay was late for a date with her friends to go skiing, which really wasn't why she was driving so fast—she always drove fast; she was always in a hurry. She'd cut her afternoon classes at King's College in Wilkes-Barre, a 45-minute drive to Big Boulder Mountain, but Harper made it in 35. The plan was to buy afternoon passes, ski for a few hours, then go party, and that night she would stay at her parents' ski house not far from Big Boulder.

Harper loved to ski, and, much more, loved to party. It was practically what she was majoring in, and it might have become a lifelong problem if it wasn't for her brief encounter with Jack Teduska.

Six

Calvin sat in an Adirondack chair on his back deck, watching the snow accumulate. Fagen was at his feet, assiduously protecting the small clearing that passed for a backyard edging up to the thick woods, hoping a rabbit or squirrel would dare to show its face on his turf. Calvin had built the deck himself, plank by plank, nail by nail, smashed thumb by smashed thumb, just after he bought the cabin 10 years ago. It was a statement of maturity—the cabin and the deck. He'd traveled the rock-and-roll circuit in search of fame and fortune, and after years of almosts and could've-beens, he settled back in the Lehigh Valley to become a gentleman guitar player. In his mind, a gentleman guitar player was a guitar player who was not rich and famous but very good at his craft.

The cabin represented roots to him, but like the abundant hemlocks that surrounded his property, his roots were shallow. He'd thought about buying a house in Allentown, but those roots would have been too deep, just in case another "almost" came along to crush the last remnants of his youthful hopes and aspirations.

As Calvin sat there sipping a Heineken, waiting for Molly, the hinges on the outside shower stall caught his attention. He had a plumber install the shower after he built the deck, and he felt an exhilarating sense of freedom standing outside, even in winter, with the warm water flowing over him, naked as a jaybird for all the world to see. But the world wasn't looking, was nowhere in sight, which is how he tried to explain it to Molly when she insisted he enclose it. The hinges were galvanized steel and weren't supposed to rust, but they did, causing Calvin to wax philosophical. *Those hinges and I are kindred spirits,* he thought. *We are both trying to get back to a stable state.* He found the idea of rusting away to stability rather ironic—and telling.

Because here Calvin was, sitting on a deck in the middle of the woods in the midst of a snowstorm, rusting away.

He chuckled at the thought and took another swig of beer. Fagen looked up, thinking it might be a sign to go chase rabbits. The dog had been Molly's idea. She thought Calvin needed a buddy to hang with, and she was right—Calvin and Fagen had become inseparable, spending all their time together when Calvin wasn't playing or giving lessons, and lately, that wasn't much time away from each other.

Calvin named him after Donald Fagen of Steely Dan, his favorite group. He loved jazz-infused rock and loved playing irregular, symphonically-paraprosdoki-an chords, the discordant clash of sounds resonating in a harmonic oxymoron of pure feeling and sensation. He longed for a world where he could make a living playing the kind of music he loved, but that wasn't in the cards. He had tried several times to reshuffle the deck, but aces and eights kept coming up.

Calvin was spending more and more time ruminating over his future—or lack thereof, as he saw it. It had been a long journey to get to this place in his life, and he was unsure where it was going. He got his first guitar in the sixth grade—an old beat-up acoustic he bought from the brother of one of his schoolmates for

20 bucks. A year later at Christmas, Calvin's parents gave him an inexpensive electric guitar and small amplifier. He formed a band not too long after that and had been playing in one band or another ever since.

By the time Calvin had graduated from high school, he'd gained a reputation as an accomplished finger master, so he bummed a ride to California from a drummer he'd met playing at the Jersey Shore the previous summer. The guy was going to the West Coast to do some studio work, and he told Calvin that he might be able to get him into the studio. He did, and Calvin spent the next 10 years between Los Angeles, Nashville and New York City, playing with some talented musicians. He played, uncredited, on numerous songs, a couple of them becoming hits. He even cut a few demos of his own material—but got no offers. His voice was gravelly like Dylan's and Springsteen's, but lacked range and resonance, and his songs were uninspiring and derivative, most coming out sounding like "Babylon Sisters" or "What a Fool Believes."

Although Calvin'd become a virtuoso guitar player, the realization that his songs and singing voice were never going to get him anywhere was like a pack of wolves salivating at his door, so he moved back to Pennsylvania, formed Calibration and settled in for phase two. Phase two included Calibration becoming a very good regional band, Calvin giving guitar lessons twice a week, playing with the Lehigh Valley Symphony Orchestra a couple of times a season and even making sporadic appearances on a local PBS television show about music. Occasionally, he'd take a solo acoustic job for afternoon business functions or dinner hours, and once in a while he'd team up with another guitar player and do gigs playing old-time country and bluegrass.

But after a few years, it stopped being fun and became work. That was until Molly showed up with her four-octave range and sublime good looks. She revitalized him professionally and personally, and other than the lost-at-sea uncertainty of his life, they were happy together.

But it wasn't happiness that was on Calvin's mind as the snow became thick. It was that uncertainty playing havoc with him, stressing him out every which way but unhinged. It was confusing and tiring, and he wanted out of the box he'd built around himself. He brushed snow off his head and arms and sang a bit of an old outlaw song called "My Heros Have Always Been Cowboys," a song about the fear of rusting away. As he gazed at the hills surrounding him, he couldn't help but wonder if he wasn't already over them.

Fagen looked up at him and barked.

"Ain't that the truth," he said.

Seven

It started early.

Jake and Jack jumped their first call at 4:45 that afternoon. A car had slid off the road, taking out two mailboxes and getting stuck in a ditch. A state trooper called for a tow, and before the company he called could record the message, the Teduska boys were already rolling. The trick was to get there and be gone before the other company showed up, so the brothers worked as a team, quickly assessing the situation, hooking up the vehicle and moving it onto safe ground. While Jack disconnected from the towed vehicle, Jake collected the fee, always cash, and then they were gone like The Flash, only no contrail or identifying tracks left behind: no written bill, no business card, no lettering on the side of the truck, no name patches on their jumpsuits, just two happy comrades-in-arms, heading into the dark of night—now you see them, now you don't.

Eight

It started early.

At 5 o'clock, Harper Fay was sitting at the bar in the Alpine Lodge drinking her second lemon splash martini, a house special during happy hour. She was feeling no pain. The skiing had been marvelous she was telling anybody who would listen, trying to talk over the country band playing an upbeat version of "You Never Even Called Me by My Name."

Nine

It was dark by the time Molly arrived at the cabin. Calvin was lying on the couch with his eyes closed when she walked into the living room. Fagen was next to him on the floor. Molly carefully maneuvered past the dog, trying not to disturb the wishful rabbit hound, and sat on the edge of the oversized sofa.

"You asleep?" she asked.

"Sort of," Calvin mumbled.

"How can you sort of be asleep?" she asked and softly rubbed his arm.

"What time is it?" he asked, slowly opening his eyes.

"After 5."

"What took you so long?"

"The roads aren't great, and those city people can't drive in snow. And traffic, of course. All those skiers who won't be listening and dancing to us tonight," she lamented.

"Don't remind me," he said gruffly.

"Is that what's bothering you tonight, pookie? The cancellation?"

"Yes. The cancellation. The cancellation and I'm a washed-up old man."

"Washed up? Not a chance. You're in your prime. I can personally attest to that."

They were quiet for a few moments, then he said, "I talked to Murry today."

"And?" she demanded.

"I accepted the job."

A big smile spread across her face. "Oh my God! Are you serious? That's wonderful! I'll bet Murry was happy."

"He was beside himself with joy."

Murry Stevens was the president and CEO of Stevens Guitars in Catasauqua. He was the fourth-generation leader of the world-renowned acoustic instruments maker, and it was his awesome responsibility to make sure the Stevens name stayed attached to high-quality products. Calvin's and Murry's paths had crossed many times, and they had become good friends. Not surprisingly, Murry played guitar, and he would occasionally sit in with Calibration. Murry had been bugging Calvin for a few years to come work for him selling guitars. Murry would tell him he was one of the best guitar players he'd ever seen, and he'd seen the best. He would invariably add, "And you can be quite charming when you feel like it. My customers will love you."

"Then your customers must be idiots," Calvin would respond.

"You're one of my customers."

"I rest my case."

Calvin had lunch with Murry a few days earlier and Murry made a big play, offering Calvin a nice salary and generous commission package. Calvin could make a lot of money; however, it would mean giving up some things, such as lessons. He hated teaching guitar to musically ungifted kids, and as far as he was concerned, eschewing those painful sessions was the only good thing about taking the job. He had wrestled with the decision and couldn't escape a feeling that accepting the position was the final sellout.

"I'm very happy for you," Molly said.

"For becoming a salesman!"

"Not a salesman. A marketing advisor and product expert," she offered.

"A salesman," Calvin replied.

"Well, you're going to be great," Molly said, then added, "Speaking of that, I have something I need to talk to you about."

"No, you can't quit your job now."

"Ha, ha! No, I looked at a cute house in Catasauqua—a three-bedroom colonial with a big yard for your buddy. Part of the basement is finished, and it would be perfect for a music room. I know you're going to love it."

"Catasauqua, eh?" he prodded. "You were confident I was going to take the job?"

"Sort of."

"Then why didn't you tell me? You could have saved me a lot of anguish."

"I knew you'd do the right thing, sweet lips. You always do. Problem is, if we don't make an offer by tomorrow, we're going to lose it," she said as she ran her hand through his hair.

"How can you lose something you never had?"

"So, what do you think? Can we go look at it tomorrow?"

"I don't want to think, and I don't want to talk." The thought of buying a house was just too much for

Calvin at the moment. At any moment, for that matter. Why was this happening to him?

"Okay, we'll finish the discussion at dinner. I made a 6:30 reservation at Close Quarters so you better hurry. You only have another hour to be maudlin."

"Why can't I be maudlin at Close Quarters?"

"Because you have a dynamic public personality that even you can't suppress."

"Do I have to be maudlin? I'd rather be irritable. I'm much better at irritable."

"You can be anything you want to be, cuddle muffin, just so long as you can do it in the next hour," she said as she leaned in and kissed him on the tip of his nose.

Ten

By 6:15, the snowstorm was dissipating and the predicted 15 inches was turning out to be four, maybe five inches of business-as-usual in the meteorological world of hand grenades—just get it close, and if not, it will still make a lot of beautiful noise.

By 6:15, Mr. and Mrs. Coffman were driving north on Route 903 in Calvin's three-year-old, midnight blue Jeep Cherokee, which gave Calvin only 15 more minutes to be irritable.

By 6:15, Jake and Jack Teduska had just finished a tow job they had jumped in Blakeslee and were heading south on Route 115, listening intently to their police scanner.

By 6:15, Harper Fay was swallowing the last vestiges of sweet intoxicants and paying the bill at the Alpine Lodge, on her way to Molly Maguire's Pub and Steakhouse in Jim Thorpe, about a 15-mile drive in her new, Chevrolet Camaro ZL1 with 650 horsepower—a Christmas gift from her parents.

Eleven

The roads weren't great but Calvin was making decent time, so Molly was confident they'd be at Close Quarters on time.

And then the first snowball smacked against the windshield.

It startled Calvin, and he instinctively jerked his head to the left. As he did, another frozen missile hit the windshield and one slammed against his side window. Calvin saw a group of three or four boys just ahead, standing by the side of the road throwing the snowballs, smiling and laughing and having a marvelous time. The deluge continued, and Calvin said, "That's it! I've had it!"

He turned the wheel hard and slammed on the brakes, causing the Jeep to spin sharply to the left where it stopped, facing the group of young miscreants. Calvin gunned the engine, and the 4x4 lurched forward. The group smartly turned tail and beat feet. As they scattered into the woods, Calvin fought to get control of the sliding mass of aluminum and steel, skidding sideways and landing in a drainage ditch alongside the road.

"Nice," Molly said as she tried to pull herself together. "Feel better now?"

"Actually, I do," Calvin responded while nodding his head slowly up and down.

Calvin tried to move the heavy vehicle forward, but it wouldn't budge, and then he tried reverse with the same results. He prided himself on being able to get out of any snow jam, so he began rocking the rugged descendant of "This We'll Defend" back and forth, jamming the transmission from drive to reverse, but he was going nowhere. He climbed out and walked behind the Jeep to discover he had put it in a culvert. There was no way it was going anywhere.

Not without a tow truck.

Twelve

Molly opened her window and yelled back to Calvin, "Are we stuck?"

Calvin gave her a look.

When he climbed back in the front seat, he said, "I guess we need to call a tow truck."

"No need," Molly said. "I called 911."

"911! Why'd you call 911? This isn't an emergency."

"The front of our car is sticking out onto the road. Don't you call that an emergency? Or would you rather wait until somebody hits us?"

A silence with a noticeable twinge of animus ensued.

Eventually Calvin said, "Well, I guess you better call Close Quarters."

"Already did," she replied. "They said they have plenty of room tonight—lots of cancellations. They told me they'd seat us whenever we get there."

"Good," Calvin said, then added, "I guess I should have stuck with morose."

"Cold or wet, tired you bet. All of this, I'll soon forget, with my man," Molly sang in a dead-on imitation of Billie Holiday.

"I'm stuck in a ditch and the girl sings a jazz classic in perfect pitch" marveled Calvin as the red-and-blue flashing lights of a Pennsylvania State Police cruiser pulled up behind them. The trooper got out and set two flares behind them, one at about 50 feet, and the other at about 100.

The trooper walked over to Calvin's open window and asked, "What happened?"

Calvin was too embarrassed to tell him the truth, so he merely said, "I slid off the road; landed in a culvert."

"I called a tow truck," the trooper said. "Should be here soon. I have to go, though. Just got a call about a bad accident. Good luck," he threw over his shoulder as he jumped into his car and sped away.

A few minutes later, Calvin and Molly saw flashing yellow lights coming up on them from behind. The tow truck pulled onto the shoulder of the road in front of the four-wheeler-formerly-known-as-Willys, and two gentlemen of questionable-looking character disembarked the battered old wrecker. Jake and Jack had been only a few miles away when they heard the call about a blue Jeep Cherokee stuck in a ditch on the northbound side of Route 903, approximately a mile north of Route 534. They arrived at the scene within five minutes.

As the brothers approached the Coffmans, dressed in dirty, black Carhartt coveralls and floppy galoshes, Molly remarked, "They look grimy."

"We're not going to dance with them," Calvin said and climbed out of his Cherokee to meet the brothers grim.

The Teduskas wasted no time. They didn't set additional flares or put out orange traffic cones, they just went to work lining up the rig to the Jeep, hooking it up and pulling it off the culvert and out of the ditch. Didn't take them but 15 minutes. Once they unhooked the emancipated SUV, Calvin got behind the wheel and straightened out the Jeep so it was safely on the shoulder of the road behind the tow truck. Jack was standing on the edge of the road, next to Calvin, still in the driver's seat. Jack was waiting for Jake, who was behind the Jeep, collecting $50 cash from Molly.

The next thing Calvin heard was a swish and a thump.

Harper Fay was burning down the highway at a high speed, the radio blasting The Killers' "Somebody Told Me," and she never saw the two flares, the flashing yellow lights, people standing on the shoulder, the Jeep's flashers, the large tow truck or Jack Teduska. Jake, who had the best view, estimated she was doing between 65 to 70 miles per hour when she hit Jack, hurling him against the large steel bumper on the back of the tow truck, like a bean bag thrown at 100 miles per hour by Jacob deGrom against a concrete wall.

There wasn't much inside Jack Teduska that wasn't broken. He laid on the pavement a crumpled mess, dead as dead can be, while Harper Fay kept on going. She knew she hit something, she felt the jolt, and she knew it was bad because she could see flashing yellow lights in her rear-view mirror. She hoped it wasn't a dog.

A doctor, on his way home from dinner, stopped and took one look at Jack and forlornly shook his head. Calvin was practically out of his mind and insisted the doctor resuscitate the corpse lying at his feet. The doctor could see that Calvin was in bad shape, so he tried to perform CPR on the lifeless body, just for show. Everybody knew it was useless, and the good Samaritan doctor finally got to his feet and in a quiet voice said to Calvin, "I'm sorry."

"This is all my fault," Calvin moaned. "I killed that boy."

Thirteen

Calvin and Molly finished their dinner and were sipping coffee in front of a warm fire at Close Quarters. After a bourbon on the rocks with a splash and twist, two glasses of pinot noir and Molly's supportive reassurances, Calvin was close to a state of relaxed.

"I should have just kept going," Calvin said. "I should have laughed it off and just kept going."

"All you did was get your car stuck," Molly said. "That's all you did. You were just one cog in a wheel of circumstances, and a pretty small cog at that."

"Still—," he said.

"Look, it's just as much my fault. I'm the one who told you that you could be irritable," she said and smiled at him.

"Do you think they'll catch that girl?" Calvin wondered out loud.

"I'm hopeful," Molly said very quietly.

Fourteen

They knew it was a girl because Jake had a good view of her. And because he was a motorhead and knew cars, he was able to give the cops a detailed description of the Camaro: make, model, year, and he even described the fancy chrome wheels. One of the cops on the scene after the accident told Calvin he was surprised Jake didn't give him the VIN number.

Jake also told the cops that the car was weaving when it sped away, so they assumed she had been drinking and canvassed the bars up Route 903 and along Route 115. A waitress at the Alpine Inn, who was outside smoking a cigarette when Harper left that afternoon, remembered the car pulling out of the parking lot, cinders flying, so they were able to get the credit card receipt she'd used to pay her bill, and consequently, track her down.

At 8 o'clock the next morning, two state troopers knocked on the door of Harper's parents' home in Bryn Mawr, an upscale bedroom community on the Main Line outside of Philadelphia. The Fays immediately called one of their neighbors, a high-priced criminal lawyer, who went to work getting Harper, if not a slap on the wrist, a pretty light deal considering she killed a man.

They couldn't prove she was under the influence because there was no way of knowing how many of the drinks on her bill she had consumed, and nobody at the Alpine Lodge was going to testify that they got her drunk and sent her on her way to kill somebody. Even a charge of vehicular homicide was going to be tough to prove because the only eyewitness who had a clear view was Jake Teduska, and he said she was going 65 to 70 miles per hour, testimony the sharp Philadelphia lawyer would have torn to shreds on cross. The only hard evidence was the wrinkle in Harper's right front fender, but even that provided no real forensic evidence because the first thing Harper did after she got her parents' phone call the next morning was to wash her car. When asked about it by the police, Harper's lawyer wouldn't let her answer, and she was never going to take the stand.

The district attorney in Carbon County wasn't the shiniest pair of shoes in the closet, so Harper's lawyer was able to wrangle a charge of negligent homicide, a misdemeanor. She was sentenced to a year on probation, a $5,000 fine and 50 hours of community service. She also lost her driver's license for a year. Harper dropped out of school, temporarily, and her parents sent her to an expensive rehab in Arizona, where she was scared to death every day she spent there. Or, more accurately, scared straight.

Fifteen

"We need to talk about the house," Molly said.

"Oh, please," Calvin implored. "Not tonight."

"We have to talk about it tonight or it will be gone. And there is one other thing: I went to the doctor today and I'm pregnant."

"What!" Calvin gasped and took a beat...or two. "Man, I wasn't looking for that."

He folded his hands on the table in front of him and stared off into space.

Molly waited patiently, full of trepidation. After a minute or so, she put her hands on Calvin's and asked softly, "So, what do you think?"

Calvin looked at her and smiled for the first time in days. He cocked his head to one side and said, "What do I think? I think we better get up early tomorrow morning and go look at that house."

It's Not You, It's Me

You

Through his face mask, and without moving his head, he could see the split end, the halfback and the quarterback, his keys in the overly complicated defensive scheme designed by a coach who believed that simplicity was the workshop of the devil. His first responsibility—his first read—was the end, making sure he didn't break loose for a long catch and run, which was tricky because teams that focused on the run game would use the split end as a decoy, hoping to draw the outside linebacker or cornerback out of the play. Occasionally, the end would start a route, then turn in and try to throw a block, and at that point, Ahmed knew it was a running play, most likely coming around his corner.

His second responsibility, or read, was the running back, first to make sure he didn't run a crossing pattern with the split end or flood Ahmed's zone. In that case, he was to cover the long man or the outside man, and the linebacker was supposed to pick up the short man. If they both went long, it was the safety's responsibility to get the inside man. If the halfback set up to block, it was a passing play and Ahmed's focus was on the split end, trying to keep the receiver from getting behind him. If the quarterback, his third key, handed the ball to the halfback, Ahmed's responsibility was to help keep the play inside and make, or assist in making a tackle. While undertaking all that, Ahmed was supposed to keep the quarterback in the corner of his eye at all times to make sure no tomfoolery was afoot.

It gave Ahmed Clark a headache. Although he loved football, he didn't particularly like playing defense, but since he was the fastest guy on the team—and one of the two or three fastest players in the state—his job was to make sure the other team never scored a long touchdown, the defensive coach would pound into him.

"Always keep the ballcarrier in front of you and turn on the jets," the coach would preach. "And don't forget to defend against the long bomb, stop the running back and keep the quarterback in check with the angle of the dangle that's inversely proportional to the heat of the meat."

Freakin' guy's nuts, Ahmed thought as he ran through his checklist.

It was the last play of the game for the 1973 Delaware State football championship with Ahmed's Hockessin Prep Pit Bulls leading the Joden Cowbirds, 21-20. Ahmed had scored one of the three touchdowns for The Pits, as they were unaffectionately referred to by everybody who wasn't a Pit Bull, and there were a few scouts in the stands that day who made notes on the young receiver's hands and footwork. Ahmed was only a junior, but he was already known for his great speed, having medaled in the 100, 200 and 400 relay plus the hurdles at the previous spring's state track tournament. College coaches in the area were starting to notice him, but the perennial question for all track phenoms was whether they could handle the toughness of a collegiate football schedule.

Ahmed was about to answer that question in spades.

When the ball was snapped, the split end took off in a sprint and Ahmed backpedaled for a few steps, then turned his body sideways to keep pace, while trying to watch the running back and quarterback. At about 12 yards, the split end broke hard to his left, taking Ahmed farther away from the line of scrimmage and his other two reads. Out of his peripheral vison, Ahmed saw the halfback crouch in a blocking stance and then break downfield as the quarterback tossed him a short, 10-yard pass, hitting the runner in stride as the halfback found a hole in the coverage and galloped through the outstretched arms of the desperate Pit Bulls.

Ahmed wheeled and took off in hot pursuit, 40 yards from the unfettered ball carrier, who was 35 yards from glory. Instead of chasing the rambling wreck-to-be, Ahmed took the angle and ran him down. He caught him on the 5-yard line, and just as he was about to dive at the churning feet of the almost-hero, an alarm went off in his head. Ahmed made a slight adjustment to his shoulders and let fly, bringing down the surprised Cowbird at the 2 in a bone-crunching tackle.

The scouts smiled and the Hockessin fans went berserk. The band played, the cheerleaders yelled, and Ahmed Clark got up rubbing his left shoulder. It was good.

Me

I see this as a tragedy, but I'm sure most people would disagree. That is, they'd argue that I've had a good life, and that may very well be—no, they'd be correct; I've had a good life, but...

I guess it's a matter of perspective.

It all started with that damn tackle. Or should I say, that's where it all ended. I know, I know, I'm being melodramatic, but you try living with this...with this nightmare for almost 50 years. Okay, it might not be a nightmare, but it's been pretty unpleasant. No, no, it's been a nightmare. If only...

Those "what ifs" and "could've beens" will kill you, man.

I probably should have said it all started with that missed tackle, because that's how it infamously became known. They might as well engrave "The Missed Tackle" over the stone Hockessin Preparatory School marquee in front of the school's driveway; might as well put a plaque across the trophy case in the hall outside the gym that reads "The Missed Tackle! Thanks, Ahmed Clark!" Maybe I should write a book titled *How to Go from Hero to Loser in a Nanosecond,* or maybe, *How to Flush Your Future Down the Hopper.* Or even better, *How to Spend Your Entire Life Reliving One Fleeting Moment in Time.*

And time does not heal all, believe me.

I remember that moment like it happened yesterday, which is no big stretch since I dream about it fairly regularly. My mind plays with it, though, adding different scenarios to enhance the night sweats, like I can't find my way out of the locker room, or I can't find my helmet on the bench, or I'm standing naked in front of the entire stadium, but most of the time it's the same old thing, me streaking downfield and diving at the ballcarrier. Then I usually wake up, out of breath.

I should have seen a shrink years ago, but what could I tell him? The reality is that it changed my life's trajectory, and not in a good way, I'm sure—at least not to me, to my stunted sense of self-worth. It was such a simple thing: I was in my ready position going through my complicated list of reads and peeking at Sandy standing with the other cheerleaders, pom-poms at her side, eyes closed and praying the play went away from me, like she always did.

Well, she got her wish.

The tight end went long and wide and pretty much took me out of the play. When the quarterback threw the ball to the halfback breaking through the line, I was a half a world away with no chance of catching him, but I was the last thing standing between us winning the state championship and a lifetime of second-guessing, although that scenario had yet to present itself; was patiently waiting on the sideline, drooling.

I knew I was fast—I had proven that at the previous year's track finals—but I didn't think I was that fast. Somehow, though, I was able to find a new gear and ran down the guy. I still don't know how I did it, and many observers, even today, say it was a miracle that I got there in the first place. I remember it so clearly—can still see it in slow motion—leaving my feet and hitting him a speck too high just as he swung his arm and shoulder, flicking me off like a horse shooing a fly with his tail. I slid off him and hit the ground hard, slamming my left shoulder into the ungiving half-frozen turf. The ecstatic ball carrier crossed the goal line with the winning touchdown while his teammates jumped up and down and hugged. I heard a loud groan from our fans as I lay on the ground screaming and writhing in pain, holding my left shoulder.

We

By the time Dr. Brody Winechal was nine, he could finish *The New York Times* crossword puzzle over his Cocoa Puffs in the morning until he got bored and gave it up a year later. He had an eidetic memory and could look at a page in the dictionary for a few minutes and then spell and define every word accurately. His school tried to enter him in the National Spelling Bee, but he wouldn't go. He said it was a waste of his precious time. Time was something that was always on Brody's mind—he had a lot to do and very little time to do it. One doesn't change the world by participating in frivolous activities, does one?

You

Ahmed Clark became an overnight sensation. "The Tackle," as it became known almost instantly, was featured in sports media reports for the rest of the weekend. *The News Journal,* the largest circulation newspaper in Wilmington, Delaware, used a 36-point Helvetica headline to get the ball rolling, with the subhead reading, "Ahmed Clark Grounds the Cowbirds." All three Philadelphia papers—*The Bulletin, The Inquirer* and *The Daily News*—had blurbs about the game with pictures of Ahmed making The Tackle. A local Wilmington TV station broadcast film of the play, the commentator closing the bit with, "Keep your eye on this boy because you're going to be hearing his name in the future."

Sunday evening, just as the Clarks were sitting down to dinner, Ahmed's head coach called and told Lonny Clark, Ahmed's father, that Tubby Raymond, the legendary coach at the University of Delaware, called and asked for the Clarks's phone number. "I told him I'd have to ask you first if it was okay," Coach Moose Moorhead said.

There was silence on the line as a shocked Lonny tried to digest the ramifications of the call.

"Well, what should I tell him?" the coach finally asked.

"Hold on," Lonny said and covered the mouthpiece with his hand.

"Coach Raymond from the university wants to call you, Ahmed. Is that alright with you?"

Ahmed's mother, Azra, laid down her fork and covered her mouth. "Oh my," she whispered. Ahmed's sister, Mya, who was three years younger, looked confused.

Ahmed had dreamed of playing football at Delaware, wearing the Blue Hens's blue and yellow helmet, the ones Michigan copied, he would tell his buddies in the locker room as they pontificated on their certain futures of glory and beautiful babes.

"You already got a beautiful babe," they would tease him. "And you're already way out of your league."

Ahmed's heart was almost beating out of his chest and his mouth was as dry as the Karapinar Desert, like it was filled with cotton. All he could manage was to nod his head up and down, slowly, in disbelief.

Lonny said into the phone, "Go ahead, Coach. Please give him our number. And thanks."

"Don't thank me," Coach Moorhead said. "Thank your boy. That was one heck of a play—never seen anything like it. Can't wait till next year!" he said and hung up.

The Clarks sat looking at each other, not touching their köfte. All of a sudden they started to laugh, a huge laugh like a loud break of thunder, and then they were on their feet, holding hands and dancing around the table.

Me

The interesting twist here in this Greek tragedy is that I was really hurt—seriously injured—and nobody believed me. That's because by the time the ambulance made its way around the track that circumnavigated the football field and pulled up on the grass next to me, the screaming had stopped and the agony was gone. When it first happened, while I was still rolling around on the ground, I put my right hand on my shoulder beneath the jersey and shoulder pads, and I could feel a bulge, like a tennis ball sticking out from under my skin. After a couple of coaches stood me up and I turned my upper body to get in a more comfortable position, which at the time didn't exist, I felt something move inside my shoulder, like a deadbolt lock sliding into place.

And just like that, no pain in my shoulder.

Only the one I would shoulder forever.

When I told my coaches I was fine, they looked at me in disbelief.

You have no idea know how frustrating that was.

We

When Dr. Brody Winechal was 10 years old, his Uncle Mo, a doctor of orifical virtuosity, Mo would joke—a proctologist—gave Brody a $500 chemistry set designed for advanced high school students. Uncle Mo told him that the chemistry lab kit bundled the hard-to-find materials and laboratory equipment for doing really cool science experiments. While other kids his age were making slime, crystals and bottle rockets, the future Dr. Brody Winechal was more interested in using metal nanoparticles to catalyze organic reactions in water by using polyelectrolyte nanoreactors and things like that. Unfortunately, for most of the experiments he wanted to conduct, he needed uranium, which, for some unfathomable reason, didn't come with the chemistry set. Highly perturbed and motivated, young Brody went to work developing an alternative catalyst. The results of his efforts earned him an article in *Scientific American* titled "Schoolboy Makes Breakthrough in Catalyze Research."

Me

In the locker room after the game, Coach Moorhead told my dad that the team doctor didn't see any damage and was referring me to an orthopedist for a more thorough examination. When I saw the orthopedist five days later and described what had happened, he looked at me with what I thought was a skeptical eye. He took an x-ray and told my parents he saw no structural damage, that I had probably suffered a severe muscle spasm, and that he was sending me to a local Doctor of Osteopathic Medicine who specialized in ultrasound therapy.

I saw the DO for the next eight months, receiving treatments on a shoulder that had been severely damaged, severely misdiagnosed and pretty much severely ignored by the powers that were. I kept Coach Moorhead up to date on my treatments and progress, although any progress I reported was more of the wishing and hoping variety because my shoulder continued to pop out every so often—like when I was playing pickup football or basketball or carrying something or reaching for a pencil.

Coach Moorhead always seemed distracted or bored whenever I visited his office to discuss my shoulder. Once, after one of those one-sided talks, I was in the equipment room, which was next to his office, and I overheard him telling one of his assistant coaches that he thought the problem with my shoulder was mostly in my head—that I was using it as an excuse for missing The Tackle.

Nice, huh?

The next year—my senior year—I didn't even make it out of the preseason. The practice before our first game, I went out for a pass and when I reached up to catch the ball, my shoulder popped out. That time, though, it wouldn't pop back in. They had to take me to the hospital in an ambulance and rush me into the emergency room. A doctor there tried to manipulate it back into place by putting his foot in my armpit and moving my shoulder around until I almost passed out from the pain. Eventually, they had to knock me out so they could move the ball joint back into its socket.

In one of my cruelest lessons of the unfair nature of life, I was walking down the hall in school a week later with my arm in a sling, and the assistant coach to whom Coach Moorhead had told I was faking the injury, stopped me and asked, "Why didn't you tell us about this? Why didn't you tell us how bad it was?"

Why don't you get your head out of your ass? I was thinking, but said nothing. I just shrugged my one good shoulder and moved on down the hall. Coach Moorhead never spoke to me about it, and since my football career was over, he probably figured there was no longer any need. I had become irrelevant.

When I finally got around to seeing a doctor not out of a Norman Rockwell painting, he told me that the ultrasound had probably done more damage than good.

But of course, by then it was too late.

You

Ahmed was in the locker room, celebrating with his teammates and coaches after winning their second straight state championship. The past year had been a whirlwind for Ahmed, ever since The Tackle had made him semi-famous in the world of high school football recruiting. He had received letters of interest and phone calls from colleges during his junior year, but after his final game as a high school player, wherein he caught a touchdown pass—a 48-yard scamper—and played stellar defense, it really heated up. His mother cooked so many meals for coaches and scouts that the Clarks began referring to their kitchen as *Azra's Restoran.*

Having grown almost two inches between 11th and 12th grades, Ahmed was 6 feet tall, but only 165 pounds. An assistant coach from a Big Ten powerhouse visited Ahmed during the season and advised him to spend the winter in the weight room, building himself up and increasing his strength. He told Ahmed that if he wanted to play big-time college football, he needed to get bigger and stronger.

Ahmed took that suggestion to heart and put on 10 pounds—all muscle. Surprisingly, when track season started, his times were slightly better than the year before when he had once again medaled in the 100-, 200-, 400-relay and the hurdles, winning two gold, a silver and bronze. With the added weight, nobody expected him to repeat his superlative performance from the previous two years, but to the amazement of all—most notably to himself—he won gold in all four events.

Fortunately for Ahmed, after he had talked to the Big Ten coach about buffing up, he joined a gym in Wilmington, a 15-minute ride from his house, where he met a trainer who was a strength and conditioning maven. The trainer put together a program that helped distribute the muscle gain proportionately between Ahmed's upper and lower body while increasing bone density and adding greater flexibility. Ahmed's legs were more powerful, and his musculoskeletal system surrounding his core was stronger and working in better harmony with the rest of his body.

Ahmed had wrestled all year over where to go to college. He felt a loyalty to Delaware, but the program was smaller and not as high profile as the Syracuses and Pittsburghs that were desirously besotted with his highly talented potential. His parents wanted him to go to Delaware; his girlfriend, Sandy, wanted him to go to Delaware; everybody in Delaware wanted him to go to Delaware, but Tubby Raymond, like the other coaches and recruiters he was meeting, expected Ahmed to play defense.

With good reason.

Ahmed had made first team all-state his junior and senior years as a defensive halfback, but on the offensive side, he was only awarded an honorable mention his junior year and second team as a senior, both disappointing but fuel for the recruiters. As a highly rated defensive back, Ahmed had a choice of many schools, but he held on to the hope of playing wide receiver. After a long winter of disheartening discussions with gridiron suitors, he was just about to give up on ever playing offense again when he met Mike Callihan, the head coach at Alabama Tech, who promised Ahmed he could try out on offense. After that apparently serendipitous but delusive meeting in the spring, he committed to Tech and signed a letter of intent just a month before graduation. He was happy and relieved, yet extremely nervous about moving so far away. Like all young people leaving home for college, he was anxious and scared—how would he cope without his life-long support system there to protect and shelter him?

One week of football practice in the grueling August heat of southern Alabama and his focus changed from one of apprehension to survival. He made friends quickly, as is common for brothers-in-arms, went to a couple of parties, got drunk for the first time in his life and soon forgot all about missing the folks back home.

Including Sandy.

Me

Two weeks after that memorial visit to the emergency room (where a doctor finally diagnosed the injury as a complete dislocation of the shoulder—duh!) was picture day for the football team. My arm was in a sling, and I was still hurting some, but Coach Moorhead sent word that he had saved a jersey for me to wear in the picture. When I got to the locker room, the team was already on the field doing light calisthenics while the photographer set up.

The shirt that Coach had left for me was thrown on the bench in front of my now-empty locker—number 74 and huge—a number and size designed for an offensive lineman, "the big uglies," as John Madden used to call them. With my ego and sense of belonging deflated like a ruptured pigskin, I bagged the picture. Nobody seemed to notice … or care. Coach Moorhead had given my number 22 and most of my self-respect to another player, and that was pretty much the end of my football career.

And in many ways, my life, in a convoluted manner that we'll get to.

Later that week, my dad took me to Philadelphia to see an orthopedic surgeon at the University of Pennsylvania Medical Center who said I needed major reconstructive surgery. He told us that the result of the multiple dislocations over time had severely damaged the structure of the glenohumeral joint and that the ligaments, capsule and cartilage surrounding the shoulder were so badly overstretched as to render the function of the joint wholly compromised, and without the surgery it would only get worse. He added that had I received proper treatment for the initial injury—isolating the joint with a surgical sling for eight weeks—I would have healed 100 percent.

A month later, I had the complicated surgery—a four-and-a-half-hour procedure—and then spent the next couple of months walking around with my arm cradled against my chest, held in place by Ace bandages. That trying experience was followed by six months of intensive physical therapy, which pretty much precluded my participation in track, rendering senior year a total washout.

Except for Sandy.

We

Dr. Brody Winechal's parents were worried about him. He was 13 years old and studying at a 12th-grade level, but he didn't seem to have any friends or interests outside of academics. To help combat that isolation, his parents bought him a dog—a two-month-old Chihuahua that Brody named Element 115, or El for short.

Brody loved El and spent a lot of time playing with him, much of it outside, which pleased Brody's parents greatly. One day when they were playing in the backyard, a sudden, unexpected storm blew up and lightning hit a tree. The tree fell across the wire that carried electricity into Brody's house, breaking it in two. The hot end of the wire swished around on the ground, shooting out sparks and catching El's attention, who chased after it. Before Brody could catch up to him, El grabbed the live wire between his teeth and lit up like a Tijuana taxi. Brody picked up a piece of broken tree limb and knocked the wire out of El's mouth, but by then it was too late. The dog's body lay on the ground, charred and lifeless, as Brody stood over him in the drenching rain, staring at the corpse.

He was trying to figure out how to turn back time.

You

Ahmed had just hit the locker room after the last workout of the day in the middle of his second week of practices when an equipment manager told him Coach wanted to see him in his office. When Ahmed walked into the office, still in his football pants and cleats and dabbing a towel against his bare chest that was sweating profusely, two assistant coaches were sitting across the desk from Coach Callihan going over the playbook. When they saw Ahmed come in, they picked up their books and hurried out of the room without any greeting or acknowledgment of Ahmed's presence, like rats scurrying off a sinking ship.

"Sit down, Ahmed," Coach Callihan said as he motioned to one of the stuffed chairs across from him.

Ahmed sat without saying a word.

"How's it going?" Coach asked.

"Good," Ahmed responded, too uncertain to add anything further.

"Good," Coach Callihan said. "You seem to be fitting in real good here, and we're all impressed with your work ethic. Keep it up."

"Thanks, Coach."

"There is something I want to talk to you about, Ahmed. You're doing fine and learning the system quickly, but right now you'd be fifth or sixth on the depth charts at receiver. That means we would have to redshirt you. In other words, you wouldn't play this year but be freshman-eligible next season. On top of that, four of the guys in front of you on the depth chart are underclassmen, and who knows what we might bring in in the next couple of years," Coach Callihan said and held a look on Ahmad.

"What are you saying, Coach?" Ahmed asked, full of apprehension.

"What I'm saying is, right now, the way things are going, you might never be a starter at receiver. Oh, you'll get playing time, no doubt about that, but you could end up being a career backup."

Ahmed didn't know what to say. He sat there staring at his folded hands resting on the edge of the desk in front of him.

"Of course," Coach Callihan added after a pause. "If you move to defensive back, where you really belong, you'd start this season."

Ahmed lost his breath.

"Not just that, but at d-back, with your speed and toughness, I feel certain you might be able to play in the NFL," Coach Callihan confided with a big smile. "Hell, Ahmed, you might make All-American and end up a first- or second-round draft pick. There are plenty of receivers out there, but not many d-backs who can play the way you do, and the good ones, like you, are at a premium in the pros."

Ahmed didn't know what to say. He felt betrayed, set up and knocked down.

"What do you think?" Coach finally asked.

"I don't want to not play," Ahmed mumbled.

"Then it's settled. Great! You made the correct decision, son," Coach Callihan boomed as he grabbed Ahmed's hand and shook it vigorously. "After you clean up, turn in your offensive playbook and report to Bob Halpern, the defensive backfield coach. You're going to have a heck of a career at d-back."

Ahmed would never have committed to play defense at Alabama Tech, and Coach Callihan knew it from square one. His only chance was to deke Ahmed with a head bob.

Ahmed left the office and walked outside. He sat on a step at the other side of the building where nobody could see him and cried.

Me

Thank God for Sandy, man. Really. If it hadn't been for her, I'd have had a hard time coping. It's like I went from having the whole world of possibilities in front of me to a deep black hole … with no apparent way out.

Sandy was my way out.

We spent most of senior year together, her nursing and supporting me, me feeling sorry for myself and developing a hard case of resentment and anger.

I was pissed, but I didn't exactly know at whom. Or at what. Life sucked, that was for sure, and I made damn sure it kept on sucking with my bad attitude and wounded sense of entitlement. I was one discouraged, unpleasant dude to deal with, but Sandy did, faithfully, uncompromisingly, propping me up and constantly reassuring me that I had value and lots of possibilities—that my life wasn't over, that it was just beginning.

And she was right. I never got to live my dream of playing football, but, as I'm sure you would say, I got something better: I got Sandy. And a pretty good life, as I'm sure you would say.

But …

I should've made that tackle. It could've been different.

Of course, my family stood by me through those tough, emotional times, too, knowing how much I was hurting, and not just physically, either, but emotionally—especially emotionally. Looking back now, it's almost sad how much of my self-esteem I put into playing football. I mean, I came from a good family. I was smart and healthy (relatively speaking, that is, if you overlooked my gimpy shoulder tethered to my dispirited chest). I had a beautiful, loving girlfriend, and I had an extremely successful family business waiting for me to arrive and take over, someday. I definitely had it all going for me.

But...

I should've made that tackle. It could've been different.

All these years later and there's still that "but."

Sandy and I went to the University of Delaware in Newark together. I studied business; she studied elementary education. I ended up at the Alfred Lerner College of Business & Economics, where I was enrolled in a five-year program to graduate with a Master of Business Administration in management. Sandy was out in four years and got a job teaching second grade in Wilmington. We lived together in an off-campus apartment after our sophomore year, much to the consternation of both sets of our parents, but Sandy moved back home after she graduated. I remained in Newark alone for my final year, where I continued to assiduously ignore football. During five years at a football school, I never went to a single game.

But that didn't stop the dreams.

I should've made that tackle. It could've been different.

You

Alabama Tech opened the 1975 season at home against East Texas, a weak team that wouldn't win a game all year. Accordingly, Tech beat up on the hapless Prickly Pears, 28-10. Ahmed started at right cornerback, as promised, and had a less-than-superlative game. He got beat for the only touchdown East Texas scored when he tripped while trying to change direction against a small scatback who deked him with a head bob and rolled into the end zone. Other than that, the biggest problem he had all day was fighting through blocks from East Texas's huge tight end. Not only was Ahmed's limited repertoire of techniques rudimentary, he was undersized at 175 pounds.

Ahmed's parents and Sandy flew down for the weekend and took him to dinner after the game. Ahmed was distracted all evening. He wanted to be with his teammates celebrating the win, and even though he was happy to see Sandy, he didn't want to miss out on the attention he knew the coeds would be lavishing on him. It wasn't so much that he was interested in someone other than Sandy, but things had changed, and Sandy just seemed irrelevant for the time being.

The time being being forever.

We

Dr. Brody Winechal finished high school in the middle of February when he was 14 because there was nothing more anybody there could teach him. He'd passed all his teachers in the math and science departments the year before—they simply hung on the next year, learning more from Brody than he did from them. He entered Harvard immediately in a special, accelerated program designed specifically for him and by summer, was taking an upper-level course load. He graduated from Harvard in four years with two PhDs: one in neuroscience and the other in applied mathematics.

All through his studies, Brody had been obsessed with Albert Einstein's theory of special relativity that proposes time is an illusion that moves relative to an observer. One of his dissertations was an examination and augmentation of that theory wherein he hypothesized implementation of yet-to-be postulated mathematical anomalies to prove its validity, a paper that only two or three people in the world could comprehend. None of that select group was on his thesis committee, but they knew the paper was brilliant by virtue of the fact that they didn't understand a word of it.

You

A few days after the East Texas game, Ahmed was leaving the football building following practice when he encountered a middle-aged gentleman dressed to the nines. The man was wearing a white, three-piece suit with a blue silk shirt and paisley ascot, standing at the edge of the parking lot leaning against a silver Bentley.

"Hello, Ahmed," the man said as Ahmed came within earshot.

"Hi," Ahmed responded with caution. Something about the guy set off an alarm in Ahmed's head, and he quickened his pace as he neared the opulent stranger.

"How was practice?" the man asked.

"It was good," Ahmed said without looking at him and kept walking.

"What's the hurry, son? I would like to speak with you if you have a few minutes. I think you'll find the time spent of great value," the man said with a smile.

Ahmed stopped a few feet from the man, looked at him, but didn't say anything.

"My name is Bo Whitney, and I'm a big supporter of the football program," he said as he stuck out his hand.

Ahmed reluctantly shook Bo's hand, weakly. "Nice to meet you," he said almost inaudibly.

"I represent a group of alumni that works with some of the players—the more gifted players, like you—to help them through their collegiate experience."

Ahmed stood still, not sure what to say or do.

"I was hoping you might like to have dinner with me tonight. I want to learn more about you and find out if there are things we can do to help you. We believe you're going to be a heck of a football player for us, and it's in our interest—in the school's interest—to do whatever we can to ensure your success."

"I don't know," Ahmed said. "I have a lot of homework tonight."

"I don't blame you for being reluctant. Hell, you don't know me or anything about me," Bo said. "So I invited Coach Halpern to join us. He should be coming out any minute now."

As Bo said that, the door to the football building sprung open and Coach Halpern bounded out. "Sorry I'm late, Bo. I see you met Ahmed."

"Yes, we've been having a little chat, getting to know each other," Bo replied. "I've invited Ahmed to join us for dinner at the club."

"Then let's go," Coach Halpern said and jumped into the backseat of the Bentley. "You ride up front, Ahmed," he added, and Ahmed reluctantly climbed into the most amazing car he had ever seen.

After arriving at the country club and talking about the team for a while, Ahmed began to relax. Bo and Coach Halpern dissected the East Texas game and asked Ahmed questions about his thoughts on the effectiveness of their schemes and coverages. Ahmed was forthcoming in his opinions but mostly talked about his need to learn the systems better and to get in better shape.

"You appear to be in fine shape, at least from what I saw on Saturday," Bo offered. "You're as fast as anybody out there, maybe faster, and you have the stamina to keep up. No, it's not conditioning that's your problem. It's size and strength."

Coach Halpern didn't say anything, just nodded.

"I work out in the weight room," Ahmed said. "I plan to really go at it hard this offseason."

"That's a good plan," Bo said. "But sometimes weight training's not enough; sometimes a player needs ... how should I put this? Sometimes a player with great potential, such as yourself, needs more professional help—medical help, if you will—to get strong enough to compete at the highest level. And we all believe that you're capable of competing at the highest level."

"What do you mean?" Ahmed asked.

"It all comes down to commitment," Bo said. "How bad does a player want it? How much is a player willing to do to be the best, to take it to the highest level? Some guys just don't have that kind of drive; they're content to be good. You're already good, Ahmed, but the question is, do you want to be great?"

"I want to be great," Ahmed said, emphatically.

"I'm glad to hear that," Bo replied. "Would you like me to help you to get there?"

"Sure. How?"

"There's a physician in town named Dr. Leroy," Bo said. "I'd like you to go see him and get his advice on your diet and workout regimen. He's an expert in physical fitness, nutrition and supplemental accelerators, and he works with other players on your team. You'll like him."

"Okay," Ahmed said. "When?"

"That's what I like to hear—enthusiasm and commitment," Bo responded. Bo handed Ahmed a card. "This is my phone number and Dr. Leroy's number. Call him tomorrow morning; he'll be expecting your call. And Ahmed, this is help from me, not your coaches or anybody in the football program. If you have any questions or need anything, feel free to call me day or night. Remember, I'm here to help you. And please don't bother your coaches about Dr. Leroy. They have enough to do already. Also, I wouldn't mention Dr. Leroy to anybody else either. We don't want to overburden him with a lot of nuisance from people who don't have your commitment, do we? His programs are only suitable for the truly gifted athletes, like you."

"I understand," Ahmed said. "And thanks. I really appreciate your interest in me."

"That's what I'm here for," Bo said, then let out a small laugh that sounded something like a sneer.

Me

I graduated with my MBA in late May 1980, went to work for my father the next week and married Sandy a month later. After that, it all became an ordinary life of an ordinary man: I went to work early in the morning, I came home and went for a run, had dinner with my wife, watched some TV and went to bed. I'd get up the next morning and repeat, ad infinitum. On weekends, I'd play golf and go to the country club for dinner on Saturday nights. In the winter, we'd ski, and twice a year we'd take vacations: one week in Rehoboth at my family's beach house and a couple of weeks in Turkey.

It was a pleasant life, one ordained for me generations before, I guess—a life I was destined to lead if it wasn't for that missed tackle. I'm convinced that that tackle was my ticket out of the mundane and pleasant, because pleasant wasn't what I was looking for. I was looking for spectacular. And maybe that's what I had but was too stupid or too immature or too wrapped up in myself to see it in front of my face.

At this point, who knows?

And it's not that I didn't enjoy the work. It was ... how should I put this? Pleasant. Challenging at times, of course, but generally speaking, relatively uneventful and ... pleasant.

If there's a more ordinary, mundane word in the English language than "pleasant," I don't know what it is.

My mom's grandfather was in the pistachio business in Turkey a long time ago. He exported the seeds—misidentified as nuts—around the world, but the United States was, by far, his biggest territory. So, in 1910, five years before my grandfather was born, my great-grandfather moved the business to Wilmington, Delaware. Why Wilmington is still a mystery in the family. With Philadelphia just up the road offering a larger port and a much more expansive transportation system, it didn't make a lot of sense. My father once told me that he believed the old man knew some people from the old country who had founded a mosque in Wilmington—one of only a few in the region back then—but nobody ever talked about it. The family had stopped going to religious services years before—lost all interest in organized religion because they felt it had become too political—so it was all just guesswork.

When my father, who was a lapsed Catholic, married my mother, he went to work for my mother's father and eventually took over the business. My dad was a smart businessman, like my grandfather, and together they built the company into a huge enterprise with more than 250 employees in the United States and Turkey.

And then I came along and didn't screw it up, which wasn't that hard to do because, let's face it, those little green seeds are addictive as hell, aren't they? Really, it would have been hard for me to screw it up, right? And I guess that's the best way to sum up my life: He didn't screw it up.

Oh, I suppose it wasn't as bad as I make it sound, but in the back of my head there was this feeling, this deeper suspicion that I was supposed to be doing something else, something more important.

Do you feel that way too? Is that part of the human condition, or was I stuck in a groove with the needle repeating the same old lyric over and over again? In retrospect, which is pretty much what I'm left with, I could have spent the rest of my ordinary life like that.

But for the dreams.

I should've made that tackle. It could've been different.

You

A few days after his dinner with Bo, Ahmed went to see Dr. Leroy. Dr. Leroy was young and looked like a bodybuilder. He told Ahmed that he had gone to Tech on a wrestling scholarship, and he'd been in practice for about three years. He explained that he knew Bo Whitney from his days on the mat. Bo had helped Dr. Leroy get into med school and made arrangements for a loan to start his practice. Bo and his group sent students from Tech his way because Dr. Leroy was really in the business of building better athletes.

Dr. Leroy gave Ahmed a cursory examination. When he was done, he sat down with Ahmed and went over his diet and workout regimen, making suggestions and giving Ahmed some brochures and samples of vitamins and supplements.

Dr. Leroy paused for a moment, then asked, "Have you ever heard of anabolic steroids, Ahmed?"

"I've heard of steroids," Ahmed answered. "But I thought they were illegal."

"Well, they're not. The NCAA doesn't test for them, and Tech, although not directly involved in dispensing them, sends many players to me to help them build up their bodies and gain strength by using safe, prescribed anabolic steroids. I recommend you start with a low dosage, three times a week, and we'll gradually increase it over the next few months until we find a level that works for you. I know your coaches don't like you doing a lot of heavy lifting during the season, but as soon as it's over, if you get in the weight room every day, you're going to see rapid growth in weight and strength. You'd come here for the treatment. It only takes a couple of minutes—a quick shot in the arm. We can do your first one today."

"That sounds all right, but steroids scare me a little."

"That's because sportswriters, the biggest wannabes in the world, guys who were never any good at sports, get a kick out of tearing down real athletes. They love to find things they can point to and say, 'See, that guy's really not that good.' They play up the negative side effects that only show up in such a small percentage of steroid users that it's not really measurable. It's all a bunch of hogwash. Take my word for it."

"Okay," Ahmed said. "But how do I pay for it?"

"You don't have to worry about that, Ahmed. You just worry about making tackles and everything will work out fine."

Ahmed got his first shot that day, and by the beginning of the next season, he had put on 20 pounds of solid muscle. By the start of his junior year, he tipped the scales at 205, and at 6 feet and still as fast as lightning, he was the prototypical NFL cornerback.

We

The course of study Dr. Brody Winechal most wanted to pursue was theoretical physics and the spatial relationship between perception and the concept of time. He realized that to achieve any real success in that field, he was going to need to gain a better understanding of the functions of the brain, so his next stop was Harvard Medical School, where he finished in two-and-a-half years. He could have done it more quickly, but his monitored research project held him back because the instructor was having a hard time keeping up. He went on to do a two-year residency in neurology at New York Hospital, Cornell University Medical College, where he wrote and published two extraordinary, groundbreaking papers on cognitive neuroscience, focusing on theories of intellective psychology and computational modeling with experimental data in analyzing neurological manifestation as covariates for conjoined and compartmentalized developmental function.

While finishing up his residency, Brody was approached by Dr. Hans Schultz from Heidelberg University's Department of Neurology to join his staff as a guest lecturer and head researcher in Germany. Dr. Schultz was one of the world leaders in intellectual neurology and perceptive sensorium. Brody spent two years working closely with Dr. Schultz, then moved on to the Neuroscience School of Advanced Studies in Switzerland, where he conducted cutting-edge research on the nervous system and its connectivity to cerebral cognizance and perspicacity.

After a year of that, Brody ended up back in New York working at the Riverdale Institute in the Bronx, an affiliate of Hudson University. Riverdale was a think tank, a research facility focused on neurological disorders and treatments. He was involved in the imaging of the centromedian thalamic nucleus using quantitative susceptibility mapping. As he wrote in his first paper at Riverdale, "The centromedian nucleus is an intralaminar thalamic nucleus, considered as a potentially effective target of deep brain stimulation and ablative surgeries for the treatment of multiple neurological and psychiatric disorders."

But Dr. Brody Winechal wasn't satisfied. He became bored and restless after a few years of what he called "programmed corporate research," where the desired results are first established and then research and experimentation are developed to create a pathway to those predetermined outcomes.

His ambitions were much greater. He was still looking for a way to turn back time.

You

Ahmed spent New Year's Eve of his junior year in Seattle, Washington, with the rest of his teammates playing against Northwest State in the Apple Bowl, where Tech trounced the Highlanders, 24-6. The win was punctuated by Ahmed's highlight-film interception and 73-yard touchdown dash, broadcast nationally for all to see before switching the dial over to Dick Clark and the climactic ball drop. A couple of weeks later, Ahmed was included in the list of Top 100 College Prospects by Street and Smith, the Bible of college football players.

And everybody was taking notes.

Including Mel Flapp, a New York City-based sports agent who had watched Ahmed outrun everybody on the field New Year's Eve.

Including Coach Callihan, who had tried to run down the sideline, jubilantly chasing Ahmed on his incredible gallop to notability, but he couldn't keep up.

Including Bo Whitney, who saw nothing but problems brewing for his beloved alma mater.

With good reason, for that perceived hell-broth was a cautionary potion of all that was to follow, as Mel Flapp was about to do to Ahmed what Coach Callihan and Bo Whitney had so masterfully done before him: deceive and exploit.

Mel knew that if Ahmed played his senior year, he'd have every sports agent in the country after him, and Mel, who ran a relatively small shop, would have a hard time competing against the big boys. So, he took his shot. He wanted to be the first to reach out to Ahmed. As soon as the Top 100 list was announced, he jumped in a taxi, sped to the airport and after two changes of planes, landed in what looked to Mel like Treestump, Nowheresville. He rented a car and high-tailed it to Alabama Tech to lie in wait for an opportunity to bushwhack, and hopefully capture, Ahmed Clark, future NFL draft pick and open spigot of mega moolah for Mel.

Coach Callihan didn't need to read the tea leaves to know that his school record-holder for interceptions and tackles would soon be up for grabs, and he desperately wanted to divert any troublesome attention that showed up on campus, so his first move was to bring Ahmed in for a chat.

"How's everything going, Ahmed?" Coach began, slowly stalking his game, like a big cat circling and watching for an opportunity to pounce.

"Good," Ahmed said in his taciturn manner. He had learned that most conversations with someone in authority that began with asking how he was doing were a telltale sign of other, bigger things to come, things that would most likely not make Ahmed happy. Actually, happy was an emotion getting harder and harder for Ahmed to find.

"You had a heck of a season, son," Coach Callihan offered.

"Thanks, Coach."

"Let me ask you something, Ahmed," Coach proffered as Ahmed braced himself, becoming irritated, not an uncommon feeling lately. "Are you happy here at Tech? You know, we get so wrapped up in the season and games, we sometimes forget to make sure you guys are doing all right outside of this building. Even in our post-season interviews, we neglect to make sure you're happy here. So, are you happy here?"

"Yeah, Coach," Ahmed said but looked puzzled, anger starting to seep in. "Of course I'm happy here. I love it here. Why do you ask?"

"Because, Ahmed, you're about to be deluged with advice and offers to, well … make a change in your life, a change that I fear will do you severe harm."

"Are you talking about the NFL draft, Coach?" Ahmed asked, relieved but still fighting off an undertow of ire. He disliked and distrusted one-on-one meetings with Coach Callihan—the guy who snaked him to Tech in the first place.

"Have you been thinking about it?"

"No, not really. I talked to my folks about it when I was home for break. They want me to stay in school."

"Good. Good. I'm glad to hear that, Ahmed. Listen, I need to warn you: There's going to be people—crooked people, people who will lie to you—who are going to try to talk you out of staying at Tech and declaring for the NFL draft. You can't trust those birds of prey. They're only out for themselves, and they in no way have your best interests at heart."

Ahmed stiffened. Having to deal with those birds of prey was nothing new for him. *Right, Coach?* he thought.

"Look, Ahmed," Coach Callihan soothed, sensing a sudden tension in his star player. "You have an outside chance of making All-American this year, but not much of one. You became known nationally too late for serious consideration. But you're a shoo-in for next year. After the game you played in the Apple Bowl, everybody will be following you from the get-go. Not a lot of cornerbacks have been going in the first round lately, but if you play like you did this year, you're a first-round pick next year, for sure. Definitely."

That made Ahmed smile—not just the sentiment, but the overly animated expression on Coach's face. What a show. Coach Callihan was a big man. At 6'3" and weighing well over 250 pounds, he looked misplaced when he got excited and bounced around, like one of those inflatable tube men that bob up and down at promotional events.

"Look, you're going to be approached by agents and reps of agents telling you you'll be a first-round pick this year, but I'm telling you, you won't be. I wish you could be, but there's no way, and those people will say anything to get you to sign a contract with them. They have nothing to lose. You, on the other hand, have lots to lose. The difference in money between a first- and a second- or third-round pick over a career is huge. If you go this year, you'd literally be throwing away millions of dollars."

Coach Callihan took a beat and let the red drain from his face. Ahmed's head was spinning as he choked back an urge to punch the man in the face ... for no immediately discernable reason. Coming from a family of means, Ahmed hadn't given much thought to the financial aspect of playing football professionally. He had concentrated on working out, building up his body and getting better at defense.

Coach Callihan leaned across his desk and looked Ahmed in the eye. He was extremely reluctant to ask the next and obvious question.

"So, how do you feel about it, Ahmed? Do you want to stay for your senior year?"

"Yes, of course," Ahmed replied, firmly, annoyed. "I don't want to leave the team. We're going to be great next year. We have a shot at a national championship and I want to be part of that," he said and pounded the desk with a clenched fist for superfluous emphasis.

"That's great," Coach Callihan said, a bit tentatively, taken aback by Ahmed's sudden show of emotion. He smiled at Ahmed as the young man stood up to leave. "But remember," Coach added, "be careful. The wolves will be circling."

One of those wolves was Bo Whitney, who took a more direct approach to the soon-to-be problem at hand. He and his associates had put a lot into making Tech a national powerhouse, and he wasn't about to stand by and let the kingpin of their defense slip away. He sailed onto campus one afternoon soon after classes resumed in January, driving a brand-spanking-new black Corvette Stingray with the top off and the radio blaring. A dignified-looking man in his mid-50s and wearing his trademark white, three-piece suit, he presented an incongruous image in the hot sportscar. But that didn't stop Bo from cruising around until he saw Ahmed leaving the football dorm on his way to an unofficial team workout—exactly where he knew Ahmed would be.

"Hey, Ahmed," Bo called. "Jump in. I'll give you a ride."

"Nice car," Ahmed said as his eyes practically bulged out of their sockets like a character in a cartoon.

"You like it?" Bo asked rhetorically. Ahmed was practically panting as they drove down the street with Bo throwing the car into gear after gear, swoosh after swoosh.

They pulled up in front of the practice facility and Bo put the four-wheeled rocket into neutral. "I have a proposition for you, Ahmed," he said. "You're getting to be quite the hero around these parts, and I'd like to use that adoration to help promote my business—and give you some compensation for your troubles."

"What do you mean?" Ahmed asked, full of trepidation. He wasn't sure he liked the way this conversation was going, but then, he didn't like much of anything lately except playing football and hitting people.

Bo picked up on the defensiveness in Ahmed and quickly said, "All you'd have to do is make yourself available a couple of hours a month to meet some of my customers, have lunch with us and get your picture taken—easy work. And for that little bit of effort, you'd get a company car—this here buckin' bronco you're sitting in."

Ahmed thought his head was going to explode.

"And naturally, you'd get a small salary, a pittance," Bo added. "Let's say a thousand a month. And of course, a company gas card to fuel this beast. How's that sound?"

"Am I allowed to do that?" Ahmed asked, still in shock but much less perturbed.

"Hells bells," Bo thundered. "There would be nothing illegal about it, more or less. It's not like I'm trying to recruit you; I'm simply letting you borrow a car. And all your compensation would be in cash, of course. I don't want to put you in need of a tax accountant. So, what do you say, Ahmed? Do we have a deal?"

"I guess so," came stumbling out of Ahmed's mouth with little forethought. "I mean, yeah, if you say it's okay and everything."

"Of course it's okay," Bo said and slapped Ahmed on the shoulder. "But let's keep this just between us, all right? I don't want other players bugging me."

"No problem," Ahmed said as his head continued to buzz.

"Oh, and one more thing," Bo added as Ahmed climbed out of the sleek speedster. "You have to be here next year if you want to haul ass in this baby. Give me your word and I'll have it delivered to your dorm tomorrow morning."

Sitting in his rented Plymouth Reliant, Mel Flapp watched Bo and Ahmed from the parking lot. He couldn't make out what they were saying, but he knew there was some hanky-panky going on when the rich-looking guy driving the Vette reached across the front seat and shook Ahmed's hand.

Me

Sandy got pregnant two years after we were married. It wasn't planned, but you know how that goes. We had talked about starting a family, and we were going to do it, but Sandy wanted to teach for five years before she had to give it up. That's right, folks, in my macho Turkish family (one side, anyway, although my father worked so many years with my mother's father and spent so much time in Turkey, he became a Turk by osmosis), the wife didn't work—she stayed home and took care of multitudes of babies.

Ha, ha, multitudes, get it? I was one of only two, and as it happened, we ended up with two of our own, both girls, and both the darlings of daddy's eye. Lydia was the first-born, and although I loved Sandy more than life itself, I couldn't believe the feelings I had watching the birth of my daughter. My love for my wife increased exponentially to a point where it scared me, and my instant love for Lydia made me as happy as I had ever been before.

Except, of course, for those dreams and the nagging restlessness that wouldn't let go.

I should've made that tackle. It could've been different.

But what the hell, man, I had a daughter!

Two years later, I had another one. Although I would have liked to have had a son, Marla was nobody's second-best, nobody's replacement. She was a terror from the get-go, and when I say a terror, I mean that in the best way possible. She wasn't bad or anything like that, just strong-willed and determined. She wouldn't back down from anything, not even from her old man.

Maybe I should say *especially* from her old man.

I loved that about her. She always knew what she wanted and went after it with everything she had, including replacing her old man as the head of the family business. But more on that later.

Both girls were beautiful, but what kids aren't beautiful to their parents? Lydia was fair and gentle, All-American looking like her mother (and yeah, yeah, I know, that's a Western European conceit, so sue me—but only on my father's half), and Marla was dark and Delphian like our Mediterranean origins, with a Sophia Loren quality, if you know what I mean.

Lydia inherited my speed and became an excellent soccer player. I was obliged to learn what the rest of the world called football (which, incidentally, is not football—it's a track meet with a ball) if I wanted to participate in Lydia's life by helping coach her teams over the years. She used that skill to get a partial scholarship to Bucknell, one of the best schools in the country for pre-law.

By the way, did I mention that both girls were smart like their mother? Well, they were, and Lydia was smart enough to get into Rutgers Law School. When she graduated, I tried to talk her into going to work for the company as in-house counsel, but she was hell-bent on defending the underrepresented. I guess living in Camden, New Jersey, for three years studying ethical and moral concepts amidst unfathomable squalor will do that to you.

"So, in other words, you're planning on starving?" I asked her.

"Not as long as I have you, Daddy," she replied. Did I mention she was a real smart-ass? Well, she was, but you probably picked up on that.

Marla was a dancer who was particularly interested in modern dance, which was okay with me because I loved jazz, and a lot of Marla's performances were set to jazz. My favorite musician was Miles Davis, and her last recital before graduating from high school and leaving dance behind was to "Venus De Milo," so that all worked out well for me since I didn't have to learn to dance or anything like that to be part of her experience.

Marla went to Delaware, like her mom and dad, and like her dad, earned an MBA in the five-year program, except she did it in four. She came to work for the company, and now she's taken over the whole operation, but more on that coming up.

After Lydia was born, Sandy insisted we go to church, so we started going to the Episcopal church she had attended growing up. I liked the Episcopalians because you could actually question scripture and religious dogma in an open discussion without being shunned or burned at the stake, and I became a regular churchgoer—not bad for an avowed agnostic, eh? At some point, I realized that I might not have been a traditional Christian, but I was a theist. I guess you could call me a Jeffersonian Christian. That's someone who believes in Christian teachings without all the miracles and supernatural stuff. Call it Christian lite.

Sandy and I got fairly involved in church activities, lending a hand at a parish-sponsored soup kitchen once a month and visiting the elderly in convalescent homes with the youth choir. Through contacts at the church, I also did some work with Habitat for Humanity, helping to build homes for the downtrodden when I could find the time.

When my mom was 64, she developed ovarian cancer, but they caught it early, and after surgery and massive chemotherapy, she survived. Sandy and I, along with my sister, Mya and her husband, Nicholas (yes, my sister married a Greek—you should have been there for that discussion with my mother, although he did, eventually, come to work for the company, which prompted my mom to comment, "We're not selling grapes here, you know!"), joined the American Cancer Society and invested time and money into raising awareness and funds for ovarian cancer research.

Hey, I'm not blowing my own horn for shits and giggles, I'm just relating my life story for your edification and to help you decide if I've had a good life or not (like it's you I'm trying to convince, right?). Well, I've tried to have a good life, anyway, and I tried to make a difference when and where I could, but let's face it, I'm a wealthy man and I could have done a whole lot more. For what it's worth, anytime I saw someone standing on the ramps at the interstate with a cardboard sign and ragged clothes, I always slipped him a ten spot.

Assuaging a guilty conscience?

Probably.

Guilt from not doing enough?

Not hardly. Oh no, the guilt was all about the story I'm trying to tell you; the guilt over not appreciating what I had and still listening to that little voice deep down inside of me, repeating that old refrain, a constant lament to remind me of what I didn't have, or what I thought I didn't have.

I should've made that tackle. It could've been different.

You

After the informal workout, Ahmed left the practice facility with a couple of his teammates. Mel Flapp was still sitting in the parking lot and watched Ahmed climb into the back seat of a late-model Japanese compact. With three large football players in the small vehicle, it looked almost comical, like piling clowns into a tiny car at the circus. Mel chuckled to himself.

Mel followed the car to a pizza joint off campus, and when Ahmed and his teammates went in, he followed—at a distance. Mel sat in a booth in a dark corner at the back of the restaurant and ordered a slice and a Coke and watched Ahmed and his buddies down two whole, large pizzas topped with everything but another pizza. They were joking around and every so often would punch one another in the arm. It looked like a typical scene out of any college in the country, the only noticeable difference being the short, bald guy in the back, closely scrutinizing the three amigos. And Mel would continue to scrutinize Ahmed until he found a way in.

That way in opened up the next morning when the black Corvette was delivered to Ahmed. The driver met

Ahmed at the door of the football players' dormitory and handed him the keys and an envelope. Mel took a photo of the exchange and another of Ahmed opening the envelope and taking out a stack of bills.

"Bingo!" Mel said quietly to himself. "Got ya, partner."

Mel watched Ahmed jump into the car and burn rubber, a-whooping and a-hollering all the way down the quiet street. Mel didn't follow, he knew where Ahmed would be when he needed him. Mel left the parking lot and drove across town to a one-hour film-developing kiosk in the parking lot of a small shopping center. To kill the hour, he went into a restaurant in the strip for breakfast: bacon and eggs with grits. The grits remained untouched.

We

Time was fleeting, a preoccupation of Dr. Brody Winechal for most of his life. Unfortunately, Brody's pursuit of harnessing and controlling time was just as fleeting, although he became more and more convinced that perception was the only reality and that the concept of time was an illusion. He saw mankind's preoccupation with time as the only true barrier to control over the trajectory of one's life, and he meant to do something about that. He was smart enough to realize he wouldn't have enough time (speaking of a preoccupation with time) to accomplish all he hoped, but he was confident he could take one giant step for mankind and lay the groundwork for a future Dr. Brody Winechal to cross the finish line. In his crusade, as he pursued the tributaries and dimensions of perception, he dove deeper and deeper into a world not yet plumbed or even imagined—he was entering a new domain of comprehension that would not only change the basic understanding of time but could add a level of existence beyond the corporeal self.

Brody's vision, simply put, would revolutionize the limitations and impositions of time; he would render time, as we know it, unessential. In his view, time meant nothing and never would again. And that vision finally found its impetus—a pragmatic direction—while he was at Riverdale working with the terminally ill.

Dr. Brody Winechal would turn back time and end suffering once and for all.

You

Mel Flapp was waiting for Ahmed Clark when he came out of his dorm later that day. Ahmed was on his way to the legally questionable informal workout arranged by Coach Callihan, but without his presence, of course, because that would have violated NCAA rules.

And Coach Callihan was a stickler for obeying the rules. When he could, generally speaking, but there were a lot of rules, and he was only one man.

Ahmed had left the top off of the Corvette, and Mel was in the passenger's seat when Ahmed reached the car. He stopped short when he saw the stranger sitting in his new babemobile.

Before Ahmed could think to say anything, Mel said in a patronizing show of disingenuous friendliness, "Hey, Ahmed. I'm Mel Flapp, and I'm the only friend you have in the world right now."

Ahmed was frozen in stone.

"Relax," Mel offered in as reassuring a voice as he could muster. "I'm here to help you, and believe me, you need help."

Ahmed hadn't moved a muscle as his mind raced away, out of control. The only intelligible thought he could put together was, *What now?*

"Come on; hop in," Mel said as he patted the driver's seat.

When Ahmed still didn't move, Mel took a photo out of the envelope he was holding, the one of Ahmed inspecting the stack of bills.

"I want to show you a couple of pictures," Mel said as he handed the print to Ahmed. "I figure it's about 1,000 bucks. Am I close?"

Ahmed looked up from the photo and, for the first time, focused on Mel. Ahmed's eyes were barely slits as he tried to wrap his head around what was happening. He studied the visage of this troubling intruder while desperately endeavoring to figure out an escape route.

"You're in trouble, son," Mel said. "That's a violation of NCCA rules, not to mention university policy. And this beauty we're...excuse me...*I'm* sitting in, well, that's another infraction. You could be kicked out of school and lose your NFL draft eligibility for a year or two. How's that sound? Want to get in now so I can tell you how we can fix this?"

Ahmed slowly got in the car, still not saying a word.

"Like I said, my name's Mel Flapp, and I'm a sports agent out of New York City. I watched you in the Apple Bowl, and I'm very impressed. I believe you could go pretty high in the draft right now if you decide to declare. I can't say first round for sure, but I think it's reasonable to expect a second-round pick," Mel said and flashed a greasy smile.

"I don't want to go in the draft," Ahmed said, weakly. "I want to stay at Tech."

"I'm afraid that train's left the station, Ahmed. You have only two choices at this point: Sign a contract with me and declare for the draft, or face the dire consequence of your miscreant behavior, which means no more football for a while and no big bucks at the end of the rainbow."

Ahmed looked like he was about to cry.

"Hey, I'm doing you a favor. Somebody was bound to find out about your arrangement with old Mr. White Suit and turn you in, or you could get hurt next season playing in this godforsaken Podunk town and never make it to the NFL. So, like I said, I'm doing you a favor."

Ahmed actually smiled a little at that remark. Everybody was trying to do him a favor.

Mel handed Ahmed his business card as he climbed out of the Vette. "I don't want you to be late for practice," he said. "It's a lot to absorb, I know. Think about it and call me tonight at the Holiday Inn. And please keep this in mind: I would hate to have to turn you in, but I will. And if you talk to anybody about our conversation—your coaches or the guy in the white suit, or anyone else, for that matter—you'll leave me no choice but to turn the pictures over to dear old Alabama Tech and the NFL. And just so nobody gets any never-to-be-heard-from-again ideas down here in swamp wonderland, I overnighted a set of these pictures to my office in New York. Face it, kid, we're married to each other now, and there's nothing you can do about it," Mel concluded, then walked away.

Ahmed sat in his new-smelling Vette for a few minutes, then went back into his dorm and threw up.

They

A short woman with dark features who is somewhere between her 40s and 60s—it's hard to tell from a distance—stands on the metal bridge-like structure and looks down at the man.

"I hate to see you like this," she says to the man. "But you look so peaceful. I hope you're happy."

Me

As it ended up, I never had to worry about Lydia living off her dad. That's because she married a rich young man from San Francisco named Theodore Mortimer Jonas III of the Jonas Shipping Lines. His family operated one of the largest fleets of container ships in the country, and Teddy, as he was called, was worth a king's ransom. In other words, beaucoup bucks, boogaloo. In a fascinating twist to this fable I'm sharing with you, Jonas was one of the shippers we had been using for years to import our delicious, addictive pistachios.

It is a small world after all, isn't it?

I don't know why I'm being so glib—this is, after all, a tragedy, isn't it? I know, I know, you need more information.

Lydia met Teddy during a ski vacation in Vermont over Christmas break during her last year of law school. Teddy was working on a master's degree in transportation and logistics at the Massachusetts Institute of Technology. One of Lydia's classmates had a ski house in Killington, and her brother, who went to MIT, was also staying at the house that week, along with his roommate, Theodore Mortimer Jonas III.

Which is how he was introduced to Lydia, with a sarcastic emphasis on elongating the name. I don't think it was love at first sight, not from what Lydia told me. Actually, she said that Teddy was reticent and a little stuck-up until he had a few, then it was good-time-Charlie, very charming and gracious and attentive to Lydia—a real Dr. Jekyll and Mr. Hyde. After Lydia returned to school, he called her. Then he called her again. Then he called her every day, and the rest, as they say, is history. Teddy turned out to be a decent guy. It amazes me how rich kids always seem to find each other. Must be some intangible quality that a has-been football player is too obtuse to recognize.

The worst part of that love story is that they moved to San Francisco after finishing their degrees. Teddy went to work for his family's business, and Lydia got a job as a public defender, naturally. A few years later, Lydia delivered a bouncing baby boy, Theodore Mortimer Jonas IV, whom Sandy and I only got to see a few times year. But Lydia was happy, so what more is there to say about that?

Marla, on the other hand, never seemed perfectly happy. She was always driven to do more, to get more, to be more (much like her father's dreams, you could say—*I should've made that tackle. It could've been different*).

It's not that she was unhappy, I don't think, but there was always something there—an itch she couldn't scratch or couldn't quite reach. She excelled in college and took the company by storm upon graduating with her MBA. She modernized our equipment, software and procedures in her first six months on the job as office manager, throwing out our abacus and mimeograph machine, ha ha! At least that's how she made it sound, like we were living in a cave and writing on stone walls with charcoal. Oh well, we probably did seem like Neanderthals to her online generation, although the technology we were using wasn't *that* old. In a world where state-of-the-art is yesterday's news before you can say it, we weren't doing that bad.

At Marla's next stop, director of supply chain management, she was just as nimble and effective in upgrading all our rickety old methodologies lickety-split, creating a streamlined system that saved the company about 10 times her salary.

Which she diligently and delightedly pointed out to me ... often.

Marla was probably the most driven and competitive person I ever worked with, and that drive had set its sights on my job, as she waited for the right time to make her move.

Which is where we're at now, but I still have more to tell you before we get there.

You

The way Ahmed had it figured, Mel Flapp was right, so he signed a contract with his only choice and declared for the 1978 NFL draft coming up in the spring. His meeting with Coach Callihan was uncomfortable and borderline abusive. On the other hand, Bo Whitney wouldn't even talk to him—he sent a messenger to pick up the car and the cash, and Ahmed never heard from Bo again, not even when he was inducted into the Alabama Tech Football Hall of Fame years later. Perhaps Bo was dead by then; Ahmed didn't know but smiled at the possibility. By the time Ahmed left Tech, he didn't really care what anybody thought anymore because he didn't believe anybody really gave a hoot about him, only what he could do for them.

Even Sandy had abandoned him, a most egregious employment of sophistry. In truth, he had abandoned her through indifference, having lost touch somewhere along the way. According to the grapevine, she was dating a guy she met in college at Delaware, and that only added to Ahmed's tortured state of mind. He should be happy—he was going to play in the National Football League and make a lot of money and have a wonderful life. But emotionally he was all tangled up.

His mind wasn't functioning the way it used to when life was simpler and he could see clearly.

Ahmed's parents were supportive but disappointed when he quit school and moved home. He helped out in the family's huge, on-site warehouse—as he had done all through high school—and worked out to stay in shape for evaluations by NFL teams that would thoroughly assess players who were eligible for the draft. At the gym, he met a guy who was able to hook him up with a supplier of steroids. He didn't want to lose three years of hard work, especially before the evaluations.

The day of the draft, Mel Flapp was at the Clark home in anticipation of his big payday, enjoying Mrs. Clark's delicious cooking and eagerly awaiting the reward for his ruthless cleverness. Ahmed's performances for the NFL scouts had been excellent, better than had been expected, and Mel had been fielding calls from NFL teams ever since. He had confided in the Clarks that there was an outside chance Ahmed could go in the first round, but the second round was much more likely. The first round came and went without Ahmed's name being called, and with each miss, Ahmed became more and more irritated. He wasn't sure why because he expected to go in the second round, but his tolerance for stress was exceedingly truncated.

With the fourth pick in the second round—the 32nd pick overall—Ahmed Clark's name was called by the Buffalo Bills, one of the worst teams in the NFL. Ahmed's heart sank.

"That's worth about half-a-mil on a four-year deal," Mel practically bellowed. What he didn't say, and why he was so jubilant, was that the pick would put about 50 large in Mel's coffers … maybe more if he could negotiate a favorable contract.

Ahmed was agitated and had to suppress his anger. He wasn't sure what he was mad at, but felt lost and forlorn as a thought occurred to him for the first time: *What if I had missed The Tackle.*

And from some deep dark place inside him, a place he didn't recognize, didn't know was there, came a voice, faint yet piercing, a disturbing refrain he didn't understand: *I should've made that tackle. It could've been different.*

Me

My father would visit our operation in Turkey about six times a year. My mother's family came from a small village east of Gaziantep in the Anatolia region, heart of pistachio country. Going back several generations, her family had acquired massive acreage of pistachio trees and became one of the largest processors and distributors of the popular seeds, and not just their own product but that of many other farms in the southeastern part of Turkey. As the business grew in the early part of the 19th-century, my mother's great-great-grandfather moved the operation to Adana to be near the port of Mersin. And that's where it remains today, and that's where my father would go, first with my mother's father, and then by himself after my grandfather began discharging some of his responsibilities.

Once a year, during our summer vacation from school, my dad would take the family with him for a two-week visit to the old country. Those trips were not only an opportunity to explore our roots and spend time with my mother's family, but they were educational as well. We would always enjoy a couple of nights in Istanbul and over the years, visit places such as Greece, Israel, Iraq and Georgia. I enjoyed those trips, so when Sandy and I started a family, I would do the same as my father had done; we'd pack up the family and go to Turkey for a couple of weeks each summer. As the girls grew older, Lydia loved the cultural aspects of the trips, but Marla's main interest was in learning as much as she could about the operation and our Turkish family members who ran things in that part of the world. I would have to drag her out of the facilities for our various excursions into the ancient lands of our heritage. By the time Marla was in college, she probably knew as much, maybe even more, than I did about our processes and people in Adana. She was smart as a whip and much more driven than I ever was.

During those trips, Marla got to know a boy named Ugur who worked part-time in the plant, and somewhere along the way, after she had come to work for the company and he was a full-time employee supervising the logistics of moving pistachio from the port of Mersin, and after they had known each other for years, they fell in love. Marla had dated in the past, but nothing very serious. Then while on a short business trip with me, the spark that had always been there, I suppose, burst into flame. They were married in Turkey, and Ugur moved to the United States and worked for the company over here. Marla was not his direct boss, but she was, if you know what I mean.

Poor boy.

They had two kids in short order over 23 months—a boy and a girl (the family tradition of multitudinous babies, right?)—because Marla didn't waste time doing anything. During the pregnancies, she took off only 20 days—10 per birth—but in truth, it was only about three days for each, working from home almost as much as when she was in the office.

Did I mention she was driven?

And a pain in the ass.

But a good pain in the ass (if there is such a thing). Marla wanted my job, made no bones about it, and by the time she took over, you could say I was ready.

Ready for what was the big question because it never stopped, only got worse as time and life kept turning me around—up, down and sideways.

And always there was that voice: *I should've made that tackle. It could've been different.*

We

Brody quit Riverdale and accepted a position as head of the research-and-development department at D. Brown Medical in Princeton, New Jersey. D. Brown couldn't believe its good fortune in landing such a well-respected doctor and scientist, perhaps the leading researcher in neurological disorders and cognitive impairment in the world. The old, prestigious company thought it had pulled off quite the coup in hiring Dr. Brody Winechal, but in actual fact, Dr. Brody Winechal had hired D. Brown.

That's because he needed a facility to conduct his R&D, and the type of development Brody had in mind was going to take state-of-the-art labs, practically unlimited resources and a huge staff to assist him. In his first meeting with the executives at D. Brown, Brody explained his project thusly: "I plan to build a brain."

You

On his first full-go practice at Bills' training camp, Ahmed was playing right cornerback. After a few plays in the controlled scrimmage, the quarterback came around end on a broken play, and Ahmed strung him out wide, denying him a lane to turn upfield. Before the QB could reach the safety of the sideline, Ahmed buried his helmet into the unsuspecting ball carrier's protective red jersey and drove him hard to the ground.

Whistles blew like a five-alarm fire, and coaches came running from all directions. One of the coaches got in Ahmed's face, nose to facemask.

"We don't hit the goddamn quarterback, you stupid son of a bitch," he screamed as the spittle flew. "See that goddamn red jersey, shithead? See it? See it?" and he got louder on each syllable. "You don't hit the goddamn red jersey, you stupid son of a bitch shithead!"

Ahmed stood still, weathering the spit shower.

"Got it, asshole? You don't hit the goddamn quarterback in the goddamn red jersey! Got it?"

"Yes sir," Ahmed managed between the expectoration bombardment.

Later that day, when Ahmed was in the shower, three huge offensive linemen pushed him into a corner over the slippery tile floor. Ahmed was naked and covered in soap and in no position to defend himself, even if he could against the mammoth big uglies. One of them repeatedly poked a finger in Ahmed's chest and said, "Listen up, 'Roid Rage. If you ever hit our quarterback again, we'll beat the crap out of you and then hang your naked ass from the flagpole out front. Understood, rookie?"

"Understood," Ahmed said meekly.

Ahmed didn't know why he'd hit the quarterback. He knew he wasn't supposed to hit him, that it was a major violation of the rules of practice, but he couldn't help himself. It was getting increasingly more difficult at times to control his bursts of anger that seemed to come from nowhere. Fortunately, that was his only significant transgression, other than a conspicuous fidgetiness that wouldn't allow him to be still. He was always moving one part of his body or another in a kinetic dance of propulsion-less locomotion.

After a week of training camp, Ahmed realized he was no longer the fastest player on the field—everybody was fast. And big. And strong. Whereas in the past, he was able to use his speed to overcome miscues, in the pros, speed was your ticket in, but wasn't any guarantee you'd stay, and miscues were frowned upon.

Seriously frowned upon.

So, Ahmed had to buckle down and learn the systems inside and out, a difficult task given his current lack of focus. But that didn't mean he was adjusting well. He wasn't. His frustration in having to absorb so much new information and trying to keep up with the other players physically was palpable. One of the veteran defensive players pulled Ahmed aside after two weeks of camp and asked him point-blank, "Are you juicing?"

Ahmed didn't know what to say, so he acted stupid, a pose that was becoming easier for him to affect. "What do you mean?"

Daryl, the veteran player, snickered. "Come on, man. I'm trying to help you out here."

At that point, Ahmed's scrotum would have contracted into his groin in a reflexive, albeit primordial defense mechanism at the prospect of someone else trying to help him, but his scrotum was nowhere in sight after years of steroid abuse.

"A lot of the guys on the team are users," Daryl continued. "So, let me ask you again, are you on the juice?"

"Yeah," was all Ahmed said.

"They're messing with you, man. I can see it—everybody can see it. You can feel it, too, I know. It's plain as day. Some guys get a lot worse reaction to the stuff than others. You need to back off or you're gonna explode, probably explode right off the team if you keep at it like that."

"I don't want to lose my edge, my muscle and size," Ahmed replied, almost apologetically.

"You don't have to," Daryl offered. "I know a cat that can help you out. Have you ever heard of HGH, human growth hormones?"

For a moment Ahmed thought he was experiencing *déjà vu*.

"No, not really."

"You get a hormone shot that stimulates growth, cell reproduction, like that, like steroids, except it's all organic, real human hormones. What you do is ease back on the 'roids and add the hormone shots to your regimen, and as you add more HGH and fewer steroids, a lot of the side effects will fade away. You'll feel better and get back on a more even keel, man."

"And it works? Do you do it?" Ahmed asked.

"Don't ask a lot of questions, rook," Daryl scolded, then chuckled. "I'll get you fixed up."

He did, and in no time at all, Ahmed was feeling better—less agitated and more in control—but the anxiety and insecurities were still playing on him. He visited a doctor another teammate recommended about his dark periods, as Ahmed called them—the increasing bouts of depression. It was a short visit; the doctor didn't bother with a physical since Ahmed had recently been thoroughly examined by the team physician at the beginning of training camp. Ahmed explained his symptoms, and the doctor never asked about performance-enhancing drugs. Instead, he prescribed a strong antidepressant. The pills made Ahmed feel sick and nauseated, and he became constipated and even more impotent, but he kept taking them because it helped with the pervasive and persistent sense of foreboding.

After another week or so of camp, a plethora of bumps and bruises led Ahmed back to the same doctor for some pain relief, and he left with a prescription for a powerful narcotic analgesic. Not too long after that, he was back again, this time for a little pick-me-up, and the good doctor prescribed a popular amphetamine known in athletic circles as greenies, and in short order, Ahmed was taking his meds like vitamins.

Ahmed's life had become a Ferris wheel of medications and a roller coaster of side effects, but his concentration and performance improved, and he had a very good run with the Buffalo Bills. As promised, Mel Flapp had wrangled him a four-year deal worth close to $500,000, 10 percent going into Mel's avaricious pocket. The Bills struggled during Ahmed's first two seasons, but made the playoffs his last two. On the last year of his contract, Ahmed made the Pro Bowl—the money year, as Mel called it—and his hardscrabble agent with a Napoleonic complex utilized that success to negotiate a lucrative five-year deal worth more than a million dollars, plus incentives. The only requirement Ahmed had given Mel was to get him someplace warm—he'd had it with the brutal weather in Buffalo—and he signed with the Tampa Bay Buccaneers, a team that had made the playoffs two out of the last three years.

More importantly, though, it was tropical.

In the third game of his first year with the Bucs, Ahmed tore up his knee and needed surgery, which ended that season for him. He had dated several women in Buffalo but remained an uncommitted bachelor. Consequently, in Tampa Bay he was alone, so his sister, Mya, who had just graduated from Gettysburg College in the spring, took a leave of absence from the family's business and moved in with Ahmed to help nurse him back to health.

Over the past several years, Ahmed had not spent much time with his family. He was too busy during the season for holidays—other than quick drop-bys—and spent the off-seasons working out in warmer climes. After just a few days with her brother, Mya was appalled at the shape he was in, not physically—he was an Adonis in that regard—but emotionally. On the phone with their mother, she told Azra that her son was a basket case and needed serious help. Ahmed overheard the conversation and confronted Mya as soon as she hung up.

"What the hell do you mean, I need serious help?" he railed.

"I'm sorry, Ahmed. I didn't want you to hear that, but I'm worried, really worried about you. Your frame of mind is—I don't know how to say this—half the time you act crazy and the other half you're morose. Something's wrong here. I see all the pills you take and the needle marks in your arms, and I'm really scared for you."

"Give me a break, will you?" Ahmed pleaded. "I just had a killer injury and major surgery. I'm off my game a bit, I admit, but I'm in great shape, other than my obvious but temporary physical limitations. You don't need to worry about me. I'll be back to normal in no time at all."

"But what's normal these days?" Mya questioned. "Don't you see it, Ahmed? Don't you realize what you've done to yourself?"

"I just want to play football," was all Ahmed could manage.

"At what cost? Is it worth your life?" Mya asked and began crying.

A thunderclap of emotions erupted in Ahmed, and without being aware that he had moved, he was holding his sister tight and crying, too.

And in the midst of the emotional turmoil, that frightening voice whispered from the deepest depths of a place he knew not, a place that scared him right down to his bones: *I should've made that tackle. It could've been different.*

What the hell's going on here, he thought. *Something is terribly wrong.*

They

A woman is at her perch above the man, watching him, as she is every year on this day.

"How are you? I hope you're well," she says to the man.

Her features are dark and attractive, although a gauze-like veil seems to surround her in a cloak of clandestine secrecy, almost like a ghost coming in and out of focus, and after a while, it's hard to tell if she's real or imagined.

She sings happy birthday to the man, then leaves.

Me

So, there I was, sailing along, semi-happily leading my ordinary, pleasant life (what, by all rights, should have been my happy life, except for … well, you know), when things started to unravel. By that time, my mother was almost 70, and the heavy doses of poison they'd dumped into her body to kill the toxic cancer cells had caught up with her; her heart gave out and she took that long ride into eternity.

My father, who was in good shape—healthy as a horse, he liked to say—when my mom passed, went downhill quickly and followed her on that unavoidable, one-way journey five years later. His cause of death was a broken heart, but that's not what it said on his death certificate. His death certificate listed cause of death as "influenza."

What a crock, but not an uncommon story. My parents loved each other dearly, and together they made a whole, her yin to his yang. Does that sound too cliché? So be it. Clichés are clichés for a reason, and this one works here. My father simply couldn't bear to live without my mother, so he died.

I was devastated, and once again Sandy helped me through it like she always did. She was the rock I held onto, my anchor, the air that I breathed and all that Hallmark card pablum, except in this case it was true. Without her ... well, without her, I don't know what I would have done, how I would have coped. And I know what you're thinking: You're thinking I was already barely coping, which is exactly my point—thank you for making it for me. Maybe now you're getting some idea how unpleasant it could be...

...or would be.

Anyway, without Sandy I doubt I'd be telling you this story. I don't know what my life would have been like, or how it would end up, but I'm guessing it wouldn't be pleasant—and maybe that's a precursor. Who knows?

But it's not that bad, really, and isn't that a hell of a way to describe your life? Hey, maybe pleasant *is* good, as good as it gets. Maybe pleasant is the best of all possible worlds, eh Candide? (Ha, ha! Right?) And maybe pleasant is really happy, only tainted through the prism of time and regret, years of doubt and second-guessing.

I told you before, folks, those "what ifs" and "could've beens" will kill you.

But pleasant it was, and thanks to Sandy, pleasant it was once again ...

... but not for long, because "pleasant" caught the 3:10 to Yuma.

We

The people at D. Brown didn't believe Dr. Brody Winechal could actually duplicate the human brain, but they were excited by the possibilities of new discoveries through his research that could help to augment their vast stock of medical equipment and devices. As a matter of fact, the initiative, with its explicit objective of replicating fundamental encephalon activity, took on the ominous ambiance of Frankenstein's lab. In short order, his coworkers, in a playful yet insolent vituperation, started referring to the top-secret project as Brody's Bumptious Brain, or The Bees. A couple of lab assistants had Bee pins made, and everybody but Brody wore one. It became emblematic of an *esprit de corps* and a badge of honor for the overworked and greatly underappreciated by their workaholic Captain Ahab, who took notice of none of it.

But the skeptical, supercilious tenor of the labs changed dramatically when the brilliant young doctor made a major breakthrough after only three years of work, although "breakthrough" hardly covered it— monumental or Earth-shattering would be more appropriate, but they wouldn't do the finding justice, either. Indeed, there are probably no adequate adjectives in the English language to describe the colossal impact of Brody uncovering another level of consciousness, a level deep below the subconscious, and a function of the brain never before detected, let alone suspected. This was a quantum leap in understanding the workings of the human brain, and therefore, the workings of the human. In simple terms, Brody had identified the foundation of what we know as intelligent life.

This development was so important and its secrecy so imperative that D. Brown had to hire an outside agency specializing in covert operations to ensure the research data didn't leak out before it was ready to capitalize on it.

Brody named his discovery Precognitive Rheostatus, or PR, and it made the study of id, super-ego and ego look like training wheels. The structure of PR was so embedded, so intertwined in all functions of the brain that detection of it as a separate entity of cognitive activity was practically impossible.

Except for Brody, boy-genius with an unmeasurable IQ, now a full-grown, yet emotionally and socially retarded man-child-genius—a man-child-genius who, five years later, would win a Nobel Prize at the age of 37. He would have been the youngest person ever to win a Nobel Prize in Physiology if D. Brown had released the data when the discovery was made, not that Brody cared. Those five years had been fast-paced and demanding as he worked to perfect his external, untrammeled brain, and a Nobel Prize was just another distraction.

He was much more interested in the implementation of his visionary and innovative ingenuity, which was in its latter stages of practical application.

Dr. Brody Winechal would finally realize his lifelong ambition to turn back time.

Bzzzzzzzzzz!

You

Mya found a holistic clinic in Clearwater that specialized in rehabilitating the mind, body and soul, as the hyperbole promised in their slick trifold brochure. One day, unannounced, after she picked up Ahmed from a physical therapy session because he still wasn't cleared to drive, she took the Courtney Campbell Causeway over Old Tampa Bay, heading the opposite direction from Ahmed's condo.

"Where we going?" Ahmed asked, practically disinterested. His physical therapy session drained him almost to the point of total exhaustion.

"We're headed to the Verdurable Vitality Vortex," Mya answered.

"The what?"

"It's a clinic that specializes in holistic methods for restoring Ahmed," she said and giggled. It had been a little over a week since they had first talked about Ahmed's drug abuse. In the interim, they had discussed ways to help him reclaim his mental and emotional health, but mostly it had been Mya trying to get him to stop using, with little success. She had told him she was looking for a doctor or an organization that could help him, so the trip wasn't a complete surprise.

"I don't want to do this today, Mya. Not today."

"What you mean is not any day, Ahmed. Well, time has come today, brother," she said and giggled again. Mya was trying to keep it light and doing her best to take the edge off Ahmed's uneasiness. "You'll like Dr. D'Swill. She's really very nice and has a great reputation. I've checked her out."

"Dr. D'Swill? Really? What kind of doctor is she? Does she chant and burn incense? Does Dr. D'Swill have a bone through her nose?"

"Dr. Althea D'Swill went to Yale."

"Oh yeah? What'd she do there, wash dishes or make the preppies' beds in the morning?" Ahmed said and laughed. His snide remarks actually pleased Mya—at least he seemed to be enjoying himself, joking about something he no doubt dreaded.

But Althea D'Swill turned out to be no joke. Her methods were rather novel and exotic, but she eschewed the usual new-age atmosphere of the medicine show-like genre: no music intended to promote serenity that did little more than give the high-anxiety sense of sitting in a lobby waiting for a root canal or ceramic waterfalls that induced an urge to pee. Her methods were straight-forward and deliberate—she pulled no punches.

"You're a junkie, Ahmed," she told him that first day. "And there's no nice way to put it. Oh, you're not hustling fixes down on Sligh Avenue—you have too much money for that—but you're addicted to drugs, just the same."

Ahmed said nothing, sitting quietly and staring at his hands clasped in his lap. They were alone in a small, hexagonal room at the end of a long corridor in the back of a building that looked like a hodgepodge of failed grad-school architectural projects. Seeing the one-story, white clapboard structure sequestered in the middle of a middle-class residential neighborhood for the first time was definitely not a soothing experience. *Maybe that was the point, to shock and distract you,* Ahmed thought, wishing he were anywhere else while listening to Dr. D'Swill castigate him amidst the sparse and confining sanctuarium.

"You're lucky to have someone who cares about you enough to try to help," Dr. D'Swill was saying. "And without some help, you're in big trouble, Ahmed, but I think you already know that, don't you? Do you want to lose your career? Do you want to end up dead?"

Ahmed looked up and gave her a crooked smile. "So what do we do to fix this?" he asked in barely more than a whisper.

"We get to work," Dr. D'Swill proclaimed in an authoritative voice. "Starting right now!"

Dr. D'Swill primarily used a methodology known as Ayurvedic medicine that emphasized lifestyle practices, such as massage, meditation, yoga, dietary changes and the extensive use of herbal remedies. She and her staff were adept at different types of massages to help restore collaborative bodily functions and positive energy flow, including techniques such as Bowen therapy that worked on soft tissue to promote pain relief and stone massages for healthful alignment and relaxation.

Ahmed went to the clinic four times a week for massages, yoga and consultations with Dr. D'Swill. He learned to meditate every morning, and with Mya's help, he improved his diet and took vitamins, herbal blends and supplements religiously.

To Ahmed's once-protective cynicism, and even more to his amazement, the seemingly snake-oil process worked, and he got off his medications and performance-enhancing drugs after months of hard work and some serious distress. Coupled with his physical therapy and ongoing fight to stay in tip-top shape, he spent six months going through hell. As Ahmed rehabbed his knee and detoxed his body, his mind and spirit followed, and by the beginning of the following year's training camp, he was in better mental and physical shape than ever before. He had dropped a few pounds, but his speed was still there and his stamina had increased significantly.

Thanks to his sister, Mya, and his deep-seated need to play football (which existed somewhere beyond his consciousness and comprehension), Ahmed was literally a new man.

Except for the troubling little voice that made no sense at all and scared the bejeebies out of him: *I should've made that tackle. It could've been different.*

Me

It started with small twitches, first in the hands that sometimes affected her manual dexterity and made it difficult to work buttons or write—not an uncommon malady in the aging process and one that easily went unnoticed, or, I should probably say, went by with little concern, so she didn't pay much attention to it. (It's my experience that women have a much easier time accepting signs of senescence than guys do, if you know what I mean.)

It didn't take too long for the twitches to spread to her arms and legs and begin to impede walking and lifting, and that's when she shared her problems with me and we became concerned. But it was when she started to slur her speech that the alarms went off, and I took her to the doctor.

Sandy was two months shy of 60, and we expected to have many more years together in front of us. I mean, come on, we all slow down as we get older. I myself was showing signs of deterioration, such as forgetting what I went into the garage for or which day of the week it was, not to mention (and I'd appreciate it if you didn't) that I couldn't hit a golf ball anywhere near as far as I could when I was younger and spryer, as they like to say. Look, we were getting old and it was showing. Nothing abnormal about that, right?

Wrong!

Our family doctor was immediately concerned, but he didn't share much with us until our second visit, after the test results came back. He told us that Sandy was suffering from amyotrophic lateral sclerosis, or ALS, more commonly known as Lou Gehrig's disease. Then he told us she was going to die.

And he was right.

Sandy died almost three years later after suffering through immense pain. When we buried her, I stood over the open grave and wished I could be in there with her … and in many ways, I suppose I was.

It seemed to me on that mournful day that my life was over, too, except for that little voice in my head that wouldn't go away, reminding me that this was only the second-worst day of my life. *I should've made that tackle. It could've been different.*

But maybe there was a way out.

You

Ahmed married a cheerleader who also happened to work for the football team, a no-no within the organization. Team personnel were not allowed to fraternize with or date cheerleaders—end of story. It was a singular rule, clear cut and definitive, and nobody on the team paid much attention to it.

Ahmed had met Delia his first year in Tampa, and they had become friends, or you might say, had become friendly. There was an obvious attraction between them, but Ahmed was, at first, a little naïve and concerned about the rule. They lost touch when he got hurt and went into a healing cocoon until the next summer's training camp, at which point a clean and healthy Ahmed took stock of his meager existence and realized something was missing: a life!

And Delia became that life.

Much to Mya's annoyance.

Mya was convinced that Delia was a shallow, gold-digging, bleached-blond floozy out to live off of her brother's fame and fortune, who, like a ravenous shark, had circled the waters searching for blood. With that proverbial keen third eye that parasitic bloodsuckers seem to innately possess, Delia had little trouble sniffing out the blood leaking from Ahmed's myriad self-inflicted wounds, and she attacked and devoured the almost lifeless prey before Mya had a chance to on-board the interloper and cut out her heart. Mya had pleaded with Ahmed to go slow and give it some time and, "For God's sake, do not marry that woman!"

"But I love her. I need her," Ahmed said.

"No you don't," Mya answered emphatically as her spirited Mediterranean blood started to boil. "You don't even know her, not really," she argued.

"She's gorgeous and sweet and cares about me," Ahmed pleaded. "What more do I need to know? You're just jealous that somebody else is going to take away your brother's attention," Ahmed joked.

Too bad he couldn't laugh away Delia, who as time went by, proved Mya right.

Ahmed played four more years for the Buccaneers, making All-Pro twice, but never getting back to the playoffs after his first year. In the middle of the last year of his five-year contract, he blew out his other knee and had to endure surgery and rehab all over again … but for the last time. On the advice of his surgeon, Ahmed retired and reluctantly walked away from his first (and maybe his only) true love.

He was no longer a football player.

Then what the hell am I?

Ahmed accepted a position as a TA (teacher's assistant) on the University of South Florida football team for a pittance, but free tuition. Much to his mother's joy, he enrolled and in two years finished his aborted bachelor's degree in business. From there, he joined a prestigious real estate firm in the Tampa Bay area and became quite successful. His parents and sister wanted him to move back to Delaware and work in the family business, but Ahmed loved Florida and wasn't about to go back to the cold Northeast.

He and Delia tried for years to have children, but a fertility doctor told Ahmed, confidentially, that his abuse of performance-enhancing drugs had damaged his testes and greatly compromised his ability to produce effective spermatozoa, rendering him, for all intents and purposes, infertile.

"They just can't make the swim," the doctor told Ahmed and Delia without revealing the cause. Ahmed was heartbroken, but Delia accepted it well and went on as if nothing had changed—and presumably never would.

And maybe that was the point.

They had a beautiful house on the bay, a big go-fast boat and an active social life. Things were pretty good for Ahmed ... except for that disturbing, tiny voice he would hear occasionally with the message he didn't understand.

And the headaches.

We

Brody's chief assistant was Dr. Barbara Steigelman-Genther, who had earned her M.D. from Johns Hopkins and a Ph.D. in computer science from Carnegie Mellon, where she concentrated in artificial intelligence. Before she was 40, she had become one of the most accomplished scientists in the field of AI, and her experience in detecting and charting the commerce of the human brain was unsurpassed. She was a shiny beacon in a field many of her colleagues felt was too sci-fi or too dangerous for conventional scientific inquiry, but not Dr. Brody Winechal, who recruited her to work with him in developing viable passageways and lobal connectors to facilitate expeditious interpretable confluences of data within zeptoseconds.

Which she did, but not in short order, comparatively speaking. It took them more than five years to identify and map all the intricate links and functions between the billions of neurons and the 1,000-trillion synapses that pass signals between the neurons. It was a daunting assignment for Dr. Steigelman-Genther, a labyrinthian and vast enterprise that her beyond-consummate skills in computer wizardry reduced to a relatively manageable undertaking. However, the biggest challenge they faced was isolating the essential protein particle fulcrums indigenous to the PR, which could be asymmetrical, opaque and fluid. It was an arduous and laborious occupation, one that would have provided an effective basis for Dr. Winechal and Dr. Steigelman-Genther to bond, but Dr. Winechal didn't bond.

Ever.

With anyone.

He just worked.

Some people—probably most people—would say that developing a replica of the brain in little over eight years was an amazing accomplishment, but Dr. Winechal would not. He was engrieved that it took so long and impatient to assimilate Brody's Bumptious Brain into an empirical application.

Bzzzzzzzzzz!

And that application became the Institute of Cognitive Realignment, or ICR, a wholly owned subsidiarity of D. Brown. However, before the company would invest the grotesque amounts of money necessary to build Dr. Winechal's machinery, Dr. Winechal and Dr. Steigelman-Genther had to face the board of directors of D. Brown and defend ICR.

After almost a decade of being the top dog in R&D, Dr. Winechal surely would have met the board members previously at one of the many business events or social gatherings D. Brown held, if Dr. Winechal attended events or social gatherings, which he didn't because he viewed them as an enormous waste of time. Consequently, Martin Berry, the CEO of D. Brown, opened the meeting by introducing the 15 directors and two doctors.

"You should all have a copy of the prospectus we prepared," he said.

The 10 men and five women who made up the board all nodded their heads and held the bound booklets in front of them in unison, like trained seals waiting for a treat.

"I hope you all had a chance to take a look at the report and familiarize yourselves with the project," Martin said. "I'm sure you're as impressed with this enterprise as we are. And as I'm sure you know, it's the most enormous, expensive undertaking that we've … well, that we've ever undertaken," he said, and the directors chuckled along with the CEO as if on cue.

"Without a doubt," Martin continued, "this project is the biggest and most expensive enterprise any private company has ever undertaken. It ought to be; it's predicated on cracking the very code of intelligent life. Not a bad day's work, eh?"

The group smiled and sighed as one.

"So, without further ado, Dr. Steigelman-Genther will now give a short, and non-technical, we hope"—

Martin paused here to wink at his audience, and the non-brilliant attendees laughed together with the harmony of a church choral group—"overview of the project. Then Dr. Winechal will discuss, briefly, the dimensions and scope of the project's application. Dr. Steigelman-Genther, the floor is yours."

Dr. Steigelman-Genther explained the process they had employed to uncover the Precognitive Rheostatus and how she had, in the simplest of terms, developed a complicated program to map it and its activity. "Dr. Winechal," she told the enthralled group, "used my program to replicate the process of the PR interacting with the rest of the brain. It sounds like a simple process, but it wasn't."

One of the directors raised her hand. "Is this … PR, is it like DNA?"

"Think of DNA as the building blocks of life," Dr. Steigelman-Genther answered. "And think of PR as the builder."

"Do you mean that PR is God?" another, somewhat startled, director asked.

"No, of course not," Dr. Steigelman-Genther replied and smiled. "But it's as close to God as we'll probably ever get." And with that, the group took a deep breath, as one.

Dr. Winechal took over and in a clipped, expressionless monotone, explained the application they had designed for the project.

"My staff named it The Hive," he told them, "and it is divided into cells that we call the honeycomb. Each cell within the honeycomb can house one patient, and we can add as many cells as needed. The number of cells The Hive can accommodate is infinite."

The entire board stiffened; their eyes opened wide.

A board member asked breathlessly, "Infinite?"

"Yes, infinite," Dr. Steigelman-Genther interjected. "But we don't expect to reach infinity." Everyone in the room laughed, except Dr. Winechal, who looked at his watch.

"The patient is domiciled in a type of liquid plasma, floating in, if you will, a cell filled with a life-preserving solution." Dr. Winechal continued. "Everything the patient needs to sustain life is delivered through the enriched plasma: oxygen, nourishment, vitamin D—whatever is needed to maintain a physical existence."

"So this is like suspended animation?" a board member asked.

"No! It is nothing like suspended animation. That is the stuff of science fiction and Saturday morning cartoons," Dr. Winechal retorted, emphatically. "The patient's brain is still fully activated and conscious, in a way of speaking, but all cerebral activity is routed through The Hive."

"In other words," the board member followed with, "they're aware of their surroundings?"

"They are aware of what their mind perceives to be real, so yes, they are aware of the surroundings that their minds, working in conjunction with The Hive, create. But no, they are not aware of the physical dimensions of our perception."

"What does that mean?" another board member asked.

"It means, simply put," Dr. Winechal said, "that perception is reality. Perception is personal, like snowflakes. No two people have the same perception of life. How do we know we are not floating in a vat of some advanced liquid right now? How do we know we are even here? Because our perception tells us we are here and that everything around us is real. Ergo, reality is flexible, and we use that flexibility to ensure our patients a better life than the one they would be facing."

"Please explain that," Martin requested.

"All of our patients will be terminally ill with no hope for surviving more than a few years. We thoroughly debrief them—intellectually, psychologically, physically—and then we connect them to The Hive, which scans their brains and absorbs all their memories and pertinent data of their lives. The Hive then uses the patient's brain to recreate their lives from any given point—what we call the trigger point, or TP. Each patient tells us where they would like to begin their lives again, and The Hive builds a program from that point on working in conjunction with the patient's brain. Their brain is still the driver of their perception, and it always will be."

A board member sitting at the back of the table who had been quiet until this point interjected, "Are you saying they're a new person with a new life?"

"No, they are the same person with the same life but with a different trajectory."

"So, what happens in this new trajectory if they get sick again?"

"That is where The Hive takes over to ensure the patient stays on track regarding their desired new trajectory. This is an organic process, and the patient's mind is in control. The Hive is simply a facilitator and guide. We could program The Hive to control all thoughts, but that would defeat the purpose of regeneration, the revival of one's inner spirit, if you will."

"Is this a virtual existence, like a game?" the board member from the back of the table pressed.

"Of course not," Dr. Winechal huffed. "The patients' new existences are as real to them as the stone was to Dr. Johnson."

"I refute it thus," added one of the more erudite board members, smiling broadly like she had just won a kewpie doll at the county fair.

"Exactly," Dr. Winechal said without anyone in the room noticing the ironic misinterpretation of Dr. Johnson's famed quip.

"So, how long do they remain in this state? How long does this new reality last? Do they ever wake up?" a less-erudite board member asked.

"They have nothing to wake up from," Dr. Winechal corrected. "They are never asleep. They are still very much alive, but living on a different level of existence than we have previously experienced, at least in any comprehensive form. The timeframe is individual. The Hive can determine, through the patient's PR, the timetable the patient is on and make adjustments accordingly. We will institute procedures to slow down the aging and deterioration process, but the duration of a patient's new existence can last as long as the patient determines. That determination will depend on the patient's constitution and will to live. We believe that 'will to live' will be the primary deciding factor in how long a patient lives."

"But can they be revived or removed from The Hive?" the director asked from the back of the table.

"No. They have chosen a different path. The purpose is to alleviate their current suffering. Why would they want to come back to that?"

The board members looked at each other and nodded their heads in animated accord.

Martin Berry thanked Dr. Winechal and Dr. Steigelman-Genther for their time and thoughtful presentation. As he was about to conclude the meeting, a board member asked, "How much do you plan to charge someone for this service?"

"It's in the prospectus," Martin said. "Ten million dollars."

Bzzzzzzzzzz!

You

The first concussion Ahmed could remember happened during his sophomore year in high school. They were playing Wilmington Friends, and he took a big hit directly to the head, helmet to helmet, after catching a pass in the first quarter. He was knocked out.

Cold.

But revived a few minutes later and walked off the field, groggy and adrift at sea. Coach Moorhead told him to get a drink of water, and on the next series Ahmed was back in. He played the rest of the game, although he didn't remember much about it. He had headaches for the rest of the season.

In college, he suffered what the team trainer called stingers, and they gave him headaches, too. On two occasions, he saw stars and had a sour taste of metal in his mouth. Coach Callihan told him that he'd had his bell rung and to walk it off. He finished both of those games but remembered not much of either.

And those were just the incidents Ahmed could recall.

In the pros, he'd had his bell rung often and spent most of those seasons with headaches, but he was never diagnosed with a single concussion. By the time Ahmed left the game, if you asked him if he ever had a concussion playing in the NFL, he would have told you "No, but I got my bell rung many times." Such were the days of euphemistic sleight of hand: If you didn't say it, it wasn't there.

Ahmed couldn't remember a time when he didn't have headaches. They were not constant and usually not of the migraine variety, but he did get some doozies now and then. By the time he was in his 40s, he was experiencing bouts of depression that he blamed on the headaches. When he started to forget simple things, such as phone numbers or people's names, he blamed those lapses on the headaches. As he aged further and started to get confused and angry, he blamed that incongruous behavior on the headaches.

He was right about the association of the headaches to his difficulties, though they weren't the root cause of his problems, obviously, but were telltale signs of what was happening to his brain and a potent harbinger.

About the time Ahmed was becoming more and more dependent on assistance, Delia left, saying it was too much trouble taking care of him.

To no one's surprise.

He was lucky his devoted sister had made him get a prenuptial agreement, and Delia walked away with almost nothing … except for an 82-year-old man she had met at the yacht club who was filthy rich, enamored with her well-maintained and glamorously groomed body, and harmlessly impotent.

Delia's ideal man.

Ahmed didn't blame the breakup on his headaches because by then he wasn't much interested in cause and effect, just survival. Mya swooped in once again to take care of her brother, first by moving him into her home in Delaware with her husband and two teenagers. They had a big house and converted never-before-used space over the garage into a small apartment. The next thing she did was take him to a qualified neurologist. In Florida, Ahmed had been seeing a friendly, easy-going general practitioner who told him he was showing signs of diminished capacity in its very early stages, nothing to worry about, all part of the aging process. They would watch it and treat him as needed.

The neurologist Mya took Ahmed to see told him he was suffering from chronic brain syndrome, a condition most likely caused by his years of playing football and taking hits to the head. The doctor sent Ahmed to another neurologist in Philadelphia who specialized in chronic traumatic encephalopathy, or CTE, a common malady in ex-football players. The specialist told Ahmed and Mya that CTE was a degenerative disease of the brain and that there was no cure, but added that they were having some success with treatments to at least hold off the inevitable. He sent them to Sunshine Care, a clinic that specialized in degenerative brain disorders.

The clinic was on the outskirts of Baltimore, about an hour's drive from Mya's home. The director of the clinic welcomed them and said that many people with CTE live healthy and fulfilling lives. He recommended regular exercise and healthy nutrition and adopting a few strategies, such as establishing a daily routine because creating a predictable structure helps life feel more stable and writing things down to help combat memory problems. He also recommended some relaxation methods, including deep breathing and stretching to help control Ahmed's obstreperously emotional mood swings. The director told them it would be greatly beneficial to Ahmed's circulation and his blood flow to the brain if he could come in at least twice a week for massages and hands-on manipulative amelioration.

"The most important thing, Ahmed," the director told them at the conclusion of the meeting, "is to ask for help. Don't be afraid to lean on your family and friends. That's what they're there for."

Mya helped Ahmed set up a routine, and he hung on for some time, even going to work in the family business a few days a week during the first few years. But as time went by, his condition worsened, and it reached the point where he could barely take care of himself. He spent a great deal of time in painful discomfort.

The good news for Ahmed was that the little, confusing voice inside his head had stopped. Or maybe it hadn't. He couldn't remember. What he could remember, though, was the nagging feeling that he shouldn't have made The Tackle. What the hell that was all about he couldn't figure out, even on his most lucid days, and that bewildering notion only added to his incertitude and futile effort to fight the terrifying disorientation.

But maybe there was a way out.

They

A woman stands at her perennial spot and looks down at the man. She doesn't talk. Everything that has to be said has been said. She is no longer conflicted over the matter and has learned to accept the reality of the situation.

But reality can be so hard to figure out, she ponders.

Me

So here we are, back to where we started. I'm a 65-year-old man, out of work, out of love and out of gas. (I was going to say out of life, but that sounds awfully dramatic, doesn't it? Of course, if you believe your life is over, I mean, if you *really* believe that for certain, then I guess nothing's overly dramatic any longer, is it?) Giving up work was the easy part; Marla took care of that. After Sandy died a couple of years ago, I lost interest in the company, in golf, in everything and walked around like a whupped pup, practically a comatose zombie—the walking dead, you might say, if you go in for that type of overwrought morbidity. By that time, Marla was practically running the company anyway, so she and my sister, Mya, and my daughter, Lydia—via Skype—sat me down and gave me a good thrashing about feeling sorry for myself and giving up and preached to me that I still had a lot to live for and all that rah-rah crap that they thought would help, but it didn't. It only made me feel like more of a failure.

Which, I guess, was pretty much how I was feeling: I failed to save Sandy. I failed to make the tackle. End of story.

During the intervention, they talked me into retiring, which was about as hard as blowing a feather off your hand. From there, I went about the business of wanting to not live. I guess they were still worried about me because each one of them called every day, and Mya and Marla took turns checking in on me at my empty, moribund house (that was, really, no longer a home). They soon started, subtly at first, talking about retirement villages and how great they are and how much fun I'd have commingling with all the wonderful people my age parked at a way station waiting for death to show up at their doorsteps, scythe in hand (although those weren't their exact words).

As great as that all sounded, I had a better idea.

I suppose, at this point, you think I sound awfully jolly for such a sad tale, so let me bring you up to speed: I made a decision that's going to fix everything.

One day when Sandy was in her final stages, Mya, my short, effervescent and tireless sister, showed up and sat us down to talk about an article she'd read in a medical journal (and what she was doing reading a medical journal is beyond me, but knowing my sister, she was probably looking for information to help Sandy).

Mya said, "The article described a procedure developed by some Einstein-like genius who invented a way of putting terminally ill patients in some kind of trance or vegetative state to alleviate their pain and allow them to live in some kind of virtual reality. I really don't understand it, not completely, and it sounds like the writer of the article didn't either. It's a little off-the-wall, I know, but I talked to someone there—it's near Princeton, New Jersey—and they told me they're having great results with the program."

I looked at Sandy and she was smiling. "Sounds wonderful, Mya," she slurred. "But I don't think I'd enjoy living in a test tube."

"It's not like that at all," Mya responded, excitedly. "The place is called the Institute of Cognitive Realignment, and it's part of D. Brown, a huge medical-equipment manufacturer. I know it sounds Star Wars-y, but this organization is for real, and it's helping people who are … well, you know."

"Yes, I know, Mya," Sandy said, shaking. "I'm dying."

"I'm sorry," Mya said. "I don't want to upset you. But truly, it's a godsend for people who are terminally ill and living with no hope." She paused and bit her lower lip. "I just want you to have some hope, Sandy," my compassionate sister, who was the physical template for my daughter, Marla, said through tears.

By that time, Sandy was confined to a wheelchair, and even though we'd gotten her an electric one, she couldn't operate it by herself. If she could have, though, I'm sure she would have gone to Mya and hugged her. But she couldn't, so all she did was cry, too.

Mya kept at it for a couple of days and finally badgered me into at least visiting the facility and meeting the staff. The trip would have been too arduous for Sandy, so we decided I'd go and report back. I was skeptical, as was Sandy, although saying skeptical was being kind for Mya's sake; it sounded like something out of a futuristic comic book, a quixotic, improbable scheme too far out there. So, I schlepped up to Princeton and with every mile, became more and more annoyed. I didn't like the idea of giving Sandy false hope with some hocus pocus alakazam scam.

Boy, was I in for a surprise.

The facility was out in the middle of nowhere, wedged between old forests and farmland, it stuck out like a futuristic design you might see on *The Jetsons*. The main part of the complex was an enormous dome that resembled a nine-month-pregnant airplane hangar—a strikingly imposing erection that sat in the middle of the grounds. It was constructed of a space-age looking material, like the mysterious metal alloy found at Roswell, New Mexico, in 1947—you know, the stuff that the government claims was from a high-altitude balloon that crashed in the desert, and any day now, after examining and testing the stuff for the past 75 years, they'll be able to identify that pesky substrate.

But that puzzle was nothing compared to what I was looking at: The dome appeared to be breathing—I kid you not—in and out, in and out, ever so slightly, almost indiscernibly, but definitely undulating. The building sat on approximately four acres, and attached to one side was a five-story office building made of glass and shiny steel, like you might see in downtown Philadelphia, a short ride away. The place was imposing with a majestic aura of profundity, like you were going where no man has gone before—ha, ha, right? Seriously, my attention was immediately caught by how neat and perfect everything appeared, like it was designed and maintained by someone with a serious case of OCD. The driveway and parking area looked like they had just been resurfaced, and the grass and shrubbery surrounding the buildings were trimmed and pleasingly symmetrical. There was nothing out of place, no litter or loose clippings or chipped concrete curbs, just tidy and immaculate and overpowering.

And maybe that was the point.

In the small lobby, more like a vestibule, at my appointed time, I met a young man wearing a clean and pressed, well-fitted white lab coat who introduced himself as Dr. Larry. I didn't know if that was his first or last name, and I was going to ask, but he briskly escorted me into a nearby, small sitting room, appointed sharply in rich leather and chrome. I sat in one of three chairs surrounding a low table, and Dr. Larry said that Dr. Steigelman-Genther would be joining me shortly—"would I like some coffee?"—and then he disappeared in what seemed like a puff of smoke.

My imagination was getting the best of me.

A few moments later, a woman came into the room carrying two steaming cups of coffee in sparkling white ceramic mugs that she set on the table. She was tall, about 5'9" or 5'10", with a slim body and a close-cropped, dark hairdo, and was wearing the same style, perfectly fitted and cared-for lab coat as Dr. Larry. She was an almost-attractive woman in a kind of sterile way, if you know what I mean, and carried a look of guarded superiority—rather stately and imperious, but she was in no way offensive. It was a strange dichotomy of messages, and I was trying to decide whether I liked her or not when she introduced herself as Dr.

Barbara Steigelman-Genther and took a seat across the table from me.

"There's sugar and cream on the credenza behind you," she offered. "And muffins, if you're hungry."

"Thank you," I said as I picked up the mug in front of me and softly blew on the hot brew. She tried to mimic my move, but a little clumsily, lacking total grace I would call it, and she gave me a tight smile that could have been interpreted as an apology for not being as coordinately suave as I.

Or maybe she was reacting to the hot coffee. Who knows?

At first blush, she was hard to read, but I decided I liked her.

"I'm Dr. Winechal's associate. He invented our process and founded ICR. I'm going to give you a tour and overview of our facility, and then you'll meet Dr. Winechal and he'll go over the details of our program," she said in a somewhat modest yet proprietary voice. This woman was a real paradox—maybe that's just how eggheads are. I wouldn't know. Maybe you do.

She said that Dr. Winechal insisted on being the point person with each of their guests, as she called them, and the guest's family and/or caregiver. "He wants to be certain there are no misunderstandings and that everybody is given accurate information. He wants our guests to be comfortable with their decision."

She continued to tell me how Dr. Winechal and she had developed the processes necessary to build what they called The Hive, which I guessed was the name of the computer and software that ran the place. She actually told me it was an external brain that functioned in conjunction with the human brain, but that seemed a bit presumptuous, don't you think?

As it turned out, it wasn't presumptuous at all. This Dr. Winechal guy, she said, had been able to harness a part of the brain that nobody else ever even knew existed, and he won a Noble Prize for it. The funny part, at least for me, was that the more this thing sounded legitimate, the more it sounded pretty far-fetched. Does that make any sense to you? It was becoming a riddle, wrapped in a mystery, inside an enigma—ha, ha, right?

But it was.

Until Dr. Steigelman-Genther gave me the tour.

Holy crap!

She led me into the dome, what she called the honeycomb. It was massive and bright, and everything seemed to be painted electric yellow with blazing, nearly blinding illumination coming from no particular source—the light seemed to emanate from the dome itself. I reached into my shirt pocket for my sunglasses, but I'd left them in the car.

"Your eyes will adjust to the light in a minute," Dr. Steigelman-Genther told me. "We try to duplicate sunlight in the honeycomb because the human brain functions better in daylight. Did you know that? Not many people do. It's one of the startling finds Dr. Winechal made. He's quite a remarkable man."

"I'd hate to have to pay your electric bill," I quipped.

That made Dr. Steigelman-Genther smile a radiant, broad, sincere smile, and it completely changed her appearance—not like kissing a frog, but like someone threw a switch, and presto, you were at your high school sock hop and you so badly wanted to ask this girl to dance, whereas before she looked like somebody you'd be afraid to approach.

It was almost an enchanted transition, and that weirded me out even more. There was something about this place …

"We don't get an electric bill," she said. "The skin of this dome is a living membrane that absorbs the sun's rays, even on the darkest days, and converts them into light and energy, something like a solar panel only much more sophisticated, functional and powerful. It also takes in oxygen. You may have noticed it breathing. It cleans and filters the air and feeds it to the guests—another one of Dr. Winechal's inventions."

We were walking along catwalks that crisscrossed over hundreds of rectangular-shaped rooms—no, not really rooms, little cells, about 12-feet-by-6, with small angles in each corner, making each one, in effect, a non-symmetrical octagon, and overall, they looked like cells in a honeycomb. In the corners between the rooms were machines that noiselessly pulsed. Each room had walls but no ceiling so we could see into each one as we moved along, and each one contained a person immersed in some kind of liquid. There were no tubes or lines connecting them to anything; they simply appeared to float in the watery substance, not moving and bobbing, but still and suspended.

"What the …"

"It's some sight, isn't it?" Dr. Steigelman-Genther asked. "It's really quite marvelous. If it wasn't for Dr. Winechal, all of these people would be dead. Instead, they're all still very much alive and leading their lives all over again."

"How long do these people live once they're here?" I asked.

"We don't know. We've only been operational for four years, and so far, we've lost only one guest. Our guests can live for many years. We put them in a kind of induced coma and slow down all their systems so they can maintain life here well beyond the expected lifespan relative to their particular condition or disease." She must have noticed the confused and overwhelmed look on my face because she quickly added, "The alternative is much worse. Our average guest wouldn't make it six months on their own."

I didn't say anything, just stared at the people floating in their cells.

"It's hard to understand, I know," she said.

Dr. Steigelman-Genther explained the process in simple terms. As she spoke, I imagined it was much more complicated than she made it sound.

When she finished, I asked, "How many guests do you presently have?" I felt funny calling them "guests."

"Right now, we have 286. We can house up to 1,000 guests in this facility; we're still growing. As a matter of fact, I'm taking you to a cell that is accepting a new guest this morning."

We walked along the catwalk for a couple of minutes without talking until we came to a spot where Dr. Steigelman-Genther stopped and leaned on the railing. There was a group of people about 10 feet away from us on the catwalk: an older woman, a middle-aged couple and a young woman in a white lab coat. The older woman and the couple were crying.

"Watch this," Dr. Steigelman-Genther said quietly.

Out of nowhere, it seemed, came a pod that looked like a car ski carrier, moving along beneath the catwalks. We were about 15 feet above the cells, and we watched the pod stop and hover over an empty cell near us. As it quietly hummed in place, a body emerged from its underbelly and slowly descended into the cell below it. The body looked like an old man, swaddled in some type of mesh material that appeared translucent, but you couldn't see through it.

Yet another paradox to ponder.

I couldn't see anything attached to the man; no harness or platform or anything connected him to the pod.

"What's lowering him?" I asked. "I don't see anything holding him."

Dr. Steigelman-Genther turned to me. "It's magic," she said and smiled that smile while holding up 10 fingers and wiggling them back and forth.

"You guys should work for Disney," I said, and she laughed.

The body penetrated the liquid and settled into place as the pod moved back to wherever it had come from.

"That's very bizarre," I said.

"Not really," Dr. Steigelman-Genther replied. "It's accomplished by using some advanced, arcane laws of physics and simple aerodynamic principles. The traft—that's short for transportation craft—creates a column of air pressure that weighs more than the guest, and by slowly reducing the pressure in the column, the guest is lowered, like an elevator. It's another innovation Dr. Winechal dreamed up to simplify our systems and keep guests 100 percent sterile while they're being loaded into their cells. Nothing touches the guests once they have been sterilized and prepared for insertion. We call the procedure the WC, for winged chariot."

"Remarkable," I offered.

"The guests' safety and comfort are Dr. Winechal's top priorities—his only priorities."

"Where does that come from in a scientist?" I asked.

"I'm not sure," she said and put the palm of her hand under her chin like she was thinking. "He once said something about the project being in honor of El. I think that was the name of a dog he had when he was young, but I don't know. He doesn't talk much about anything other than work."

"How do you keep the cells sterile with those open ceilings?"

"They only look open. They're actually covered with an invisible screen, like a force field from *Star Trek*, if that means anything to you."

"Oh yeah! I'm no Trekkie but I grok force fields," I chimed in, then waited for her reaction to what I thought was a clever and germane allusion to the sci-fi genre we seemed steeped in, but nothing. (Anything from you, or am I just an old fart and nobody reads anymore?) "Only I thought they were made up, a creation of Hollywood," I added.

"They were, until Dr. Winechal, who had never heard of *Star Trek*, implemented them."

"I don't see any computers or equipment running this place," I observed.

"Like most people, I'm sure you think of computer systems as hardware and software, correct?"

I nodded in the affirmative.

"In Dr. Winechal's system, they're one thing; the machinery and operating system are one, and it's all part of the dome. The skin of the dome is built out of trillions and trillions of tiny little processors—it literally is magic," she said and smiled again. *I could grow accustomed to that smile,* I thought, but I doubt she gets much chance to use it around here. "That's why we call it the honeycomb—because it really is a living, organic world unto itself."

"Very impressive," I said.

"Dr. Winechal's genius is impressive, yes, but in person, I should warn you, he's a bit dry," Dr. Steigelman-Genther confided. "He's not a people person, but you'll find him honest and thorough."

"How do you feed and care for your guests?" I asked. "I don't see any feeding tubes or oxygen masks. I don't see any wires connecting to the brain or any coupling to the … what did you call it? The Hive?"

"The liquid the guests are immersed in supplies them with oxygen, sustenance, everything they need to maintain a physical existence through the diffusion of a whole-body ingestion-like process—another one of Dr. Winechal's creations. It monitors and sustains all the body's systems and is in continuous communication with The Hive through those small accelerators you see in the corners of the cells. As far as brain activity, the guests have microchips implanted throughout their brains that transmit to, and receive from, The Hive instantaneously … although it's probably more accurate to say simultaneously. The transmission signals are so fast as to have almost no lapse of time between them—the speed of the messages is immeasurable."

"Wow! I don't know what else to say."

"Good. Then I've done my job," Dr. Steigelman-Genther concluded with one last smile. "Now I'll turn you over to Dr. Winechal."

You

When things seemed all but lost, Mya sat down with Ahmed on one of his increasingly few good days and told him about an article she'd read in a medical journal. She had been conducting research to try to find anything that could help her brother, and she had stumbled upon this piece about a procedure developed by a doctor in New Jersey who invented a way of putting terminally ill patients in some kind of trance or vegetative state. The article was hard to follow, but the idea of eradicating or easing her brother's pain and suffering was enticing, even though it sounded pretty far-fetched. The article said that the process the clinic was running eliminated the awareness of pain and allowed a patient to live in some kind of virtual reality. The writer of the piece had interviewed a Dr. Barbara Steigelman-Genther, who said they were showing great results.

The organization was called the Institute of Cognitive Realignment, she told Ahmed, and it's part of D. Brown, the big medical equipment manufacturer, located in Princeton, New Jersey. She said she talked to a Dr. Larry from ICR on the phone and had made an appointment for Ahmed and her to visit.

"Would you like to go see the facility and meet these people, Ahmed?" she asked. "We don't have anything to lose by spending a day going up there and back, and maybe we'll find something that will help you. What do you think?"

Ahmed didn't think much about anything anymore, and he was having trouble following Mya, but he wanted to make his sister happy so he nodded yes.

Three days later they were on the New Jersey Turnpike, only a hop, skip and 73-yard touchdown dash away from getting the grand treatment that would convince Mya it was the right place for Ahmed.

Me

When I met Dr. Winechal for our introductory meeting at ICR, the first word that came to mind was nondescript. Really, he was probably the most nondescript-looking person I'd ever seen. Okay, that may be a bit of an exaggeration, but he was shockingly average-looking. He wasn't tall and he wasn't short.

He wasn't fat and he wasn't thin. He wasn't handsome and he wasn't not handsome. He was just plain nondescript.

Sorry, but that's the word for it.

I mean, he didn't wear glasses sitting crooked on his nose, held together at the bridge by tape, or sport a pocket protector full of various writing utensils and devices of measurement and calculation. His hair wasn't mussed but was parted on the left side and neatly combed. His lab coat and tie were clean and crisp like everybody else's I met that day, and the overall effect was that he looked exactly not like a mad scientist.

It was kind of disappointing.

"What do you think of our facility, Mr. Clark?" Dr. Winechal began.

"It's very impressive," I replied.

"Do you think we would be a good fit for your wife?" he continued, and his questioning led me to believe that he had taken a sales training course. Why not? The guy was obviously a perfectionist.

"So far."

"It would be your responsibility to ferry Mrs. Clark to this facility. Once she is here, she is in our care. We take care of everything from that point on. Once your wife arrives here, there is no turning back. You will never see her again, except if you visit and view her from the catwalks. Most people do that once in a while. It is troubling to see your loved one in that position. It is like she is dead, and to you and your family, she will be dead. This experience is for her. You will have the satisfaction and peace of mind knowing she is comfortable and trouble-free. Do you understand that, Mr. Clark?"

"Yeah," I said.

"Do you understand the fee is ten million dollars, nonrefundable once you sign the agreement and release?"

"Yeah."

"Do you understand that your health insurance will not cover our fee? Do you understand the fee is out-of-pocket?"

"Yeah, I got all that from the material you sent me."

"Is the fee something you can afford, Mr. Clark?"

"It's not a problem. We're well off."

"Do you have your wife's power of attorney, Mr. Clark?"

"If we decide to do this, I'll get it."

"Once you decide to have your wife join us, you will have to come in and meet with our attorney and notary to sign the agreement and release. At that time, our attorney will go over the details of the documents with you. Please feel free to bring your attorney. We encourage you to do so. After you sign the documents, you will need to wire the fee into our account. You should make the necessary arrangements with your bank before the meeting and activate the transfer from here. Is that clear, Mr. Clark?"

"I understand."

"Good. Now that the business is out of the way, do you have any questions?"

"Only about five million," I said and laughed. Dr. Winechal did not. He kept the same noncommittal look throughout the entire meeting. He didn't look stern and he didn't look friendly. He looked ... well, nondescript.

He answered my questions for the next hour, and by the time I left, I was convinced this was the right place for Sandy. Unfortunately, Sandy died before we could navigate the preadmission labyrinth.

You

On Ahmed's good days—and none of his days were really good any longer, they were more like marginally okay days—he wasn't sure about Mya's plan, and on the other days when he was barely aware of anything going on around him, the point was moot. Mya had made up her mind and Ahmed was along for the ride.

Wherever it was going, he couldn't have told you.

Mya obtained power of attorney over Ahmed's affairs, a relatively simple matter given his obvious state of mental impairment, and completed the preadmission requirements to have her brother committed to the Institute of Cognitive Realignment under the care of Dr. Brody Winechal.

Other than the technician-guide with her, Mya stood alone on the catwalk a couple of weeks later, watching her brother being lowered into his cell. She had a pretty good idea of what he was going through. In their meeting with Dr. Winechal a month earlier, he had explained the process in detail. Ahmed was admitted and placed in a private waiting room that looked like a hospital room, only much nicer. There he remained for a week while he was thoroughly examined and evaluated by doctors of various specialties. Minute electrodes were implanted in his brain with tiny needles that required no cutting nor caused any bleeding. According to Dr. Winechal, Ahmed would feel nothing during the process of connecting him to The Hive. Lastly, Ahmed was scrubbed and wrapped in a protective coating of a special mesh film and transported via the traft to his cell, where he would remain for the rest of his life—a concept that was still a bitter pill for Mya to swallow.

But the alternative was much worse, and she was grateful for Dr. Winechal's miraculous work as she stood on the catwalk in the bright honeycomb.

The hardest part in the process for Ahmed had been picking a TP—the trigger point where The Hive would send him during the transition. Dr. Winechal described the Precognitive Rheostatus as a computer that records everything that happens in a person's life and stores that information forever. "Once we tap into the PR we can recreate a life down to every single detail. It's all there just waiting to be uncovered," Dr. Winechal said.

"So, he'll relive his same life?" Mya asked, startled.

"No, not at all," Dr. Winechal responded. "He will be starting on a new track from the TP, and his mind will control the trajectory, just like in his previous life. It is complicated, but Mr. Clark will have a new experience, much better than his previous one. Most patients pick a TP where they became sick, or where the sickness originated, and some go back even further to a point of significant transition in their lives. It is all very personal. The Hive facilitates the new course, like an air traffic controller does to an airplane, making sure it stays on the flight plan."

During Ahmed's week of preparation as he faded in and out, he mumbled a couple of times, "I should've made that tackle. It could've been different." In and of itself, that didn't make a lot of sense, but by talking to his sister and with a little research and help from Ahmed's PR, the team at ICR was able to determine Ahmed's TP.

Ahmed had been sedated for transporting to his cell, so he was relaxed but awake. Dr. Winechal had told them it was important that the patient be conscious during submission so that the lungs could continue to operate functionally and not seize and drown the patient. He explained that although The Hive is in control, there was a slight chance that the subconscious could momentarily override its signals and put the body into the panic mode of drowning, which could be disastrous. With the patient conscious, The Hive would remain in control, and Ahmed would feel nothing except a slight sensation of congestion. Then he would drift off peacefully and regain consciousness on his new plane of existence.

"It's a simple procedure and not harmful or uncomfortable for the patient," Dr. Winechal explained to Mya and Ahmed.

Mya thought it was interesting that Dr. Winechal always called them patients, while Dr. Steigelman-Genther insisted on referring to them as guests. "Tells you a lot about them, doesn't it," she said to Ahmed on the way home from their initial visit.

In Ahmed's deteriorating and distorted state of perception, everything was blurry, but he was aware of being moved and lowered into what felt like a warm bath. He had the sensation of the liquid washing over him, and he could sense a heaviness in his lungs as he drifted off to sleep *then leaving my feet and hitting him a speck too high just as he swung his arm and shoulder, flicking me off like a horse shooing a fly with his tail. I slid off him and hit the ground hard, slamming my left shoulder into the cold, half-frozen turf...*

Me

I told you I made a decision that would fix things, didn't I? Can you guess what it was?

Okay, I'm sitting in the small meeting room at ICR again talking with Dr. Winechal, and I just told him I want to take the plunge.

"But you are not sick," Dr. Winechal protests.

"Look, doc, I'm very sick. I'm sick at heart and I'm sick of living. If you don't help me, I will surely die just as Sandy did. I have no hope left and I'm begging you to please help me."

"This is very unusual," Dr. Winechal said and looked extremely uncomfortable.

Man, that's the first time I've seen any emotion out of this guy.

"I'll pay you twice as much—20 million—will that do it?"

"This is not about money," Dr. Winechal said as he shifted in his seat. "It has never been about money. It has always been about helping people."

"Well, doc, I'm people and I desperately need your help. Isn't sickness of the mind the same as sickness of the body?"

Dr. Winechal stared into space for a few minutes, like I had short-circuited his internal programming. I could almost see smoke coming from his ears as the synapses in his brain opened and shut in frantic chaos.

"Who do I need to talk to, doc? Who can make this decision?"

"I make all the decisions here. I am autonomous."

You are auto-something, for sure.

We talked about it for some time, and he told me he wanted to discuss it with his associates and give it some thought.

"I'm not leaving here today without getting this done," I said, and now, a couple of weeks later, I'm about to be lowered into a vat of hope and promise for a better life, and from some dream-like place comes that old familiar voice *I should've made that tackle. It could've been different.*

I'm very relaxed and hazy as I float down into my new home. I can feel the liquid surround me and fill my lungs as I drift off to sleep, *and he caught him on the five-yard line, and just as he was about to dive at the churning feet of the almost-hero, an alarm went off in his head. He made a slight adjustment to his shoulders and let fly, bringing the surprised Cowbird down at the two in a bone-crunching tackle...*

They

Marla was livid after reading the letter from her father that was sent to her by his attorney. The letter explained what he had done and apologized for not including anybody else in the decision.

She immediately called the lawyer.

"How could you have let this happen without talking to me first?" Marla said in an undisguised voice of agitation.

"I was your father's lawyer, not yours. It was his wish not to tell anyone about his decision. Although I strenuously argued against it, I had no choice. I hope you can understand that your pique is not with me."

"But we thought he was in Europe on a vacation."

"That's the way he wanted it. I'm sorry."

Next, Marla called the Institute of Cognitive Realignment and insisted on talking to the head person, which she did, but only after threatening to sue.

"It is not our responsibility how a patient informs, or does not inform, his family," Dr. Winechal told Marla after she vented her displeasure over what she saw as ICR's complicity in her father's demise. "We have a signed, notarized agreement from your father, Mrs. Clark-Gonul, and it protects us completely. We have no vulnerabilities. Nothing we have done for your father is actionable, and there are no damages."

"But you took away his life."

"On the contrary, Mrs. Clark-Gonul. We gave him the life he always wanted."

"What are you talking about, 'the life he always wanted?' My father had a wonderful life; he was a happy person. He was just going through some hard times after my mother died, is all. He would have been fine if you hadn't lobotomized him!"

"We did not lobotomize him, Mrs. Clark-Gonul," Dr. Winechal said in a steady, even voice. "I do not want to be indelicate, but maybe you did not know your father as well as you think you did. Perhaps your mother's death was simply a tripping switch that exposed a life-long condition of pain that nobody else knew about."

"Is that what you're saying, that my father lived his life in some kind of pain?"

Dr. Winechal paused, then said, "What I can tell you for certain, Mrs. Clark-Gonul, is that your father is happy now."

We

We visit Dr. Winechal to try to fix this unmitigated disaster. This is not what we were promised. Who are we? I mean, we don't know, not for sure, who we are anymore. Why do we have conflicting messages rattling around in our brain, or hints of another life we were supposed to have? Why are we so confused and bewildered by our lives, and why is it so damn painful? Something went terribly wrong, and we want answers.

"This isn't working, Dr. Wincchal," wc say.

"What seems to be the problem?" Dr. Winechal asks with a twinkle in his eye.

"We want out. This isn't what you told us it would be—this is a nightmare. We've changed our minds and want out of here!"

"There's no turning back. I told you that," he says and smirks. And then he sings, "When you're a disembodied spirit, you're a disembodied spirit, you're a disembodied spirit all the way," and laughs. This is strange. There is something very strange about Dr. Winechal.

"When did you get a sense of humor. What gives?"

"When you gave me one."

We think about that for a moment, then ask, "Are you sure you did this right?"

"Abso-freakin'-lutly," Dr. Winechal responds in a playful, singsongy voice and smiles.

Hey, this guy doesn't smile.

"It's like there are two people in our head, doc. We can't tell what thoughts are ours, if you grasp the gist of our aberrant predicament. Do you? Our gist is that your toy is broken, and we feel like the toy. Got it? We mean, we don't know who's real or what's real anymore, doc."

"Who of us knows what's real?"

"What's going on? Please help us. There must be a glitch in the system."

"Sounds like it," Dr. Winechal says while playing with a paper clip.

"So, you're admitting it? You screwed up?"

"Looks like it," Dr. Winechal agrees, then picks up a rubber band and shoots the paper clip across the room. The paper clip hits the far wall and he yells, "Bullseye!"

We look at him in disbelief, shaking our head. "Look, doc, there must be something you can do. Can't you tweak the system or reprogram the software? Something? Anything?"

"Nope," Dr. Winechal says as he picks lint off his lab coat. "The problem is, I don't even know that there's anything wrong. I believe you're doing swell and everything is going great and that you're happy. I'm obviously obliviously wrong." Then he breaks into song again: I'm singing in the rain, just singing in the rain. What a glorious feelin', and I'm happy again!"

"You're messing with us, right?"

"Not at all. And by the way, you're screwed, m' boy."

"What? Don't you feel any accountability for our situation? Don't you have an obligation to help us?"

"Wish I could, but can't."

"So in other words, you won't help us?"

"*Nada que puedo hacer,*" he says and twirls a pen on the table.

"Where'd this new personality come from? Seriously. We mean, what's going on with you?"

"You're what's going on with me. It's your show, Ahmed. You're the writer, director, star actor; it's all you. I can be whatever you want me to be—I have no control over anything any longer. In other words, make of it what you will, *compadre.*"

"What do you mean?"

"I mean: You control everything. If you don't like the ride, stop the merry-go-round and get off."

"We can do that, just walk away?"

"Not exactly walk away; more like disintegrate away," Dr. Winechal quips and laughs.

"Yo, doc, come on, man! Be serious. You did this to us. You promised peace, you promised contentment, but we don't know who we are, what we are. Do we even exist any longer?"

Dr. Winechal picks up the pen and examines it. "You are not the first person, and you won't be the last, who was ruined by a lifelong obsessive preoccupation with an insignificant event that was allowed—no, was encouraged—to distort everything else, poor boy."

"What?"

"Did you hear the one about the guy who was waiting for his wife to give birth?" Dr. Winechal asks.

"No," we say.

"After she does, the doctor informs him that his son was born without a body—no torso and no arms or legs. "Your son is just a head," the doctor tells him. The father is mortified and embarrassed, but he loves his son and raises him as well as can be expected. When the son turns 21, the father carries him in the crook of his arm down to the corner bar where he orders himself and his son a shot of whiskey. While all the bar patrons looked on with curiosity and the bartender is shaking his head in disbelief, the father drinks his shot, then picks up the other shot and feeds it to his son and shazam! a torso pops out of the son. 'It's a miracle,' the father shouts as the bar goes silent, then bursts into cries of joy. 'Let's have another,' the father says, and the bartender sets it up. The father pours it down his son's throat and shazam! two arms pop out. 'Oh dear Mother of God,' the father exults as the bar goes wild in cheers and huzzahs. Trembling and in tears, the father orders another shot to celebrate this unbelievable event. The boy grabs the whiskey with one of his new, trembling arms, shoots it, and shazam! two legs pop out. By now, the bar is in total chaos and the father is ecstatic, falling on his knees and thanking God for this wonderful gift. The son stands on his new legs, wobbly at first. He stumbles to his left, stumbles to his right, and then stumbles out the front door and into the street where a truck runs him over and kills him. The bar falls silent and the father moans a great moan of pain. The bartender sighs, leans across the bar to the father and says, 'He should have quit while he was a head.'"

"What's that supposed to mean?" we ask.

"You should have quit while you were ahead."

They, in the Future

"Ahmed Clark has terminated," Dr. Barbara Steigelman-Genther tells Dr. Brody Winechal.

"Our longest-living resident," he says.

"Yes. I assume you'll call the family," she says.

"Yes."

A woman answers the phone: "Hello?"

"Is this the family of Ahmed Clark?" Dr. Winechal asks.

"Yes."

"This is Dr. Winechal from the Institute of Cognitive Realignment. I have an update on Mr. Clark: He is dead."

"He's dead? Did you say he's dead?"

"Yes."

There is silence on the other end of the phone. Finally, the woman says, "He died … is that what you're saying?"

"Yes, at 6:03 this morning."

"Oh, no. That's terrible," she groans, then pauses again to collect herself. "Can you tell me the cause of death, Dr. Winechal? Did he suffer?"

"He was an old man. Mr. Clark had been with us a long time, longer than any other patient. We monitor our patients' vital signs, of course, and your father's systems were in a weakened, deteriorating state. We have no data on specific failures. Our systems are not programmed to diagnose precise causation. It is possible he simply stopped participating."

"What do you mean, 'stopped participating?'"

"You may request an autopsy to be performed, if you wish, for a charge."

"No, that won't be necessary. Can you at least tell me if he was content? Was he happy?"

"Happy? Of course he was happy. All of our patients are happy. I can assure you that he received 100 percent satisfaction. He got exactly what he asked for."

The Dollhouse

Barry was upset with himself for being late. He was walking toward the stands when Michael ran up to him on the way to first base.

"Hi, Dad!" Michael yelled and waved his gloved hand at his guilt-wracked father. Michael was wearing his Little League uniform: black knickers, red stirrup socks and a red jersey trimmed in black with the number 21 over his heart and splashed across the back.

"Hi, Son," Barry said. "Sorry I'm late. I got tied up."

"It's okay, Dad. I'm glad you're here," Michael said and gave Barry a big smile.

Barry's heart melted a little.

"What's the score?" Barry yelled to Michael as he made his way onto the infield.

"Two-two, top of the seventh. We're gonna get 'em this inning, Dad!"

Oh great! Barry thought. *I get here in time for the last inning. What kind of father am I?*

"Go get 'em, Son," Barry said, softer than he wanted. For some reason, he wasn't able to modulate the volume of his voice, as if he were talking through a wad of cotton.

The first batter from the opposing team hit a soft fly ball to left field for the first out of the inning. The second batter struck out, and Barry clapped along with the other parents in the stands. Barry squinted, trying to make out who the pitcher was, but he couldn't identify the boy, which was strange because he knew all of Mike's teammates. Barry looked around the field and couldn't figure out who any of the other players were, either. All of their faces were a bit hazy, as if he were looking at them through some kind of veil.

"Better get my eyes checked," Barry said out loud to no one in particular.

The people standing nearby acted as if they didn't hear him.

The third batter hit the ball to the right side of Michael at first base. It didn't appear that Michael had any chance of making a play, but at the last moment, he dove and caught the ball in the webbing of his oversized first-baseman's mitt. Lying on the ground, he tossed the ball to the pitcher covering first for the final out of the inning.

"Great play!" Barry yelled, and Michael gave him another smile. Barry thought his heart was going to break.

Michael came to bat third in his team's half of the inning. With one out and a man on first, Michael hit the first pitch hard between the second and third basemen to put his teammate on third base and himself on first. The next batter lofted a floater to center field for an out, but the boy on third was able to beat the throw to the plate, giving Michael's team the win.

Michael's teammates converged on the player who scored the winning run, celebrating with him and the parents emptying out of the stands. Barry got lost in the confusion, and by the time the excitement subsided, he couldn't find Michael. He walked around the field, but the boy was nowhere to be seen.

Barry's heart sank.

He grabbed his cellphone and punched Michael's name on his favorites list.

"Dad?" Michael answered.

"Yeah, it's me. Where are you?"

"I'm home, Dad," Michael said. "Where are you?"

"I'm at the ballfield. I looked all over for you after the game, but I couldn't find you anywhere."

Michael didn't say anything.

"I was hoping I could give you a ride home, and maybe we could stop for ice cream on the way to celebrate your big win. I know your mother wouldn't like that. She'd say I'm spoiling your appetite," Barry said with a laugh.

"Are you okay, Dad?"

"I'm fine, Mike. I just wanted to spend a little time with you, that's all."

"I'd like that," Michael said. "Is everything all right?"

"Sure, everything's fine. I just wanted to spend a little time with you, that's all. No problems; nothing special I needed to talk to you about. Don't worry about that. I just wanted to spend a little time with you, that's all."

"Okay, Dad. We'll do that. Soon."

"Hey, you know what? Let's get that celebratory ice cream after dinner. What do you say to that?"

"That sounds great, Dad."

"It's a deal," Barry said.

"Dad," Michael said. "You know I love you."

"Of course you love me, and I love you. See you when I get home, Son."

After they hung up, Michael sat on his screened-in back porch, staring at the playhouse he and his dad had built for Amanda more than 20 years ago. They designed it to look like a dollhouse, and that's what they called it: The Dollhouse.

Cindy, Michael's wife, came onto the porch and asked, "Who were you on with?" But one look at Michael and she knew.

"Dad," Michael said after a pause.

"I thought they took his phone away," Cindy said, a look of apprehension on her face.

Michael shrugged his shoulders and continued to stare at the dollhouse. His dad had packed up his tools, and he and Michael's mom had made the seven-hour drive from Michael's boyhood home in suburban Philadelphia, the home his dad lived in until Michael's mom died two years ago. Michael sat there remembering how they had worked on that dollhouse for a week, how his dad had talked to him about life and the capricious nature of being, but now it was in bad repair and probably unfixable. Cindy had been bugging him to get rid of it, but he just didn't have the heart.

"Oh, Michael," Cindy said. "I'm sorry."

Michael continued to stare at the dollhouse, tears rolling down his cheeks.

Dick and Jane

Storing Memories

His name was Richard, but he preferred to be called Rich.

Jane called him Dick.

He didn't like being called Dick, but Jane said that everybody in the town where she grew up who was named Richard was called Dick, and it was a lifelong habit she couldn't break.

How hard is it to substitute Rich for Dick? he wondered. *How much intestinal fortitude do you need to get that monkey off your back?* But Dick had learned that arguing with Jane was like trying to reason with an angry skunk, so he let it go.

Dick had learned to let a lot of things go.

Dick and Jane had a daughter named Little Nell. After Little Nell's first birthday party, when Dick and Jane were lying in bed talking about their cherished child, Jane asked Dick if he ever wondered how Little Nell got her name. Little Nell was not a nickname; it was the girl's real name, and it said so right there on her birth certificate, but Dick never gave it a second thought. Jane had made up her mind on the name, and well, you know, that angry skunk thing. They both had a few drinks that night, and Jane wanted to talk. Or more accurately, she wanted to mess with Dick, as she appeared to find a certain amount of enjoyment in tormenting him when she was drinking.

And sometimes when she wasn't.

"I named her after a bar at the foot of Ajax Mountain in Aspen called Little Nell," she began and went on to tell her story. Jane had lived in Aspen, Colorado, between her freshman and sophomore years of college, and in November of that year, before the ski season officially opened, a band named the Hawks came to Little Nell to work on new material for an upcoming recording session and tour. The Hawks had a hit record that summer called "Take it Hard," and Jane was a fan—especially of their front man, Jesse Felden.

Little Nell had an informal setting—no raised stage or other barriers between the band and audience, just a dance floor, tables and a long bar at the other end of the large, alpine-ambianced room. The Hawks played at Little Nell for a week, and Jane took advantage of the casual environment to get to know the members. Between sets of their last performance before they broke camp, Jane gave Jesse a blowjob in the storage room behind the kitchen. It was such a momentous occasion in her life that she wanted to commemorate it in some meaningful way, and that's how Little Nell got her name.

"Jesus Christ! Why the hell would you tell me that story? Now every time I hear my daughter's name I'm going to have a mental picture of your mouth around some guy's dick," Dick said.

"I wanted to share it with you," Jane explained. "No secrets, remember? And don't think of it as something dirty. I didn't know you then and it was a *big* night for me. Try to be a little understanding, will you please. And besides, you know Jane loves Dick," she said and rolled away from Dick and fell asleep with a smile on her face.

Yeah, you love dick, Dick thought as he tossed and turned, unable to sleep, his mind percolating with the image of his wife's adventure in fellatioland. And what disturbed him most was that it kind of turned him on.

O Tannenbaum

"My wife seems to enjoy hurting me," Dick told the therapist.

This was not a new thought for Dick. Jane had been up his ass ever since they met as undergraduates at Fairleigh Dickinson University in New Jersey a decade earlier. At least that's how it felt to Dick. The question was: Why did he endure it?

Which is why he was seeing a therapist. He had tried to persuade Jane to join him in couples counseling, but she didn't see any need for it. To her, their relationship was like all others: sometimes smooth, sometimes rocky, "but that's the way it works, right? If you're having problems dealing with life, then by all means, go see someone. But don't drag me down into your lagoon of murky creatures," she'd said.

You mean like the one from the Black Lagoon I'm living with? Dick had almost said. Dick almost said many things, but there was a persistent fear of condemnation, like a nest of wasps hanging over his head in a tree outside their front door. No point in trying to knock it down and get stung; better to walk around it, even though it's a major inconvenience and messy when it rains or snows. And besides, why piss her off? You never know—she could turn at any second, rip off her clothes and lead him into another breathless session of passionate, uninhibited sex. She was a wild woman who could take Dick places he'd never dreamed of before meeting her.

And that was why Dick endured the abuse.

"How does that make you feel?" Doctor Bob asked. Robert Dunsberg was a University of Pennsylvania-trained psychiatrist who specialized in battered men, he liked to joke. Forty-eight years old and in practice by himself for the past 15, he wore thick, black, horned-rimmed glasses, had a dense head of salt-and-pepper hair that was permanently mussed, took copious notes and drank sparkling water that he kept in an old-fashioned seltzer bottle on the corner of his desk. The guy was a poster boy for shrinks—a living, breathing cliché.

"You're kidding, right?" Dick mocked. "Is that the best you can do? What's that, Psych 101?"

Doctor Bob laughed. "Okay, you got me. I can see I have to go to my A material right off with you. Why don't you give me an example of what you mean?"

"Like at Christmas," Dick said as if he'd been interrupted in mid-sentence. "She was supposed to leave work early and pick up Little Nell at my mom's on her way home. We were going to meet at around four that afternoon and go shopping for a Christmas tree. She didn't show up and when I finally called, she told me she had gotten tied up at work—tied up being a fairly loose interpretation of going to a bar for an impromptu Christmas party that may or may not have included people other than Jane and some guy named Todd."

Dick told Doctor Bob about his mounting anger as he called her back after a while and she said she'd leave right away. Dick was becoming more agitated as he went on with his tale about his elusive tail. Later that evening, he had called her once more and she said she'd been delayed again with an important job, evoking images of the storage room behind the kitchen at Little Nell. He was getting increasingly steamed, exasperated by his purposeful drinking. He finally called her for the finale of the three-act drama and told her not to come home, that he had asked his mom to keep Little Nell and that he was drunk and possibly dangerous.

"She walked through our door 20 minutes later—about the time it would take to get dressed and drive home," Dick told Doctor Bob.

"So, you assume she had an affair that night?" Doctor Bob asked.

"Yes. No. I don't know. Maybe. I hope not. She never admits or denies anything, and she seems to find some perverse satisfaction in antagonizing me, toying with me, like a cat playing with a mouse. I'm probably the worst guy to ask about Jane. That's why I'm here. My mind's a jumble when it comes to Jane."

"What happened when she got home?" Doctor Bob asked.

"We had a huge fight that ended ... well, weird." Dick said.

He described the evening to Doctor Bob in all its graphic, grotesque detail: Dick, drunk, confronted Jane when she came through the door, before she could barely get her coat off.

"Who's Todd?" he demanded.

"Just a friend. Why? Are you jealous?"

"Did you suck his cock?"

"What do you think?" Jane challenged, coquettishly tilting her head to one side with a small smile on her tight lips, antagonizing Dick even further.

"I think you're a whore who'd do anybody, you skanky cunt!" Dick said through clenched teeth, confronting Jane for the first time ever, but too intoxicated to grasp the earth-shifting profundity. It was the only time in Dick's life he had used the c-word, a universally accepted combustion accelerator in emotionally-amplified couples' communications, and he wasn't entirely sure he understood the complete connotation of skanky.

But Jane got it, and her countenance changed abruptly. She spit in Dick's face.

Dick acted without thinking: He slapped her, not terribly hard but with emphasis, like an old black-and-white movie slap, an anachronistic reaction from some primal crevice of his battered masculine psyche.

Jane's nose began to bleed profusely, disproportionate to the blow she suffered, but she had warned Dick on several occasions during their often-rough lovemaking that her family possessed glass noses, and they all had broken them at one time or another, some more than once. Dick felt immediate and painful remorse, recriminating himself for his lack of self-control in losing his temper and hurting Jane. He took her in his arms and walked her to the bathroom as she leaned her head back to abate the flow of blood.

Somewhere along the way, she turned and hugged him. She brought her lips to his in a passionate, protracted kiss while her blood ran down their meshed faces and intertwined bodies, dripping onto clothing and the tile floor. In an awkward dance of unquenchable lust, she stripped, then fumbled with his shirt buttons and the belt and zipper on his pants. Her uncontrollable, obsessive hunger covered him with a primitive desire to copulate avidly, immediately, almost violently, as they lay on the floor furiously fornicating; slip-sliding on the coagulating blood spill.

By the time they were finished, lying in the gory mess of Jane's retribution and breathing easier, the blood in her nose had clotted and the emergency passed, washed clean by the exchange of carnal bodily fluids, emancipated momentarily from all guilt and regret, floating in the wake of a thunderous explosion of original temptation, content and satisfied, their essence briefly nourished and sustained—smiling.

It was the best sex they'd ever had.

Butter Days Ahead

"Wow," Doctor Bob said. "I want to ask how it made you feel, but I don't want to upset you."

"It made me feel manipulated," Dick answered. "Grateful, extremely grateful. But manipulated."

"I believe Jane uses sex to control you," Doctor Bob offered.

"Duh!" Dick responded. "Do you think?"

Doctor Bob smiled.

"It's not simply the sex act, or acts, not just the intercourse," Dick said. "It's the way she approaches sex, her absolute inhibition, her uncompromising industry. She's extremely brave when it comes to the raw exploration of sexual indulgence. But there always seems to be a troubling undertow—a subtle but unmistakable menacing threat. It can be wearying—incredibly fun and exciting, but wearying.

"It's like living in a porno movie," Dick continued. "I mean, that wasn't even the first time we soiled the floor."

"Do tell," Doctor Bob encouraged. Enthusiastically.

Dick and Jane had been having an ongoing argument about butter. Jane liked to keep it out on the counter so that it was soft and spreadable, but Dick wanted it stored in the refrigerator where it wouldn't get rancid and give them salmonella poisoning.

"You can't get salmonella from dairy," Jane teased. "You shouldn't have dropped out of college. Maybe you'd have learned that."

A relatively harmless yet oft-used barb to soften Dick up for the kill.

Jane undid Dick's pants and pulled them down to his knees. With an index and middle finger, she scooped some of the soft butter from the dish and spread it on Dick's dick, already erect and fully attentive.

"If we kept the butter in the refrigerator, I wouldn't be able to do this," she purred in his ear, then got down on her knees and licked the butter off his cause célèbre until he exploded in a milky confluence of passive and aggressive substances of gratification, rendering a salty solution of sensual sensation.

Jane stood up, licking her fingers. "Well, I guess that's my daily requirement of protein."

"But you can't do *this* with soft butter," Dick said, opening the refrigerator and taking out a stick of butter. Unwrapping it, he reached under Jane's enticingly short skirt to pull down her panties, but there was nothing there to grab."

"Where's your underwear?" he asked, disturbed.

"I thought it'd be sexy for you," she said.

"But we're getting ready to go to work."

"Come on, now. Don't spoil the moment."

Dick obediently did as instructed and reached the butter stick up between Jane's legs and roughly shoved it into her passageway of opportune deviation. Jane groaned, first from the cold, hard intrusion, then, as her vaulted sanctuary realized it was being righteously pleasured, with uncontrollable delight.

She squeezed her thighs together as the butter began to melt and drip down her legs and onto the floor. Without any further touching or provocation, her knees buckled, and she let out a harmonious moan of exhilaration and satisfaction.

They cleaned up and left for work without speaking another word, save, "Have a nice day," and "You, too."

Thus ended the debate. Dick had made an excellent point, but the butter remained out on the counter. He was both unhappy and pleased and still afraid of getting salmonella, but figured that's the price you pay …

For what? scared the hell out of him.

Janie's Got a Gun

"Does Jane often go without underwear?"

Dick stared at Doctor Bob for a moment, thinking, *That's an interesting thing to ask.*

"I don't know. I grab her ass every morning now to check, but she could take them off in the car. It's become a sort of game. Sometimes she puts on my boxer shorts, and other times she'll wear an old-fashioned girdle or laced corset. One time she was wearing crotchless panties."

"Does her underwear symbolize anything for you?"

Once again Dick stared at Doctor Bob, amused. "No, I don't think so, but not wearing any symbolizes a lot, like she's either a promiscuous vamp or sadistically out to drive me crazy. She's most definitely an exhibitionist, and I think she likes to flash the doctors."

"Doctors?" Doctor Bob asked, wide-eyed.

"Jane's in pharmaceutical sales and calls on doctors every day. She almost never wears a bra because she says doctors like to stare at her nipples. She sits in her car before appointments to make sure they're prepped for the show."

"What if the doctor's a woman or if Jane has to deal with a female office manager?"

"Jane says women stare at other women's boobs almost as much as men do, but for different reasons."

"Competition," Doctor Bob suggested.

"Probably, but she's never explained it fully. I think she sees it as something more complicated, with a sexual component. Everything has a sexual component as far as Jane's concerned."

"And apparently a danger component as well. Does Jane scare you?" Doctor Bob asked.

"Are you kidding? To death! Especially now."

"Why now?"

"Because she bought a gun," Dick said.

"A gun!" Doctor Bob exclaimed. "Why did she buy a gun?"

"She told me it was for protection. She was afraid of intruders in the house, and she wanted to be able to protect me and Little Nell."

"Do you believe that? Do you think you need protecting?"

"Yeah, from Jane. She showed it to me: It's a snub-nosed, chrome-plated, pearl-handled .38-caliber revolver that holds six shots. She's very proud of it. And she won't tell me where she keeps it."

"Why?" Doctor Bob asked, alarm in his voice.

"She said she can no longer trust me to control myself since the Christmas incident, and she thinks I could be dangerous. Isn't that a hoot?"

"Oh, this is not good, this is not good at all," Doctor Bob said, shifting in his seat. "We need to talk about this. Aren't you concerned for your safety?"

"On one level, yes. On another level, she treats me differently now, like I'm more respectable, almost like I've earned some dignity and viability. I like the feeling. I like the idea that she feels she needs a gun to protect herself from me, like I'm in charge."

"But you're not! You've challenged her and she apparently isn't doing well with it. You're playing with dynamite, Dick," Doctor Bob warned, still squirming. "I think you should consider a separation until you two can work through these … um … difficulties. I think you're in danger. I think you need to get out of that house."

"I said something like that when she showed me the gun, but she assured me I was in no danger, that she loved me and that she would never do anything to harm Little Nell's father, unless, of course, I misbehaved and disrespected her again and she had to protect herself. Then she took off her clothes and … well, you know."

Cordless Drill, Apparelless Driller

Dick was the general manager of a Tools Galore Hardware Store, the national chain with the cute jingle about bringing it all home to your home, the one you hear ad nauseam on TV and radio. He had been with them since he dropped out of college after his junior year and had worked his way up the ladder, as they liked to say at corporate headquarters—a rather lame attempt at humor referencing ladders, a part of the inventory at the old, conservative company.

Dick had, on more than one occasion, been offered positions in corporate management, but had to turn them down because of Jane's job. Accepting a promotion would have required relocating, and Jane made more than twice what he did and wasn't about to give up a territory she had nurtured for years with hard work and hard nipples.

The store was in Oxnarb, about 10 miles from Morristown in central New Jersey. Dick, Jane and Little Nell lived in a relatively upscale neighborhood in the new section of Oxnarb, a mile-and-a-half down Sassafras Street from Dick's parents, who still lived in the house where he grew up. The only reason Jane had agreed to live in Oxnarb was because they got free day care from Dick's mom, who picked up Little Nell early every morning and kept her until Jane fetched her on the way home from work. Oxnarb was a quiet little community with a big park, lots of oak and maple trees and a well-practiced, Middle-America image of peace and tranquility.

Jane was the exception that proved the rule.

Jane almost never visited the store, so it was a surprise when she showed up in the middle of the afternoon on a cold February day. Dick was in the back with a customer when he saw her come in and walk up the aisle toward him. She was wearing a long winter coat, buttoned to the neck, and as she approached, began undoing the buttons, from the top down. Being an unpleasant, blustery weekday, there were no other customers in the store, and only one clerk on duty in the back room gathering supplies to restock shelves.

From Jane's angle, she couldn't see the customer to whom Dick was showing a cordless drill and demonstrating its features on a workbench against the back wall. By the time Jane undid the third button, Dick could see she wasn't wearing anything on top, and two more buttons down, he could see she wasn't wearing anything on the bottom, either. He made a move toward her, but she quickly slid the last button from its hole and swung the coat open.

"No, Jane!" Dick shouted, but it was too late. Jane stood a couple of feet away with the sides of her coat held open and in full view of Dick's customer.

Jane looked at the customer without a trace of unease. "How you doing?" she asked as she let go the sides of the coat. They swung back into their relaxed position, covering most of her body. You could still see she was naked, but the vital areas were covered, mostly.

The customer couldn't stop smiling.

Jane, in her early 30s and having endured two failed pregnancies and carrying Little Nell to term, still looked awfully good. She was a solid nine/nine-and-a-half with a voluptuous body and libidinous bearing, and she worked hard at keeping a voluptuous body and libidinous bearing. Dick, on the other hand, hovered between a five and a six. Everything about him was average: average height, average weight, average eyes and hair color—a total average Joe. Dick couldn't figure out what Jane saw in him, other than an easy target, one she had in her sights today.

Standing between Jane and his customer, Dick was confused by the confluence of conflicting feelings boiling up in his battered emotional state of mind. "What the hell, Jane!" he half-hissed. "Please leave."

"Sorry. Thought you might be in the mood. Didn't mean to interrupt," she teased and smiled back at the customer.

Dick glared at her as he set down the drill and leaned against the workbench, exasperated. "Get out," he said.

Jane picked up the drill, pulled the trigger and fired 3,000 revolutions per minute of razor-sharp, high-speed steel into the middle of Dick's spread hand resting on the nicked and rutted wooden benchtop. Dick screamed as the customer grabbed Jane's arm and pulled the drill away. Blood gushed out of the open wound.

"My bad," Jane said. "Just thought you'd like a little skanky cunt." And with that, she turned and walked out of the store.

Waiting for a Girl Like You

Dick sat in Doctor Bob's office, explaining what had happened.

"What was the damage?" Doctor Bob asked after Dick had finished his gory story, pointing to his bandaged and elevated hand.

"I broke my middle metacarpal, one of the bones attached to the ring finger," Dick said.

"I went to med school; I know the middle metacarpal," Doctor Bob replied. "That can be a dangerous injury. What's the prognosis?"

"Fortunately, I was only using a quarter-inch drill bit in my demonstration, so the damage was minimal. I didn't hit any flexor tendons—no permanent harm. I will need to go through physical therapy after it heals, though—not looking forward to that."

"You keep using the pronoun I," Doctor Bob said. "Why is that? You didn't drill your hand, did you?"

Dick thought for a moment. "I suppose it's because I feel guilty—I have a hard time blaming her. That's funny isn't it? She comes in unannounced, naked, embarrasses me, drills a hole in my hand, and I feel guilty."

"That's how she controls you," Doctor Bob observed. "She plays on your insecurities, your need for approval. And since you confronted her at Christmas, she's turned up the heat. I'm afraid it's not going to stop, that it may get worse. As long as you carry that guilt, she owns you."

Doctor Bob paused, letting that sink in. "Why do you feel guilty over this incident?" he finally asked.

"She was arrested."

"Oh? Did you call the police?" Doctor Bob asked, hopefully.

"No, my clerk did. He came rushing out of the back room when he heard me scream and saw all the blood. He called 911 before I could stop him."

"What happened to her?"

"The police and an ambulance showed up within a few minutes. My customer and clerk gave statements to the cops as the paramedics attended to me. While all that was going on, they picked up Jane a couple of miles from the store after she ran a red light. When she saw the cop car, she took off, drove up on a couple of curbs to maneuver through traffic and was finally caught at a busy intersection she couldn't get through. She was charged with creating a public nuisance, indecent exposure, open lewdness, reckless endangerment, assault and battery, speeding, reckless driving and avoiding arrest."

"Wow. That's a powerful lot of guilt."

"Her father's a hotshot lawyer from Bergen County and he bailed her out. He proceeded to file a domestic violence complaint against me on Jane's behalf. The next day, the cops came to my store and arrested me."

"Oh, my," Doctor Bob exclaimed, rubbing his forehead. "I can't imagine they held you very long."

"No, only a couple of hours. They didn't believe the charge had much credibility—just a lawyer's maneuver to extract a favorable settlement for his client."

"Did it?" Doctor Bob asked.

"Too soon to tell," Dick said. "Stay tuned."

And Doctor Bob did, asking a profusion of questions over the next couple of sessions. Dick knew Doctor Bob was worried about him and had his best interests at heart, but he also believed Doctor Bob was enjoying Dick's exploits, probably the most exciting stuff Doctor Bob had ever heard, sandwiched between "Mommy never loved me" and "I was never good enough for Daddy" tales of woe. It occurred to Dick that he should be charging Doctor Bob for the 45-minute hour they spent together each week.

Dick told Doctor Bob that the night of the drilling incident, he went home, packed up for himself and Little Nell and moved them into his parents' house. When Jane was released from jail and found them gone, she started calling and texting him. The voicemails and texts got more disturbing as the night went on.

Dick explained that Jane had a very difficult time getting pregnant, and when she did, she had trouble keeping the babies. "So Little Nell is extremely important to her, like a valuable possession. She cherishes her, and when she realized I took her and left, she went nuclear."

Dick showed Doctor Bob the last couple of texts he received that night, before Jane showed up at his parents' front door, waving her stylish gun à la Annie Oakley. The penultimate one read: *i know where you r asshole on my way.* The last one read: *better duck motherfuck im packing.*

"Oh my god!" Doctor Bob said. "What did you do?"

"I called her father and he had a friend of his—an off-duty state trooper—pick her up and take her to her dad's. You know the worst part of all this? I still wanted her. I mean, I wanted her even as she drilled a hole in my hand. I wanted her even as she waved that ridiculous gun outside my parents' door. Both times I was turned on and I wanted her right there. Is that sick, or what?"

Dick had been looking down at his hands, but now raised his head and looked Doctor Bob in the eyes. "Am I in trouble, Doc?"

"Yes."

Swing Your Partner, Do-Si-Do

"Jane's been stalking me," Dick said at another session. "Every time I turn around, she's there, in the background but in plain sight, always smiling at me. And she's still sending me threatening texts. I changed my cell number, but somehow she got it and started sending messages to the new number. Most of them are about Little Nell, how she wants her back and how's she's going to get me."

"What are you doing about it?" Doctor Bob asked, alarmed, his usual posture of late in sessions with Dick.

"We went in front of a judge and my lawyer showed him the texts. The judge issued a restraining order."

"That's about as useful as a parasol in a hurricane," Doctor Bob smirked. "How's that working?"

"It's only been a couple of days, but I haven't seen her. I'm keeping my fingers crossed."

"Crossing your fingers won't help. You might want to consider hiring a bodyguard for the time being—at least until you're able to work this out, if you can ever do that."

"Ever? Really?" Dick moaned. "That seems awfully drastic. And expensive. Do you actually think it's necessary?"

"She drilled a hole in your hand and she bought a gun for no other purpose that I can see other than ... oh, I don't know, to cleanse her soul. And I believe you're the cleansing she has in mind. Until she is incarcerated or somehow restrained, I think you're in grave danger."

Dick stared at Doctor Bob. "That's probably not going to happen," he finally said with a vague mixture of dread and acceptance.

"Why?" Doctor Bob asked, distressed.

"I told you: Her dad's a good lawyer. He's making this out to be a case of battered wife syndrome, and he's painting her the victim. My lawyer says we're going to have to make a deal. He says she'll probably get a suspended sentence and some community service time, plus she'll have to deal with the problems of the traffic tickets, but that'll be a separate issue. What a joke!"

"Humph," grunted Doctor Bob.

Dick gave him a crooked smile. "In spite of all this nonsense, I still think about her all the time. I still think about having sex with her all the time."

"This isn't nonsense Dick, and your thinking it is … well, that's the main problem here, not Jane. Do you understand that?"

"I guess."

"Why did you come to me in the first place?" Doctor Bob asked, lightly tapping the end of his pen against his brow.

"Because I was confused about my feelings about Jane. And about myself, too. About everything in my life, I suppose."

"Because you were afraid that Jane was trying to control every aspect of your life, is what you told me. You said she was like a drug that you couldn't kick."

"Yeah. I remember. Boy, that seems like a long time ago now. It's only been a couple of months, but my life has changed completely. My life has turned upside down."

"Or maybe it's turned right side up?" Doctor Bob offered. "However, you're practically in a no-win situation right now. You've shattered Jane's illusion of control, and now you've taken away her daughter, another of her likely delusions of control. Tell me about her relationship with Little Nell."

"Man, Jane is obsessed with her," Dick began. "She would tell me that she was going to save Little Nell from the cruel world, that she was going to make sure Little Nell's life was perfect. But I guess to understand that relationship, you need to know something about Jane."

Dick proceeded to give Doctor Bob a quick synopsis of Jane's life. She was raised in a stylish neighborhood on the right side of the tracks in Eastwood, New Jersey. Her parents were well off, but not Gulfstream V wealthy—considered rich by their middle-class friends and middle-class by their rich friends. They belonged to the Bridgewood Country Club and had a beach house in Harvey Cedars on Long Beach Island in Ocean County, about a two-hour ride south.

Jane grew up hanging out at the pool at Bridgewood, going to school and country club activities and spending weekends on the beach. Her parents were a chic couple: her mom glamorous and always dressed to the nines; her dad handsome, prosperous and perpetually tanned. Jane was an only child, lavished with material attention. She was good-looking, popular and did moderately well in school—she had the perfect life, or so it seemed.

Then one day when Jane was 13, while rummaging through her mom's closet looking for something—she couldn't remember what—she found a photo album tucked in a stack of sweaters. Jane told Dick this story when they were in college, after seeing each other for a few months. They were in her bed and had just made love. As they lay there not speaking, soaking in the postcoital satisfaction of their spectacular union, she drifted off into what looked like a trance. Dick asked what was wrong and she told him about the album, speaking in a soft, low voice, almost like she was drugged.

The album contained X-rated Polaroid pictures of her mom and dad with another couple, a couple Jane knew. They had visited the beach house on more than one occasion. It took Jane a few moments to fully grasp what she was looking at, and when it hit her, she ran into her parents' bathroom and threw up.

Jane told Dick that what upset her most was that her parents had been wife-swapping while she was sleeping in a nearby room. And how many other couples had there been? Or parties? Or orgies? And why would her mother take pictures? And why would her mother keep them?

Jane wondered if her mom hadn't actually expected Jane to find the album. It wasn't hidden very well, and Jane often went in her mom's closet looking for things to borrow. But why? How demented was all this? How sick did it get?

That night was the only time Jane ever talked about it. Once, after they were married and she was down in the dumps because she was having trouble getting pregnant, Dick brought it up, suggesting she might be suffering from some psychological repercussions.

"What are you talking about?" she asked.

"You know, the photo album you found hidden in your mom's closet. Maybe you're having some reaction to those unresolved issues; maybe that has something to do with your difficulties in conceiving?"

"Don't be silly," Jane admonished. "I should have never told you that. It was no big deal, and you're blowing it way out of proportion. I think you misunderstood me."

And that was the last word ever spoken about it.

"She finally got pregnant but miscarried twice before Little Nell," Dick told Doctor Bob. "Jane was determined to get pregnant—scary determined."

"I see," Doctor Bob mumbled, nibbling on the end of his pen while looking down at his notes. Finally, he looked up at Dick and said, "I think Little Nell represents something to Jane beyond a normal mother/daughter relationship. I think Little Nell's become a pathological obsession with her. I think she wants to save Little Nell from the world, like she wishes someone had saved her. And it's my guess you were going to be the savior of Jane, but you ended that charade at Christmas.

"From what you've told me, it seems that you were the perfect antidote to what Jane must have seen as the ostentatious and immoral life of her parents. At one time, she held them in great esteem, but the album she found inverted her world in what must have been an unbearably painful deconstruction of everything she'd held to be true. To survive, Jane created a whole new persona to hide behind, one consistent with the world of her parents as she now envisioned it.

"She became aggressive, flirtatious and promiscuous. But she wasn't altogether comfortable in that role, and along comes Dick: solid, quiet, down-to-earth, a refreshing, safe change—the antidote to the conflicting emotions she must have been feeling. And most important, she believed she could control you, because control is ultimately what Jane craves—control over a life that spiraled out of control by those pictures.

"Unfortunately for you, Dick, when you confronted Jane at Christmas, you shattered that illusion. Now you're a constant reminder of her lack of control, like you've become a disease that she needs to rid herself of. In so doing, she thinks she can be healthy again. Of course, that's a fantasy, but very real to her, and she will focus on it to the exclusion of all other rational thinking.

"The irony here is that you're the one who has a disease—a disease named Jane, a disease you can't shake, even after the most bizarre, painful reminders that you're in deep doo-doo."

"Come on, Doc. Don't throw those psychological terms at me," Dick joked.

Doctor Bob smiled. "You're not the victim here, Dick."

"What do you mean? What the hell do you mean? How am I not a victim here?" Dick demanded.

"Because there are no victims in these kinds of situations. You knew from the beginning that Jane was damaged goods. She told you as much when she confided in you about the photo album, and you would have seen plenty of other signs along the way. No, you were a willing participant, an eager participant. Jane fulfilled some deep-seated need, some self-destructive pathology of your own, a pathology you have yet to acknowledge, let alone deal with. You were both damaged goods, as most of us are. We all carry a certain amount of baggage, baggage that is mostly externally created in childhood, but becomes internally managed, nurtured and protected in adulthood. We do that out of anxiety, an anxiety over losing a comfort that may not be altogether pleasant but feels safe. Most people sacrifice the opportunity of fulfillment for that comfort and safety, but that comfort and safety leaves them empty and frustrated. They live their lives in fear, a fear of the unknown, and that unknown is the ultimate terror that debilitates most of us. And it's that fear that drives you now, combined with the fear of being ordinary again. Simply put, Jane makes you feel alive, important, vital—all bogus feelings but staunchly defended and protected by guess who? It's a painful place for you, but the rewards appear to be worth it, even though they're obviously not."

Doctor Bob paused, like he was waiting for Dick to agree or refute his analysis, but Dick sat there disconcerted and dispirited. Doctor Bob ran a hand through his hair and continued: "You've convinced yourself that you're a victim, but it takes two to cha-cha, and you're in the midst of a disastrous dance of imminent suffering. Worse, you've accepted that self-serving rationalization, and now you're working hard to internalize that deception forever, building a wall to create what you think is a safe haven but is really a blockade against health and happiness. On the other hand, you can start taking responsibility for yourself and start to get better.

"Maybe. If you want to. But I'm not convinced you want to. I fear you're like a drug user—you've fooled yourself into believing you know what you're doing, that you can control it. But it might be too late for you, Dick. I don't know. You might be in too deep and unable to get out."

"I can get out," Dick protested.

"We'll see," Doctor Bob said.

Hit Me with Your Best Shot

Dick felt something warm. He couldn't identify where it was coming from, only that it was pleasurable. Still mostly asleep, he slowly stirred and gradually became aware of his surroundings. He was in his first-floor bedroom at his parents' home. The window next to his bed was wide open and the first thing Dick noticed was the wind blowing the curtain. The second thing Dick noticed was Jane blowing him.

Like a splash of cold water, the vison of Jane with his extended member in her mouth brought Dick to full awareness. His initial impulse was to rush Jane and hold her down as he screamed for his parents to call the police, but he decided to be polite and let her finish, sealing his fate.

When her job was done and he lay spent and momentarily disabled, Jane looked up at him and winked—a wink that sent a spasm of terror down Dick's spinal column. Jane had been using her left hand, but now she raised the right one that had been buried in the sheets. Dick instantly saw the flash of shiny chrome as she fired a shot at his head. Only about five feet away, she missed him by a hair, the bullet traveling through his pillow, mattress and box spring.

Dick instinctively lunged at Jane and grabbed her arm as she aimlessly fired two more shots, both into the ceiling, traveling through joists and harmlessly resting in the floorboards of Dick's parents' bedroom. Jane wrestled her hand free and kneed Dick as hard as she could in his recently preoccupied genitalia. In one spectacularly graceful movement, Dick punched Jane squarely in the nose, bent over and threw up. Meanwhile, Jane fired two more wild shots, one breaking a lamp on the nightstand next to the bed, and the other splintering the top edge of the headboard.

Dick pulled himself up and started toward Jane with a knowing smirk on his face. Jane lifted the gun to eye level and fired her last shot into the left side of his chest.

"Damn!" Dick said as he fell back into the disheveled bedclothing, his right hand covering the wound, blood running between his fingers. "I miscounted."

Jane stood over him grinning, blood gushing out of her nose and Dick's spilled seed dripping from the corner of her mouth.

Wham Bam, Bam-Ba-Lam

Jane was jailed at Sparta Mountain Women's Reformatory in Northwest New Jersey near the Pennsylvania and New York junction. Only about 50 miles from Oxnarb but lightyears removed from the life she had known with Dick and Little Nell, not just in terms of her incarceration and the attendant inhibitions to her independence, but the culture and attitude of the region where the forlorn facility was tucked away. Not to mention her fellow inmates.

You might assume that the average person from a soft, privileged background would suffer a depression and near debilitation from the cultural shock of finding herself in a cold, hostile state penitentiary environment, but not our Jane (always the chameleon), who easily figured out how to use the lay of the land to her advantage. She slipped into the system and lifestyle with barely a hitch in her giddy-up. If Jane was anything, she was resourcefully focused—dangerously focused. But then, everything about Jane was dangerous, wasn't it?

Her first move was to ingratiate herself with the queenpin of the yard, the shot caller in yard-dog vernacular, a woman named Betty. Jane did that by making love to Betty; Jane's first lesbian experience. And it wasn't too bad   she found it almost enjoyable. It didn't provide the same sense of ownership that humping a man's vulnerability offered, but it was sexually satisfying, to a degree. That's because Betty wasn't what you're thinking. She wasn't Big Mama. Just the opposite: tall, about 5'10", full-bodied but not fat, nicely curved and sculptured. She was light-skinned, mocha-colored, with a hard, intimidating presence—a hard walk and a hard talk, but a pleasant smile and a look in her eyes that seemed incongruous with the more apparent exterior manifestations. Jane detected something about Betty that was attractive and alluring, so a romp in the sheets after lights out was more fun than facilitating, as if anything Jane did was not facilitating to her agenda.

After their first encounter, Betty gave Jane a tutorial on the process for easy living inside the concrete and barbed wire. "The COs can make or break your life in here …"

"COs?" Jane asked.

"It stands for correctional officers, truly a misnomer, a spurious definition if there ever was one. We generally call them screws, because that is what they are after, both literally and figuratively."

Jane sat up straight and looked Betty squarely in the eyes. Gone was Betty's urban-prison patois, replaced by a crisp, properly enunciated speech pattern.

"You're educated," Jane remarked, practically an accusation.

"I have a master's degree in education."

Jane was speechless.

"I was the principal of an elementary school, working on my doctorate."

"Why the act?"

"How long do you think I'd last around here if I spoke like this?" Betty perfectly articulated in the King's English. "How long do you think I'd be controlling the gangs in here?"

"It can't be just that act that gives you power," Jane observed. "There's got to be more to it than that.

I mean, you were able to get me into your cell tonight. That's beyond simply controlling the inmates."

"My lawyer knew someone in the state's corrections office and she hooked me up with the warden," Betty answered while picking at a toenail.

"When you say hooked me up ..."

"I'm fucking the warden," Betty said with an impish smile that lit up her handsome face.

"Oh," Jane replied, somewhat startled, not just at the intimate revelation but with the ease in which it was delivered.

"It's no big deal," Betty added in school-teacher English, then lapsed back into her yard dialect: "Evbody know it—evbody know who fuckin' who, screws and res'dents. And dair's lots a fuckins goin' on."

"Really?" Jane asked. "Sounds exciting," and she rubbed her hands together in mock enthusiasm as they smiled at each other. Jane's face grew more studious. She cocked her head to one side like a young schoolgirl trying to figure out a complicated geometry theorem. "But most of the guards are women," she finally concluded, a question disguised as a statement.

Betty didn't look up, still fidgeting with her toes. "Gee, that's interesting," she teased.

Jane laughed and asked, "How long you in for?"

"All day and all night," Betty replied, disinterested.

Jane looked puzzled.

"That's life, sweetie. I'm in here the for the rest of my life," Betty admitted quietly, looking up at Jane and biting her lower lip.

"Life?" Jane asked, somewhat surprised. She contemplated that for a minute, then said, "Can't you get paroled?"

"I'm L-wop."

Jane looked perplexed once more.

"That's life without parole. Besides, even if I were eligible, the warden would never let me go as long as he likes poking me a couple of times a month," Betty said and gave a tortured laugh at her painfully pathetic joke.

"What did you do?" Jane asked, drawing her words out.

"I killed the son of a bitch!"

"You killed the warden?"

"I killed my husband," Betty said, giggling. "I'd like to kill the warden, too, that son of a bitch. I'd like to cut off his dick and stuff it down the son of a bitch's throat until he gags to death."

"Why'd you do it?" Jane probed, enjoying this part.

"Because the restraining order was useless."

Jane gave her a knowing look, then asked, "How'd you do it?"

"The son of a bitch came over one night and forced his way into the house, then forced himself onto me and proceeded to pass out on the couch, drunk and apparently very satisfied. I stabbed him through his carotid artery with an ice pick. The son of a bitch ran around the house holding his neck with the ice pick sticking out between his fingers, trying to scream until he bled out. It didn't take very long, and I just sat there watching him, rocking back and forth and humming to myself."

"Didn't you plead battered woman syndrome?" Jane asked.

"Well, there were some extenuating circumstances."

"Like what?"

"I sort of shot a cop."

"You sort of shot a cop?" Jane exclaimed. "How do you sort of shoot a cop?"

"When I knew the son of a bitch was good and dead, I took his money and car and headed south. I had no idea where I was going, but when a cop pulled me over downstate, I grabbed the gun the son of a bitch always kept under the driver's seat and blew off a good portion of that poor cop's head."

Jane was flabbergasted. "Why'd you do that?"

Betty sat up straight with a look of confusion. "I don't know; I can't figure it out. My lawyer's expert testified I had a psychotic episode, that I was suffering from reality detachment, a temporary disassociation from my immediate surroundings and emotions, but the prosecution's expert said I knew exactly what I was doing, that I was completely cognizant of my actions when I killed that cop in cold blood." Betty paused and stared straight ahead, out past the bars of her cell. "He was right, too—I knew what I was doing when I pulled the trigger. I remember being calm and deliberate," she almost whispered, tears streaming down her cheeks while she played with the end of one of her long curls.

Jane took Betty's hand and kissed it while softly stroking her arm.

"So, what are you in for, Blondie?" Betty asked after a while.

"I shot my husband."

"Now why did you do that?"

Jane thought for a moment, then replied, "Because he was a son of a bitch!" and they laughed out loud at that one, howling in unison.

In All the Old Familiar Places

Thanks to bad aim, Jane, unlike Betty, would not spend the rest of her natural life at Sparta Mountain Women's Reformatory. Much to the surprise of both Dick and Jane, Dick survived. Jane had barely missed his heart, but the bullet shattered a couple of ribs and punctured his left lung, causing massive damage and internal bleeding. He was in the hospital for three weeks, undergoing two surgeries and multiple transfusions.

Jane pleaded not guilty and her lawyer—not her dad on this one—offered an affirmative defense, arguing that Jane was suffering from battered wife syndrome, and as proof, Dick had broken her nose twice. Jane had acted in self-defense.

Dick's lawyer told the jury, "This self-defense justification has a few wee holes in it: First, he broke her nose after she had fired three shots at him trying to kill him; second, it happened at 3 in the morning when Dick was sound asleep; and third, she broke into the house he was living in at the time. Not to mention, she had to wake him up to commit her act of self-defense, and you all heard how she accomplished that." A couple of the male jurors suppressed snickers at the reminder.

If Jane had been convicted of first-degree attempted murder, she could have been sentenced to a very long prison term, maybe life, but the judge gave the jury the option of finding her guilty of second-degree attempted murder, which they did, and Jane was sentenced to five to 10 years. Ten of the jurors wanted to convict her of first-degree attempted murder, but two held out for second degree and finally, after three days of deliberation, prevailed. They were both male, unmitigated horndogs who spent most of the trial focusing on Jane's batting eyes and her legs under very short skirts, crossing and uncrossing.

As a result of her conviction, Dick was granted an uncontested divorce and given sole possession of his car, the boat, their home and everything in it except for Jane's clothes, personal effects and a couple dozen of her mementoes and belongings. She had a company car so that wasn't an issue, and she was allowed to keep her IRA and Roth accounts. They were ordered to split their savings and investments three ways: one share each for Dick and Jane and one share for Little Nell, put into a trust with Dick as trustee. Dick was given custody of Little Nell, and Jane was granted visitation once a month. The order was temporary until Jane was released from prison and would be reviewed at that time.

The visits went smoothly, albeit awkward and inhibited, but were relatively routine for several months. Then, at the end of one visit, Jane whispered in Little Nell's ear, "Don't worry, baby, I'll be out of here soon and rescue you." As they were leaving, Jane winked at Dick and quietly said, "I'll be seeing you." It caught Dick off guard and ruffled his feathers as only Jane could. The woman scared the snot out of him. Unfortunately, she still excited the snot out of him, too, and he walked out of prison that day with a semi.

Little Nell was agitated and distracted all the way home, crying intermittently. That night, Dick questioned her about what was wrong, and she told him what Jane had said. Dick called his lawyer and they ended up back in front of the judge, who suspended Jane's visitation rights and added that he would re-evaluate the situation in a year.

Jane wasn't going to wait a year.

La La How the Life Goes On

Dick told Doctor Bob about it at their next session. "It's probably best for now, at least until Little Nell is older and can start to understand what's going on with her mother," Doctor Bob said. "I never thought Jane belonged in prison," he added. "I thought she should have been committed to a mental-health facility."

"I think her lawyer had a bad strategy," Dick said. "But it doesn't really matter now, does it? I don't have to worry about it for a year, anyway."

"I hope not," Doctor Bob mused aloud. "So how are things?"

"Good. Real good," Dick offered. "Little Nell's with my parents for two weeks at their beach house in North Carolina, so I'm batching it."

"Oh?" Doctor Bob commented dramatically while playfully raising an eyebrow. "And how are you *batching* it?"

"I had a date," Dick practically gushed.

"Really," Doctor Bob elongated through a smile. "Tell me about it."

"I met her online. She's never been married, a few years younger than me and she's the office manager at a medical practice in Morristown. She likes to read, cook, garden and gamble—the casinos are her one big vice. She calls herself a slot-slut and can spend an entire weekend in Atlantic City without leaving one of those almost-forgotten palaces, hitting the thrilling magic buttons of exhilaration while watching the blinding lights of unbridled excitement, as she describes it. She's very cool."

"She sounds very cool," Doctor Bob said with what might or might not have been sarcasm, depending on what you wanted to hear. "Tell me about your date. You didn't go to a casino, did you?"

"That's funny. No, we had dinner. It was a wonderful evening. We kissed goodnight."

"Oh, my. How was the kiss?" Doctor Bob asked, sitting up and leaning forward.

"Do you mean was it like Jane?"

"I didn't mean anything in particular. I was just curious about how it felt to kiss a new woman."

"It was … okay. Different, for sure. Not like Jane, of course. But okay."

"Well, okay is okay for a start, isn't it?" Doctor Bob chuckled. "Since you brought up Jane, did it make you think of her?"

"Not really," Dick lied.

"Good," Doctor Bob said, not believing him. "But I must tell you, Dick. I'm a bit concerned about this woman's gambling problem."

"I didn't say it was a *gambling problem*. She just likes to play the slots. A lot."

"I'm concerned," Doctor Bob continued, "because gambling can be a character flaw, a bellwether for more serious problems. I don't want to throw water on your new flame, but you should be careful. Maybe we should talk about what you find attractive in this woman."

"What I find attractive?" Dick responded, quickly. "Do you mean, is there something wrong with her, something dangerous I like, something I find alluring that I can't resist because of *my* character flaw? Is that what you mean, Doc? Like I'm trying to replace Jane with another deranged counterpart to all my niceness—is that what you mean?" and Dick snickered. "I don't know, I'm just comfortable with her," he added as his voice trailed off.

Doctor Bob gave Dick a concerned but sympathetic look. "Comfortable," he said and scribbled some notes. "Well, let's talk about that next time," he added and scratched his nose. He had no way of knowing it was the last time they would ever speak to each other.

Hello. Is It My Thing You're Looking For?

When Dick got home that evening, the first thing he did was grab a beer from the refrigerator. He didn't normally drink during the week and usually only a few beers and maybe a glass of wine or two with dinner on weekends, except on special occasions, but he was troubled by his session with Doctor Bob. He walked into the living room and threw himself on the couch. There was something—he wasn't sure what—in the air that he couldn't put his finger on … something that gave him a feeling that he couldn't quite identify but knew well. Whatever it was, it was definitely something very familiar and something that made him a little uneasy as he sat in the empty room contemplating the day and his troubling conversation with Doctor Bob.

Dick heard a board creak from the stairs above and it hit him like a ton of cinder blocks: That something he couldn't put his finger on: It was a scent, a scent he did, indeed, recognize: an expensive perfume, and in that instant, he knew he had to get out of the house. He jumped up and started to make a move for the kitchen and back door when he was confronted by the jarring sight of a woman with short black hair standing at the bottom of the steps, pointing a gun at him. It took his conscious mind a few seconds to catch up to what his subconscious had known from the moment he stepped into the house: It was Jane, grinning that same grin she had grinned the last time he saw her with a gun in her hand. *So what else is new?* he said to himself and smiled as his heart raced and fear gripped him in a tight embrace of bad karma.

"You look pleased to see me, Dick. I'm very pleased to see you," Jane said and lifted her tank top, exposing her still-firm breasts, nipples standing erect and welcoming.

Dick got a hard-on.

Jane walked over and rubbed his last vestige of hope until he exploded in a spreading wet stain on his thin, khaki-colored shorts.

"Ain't we got fun," she cooed.

Humming Along

Alternately, and in no discernable pattern or configuration, Jane planned to be the model prisoner, serve her nickel and get paroled, or break out of the Sparta Mountain Women's Reformatory, kidnap Little Nell and move to a remote location under an assumed identity. The former plan was the one she had when she was thinking clearly, but the latter was the one that possessed her. Consequently, she worked that plan just in case, and that started with Betty, the key to her escape.

Betty wanted to have Jane assigned to the library so they could work together. Because Jane had a college degree, the library was a natural choice, and it was the easiest duty in the phallusless calaboose. But Jane, initially assigned to the yard crew as all new residents were—landscaping or shoveling snow, depending on the time of year, and cleaning the yard and fenced-in walkways—had done her research, and kitchen duty offered the most advantageous opportunity to plan her possible (or imminent, depending on her prevailing state of mind) premature departure.

Betty, though suspicious of Jane's motives and concerned by the potential danger she could be bringing upon herself, pulled the necessary strings (the one string in particular attached to the warden) and had Jane assigned to the mundane tasks of mopping floors, washing dishes, stacking shelves, simple food prep and spooning out the slop that passed for sustenance to the epicurean-challenged hordes. And in Jane's inimitable talent for opportunistic manipulation, it didn't take her long to curry favor from the head CO in food services.

Guess how she did that?

Jane's plan was to go out in the afternoon, for two reasons. In the afternoon, at the end of the day shift, the guards and support staff were slightly less diligent in their observations and awareness—not a significant drop-off in competency levels, but there all the same, and every little bit of an advantage Jane could get, she'd take. The second reason was that she needed to grab Little Nell in the least amount of time after her escape—the longer it took, the longer the authorities would have to discover she was gone and mount a coordinated search—and the most advantageous time to accomplish that objective was at the end of the day when Dick would be getting home from work with her baby in tow.

Obvious to Jane from jump, she was going to need accomplices inside and outside the prison. The food services head guard, without knowing it, would serve adequately as the inside man, but Jane needed to find and enlist an outside contact, which is why she chose kitchen duty in the first place—and why Betty was suspicious. The kitchen received five deliveries every day, four of them early in the morning: dairy products such as milk, cream, butter, eggs and ice cream; fresh produce that the cooks would wring every ounce of nutrients out of before serving; meat, chicken and fish from a wholesale butchery; and bread, rolls, bagels and muffins from a local bakery. Only one delivery came in the afternoon: prepared foods and dry goods from a large food distributor in Phillipsburg, about 50 miles southwest of Sparta Mountain Women's Reformatory, and that lucky delivery fellow was Jane's targeted outside man.

But he turned out to be more boy than man at a rather naïve 21 years old, which you wouldn't have thought since Noel had served almost a year in a juvenile detention center in Jersey City alongside a cadre of hard-asses and hard-luck gangbangers, mostly all serving time for possessing or selling illegal substances, which is why Noel had been in attendance—both for holding and distributing, but such a small, innocuous amount that a more strategically beneficial birth might have rendered a simple yet expensive slap on the wrist and community service. Unfortunately for Noel, or to his good fortune, depending on your point of view, even with that valuable education, he remained relatively innocent, trusting and vulnerable.

Jane liked that in a man.

She took her time getting to know Noel, smiling at him when he showed up in midafternoon pushing large rolling shelves full of spaghetti sauce, canned fruit, condiments and other foodstuffs, along with various and sundry paper products, eventually offering a few words of greeting as he passed by her while she bent over a sink scrubbing pots and pans, soon becoming pleasantries of a more familiar nature until Noel's day revolved around the anticipation of seeing Jane's smiling face, her flirtations and apparent interest in him. He was completely smitten and possessed by wild fantasies of him and Jane in the storage room—fantasies he had no way of knowing were one of Jane's specialties and most assuredly in his immediate future.

A future that came sooner rather than later, and it wasn't long before Jane was helping Noel—with the head COs knowledge and protection because the head in his title was not the only head in his life—stack his products on the line of shelves in the back room a couple of times a week, where Jane would introduce Noel to sensations he had previously thought he knew but, much to his pleasure, were beyond his former callow understanding of the workings of the world. His life had become a sexual fantasy thanks to Jane, and he would have done anything to keep those fantasies real and palpable.

Which of course, he did.

Jane had planned her escape down to the smallest detail, and after several months of preparation where all her calculated moves and behavior had become routine, expected and accepted by her fellow inmates and kitchen staff, she was confident she could pull it off and was physically and mentally ready. But she hadn't yet reached the emotional impetus necessary to make the move—not until Dick took Little Nell away from her, that is, and cast the last, proverbial straw onto the well-humped back of this libertine camel, sending Jane into a profound delusional state of monomaniacal rage; a complete break with all rational thought that was either temporary or permanent—solely a matter of perspective and lawyering skill.

Slip Sliding Away

All Jane needed was shit on a shingle.

For dinner every other Wednesday, the prison served creamed dried beef on toast—S.O.S. from World War II cuisine—or more colloquially, shit on a shingle. So, the next time a Shitty Wednesday (in penal parlance) rolled around, Jane was locked and loaded. On that fateful, much anticipated day, after lunch had been cleared and cleaned, Jane helped mix the thick cream sauce for the universally disrespected dish in large, stainless steel bowls on a long table in the middle of the kitchen area, just across a narrow aisle from the silverware organizer that was attached to a smaller table.

The entire plan depended on Noel, and he was to give Jane a signal when he arrived in the afternoon to let her know if the coast was clear. On the first Shitty Wednesday after Jane's epiphany, the signal was a no-go, signified by Noel pulling on his ear. The plan called for Jane to create a disturbance, fake an injury, sneak out of the kitchen through the loading dock and hide in the back of Noel's large, walk-through delivery truck. But in order to exit the premises without being detected by a guard doing his duty and diligently checking the contents of all vehicles leaving the compound, they had to wait for Fat Prick (as Noel called him) to be on the gate. His real name was Frank Prit, and he always busted Noel's balls, asking him if he was delivering tacos or if he had a load of illegals in the back. Most guards would go through every rack in the truck thoroughly, plus check the bag drum by poking around in it with their nightsticks.

Only three of Noel's deliveries were to large institutions—the prison, a high school and a hospital—all the rest were to restaurants and bars whose orders were much smaller, and none had loading docks. Accordingly, their orders were packed in oversized, bright red nylon bags with leather handles and see-through label holders on the side that held the restaurant's name. Noel could easily carry three or four bags at a time, and after he unpacked them in the restaurant, he would throw the empty bags into a big, blue bag drum, bungie-corded to the right, back corner of the truck.

Fat Prick never checked the bag drum—he was too lazy. He would merely step into the truck, take a quick look around, hurl a couple of insults disguised as jokes at Noel and wave him through with a badly fractured *hasta luego* or some other mangled Spanish salutation. By the time Noel reached the prison each day—his last stop—the bag drum was usually about three-quarters full of empty red bags. Fat Prick never seemed to even notice the bag drum, let alone walk back to it.

On the next Shitty Wednesday, Noel walked into the kitchen at 2:20 p.m. and smiled at Jane. He scratched his chin, and Jane smiled back.

It was on!

Noel scratched his chin with three fingers, indicating he had three racks to deliver. Jane would make her move after he rolled in the third rack. She was busy mixing cream sauce as another detainee helped Noel unload his products in the storage room under the watchful eye of Camila, a middle-aged guard who was responsible for manning the surveillance cameras in the kitchen area. Camila had almost 20 years on the job, but after recuperating from knee-replacement surgery on both knees, was assigned to kitchen detail where she sat for eight hours a day, Monday through Friday, in the small office next to the storage area and monitored 16 screens that covered the dining hall, kitchen and loading dock. Noel had become friends with Camila, stopping to chat a couple times a week, bringing her small gifts, such as candy bars or postcards from his family in Puerto Rico. So, when he started enjoying erotic activities with Jane in the storage room, where they tried to hide from the camera, Camila was watching and would put her right hand in the accommodating front pocket of her loose-fitting utility pants and discreetly masturbate. Being island kinsman, Noel and Camila shared a conspiratorial relationship, and Camila was only too happy to let Noel in on some of the perks of a women's prison: not to mention, her covert participation was, currently, her entire sex life.

During Noel's visits with Camila, he checked out the monitors and discovered there was a small space—about three feet high and one foot wide—at the bottom left corner of the loading dock door, a blind area in surveillance that convicts called "in the cut." While inconspicuously studying the monitors as he chatted with Camila, Noel figured out that if he parked his truck about six inches over the white line designating the delivery zone in front of the dock, it would block the view of the camera to his passenger door. When she was ready, Jane would have to curl up and slither through the cut in the camera's angle, crawl under the back of the truck, slide stealthily along its side and quickly slip into the passenger-side door of the cab. Jane had been practicing the moves in her cell after lights out.

A few minutes after Noel brought in his last rack, Jane started sneezing, something she had taught herself to do on command. As the sneezes grew more animated, her body convulsed and buckled, backing her into the utensil table and knocking it onto the floor—scattering forks, knives and spoons hither and yon. Jane acted startled and abruptly jumped forward, bumping the long table in the middle of the room and sending bowls of the thick cream sauce all over the kitchen floor, covering the displaced silverware in a gooey mess.

Everyone else in the kitchen stopped what they were doing and darted around, sliding on the slippery floor, trying to figure out how to handle this unexpected yet perfectly orchestrated emergency. The guards came running into the kitchen shouting for everybody to freeze, and they all did, except for Jane. Who fainted. Ostensibly.

Jane dramatically and strategically fell to a clean spot on the floor, and one of the COs immediately came to her assistance as the others began to organize the massive clean-up. The female guard helped Jane stand up and offered to take her to the infirmary, but Jane said she was all right; she just needed to rest for a few minutes. The guard helped her to a chair in the back of the room not too far from the loading dock, an area normally in plain sight, but in the confusion of the moment, isolated by the mayhem.

Meanwhile, Noel finished unloading and pushed the last rack of the day back into his truck, fastened the rack in place, shut and secured the back doors and drove away. When he got to the front gate, he stopped and Fat Prick lumbered in. With one foot in the door well and the other on the landing, leaning his large girth against the dashboard, he asked Noel, "How many Puerto Ricans does it take to change a lightbulb?"

Although Noel had heard the joke many times, he smiled and said, "Don't know, Frank. How many?"

"Just Juan," Fat Prick said and laughed hard.

"Good one," Noel responded, laughing along with the condescending Neanderthal whose limited self-awareness allowed him to believe he was being open-minded and friendly.

"Everything okay today?" Fat Prick asked, looking around. Pausing for a moment, his eyes fixed on the interior of the truck. Noel's heart skipped a beat and beads of sweat dotted his forehead.

"Hey, you have a couple of bags on the floor back there," Fat Prick unexpectedly observed. "I'll get them for you," he said and even more unexpectedly, slowly lifted his great portlyness and started to move toward the back of the truck.

Noel's stomach turned over and he thought for a moment that he was going to ralph all over Fat Prick. He swallowed and said, "No, no, don't bother yourself. I get them," as he jumped up and moved swiftly to the back, grabbing the errant bags off the floor and throwing them in the blue bag drum. "Thanks anyway," he managed to say through a mouth full of cotton.

"I never saw you move so fast," Fat Prick said as he carefully studied Noel. "Must have struck a nerve, huh? You people must take a lot of pride in keeping things neat and clean for us white folk," he joked and belched out a congested-sounding laugh.

Noel almost pissed himself with relief. "You a real card, Frank. Got to get going. I'm late, as usual."

"Okay," Fat Prick said. "*Adios amigo*," which came out sounding like aldeeose almay-go.

"Holy sweet Jesus!" Noel said out loud as he drove away from the prison.

Lip Sliding Away

Noel took the Evelyn exit off the interstate and pulled into a convenience store/gas station, parking his truck in a corner near the back, out of sight of the store's front door, the street and surveillance cameras.

"All clear," he softly announced to the back of the truck. "You can come out now."

Jane stood up slowly and stiffly in the bag drum, knocking several bags to the floor. She started to remove herself from the tangled web of red nylon, but her body parts had become unmalleable from being balled up for so long. Noel walked to the back of the truck and gave her a hand.

"You okay?" he asked.

"Yeah, but that guard scared the shit out of me."

"Me, too. I couldn't believe it. That fat prick never takes any interest in my truck. We was lucky."

"No such thing as luck," Jane said as she stretched her legs. "You make your own luck, and you were terrific," she added and gave him a soft pinch on the cheek. The move caused pain in her arm, and she grabbed it with her other hand and stretched it over her head. The plan was for Jane to stay hidden in the bag drum until they got to the convenience store. That way, if Noel was stopped by a cop during the getaway, he could still plead ignorant to Jane's presence in his truck. Then, the ruse went, when Noel went inside to buy a snack, Jane must have sneaked out of the truck and disappeared into the sameness of the suburban environs.

While Jane limbered up, Noel put on his work gloves and exited through the passenger door. He came back a few minutes later with a plastic grocery bag and handed it to Jane. From it, she pulled a gray, oversized sweatsuit, a pair of dark sunglasses and a roll of bills rubber-banded together.

"How much is here?" she asked.

"Three hundred and seventy-eight," Noel said. "It's all I could scrape together. I was up all night washing my fingerprints off 'em," he said with a hopeful smile. "I wish it was more."

"It's enough. It's perfect. You did great. Thank you," and she leaned over and kissed him on the tip of his nose. "I don't know when—it might be a while—but I promise I'll get it back to you, plus interest. Guess what the interest will be?" Jane said in a lilting, teasing voice.

She then reached in the bag to take out its last item: a gun—of sorts.

"What the hell's this?" Jane snapped. "It's a fucking toy!"

"Listen, Jane, please," Noel pleaded. "If I get caught helping you escape, I get, maybe, couple of years. I might even, maybe, get lucky and pull, you know, a suspended sentence. But if I give you a gun and you use it—and I know you gonna—I be charged with aiding and abetting and pull major time, maybe life if you kill the guy. I love you Jane, but I can't take no chance like that. I'm sorry."

"But it's a fucking toy!" Jane insisted. "What am I going to do with a fucking toy?"

"I bought it at an Army/Navy store, and the guy said he sell lots of them to people scared of guns but wanna scare intruders and burglars and like that. It's an exact replica of a Smith & Wesson 9 mm, and *it is* scary looking. Look at it—if you don't pick it up, cause it's real light and all, you gonna think it's the real deal. Anybody you point it at will. Definitely."

Jane turned the black facsimile over in her hands a few times as she assessed the situation. "I guess it will have to do," she finally said. "I get it. I do. I don't want to get you in any trouble, Noel," and she gently rubbed the side of his head.

Noel handed her a key, then took off his work gloves. "It's a gray Nissan, parked two spaces over. Got a full tank and ready to go," he said, standing sheepishly in front of Jane like a little boy trying to please his mother.

"Is it stolen?" Jane asked, though she very well knew the answer.

"Of course. My boy Martin grab it a couple hours ago from Angel of Mercy Hospital a mile or so from here. He took it from an employee parking lot, and they work 12-hour shifts, so it ain't gonna be reported missing till probably after midnight, maybe middle of night. You got plenty time. Just leave it anywhere when you done with it. But don't push it. Once it hit the hot sheet, you in danger of getting picked up."

"How'd he get the key?" Jane asked.

"It was in one of those little holders you hide under the bumper."

"Really? Do they still make them? I haven't seen one in years. They're magnetic, right? I wouldn't think they'd work because bumpers aren't made of metal anymore," Jane said, looking puzzled and a bit suspicious. "A magnet wouldn't stick to the plastic or rubber or whatever composite they're made of these days."

"Plastic tray, double-sided tape, Jane," Noel explained, broadly smiling because he knew something Jane didn't. "You gotta move with the times, girl."

"Oh," Jane muttered softly to Noel's delight. "Your buddy sounds like he knows what he's doing."

"My boy Martin's a pro. It what he do."

"What did you have to pay him?"

"*Nada*. I took care of him when we were in together. He owe me big time."

"And now I owe you big time," Jane whispered as she knelt in front of Noel and undid his pants, giving him one last ride on her lip slide.

Home Sour Home

Jane drove to the Morristown Mall and went shopping. She purchased a new outfit, one more Jane-like than the bulky sweatsuit she was wearing, some makeup and a bottle of perfume. She really missed her perfume and couldn't wait to shower and rid herself of the prison smell she'd had to endure. She also bought a couple of pairs of expensive underwear made of natural fiber. She couldn't get out of the prison-issued, synthetic granny panties fast enough. Like most of her fellow inmates, she detested them; they were degrading. On the way out of the mall, she stopped at a drug store and bought hair dye and a brush.

She drove to Dick's house—her house until the son of a bitch took it away, along with her darling little girl, logic be damned. "But we're going to change all that today, Baby," Jane said out loud as she parked the car at the curb two houses down the block and carefully made her way around to the back. She found a house key in one of those fake rocks in a small landscaped area behind the garage. "You're such a prisoner of habit, Dick," she said and smiled to herself. "Everything always has to be perfect and exactly where it belongs. And that's all I'm doing—returning things to where they belong."

She went upstairs and took a shower, then cut her hair and dyed it over the bathroom sink. When she was finished getting dressed, she nosed around Little Nell's room, going through her things, holding her pillow and clothes to her face and soaking in her dear, dear daughter. She hadn't completely mapped out her next move after Dick and Little Nell got home. She'd have to do something about Dick, then call her father for money and help in getting fake ID—surely, he'd help her. Maybe she'd drive to Philadelphia or Baltimore and hop a bus going west where she and Little Nell could lose themselves in the mountains and woods. Her plans were vague, but rationality was not a top priority at the moment—she was fixated on getting Little Nell back, then all the other pieces would fall into place. Surely they would.

Jane felt comfortable back in her old home, almost at peace, but when she heard Dick arrive, obviously alone, the rage returned. In Jane, rage evinced itself in strange ways, most notably in a marked inability to see through to the consequences of her actions. Or maybe, at that point, she just didn't care. When Dick encountered her at the bottom of the steps in her new, provocative outfit—leather sandals, tight shorts and a skimpy tank top—sound reasoning had been replaced by a pervasive, blinding malice that (as was often the case with our salacious gal-everyday) manifested itself in a perverse, meretricious lust—she couldn't help but lift the tank top and set Dick afire.

After their brief encounter with situational deviance, Jane asked about Little Nell.

"She's with my folks in North Carolina," Dick told her.

It was Wednesday night and Jane knew that Wednesday night was "pasghetti" night, Little Nell's favorite night of the week. *She wouldn't miss it unless she was away,* Jane thought, so maybe Dick was telling the truth. She hadn't counted on this contingency in her plans. *But it's hurricane season,* she thought while following along her convoluted, disjointed cognitive path, and Dick's parents would never take Little Nell to the Outer Banks during hurricane season.

"You're lying," Jane said.

"No. I'm not, Jane. I swear. They left on Saturday morning for two weeks."

"I don't believe you. Let's take a ride," Jane said and pointed the gun toward the back door.

"Where we going?" Dick asked.

"Shut up, Dick. I'm in no mood. Let's go," she warned, waving the gun again, impatiently. Dick carefully made his way into the kitchen with Jane two steps behind, pointing her pretend weapon at his back. When they reached the back door, Dick plucked his car keys off a neat row of hooks, all with perfectly arranged labels above them: Car, Store, Parents, North Carolina and Cabin. Jane took the cabin key off its designated hook and let out a small laugh. "You anal bastard," she said to no one in particular and followed Dick out the door, her mind in a white-heat hunger for final, yet gratuitous, revenge.

Fifteen minutes after they left, a New Jersey State Trooper cruiser and an Oxnarb patrol car pulled up in front of the house where Dick and Little Nell used to live.

Lulu Was a Lulu

Dick drove to his parents' house with Jane in the passenger seat holding her firearm *sans* firepower. The place was dark. *Where the hell are they?* Jane thought she was thinking to herself but actually said out loud. She was doing a lot of that today.

"I told you, they're at the beach," Dick responded to the unintended redundancy, his voice shaking a bit.

"Can it, Dick," Jane snarled. "We're going to the cabin."

"They're not there, Jane."

"Well, even if they're not," Jane taunted, "can't we have a nice time together, enjoying nature and all its cute critters and abundant flora?" Once again Jane thrust the ersatz handgun toward Dick. "Drive!"

The cabin was in the Northwest Poconos, about a two-hour drive. Dick and his dad used it for hunting and fishing. It was in the middle of the woods with the closest neighbor a half-mile away and any commercial civilization a 20-minute ride on unpaved roads. It was completely isolated—no cable or TV reception, no Wi-Fi or internet, no cellphone service—no nothing to connect it to the rest of the world besides the occasional hunter passing through.

The cabin made sense to Jane in her current state of disorientation or detachment or delusion or whatever the correct description for her current psychological identity. She hadn't seen the boat at Dick's. He usually kept it behind the garage when it wasn't in storage for the winter, and they never pulled it all the way down to North Carolina, if for no other reason than Dick, in all his OCD glory, didn't like to run it in salt water. They did, however, haul it up to the cabin, where they would spend a few weekends each summer boating on any one of the myriad lakes in the region.

"Where's the boat?" Jane asked.

"It's in the shop," Dick answered nervously. "The throttle's been sticking, and I almost killed myself last week trying to bring her down while docking."

Jane smiled sarcastically. "Good answer."

"Look, Jane, Little Nell's in North Carolina, like I told you. The boat's in the shop and there's no one at the cabin," Dick reaffirmed, frustrated.

Jane thought for a moment, then started singing:

Lulu has a boyfriend,
Her boyfriend has a truck.
Lulu likes to shift the gears,
Her boyfriend likes to...
Bang, bang Lulu,
Lulu bangs...

Jane stopped abruptly. "You're not singing, Dick! Do you forget the words?" she asked, mockingly. "Sing!" she demanded, and in what was becoming an almost nervous tick, shoved the pistol toward him. "Lulu" was a sea shanty Jane had learned at summer camp when she was in her early teens and taught to Dick on the long rides to the cabin. They would make up their own verses and then join in on the choruses. It became a fun competition to see who could create the dirtiest lyrics. Jane started singing again:

Lulu has a boyfriend,
Her boyfriend has a truck.
Lulu likes to shift the gears,
Her boyfriend likes to...
Bang, bang Lulu,
Lulu bangs all day.
Who's gonna bang for Lulu,
When Lulu bangs away?

Dick had joined in on the chorus as ordered, at first with little commitment, but as the old, familiar scenario unfolded, his anxieties, inexplicably, dissipated along with his reluctance to play along. He began to sing louder, and he took the lead on the next verse:

Lulu likes the movies,
The one that's at the mall.
Every time the lights go out,
She grabs her boyfriend's...
Bang, bang Lulu,
Lulu bangs all day.
Who's gonna bang for Lulu,
When Lulu bangs away?

Jane's frown melted as the timbre in her rather melodic voice joined Dick's more discordant trill, raising a collective chant in what sounded like, for all intents and purposes, a supplication for what was, but what was never to be again. Jane jumped on the next verse with relish:

> *Lulu joined the circus.*
> *She has her favorite stunt.*
> *Lulu likes to lift her dress,*
> *And show the boys her...*
> *Bang, bang Lulu,*
> *Lulu bangs all day.*
> *Who's gonna bang for Lulu,*
> *When Lulu bangs away?*

It was Dick's turn, and he couldn't hide his absolute enjoyment. For a moment in time, it was like the old days, the great days before his wife went batshit crazy:

> *Lulu is a barmaid,*
> *She works down at the dock.*
> *Lulu likes to serve the drinks,*
> *And sometime suck a...*
> *Bang, bang Lulu,*
> *Lulu bangs all day.*
> *Who's gonna bang for Lulu,*
> *When Lulu bangs away?*

Now it was Jane's turn, but she just looked at Dick and shrugged her shoulders, like she was out of verses, or out of energy, or out of caring. Dick didn't seem to notice and jumped right in with a blind but misplaced passion:

> *Lulu has a boyfriend,*
> *Her boyfriend has no class.*
> *Every time she turns around,*
> *He shoves it up her...*
> *Bang, bang Lulu,*
> *Lulu bangs all day.*
> *Who's gonna bang for Lulu,*
> *When Lulu bangs away?*

Jane didn't join in on the chorus, and Dick mumbled through the last couple of lines, alone again. Somewhere along the way, Jane had grown morose and lost interest, falling into a depression-like stupor. Perhaps it was regret, which seemed unlikely given Jane's sociopathic tendencies, or maybe it was the heavy and inevitable sadness of reality settling in after the excitement and euphoria of her great escape, or maybe it was something else, as she sat staring out of the front windshield for the rest of the trip.

As Jane zoned out, Dick contemplated making a grab for the gun, jerking the car in a hard swerve first and catching her off balance. But the wound from his last encounter with Jane and a gun still hurt on occasion, and the emotional scar had yet to fade into a distant memory.

By the time they reached the empty cabin, it was dark, and with a thinly cloud-covered eerie moon, it looked like a setting for a Hollywood slasher movie.

You could say, the perfect setting.

The First Cut Is the Deepest

"The cabin" was an apt description for the place: It wasn't much more than that. It consisted of one large room and a sleeping loft, covered in cheap, T1-11 siding stained dark red under a peaked roof covered in tin that when it rained, sounded like the hammers of hell cutting through the peaceful woodland. It did have electricity, though, installed only a few years earlier after Little Nell was born, at Jane's insistence so they could have a working bathroom, a refrigerator and a few other Calvin Coolidge-era conveniences. It took a great deal of time and money to get the power company to run the line, but the effort allowed Dick to throw a light switch when they entered the hunting shack together for the last time.

Jane grabbed one of the wooden Windsor-back chairs from the old, banged-up kitchen set and set it in the middle of the room. She marched Dick over to it and instructed him to strip.

"What?" Dick heard himself say, but it felt like he was watching the scene from above, out of his body and observing the theater-of-the-absurd production.

"Take off your clothes. You remember how, don't you?" Jane barked like a drill sergeant on Parris Island.

Dick stripped and stood naked in the middle of the room, shaking on the hot, late-summer night.

"Sit down," Jane ordered, and when he dutifully obeyed, she walked over to a cabinet against the back wall where he couldn't see her, only taking her eyes from him for seconds at a time, darting her head back and forth between Dick and the cabinet. From one of its drawers, she extracted a length of rope and a roll of duct tape.

Jane knelt behind the chair, set her (as it turned out) effective toy on the planked floor and tied Dick's hands together. Then she carefully and skillfully looped the rope through a few of the spindles on the chairback and down under the seat, around the middle stretcher and then back up. She finished her focused labors by tying the end of the rope around Dick's hands and spindles again for luck.

"I want to thank you, Dick, for teaching me how to tie these terrific knots during all those happy boating excursions." Dick knew knots.

"Don't mention it," Dick responded and laughed. For some reason, he, or at least the incarnation of him sitting in the chair below, thought it was funny.

"I won't," Jane said, ripping off a piece of duct tape and covering Dick's mouth.

"Mumph, mumph," Dick Below said, to the delight of Dick Above.

Jane sat the plastic gun on Dick's lap over one of those old, familiar places, and Dick Below's eyes bulged when he realized it wasn't real. Dick Above didn't think any of it real, just a play developing in amusing anticipation as Jane stood in front of Dick Below and slowly, invitingly, removed her clothes—all but her sexy new undies. She picked up the gun and walked over to the brick fireplace, opened the ash dump door at the bottom of the practically pristine firebox and dropped it where it disappeared into a deep pile of dust, never to be seen again.

Returning to Dick, she slipped off her panties and placed them over his head with the crotch covering his eyes, nose and mouth. Both Dick Below and Dick Above got erections.

Jane went back to the cabinet and pulled out a six-inch hunting knife with a white bone handle. Dick's dad had given it to Dick when he was inducted into the Order of the Arrow, because earning his Eagle Scout badge wasn't enough. *Nothing was ever enough for poor Dick,* Jane thought. *He would have been so much better off with a sibling, especially a sister. Maybe she would have taken up most of Dick's parents' time trying to keep her pristine, and Dick would have had some freedom to be flawed.*

"Oh well," Jane said aloud and tested the edge of the blade: *Sharp as ever, as it should be. As it must be,* she thought and smiled a devilish smile while walking back to Dick where she proceeded to stick the knife between her teeth and straddle the chair facing him, sliding down over his final pronouncement for one last turn on her shattered trust.

It didn't take long. Dick's surging semen erupted in a detonation of ardor and fury, hitting its mark and thunderously ricocheting back down the length of his rock-hard culmination, dripping out of Jane's vivacious swan song.

Dick's mind cross-wired into a malaise of unanswered questions: Why he had dropped out of college in his first act of rebellion against insufferable and impossible expectations, and then married Jane against his parents' wishes, in spite of their disdain for Jane's apparent impious attitudes and demonstrative behavior; how he needed, craved Jane's affirmation, an irresistible and absolute validation, a light through the darkness …

… as Jane took the existential knife out of her mouth and in one quick and deliberate motion, cut Dick's throat. The clean, shiny blade sliced deep, leaving a gaping hole from ear to ear, like a wide-open smile, emitting a distressful gurgling sound while releasing a gushing fountain of dark red blood.

"How's your skanky cunt now, Baby?" Jane breathed into the open leg hole of her panties. Dick Below fought hopelessly for his life, struggling against the expertly tied rope, while Dick Above applauded the virtuoso performance, slowly drifting away, fading out on cue in the grand finale as Dick Below desperately strained for his last gasp and finally, almost heroically, surrendered to the unavoidable diegesis as the curtain dropped.

Watching the light fade out on Dick, Jane noticed, for the first time, a shining brightness enveloping the room from behind. Climbing off the lifeless remembrance of times gone by, she walked out onto the front porch, where she was surrounded by five police cars with their lights shining in her eyes and several officers with weapons drawn, crouched behind open car doors and trees.

"Drop the knife," a Pennsylvania State Trooper ordered through a bullhorn.

Standing naked, covered with Dick's blood commingling with the last dollop of his ultimate incorrectness dripping out of her, Jane dropped the knife, its keen point sticking deep into the weathered porch deck, oscillating from the sudden impact.

"Hiya, boys," Jane said, smiling broadly with self-satisfaction. "How y'all doing tonight?"

Epilogue (or What, No Spot?)

Pennsylvania and New Jersey fought over jurisdiction, and to Jane's good fortune, Pennsylvania's first-degree murder charge trumped New Jersey's escaping prison and grand theft auto. That's because her father hired the best Philadelphia insanity-plea lawyer he could find, and the guy earned his grossly exorbitant fee in short order. His first action was to file a motion to exclude all prior bad acts from New Jersey on the grounds that the prejudicial effect outweighed the probative value.

More to Jane's luck, the judge assigned to the case was having his own problems with some sticky matters involving a bit of ass-grabbing and inappropriate innuendo with his female clerks, so he was inclined to bend over backward to demonstrate his sensitivity toward women's issues.

And Jane's lawyer was most definitely making this a woman's issue. Since Jane had last been to court, the country's attitude toward abused and battered women had taken a 180-degree turn, and her lawyer meant to exploit that change to the fullest. He enlisted the aid of a group based in Philly called Women Against Sexual Predators, or WASP. They organized marches in front of the Monroe County Courthouse in Stroudsburg and the nearby jail where Jane was being held, carrying picket signs that read things such as "Jane Got Dicked" and "Our Vaginas Are Our Shields" (whatever that meant). They marched daily, chanting over and over again, "Your sins won't wash. Sting like a WASP. Your sins won't wash. Sting like a WASP. Your sins won't wash. Sting like a WASP."

In short order, everybody who worked in the area got sick to death of them. Everybody, that is, except the national media out of Philadelphia and New York. Most days, only 15 to 20 people showed up to demonstrate, but when you watched it on the 6 o'clock news, it looked like hundreds. The case caught on and produced a national furor over poor Jane, who had finally lost her mind at the hands of an abusive husband, who was originally and unfairly sent to jail because the white-male-dominated court system gave women's problems little credence.

Jane was the perfect representative for the drama playing out nationally. From the time the cops picked Jane up at the cabin, she claimed to remember nothing after being told she could no longer see Little Nell. The three experts hired by Jane's attorney submitted reports claiming Jane was suffering from hysterical amnesia and was temporarily insane when she killed Dick, and therefore, not legally responsible for her actions. The prosecution's expert couldn't shake Jane's story and reluctantly was compelled by professional ethics to agree with the other psychiatrists.

As a result, Jane's case never went to court. With the grateful judge's blessing, the two sides agreed that

Jane would be sent to a secure mental health facility in Bethlehem, where she would be treated until declared safe to rejoin society, regardless of the duration of her stay.

It wouldn't be long—20 months, to be exact. Jane's first therapist was a woman in her mid-40s, whom Jane spent several months trying to seduce. She never got any further with the reluctant, uptight psychologist than some kissing and light petting in her office one afternoon. The woman resigned a few days later, replaced by a young man in his late 20s—a fastball straight to Jane's wheelhouse.

His name was Mark, and it didn't take Jane long to introduce him to her special skill set. Naturally, Mark fell in love with Jane and declared her sane after only 18 months of treatment. It took two more months of paperwork and filings for Jane to be released back into the wild, with the stipulation that she visit Mark twice a month in Bethlehem for the next three years.

Mark wanted to marry Jane; Jane wanted to get as far away from Mark as she could, so after six months of making the two-hour trek back and forth to Bethlehem, Jane told Mark she would not be coming anymore, and if he reported her, she would tell them he had taken advantage of her vulnerability and forced her to have sex with him.

Mark was heartbroken, but he dutifully kept sending reports to the court every month. The silver lining for Mark was that the Commonwealth of Pennsylvania continued to pay him $300 a month for the next 30 months.

While Jane was serving her time in Pennsylvania, the pragmatic governor of New Jersey, not wanting to face the national outrage that was scorching the land, gave Jane a full pardon for her attempted murder conviction. The state's attorney general publicly announced he would not be filing charges against Jane for leaving prison early, as he put it, in light of the governor's pardon.

On top of that, the auto-theft complaint was withdrawn by the car owner. New Jersey had also given up trying to figure out how Jane had engineered her escape. The obvious suspect was Noel, but they couldn't prove anything against him. The state police wanted Noel to take a lie detector test, but his employer (who stood behind him 100 percent and had the good sense to assign him to a new route immediately after the authorities started showing interest in him as a suspect) had his lawyer get a court order to cease and desist harassing Noel—there was simply no evidence, and therefore no basis, to suspect that he was complicit.

Noel eventually married a voluptuous, blonde, white woman who reminded him of Jane and had two beautiful babies. He never stopped thinking about Jane, but he had learned to live by the philosophy of love the one you're with. He never saw Jane again, and she didn't keep her promise to return his money. Why would she? She didn't remember a thing.

Camila, too, was investigated, but she agreed to a lie detector test and passed. Fortunately, they didn't ask any questions about the unintended (and unknown to two of its participants) yet fortuitous *ménage à trois* and recordings from the surveillance cameras, which were seized immediately after discovering Jane was missing because the tapes automatically erased every 24 hours, backed her up: She didn't see anything. She continued to work in the kitchen, although the job had become much less exciting without Jane around. Camila was a guest at Noel's wedding—a friend of the groom.

Fat Prick's lie detector test didn't go as well, but the results were inconclusive. He stumbled on the part about checking the contents of the truck, but not badly enough to make the authorities believe he was part of a conspiracy. The conclusion was that he must have done a poor job of checking the bag drum, which is where they suspected Jane had hidden. Fat Prick was transferred from the front gate to another part of the prison. He retired seven months later with his full pension and went to work as a security guard for a retirement village, where he spent most of his time kibitzing and getting fatter.

Although the authorities didn't interview Betty, the warden was suspicious of her involvement because she was the one who got Jane assigned to the kitchen. He interrogated her aggressively, but then Betty took him on a trip around the world, and the subject was never again broached. Betty would miss Jane for the rest of her life.

The police didn't find, and therefore knew nothing of, the sweatsuit Noel had given Jane because she had astutely folded it neatly and put in on a shelf in Dick's closet along with his other neatly stacked workout clothes. They did, however, find Jane's prison garb—her white kitchen uniform, bra, panties, socks and sneakers—stuffed in the dirty clothes hamper, as they were supposed to. The acquisition of the money Jane used to go shopping was a more troubling matter, but the police eventually came to the conclusion that money was probably one of the easiest commodities to accumulate in prison, especially for someone with Jane's gifted wiles.

Jane's dad found a young lawyer who specialized in child custody battles to help Jane get Little Nell back. Jane thought he was sweet and down-to-earth and eventually introduced him to her extraordinary world of amusement and amazement. He, of course, fell in love with Jane.

Coincidentally, his name was Richard.

Jane called him Dick.

See Dick run.

The Other Side of the Tracks

First Beer

I'm sitting in first class on an airplane getting ready to take off from O'Hare in Chicago. Why I'm in Chicago and why I'm sitting in first class are details not germane to this story, but suffice to say I'm on a business trip and was bumped up to first class thanks to my frequent flyer miles. I have a lot of frequent flyer miles because I travel a lot, and on those journeys I've met some interesting characters.

This trip being no exception.

His name is Monty, and he also seems to be traveling on business. Apparently, he has not been bumped up to first class; he simply bought a first-class seat. I can see that from the ticket and boarding pass positioned side-by-side on the screen of an open tablet he lays on his fold-out table, which tells me the guy is a high roller, out of my league. I never in my life purchased outright a first-class ticket, so I'm taken aback when he orders a beer, too. I would've expected him to be a single malt scotch drinker, maybe some arcane Russian vodka, but I was pleased to learn that we can relate on one of life's most basic defining characteristics: We are both beer drinkers, and that's a special kind of no-nonsense, unpretentious bond—just a couple of guys having a beer ... or two ... maybe three.

I'm guessing you know how that goes on a long trip at six miles high in the sky. Or maybe not. Maybe you don't travel, or maybe you're a single malt scotch drinker and don't get it. Allow me to elucidate: The best explanation I've ever come across regarding multiple beer consumption was penned by Toni Morrison in Song of Solomon when describing a woman in a relationship where the lights have dimmed: "She was the third beer. Not the first one, which the throat receives with an almost tearful gratitude; not the second, that confirms and extends the pleasure of the first. But the third, the one you drink because it's there, because it can't hurt, and because what difference does it make?"

Monty and I are in the "almost tearful gratitude" mode, cruising along, exchanging pleasantries, when he leans over and says, I'm from Northeast Pennsylvania, a relatively small town called Junction. Ever hear of it?

No. I haven't.

Well, there's probably no reason you would, unless you're a fan of the incongruous and bizarre.

I kill my beer and wait for the story Monty evidently is about to tell. He's a big man with a deep voice and sort of reminds me of Fred Dalton Thompson, the actor and U.S. senator. I'm sure you remember him. He made many movies and played the DA on Law and Order for a few years. You'd definitely recognize his voice. It was a deep baritone that reverberated like the voice of God, and that's something like how Monty sounded—and looked a little like him, too.

Anyway, we order another beer "to confirm and extend the pleasure of the first."

Second Beer

Monty resumes:

The town was founded by railroad men, right on the tracks, sometime after the Civil War, but before the turn of the century. The exact date escapes me at the moment, but you can look it up if you want. It's not important, but what is important is that the town was built for the purpose of making life easier on the men owning and running the railroad. This was during the Industrial Revolution when we were shipping anthracite coal by the trainload down to the steel producers to fuel their blast furnaces that smelted the iron ore that was used to build skyscrapers and battleships. It was a heady time in our part of the country. Some people were getting filthy rich, and anybody who wanted a job had one, although working in the coal mines or the blast furnace shops was less than safe. You had a pretty good chance of perishing in one of those hell holes.

The president of Mauch Chunk Railroad, a man by the name of Leon Fieldershmidt, built a mansion on a small hill about a half mile from the junction of tracks that would come to divide the fledgling town in two. His partners and upper management followed suit and built houses near the president's—not on the hill, of course—and before long, middle management was building smaller homes on the same side of the tracks. About this time, the workers for the railroad, many of whom still spoke with accents from their lands of origin, began building more modest domiciles on the other side of the tracks. Eventually, the junction was a full-fledged municipality, complete with two sides of the tracks, their relative importance subject to the perspective of the chronicler.

The town of Junction was literally built over a junction of tracks, hence the name. Leon Fieldershmidt, who everybody called The Lion—not to his face, understand; he was a no-nonsense sort of fellow who would not have stood any frivolous nickname—built a marvelously engineered structure over the junction of tracks that was called The Switch House. Not only did The Switch House house the myriad switches and mechanisms necessary to keep trains from colliding into one another at the confluence of rails, it was four stories high and officed most of Mauch Chunk Railroad's management. A busy place with a large rail yard not too far down the line on the other side of the tracks, people would come and go all day long.

As the town grew, it incorporated and subdivided the undeveloped areas within the municipal boundaries into building plots, all except 200 acres that The Lion kept on the northeast corner of the town along Elbow Creek. Leon wanted to build something for the community—for his workers—but wasn't able to get it done before his untimely death at age 58. However, in his will, he bequeathed the land to the town with the proviso that it could only be used for a park and recreational area.

Now, this was in the early part of the 20th century when William Taft, the rather rotund president of the United States, was becoming an enamored devotee of the Scottish game of golf, and America was following closely in his footsteps. Howard Pimpleton, who everybody called Pimples—not to his face, of course, which was, by the way, as smooth as a baby's bottom—was elected mayor of Junction in 1908, and was, himself, an enthusiast of the royal and ancient game. Pimples, as it turned out, was also a very designing man, and after meeting in secret with the town council—a group comprised exclusively of railroad men—hatched a plan to develop the land left by The Lion into a golf course. Their rationale, sanctified by the town solicitor—who also happened to be a lawyer for the railroad—was that a golf course *is* a recreational area, and even though the club would be private, residents of Junction could join at a reduced fee. Even at a discount, though, the fee would be too much for the folks from the other side of the tracks.

As you might expect, the golf course became a symbol of the dichotomy between the haves and the have-nots, and produced a certain amount of resentment among the residents from the other side of the tracks—those not employed as cooks, waitstaff, kitchen help, caddies and other important jobs to enhance the enjoyment of the good families from the other side of the tracks, of course. That hypogean acrimony simmered for over a century as the town of Junction congealed into the perfect embodiment of 21st century America: a house divided against itself.

Then along comes Precious Maggy Harding.

Third Beer

The flight attendant comes by and we order another beer, or I should say, Monty orders us another beer because he doesn't bother to ask if I want one. That's the great thing about the brotherhood of beer drinkers: an unspoken, co-pacetic understanding.

When the attendant brings the drinks, I take a sip because it's there, and Monty continues with his story. My mind is getting a little foggy, but this is what I'm pretty sure I'm hearing:

Precious Maggy Harding became a loose spike in the tracks of the folks who had run Junction for well over a century and was generally regarded as a troublemaker and a threat to the peace and tranquility of the people from the other side of the tracks. What was most troubling was that she, too, lived on the other side of the tracks, but that didn't stop the patricians from referring to her in all manner of degradation, most notably as The Precious Hard-On, vernacularized further to Stiffy—but never to her face, of course.

Stiffy was the daughter of a doctor from Uganda and a nurse from an Irish Catholic family in Delaware County. Her parents met while her father, Damba Birungi, was in med school at Thomas Jefferson Hospital in Philadelphia. Stiffy had an older sister and a younger brother, and they lived as good a life as could be expected in an upscale neighborhood in the Scranton area, where Damba worked as a gastroenterologist for a large internal medicine practice.

Damba was at Jefferson when one of Idi Amin's Public Safety Units murdered his family: parents, an older brother—who was in grad school at Cornell and had just returned home for a short visit—and his two younger sisters. It was a senseless tragedy that would haunt Damba for the rest of his life over his perceived failure to not be there to protect his family (although if he had been there, he, too, would be dead, so it was a rather convoluted exercise in the restitution of self-worth).

But that wasn't Damba's only untenable baggage clunking along behind him. He once confided in me that while an undergraduate student at New York University in New York City, the Black students on campus made a big deal over him and his brother, Mukisa, who also attended NYU as an undergraduate, for being African nobility. He told me it was true that his family had descended from tribal leaders and that he and Mukisa were princes in the royal house of Birungi, but that was not exclusively from where their power and money had derived.

"Oh no," he said over a delightfully dry sherry one evening. "We made our fortune and amassed great power in the slave trade business. How's that for the honorable aristocratic son of Afrika? All those students who thought Mukisa and I were so cool didn't know, and apparently didn't care to know, that our family had put their ancestors in the chains of inhuman servitude."

I'll tell you, that was an interesting conversation, and it got even more interesting—and ironic. Damba told me that he and Mukisa would never have associated with any of those NYU students if they were in Uganda.

"Why?" I asked. "Because they were below your station?"

"In a manner of speaking, yes," he said. "It's because they had black gums."

"Pardon me," I said, a bit shocked. "Did you say you wouldn't associate with people with black gums?"

"Yes, that is correct," Damba said. "You see, we have pink gums, and pink and black don't go well together—other than in the movie *Grease,*" And with that, he gave out a loud laugh at his own joke.

It's too bad Damba liked his sherry and liked to tell that story after he liked his sherry a wee bit too much, but I suppose that's how most legends are born.

Stiffy went to law school at Villanova and became a successful—and rather wealthy—personal injury lawyer in Luzerne and Lackawanna counties, where she specialized in defending the have-nots, playing on guilt and sanctimonious altruism empowering juries to play Robin Hood. It didn't hurt that her husband, who is a descendent of Leon Fieldershmidt and inherited his great-great-grandfather's house on the hill in Junction, is a county judge known covertly as The Hammer—for obvious reasons—and who, clearly, couldn't hear her cases. But influence can be a slippery snake, manifesting itself in the most subtle and concomitant manner. Stiffy and her husband raised a family and had a good life … until the great awakening.

In working on a case against the railroad where Stiffy represented an injured trackman—a case her great-great-grandfather-in-law would not have smiled upon, believe me—she uncovered an interesting document in the archives stashed away in a dark corner of the basement in Junction's municipal building. It was an almost unreadable copy of The Lion's last will and testament attached to an equally compromised copy of the original deed to the property that would become the Iron Horse Country Club.

As Stiffy tried to decipher the language of the old and decaying documents, she became intrigued by the clause granting the property to the borough. She dug deeper until she uncovered the misrepresentation by Mayor Pimples and his cadre of enablers in their most egregious and scandalous interpretation of the will. She was outraged, and it lit a fire in her of such intensity that Old Pimples should be thanking his lucky stars he'd been dead for 75 years.

That day, Stiffy made up her mind she was going to change things, to realign the tracks, if you will. The Borough of Junction had a mayor and five council members, and she decided to run for one of those seats, the one being vacated by Horace Blimbly, who came from the other side of the tracks and who everybody called Blumpy because he was as round and plump as old William Taft—but never to his face, if you know what I mean.

Blumpy had been on council for as long as anyone could remember and at the ripe old age of 90 was hanging it up, so Stiffy set her sights on winning that seat in the November election, six months away. Her competition was light in numbers and cognitive ability. Accordingly, she won rather easily, garnering most of the votes from the other side of the tracks where the folks identified with her simply on the basis of her skin pigmentation and enough votes from the other side of the tracks to validate her victory.

You could call Stiffy's win a precursor to the great awakening because it was a major step for Junction to have a woman on council, let alone a woman with an identifiable skin pigmentation.

Not until her second year in office did Stiffy bring up the golf course and its shady origin. Now, this was only a few years after Barack Obama had unearthed, or should I say awoken, the simmering divide within the country, and people of all breeds were ... how to put this ... transitioning in their thinking and sensibilities. One of the more divisible manifestations of that discordant emergence was the torn and tattered notion of restitution for families of former slaves, an idea with durable-enough legs to fester since the end of the Civil War—durable enough for Stiffy to grab onto and exploit for bigger and better things, the antithetical value of those bigger and better things made manifest in a most unintended yet flagitious manner.

Oh yeah, Stiffy was on a crusade for sure, saddling that mount and spurring it to a pitched frenzy of pious indignation, like Calamity Jane riding roughshod straight into the center ring of Buffalo Bill's Wild West Show.

First Tequila

As I'm unceremoniously finishing beer number three, Monty tries to order two shots of tequila, but the middle-aged yet buoyant flight attendant gives him a big smile, a smile she had apparently practiced for years of putting up with over-testosteroned Mr. Monopolies-to-be, and tells him no tequila and no shots—airline policy. Undeterred, Monty grabs a briefcase from under his seat and pulls out a small bottle of russet-colored liquid, then produces a couple of plastic nip glasses.

You come prepared, *I say with what I'm sure is a conflicting look of disbelief and appreciation. It has been a long week, after all, and I do happen to have a certain fondness for the nectar of agave. Just how does Monty know that? I wonder. He didn't ask.*

I was a Boy Scout and took it seriously, *Monty says as he pours us each a shot.* Here's to the nights we'll never remember with the friends we'll never forget, *Monty toasts as we touch our jiggers together and shoot the hope of redemption. Monty stows the bottle and small glasses in the seat-back pocket in front of him and continues:*

Needless to say, Stiffy got everybody's attention when she brought up the duplicitous behavior of the town's progenitors, which became a cause célèbre on both sides of the tracks, but from different perspectives, naturally. Unfortunately, she didn't have the votes on council to do anything about the outrageous injustice—the town's original sin. So, she ran for mayor, winning by the smallest of margins—just a few votes.

And that's when the fun really began.

Monty gives me a smile that possesses, from my embryonic-inebriation perspective, an iniquitous connotation, then says: You see, when all the votes were tabulated, more people had voted than the population of Junction, and to make matters worse, not only did Stiffy win the mayoralty, but she tugged along three new council members, all from the other side of the tracks. As to be expected, the folks from the other side of the tracks were outraged and ready to grab torches and pitchforks. Consequently, the next council meeting, a week after the election, was quite a show.

The discussion started off with a bang after the perfunctory opening business, delivered with great conviction by Bartholomew Farthington, who was from the other side of the tracks and who was better known as Bart the Fart, or simply The Fart, but only behind his back, of course. "This whole election was total malarkey—fraught with fraud," he said. "There's something definitely cattywampus going on around here!" The Fart had been on council for more than 15 years and was not up for reelection, so he was safe for the next two years anyway. But he could read the writing on the wall, and he wasn't going down without a fight.

The Fart rubbed one of his chins as in deep thought, then continued, "There's a skattlewog among us trying to bamboozle this town right off its very foundation."

"As is greatly needed," Stiffy stated stately, her smooth skin and electric eyes contrasting the milky, dull ambiance of the presiding coven.

"I'm no nincompoop," The Fart countered. "I know felonious shenanigans when I see them."

"What are you saying, Bart?" Stiffy asked with a severe, prune-faced look, distorting her normally attractive physiognomy.

"I'm saying that there's something rotten, not in Demark, but right here in Junction," The Fart challenged. "And you know exactly what I'm talking about, Precious."

"Are you accusing me of something, Bart?" Stiffy asked coldly with laser beams shooting from her wide, terrifying eyes.

"I'm accusing somebody of something that's not according to Hoyle—somebody, or somebodies, are not playing fair," The Fart said and snorted, scratching the top of his balding head. "How can you have more votes than people? Can you explain that?"

"Obviously, the census data is off," Stiffy told him, throwing her shoulders back and pulling herself up straight, like a rocket ship about to take off. "There must be a glitch in the system. You do know, don't you, Bart, that some people, some of our newest residents who came from places where governments are corrupt and dangerous, are reluctant to provide accurate information to officials out of fear. I would estimate that the actual population of Junction is at least 10 percent higher than the recorded numbers. That's the real glitch, Bart: fear."

"Hogwash! Pure hogwash!" The Fart groaned. "The glitch is a lot closer than some mysterious snafu in the system. It's more of the living, breathing variety of glitches, regardless of how much kerfuffle you try to make." He punctuated his remarks with a wagging finger pointed at council.

Everyone on council, except Stiffy, was old friends of The Fart, and all five (including the about-to-be-former mayor and town solicitor) hula-hoop-era men with no discernable skin pigmentation nodded, their heads as one.

"We need a recount," The Fart emphasized, shaking his head vigorously as his elephant jowls bobbed up and down. "And even with a recount, we know what you did to rig the election," he said and looked directly at Stiffy, timorously blinking his pumpernickel eyes.

"What I did?" Stiffy asked, incredulously.

"Yes, what you did, and you know it, so don't play dumb," The Fart refuted. "You got your people from the other side of the tracks, the side of the tracks you don't live on, by the way, to go house to house and help fill out ballots for folks who had never voted in any election before—probably a lot of illegals," and with that, he spread his hands compliantly toward the large audience that had come out looking for a good old-fashioned whack-em-up.

"We did no such thing," Stiffy retorted stiffly. "Canvassers simply collected ballots from the neighborhoods to deliver to Borough Hall, which is legal now, Bart. It's not 1950 any longer. Those good old days are over."

"Yeah, the good old days when you could trust your neighbor and rely on honest men to do the right thing," The Fart lamented.

"I would probably not hang my hat on that honest men thing, Bart," Stiffy rebuked. "As I've previously pointed out—much to your chagrin, as you've amply voiced—those honest men have been screwing the people of Junction for over a hundred years."

"And, so now it's your turn, eh? You've come a long way, Baby, is that it?" The Fart asked sarcastically and let out a loud guffaw. "Just a lot of gobbledygook, if you ask me."

"This is getting us nowhere," interjected Mayor Rodger Trout, who was from the other side of the tracks and had been mayor of Junction for more than 20 years, as his father had been for 32 years before him. The Trouts were offspring of a minor partner of The Lion, and all the descending Trout men continued to work for the railroad to this day. Rodger Trout, the last in that line because he was a bachelor well into his 60s, and who engendered much speculation as to the circumstances of that bachelorhood, if you catch my drift, was about as dull and nonthreatening as a potted plant, and everybody called him Fish Face. They called him Fish Face not because of his name, interestingly, but because whenever he was confronted with a decision he couldn't defer or delegate, his mouth puckered up with the middle of his lips scrunched together and pulsing, like a guppy in a fish tank exploring the edges of its universe. It goes without saying that nobody called him Fish Face to his fish face, which was relatively easy because Fish Face hardly ever spoke to anybody if he didn't have to, and hardly anybody ever spoke to Fish Face if they didn't have to.

"What we need here is a recount," Fish Face added to the astonishment of all—he never made pronouncements or suggestions or any comments of substance, so his unexpected (albeit self-serving) declaration of involvement came out of left field. The room fell quiet with anticipation as everybody sitting at the dais looked nervously back and forth at each other (except Stiffy, of course, who wore a predictably cynical expression).

"Exactly! And with proof of residency," The Fart emphasized with great gusto after a dramatic pause of trepidatious reflection on venturing into unknown territory. "People have to prove who they are. It's only reasonable."

"Reasonable for whom?" Stiffy interjected quickly. "Jim Crow?"

"Let the record show that we're—what is it now—17 minutes into the meeting before Mrs. Harding played the race card: a new record," The Fart said, and part of the room laughed along with him. Stiffy did not and threw up her hands in frustration.

Marvin Schimel, who was from the other side of the tracks, was the recording secretary for council and kept copious notes. Nobody called Marvin anything but Marvin because he was remarkably nondescript. Marvin dutifully tapped out the entry into his laptop.

"Perhaps you can explain to me, Precious, how having to prove who you are to get Medicaid or welfare is not racist but having to prove who you are to vote is," The Fart confronted.

Stiffy stiffened. "We're not trying to suppress people from getting the benefits they deserve," she said.

"You mean you're not trying to suppress dead people from voting," The Fart snortled.

"You're impossible," Stiffy said and shook her head deliberately.

"All right now," Fish Face intervened. "I believe a recount is in order. Do I hear a motion?"

"There's nothing in the municipal code that calls for, and therefore allows, a recount," Stiffy offered in a clipped assertion.

"There's nothing says you can't, either," The Fart replied snidely. "Enough lollygagging. I make a motion we conduct a recount."

"I hih-cond that motion," hiccupped Marlin Popovich, who was from the other side of the tracks and who everybody called Hiccups because everything he said sounded like a hiccup.

"Wait a minute," Stiffy chimed in. "This is completely out of order!"

"Everybody in favor of the motion on the floor please signify by saying aye," Fish Face pursued while ignoring Stiffy, and all four non-Stiffy council members responded with aye, except Hiccups who said "hih-ya."

"All those opposed."

"Everybody in this room should be opposed," Stiffy answered. "Everybody in this town should be opposed. It's time we moved out of the 19th century. On behalf of everybody with a brain, on behalf of everybody with

half an ounce of honor and decency, I vigorously op-
pose!"

"Noted," said Fish Face as Marvin Schimel typed
away.

"Mr. Apate, would you please handle the legal language necessary to engage Schurke and Associates,
the borough's accounting firm, to conduct a recount of
the election?" Fish Face adjudicated.

Nedward Apate, who was from the other side of the
tracks, was Junction's solicitor—everybody called him
That (insert appropriate adjective) Apate, and everybody feared him. He was known for being ruthless and
cunning and not at all a nice guy.

"I'm afraid Mr. Apate is going to be too busy defending the lawsuit I plan to file in the morning to stop
this illegal action," Stiffy said.

"File away," The Fart challenged. "Go ahead and
waste the people's money on your confounded crusade
and expose what you are really all about, what your
true agenda is."

"May I say a few words, Mr. Mayor?" came from a
woman sitting in the middle of the audience as she
stood and raised her hand.

"Well, it's not really public comment time ..." Fish
Face equivocated and looked up and down the table for
support, but all council members were otherwise oc-
cupied, either staring at their folded hands resting on
the table in front of them or pretending to make notes,
including The Fart and Stiffy. It seemed that nobody
wanted to deal with Hazel Colbert, who was known
for her arcane erudition. Fish Face scrunched up his
lips and looked like a guppy in a fish tank exploring
the edges of his safety, which seemed to be closing in
on him. After a few moments of what appeared to be
thoughtful contemplation, but was really a stall while

hoping the world would end, Fish Face said, "...but in respect to you, Hazel, I think we can make an exception this one time." (This one time being a rather regular occurrence at council meetings when a more nonaligned and impervious voice of inscrutable equitability was called for.)

As Hazel Colbert, who was not from either side of the tracks because she lived on the tracks, slowly made her way to the small podium (which was placed in the front of the room as far away from Fish Face as possible), the room emanated a noticeable buzz of anticipation. She was a retired English teacher who had risen to the position of principal at Junction High School, but had still taught classes, was childless, never married and dedicated to the school for almost 40 years.

When Hazel retired, the town (by then the owners of the old, decaying Switch House) hired her to live in and attend to the care and maintenance of the anachronistic monstrosity, which Hazel took on with an almost monomaniacal dedication. The old structure had been neglected for years before Junction applied to the commonwealth to have it declared a Building of Historical Significance and was awarded a continuation grant to refurbish, preserve and sustain the hubristic erection, funds that Hazel used with determined rigidity, and anybody who got in her way was dealt with industriously and swiftly and with little concern for propriety. So, as you might expect, it wasn't long until folks started calling her the Switch Witch, but never in front of her, not surprisingly.

Some of the young ruffians in town had their own take on the Switch Witch after one particularly rambunctious Mischief Night when they soaped up the windows of the hideous excrescent, and in a most ill-advised protest of pending post-pubescence toil and trouble, spray-painted in huge white block letters Witch Hazel on all four walls of Junction's most grand, yet nevertheless indecorous, statement. As might have been expected by a more accomplished outlook on life's not-so-serendipitous possibilities, the ever-vigilant Switch Witch caught the rascals in mid-vandalization of the last wall and hauled them to the police station.

The first juvenile court in the history of the town was convened, and the hooligans were charged with the arduous task of scrubbing off the not-ready-for-street-art defacements, giving rise to a more ungracious moniker for Hazel Colbert, forever after known in the expanding circle of Junction's would-be juvenile delinquents as the Switch Bitch.

The Switch Witch's head barely rose above the podium as she stood in silence for a moment surveying the room. Her eyes moved back and forth between the audience and the dais, slowly yet expressively. With both hands, she smoothed what used to be her jet-black hair but was now mostly gray and cleared her throat. As always, she was dressed from shoulder to toe in black, as if she were trying to live up to her sobriquet. With her rather pronounced chin, you could put a pointy hat on her head, and she'd have a reasonable resemblance to Margaret Hamilton in *The Wizard of Oz.*

Do you know who that is? he asks, breaking from his story.

The Wicked Witch of the West? I sheepishly ask while I take the last sip of beer in my cup.

Good, you're still with me, he says, then continues:

"You have nobody to thank for your troubles, nobody but yourself, that is," the Switch Witch began in her usual opaque manner.

"Pardon?" Fish Face asked.

"Oh come, Rodger," the Switch Witch scolded. "Don't tell me you've forgotten your studies of *The Odyssey*, when Odysseus is confronted by the Cyclops?"

"It's been a while," Fish Face mumbled.

"Well, allow me to refresh your memory," she said and smiled. She still loved teaching.

"I had planned to be a doctor when I started college, and so, as required for pre-med, took an anatomy class during my sophomore year. The professor, Dr. Sirimole, who we all called Sir Mole, but not to his face, of course, was a brilliant teacher who loved to quote Shakespeare and would allude to the masters to make his points. I loved his class, not so much for the anatomy, but for the rapt ecstasy he evidenced in his presentation of references to classic literature, and as a matter of fact, it was he who inspired me to change majors and eventually become an English teacher. One day, while lecturing on the mechanics of the eyes, he brought up the fable of Odysseus and the Cyclops."

The Switch Witch paused here, took out a small, embroidered hanky and dabbed the corners of her mouth, most likely for dramatic effect, which she was good at. "As I'm sure you will recall," she continued as she scrupulously raked over the room, "the Cyclops had captured Odysseus and his men and locked them in his cave, where he proceeded to eat them, one by one, over a couple of days. Odysseus was able to get the Cyclops drunk, and when the monster finally passed out, Odysseus drove a spear deep into his eye. While the Cyclops endeavored to grapple with his newly acquired handicap, Odysseus and his remaining men were able to escape by hiding under the bellies of the Cyclops's flock of sheep going out to pasture.

"And here's where it gets interesting," she teased. "What Sir Mole told us on that morning of foundering naiveté was that as Odysseus and his men were fleeing in their boat, the Cyclops threw a boulder at them, but missed. 'He missed,' Sir Mole said, 'because he was a Cyclops, and Cyclops have only one eye. Therefore, because they have only one eye, they have no depth perception, and that's why the Cyclops missed Odysseus's boat. You see,' Sir Mole concluded with a triumphant swell of his chest and a broad smile of satisfaction, 'we have two eyes that allow us to see things from different angles, giving us the ability to judge distances, something the Cyclops was unable to do with only one eye.'

"A boy in the back of the room raised his hand, and when Sir Mole called on him, asked, 'Is it possible that the spear in the Cyclops's eye, the one that blinded him, contributed to his missing Odysseus?' That classroom became almost as horrorstruck as this room is tonight," the Switch Witch finished and stared at Fish Face.

"And your point?" Fish Face finally asked with great trepidation.

"That the obvious is sometimes not so obvious, even when you don't have a spear in your eye. It's what happens when you let the Tin Man make decisions as opposed to the Scarecrow," she said, then slowly walked back to her seat.

"Thank you, Hazel. That gives us all something to think about," Fish Face said as the rest of the folks on the dais diligently worked at having no expressions on their faces.

Fourth Beer

My focus is on my empty beer glass as I contemplate what it must feel like to have a spear in your eye, fighting a somewhat cobwebbed confusion and intrigue with a pinch of disquietude, looking much like Nietzsche staring into the abyss, I suppose. Monty lifts his empty glass and gives me a look that asks, Shall we?

Apparently, we shall, and order another brew...because it can't hurt.

Stiffy did, indeed, *Monty pursued*, file a lawsuit to stop the recount, and the case made it all the way to the Pennsylvania Supreme Court. In Pennsylvania, as you may know, or maybe not, the Supreme Court is made up of seven justices who are elected, and thanks to Philadelphia and Pittsburgh—their large populations inexplicably always voting in the same direction regardless of the issues—the court has a tendency to list left, if you know what I mean. As a result, Stiffy won the case, probably as much for the composition of the adversaries as for the actual matter before the court.

So, the recount was stopped, and Stiffy and her new council were installed into office on January 1. Their first order of business was to rescind the lease to the Iron Horse Country Club. In The Lion's will, it clearly stated that the property on which the club sat, the piece of land The Lion had envisioned as a pastoral respite for the good people of Junction, the good people who had worked so hard to make him filthy rich, could never be sold and should always remain in the ownership of his beloved town.

Old Pimples and his posse couldn't figure out a way to subjugate that clause, so they wrote a contract that leased the land to the Iron Horse Country Club for $100 a year. Surreptitiously, that agreement was written "Until Forbidden," which meant that it would continue in perpetuity, unless Junction ever came to its senses and canceled the let.

And of course, Stiffy and her band of crusaders brought the town to its senses, but only for a very short period of time.

In due course, which was no surprise to anyone, the Iron Horse Country Club fought council's decision in court, and that case, too, eventually landed on the bench of the state Supreme Court, where once again identity seemed to trump substance. Although in this case, the decision was at least grounded in law—and the correct one.

Council had given the country club six months to vacate the property, but it took almost a year for the legal entanglements to get untangled, and in the end, the club had to scramble to close down and settle accounts before Junction could foreclose and claim whatever assets were left. In short order, the town took back the land, and the Iron Horse County Club chugged into the good night with tail placed firmly between legs. Unfortunately for the borough of Junction, its night wasn't to be so good.

Somehow Stiffy, on her way to the land of righteousness, made a disturbing U-turn that, to many, rivaled Old Pimples's disgraceful misconduct when she made a proposal at the next council meeting after the decision from the state Supreme Court was handed down. Stiffy reasoned that the land bequeathed to the borough for the enjoyment of its residents had been immorally and fraudulently misappropriated, and the best way to counterbalance that malfeasance was to give the land back to the people.

"We have an idea that may help balance the scales and attempt to make amends for some of the outrageous and dehumanizing treatment of many of our citizens' ancestors at the hands of imperialistic conceit like the natural order or manifest destiny and other linguistic sophistry to justify white, Western European dominance," Stiffy stated with a smug look of defiance.

"Oh boy! Here we go," The Fart puffed.

"I propose we subdivide the golf course acreage into building plots and allot the housing to needy families of color, those with roots in slavery, restitution, if you will, for their incalculable losses," Stiffy unwisely followed.

A loud rumble went up from the audience with several cat calls of noticeable disapproval, along with a more reserved yet conspicuous clamor of endorsement. If the town wasn't divided enough already, Stiffy, in remarkably few words, ushered in a whole new frontier of disaffection and distrust.

"Are you going to get a piece of it?" a woman with a noticeable Spanish accent shouted from the audience.

"I would not be eligible," Stiffy said calmly. "In order to be eligible, your household income will have to be below a certain level, and that level and other particulars will be determined by a committee I will appoint to oversee the process."

"It's a good thing," the woman cracked, "because ain't nobody in your family never wore no chains," she added, eliciting a laugh from many of the excited attendees.

"On one hand, you have your chainees," The Fart interjected, holding out and splaying his right hand. "And on the other hand, you have your chainers," he added, holding out and splaying his left hand.

That prompted even more laughter.

"Forgetting for a moment that your idea is galactically stupid, how exactly do you propose to determine and verify who is a descendant of slaves, Mrs. Harding?" The Fart went on. "Or are we simply going to take their word for it, like we did in the last election when anybody with a pulse, and some without one, voted? Bumfuzzle us once, shame on you. Bumfuzzle us twice ..."

"We've worked out a plan we think will solve that problem," Stiffy interrupted while paying no notice to The Fart's provocation.

"Come one, come all," The Fart announced in a ringmaster's voice. "Step right up, ladies and gentlemen, and watch Mr. Kite dance and sing! And pay no attention to the woman behind the curtain."

Stiffy looked down at the tabletop and shook her head while about half the audience laughed and the other half groaned.

Second Tequila

Monty pulls his magic decanter from the seat pocket, along with the two shot glasses, and carefully pours us another tequila.

Drink to life and the passing show and the eyes of the prettiest girl you know, *Monty toasts and raises his glass.*

We throw the tequila down our over-stimulated throats. Monty holds his drained glass up to his face and examines it like he's left something inside but can't quite remember what it was. He holds that pose for what seems like an eternity, making me restless. Although my mind's a bit off-kilter, through the gathering clouds my curiosity is about to beat the crap out of the cat.

And? *I finally blurt out.*

Oh, it became a real bubbling brouhaha, *Monty Picks up.* Stiffy announced that they would be developing the old country club parcel into approximately 750 building plots—each containing a three-bedroom home and two-car garage—which would be awarded to deserving members of the community through a raffle.

"The homes, roads and all excavation will be paid for with county, state and federal grants, plus some corporate donations," Stiffy explained.

"You found some virtue signalers, did you?" The Fart baited. "And would it be completely out of order for me to ask how you plan to determine who are deserving members of the community?"

"We'll be using the BIPOC designation for eligibility in the lottery," Stiffy said.

"I assume BIPOC is an anagram for some ultra-progressive group of freeloaders?" The Fart asked belligerently.

"Freeloaders? Really, Bart," Stiffy said with much repugnance. "BIPOC is an acronym for Black, Indigenous, and People of Color, a classification accepted and used by the federal government."

"Oh, well then, why didn't you say so?" The Fart chided. "If the feds are using it, you know it's got to be good. As in, we'll give you lots of free stuff as long as you continue to blindly vote for us. Just how do you plan to decide who fits into this nifty BIPOC group?"

"That's actually a good question, Bart, and one I've researched thoroughly," Stiffy explained. "It's a very complicated subject, but I've found that the simplest and most universally accepted test is the one-drop rule—any person with even one ancestor of Black ancestry is considered Black, and the same for the indigenous and people of color."

"So, that would probably include more than half the population of the country," The Fart mocked.

"What a progressive notion, Bart," Stiffy mocked back. "If your eligibility is not apparent by skin tone, you have to be able to prove it with some type of documentation, which won't be as hard as it sounds since all government agencies—public schools, the armed forces, criminal records and such, not to mention church and community archives—usually designated race."

"This is a joke, right?" The Fart asked. "I mean, you can't be serious!"

"Serious as the plague," retorted Stiffy as she jutted out her chin. "In order to enter the lottery, you have to be a resident of Junction and be able to prove it, plus produce legal identification. If your skin color is not definitive, you must produce documentation of who in your lineage is BIPOC."

"Prove who you are, eh?" The Fart sneered. "What a novel concept. Too bad you only thought of it now. This whole idea is crazy! Much hullaballoo about nothing."

"Excuse me," came from a skinny, tie-dye-aficionado-looking woman in the audience. "I identify as an indigenous person but can't produce any documentation to that fact."

"And so it begins," The Fart said, chuckling. "Send in the clowns."

Sonja Karnowski was a local eccentric from the other side of the tracks, one of the last of a fading generation of would-be hippies who missed out on the '60s and everything that short but tumultuous period of time was about, who erroneously believed that long hair, Woodstock-era attire and classic rock qualify as bona fide credentials to the love and peace movement …

… a movement that was, really, more about loveless piece, if you hear me, *Monty interrupts his story.*

Oh, I shear you, *I respond in a slight slur.*

Apparently, Sonja was taking a bath one day while listening to "You Keep Me Hangin' On" by Vanilla Fudge on her radio that was perched precariously at the edge of the tub when it accidentally *(and here Monty makes air quote marks around the word accidentally)* fell into the bath water. Unbeknownst to Sonja, and perhaps to her vexation, the radio was plugged into a GFCI outlet—you know, a ground fault circuit interrupter—and the circuit cut off almost immediately after it sensed the overload, but not immediately enough, and Sonja was knocked out, or so her story goes.

When Sonja awoke, miraculously she was a Munsee Delaware Indian, and further, she was the High Princess of the tribe. According to Sonja, her name in Munsee language, roughly translated, means Bosom of Hope, which translated into Tiny Titties in Junction-speak, mainly because she had … well, you can figure that one out.

Stiffy placated her, as did most of the town because she freaked the bejesus out of folks. "Yes, Bosom of Hope, we all know that."

"I just want it on the record that I'm applying as a Native American, is all," Tiny Titties said.

"There's no such thing as a Native American," rebuffed The Fart. "Indians came over the Bering Straits way back when they were connected to Asia by ice, so what we have here are Mongolian immigrants, not Native American. And they came in illegally, to boot," The Fart said and laughed loudly.

Stiffy shot him a hard look, and Tiny Titties started to cry.

"Don't worry, Bosom of Hope," Stiffy soothed. "You may enter the lottery."

"Hey, my dad told me he dated a Japanese girl while he was stationed in Japan after the war. Do I qualify?" The Fart asked facetiously.

"May I say a few words, Madam Mayor?" came from the Switch Witch.

"Well, it's not really time for public comment," Stiffy equivocated and looked up and down the table for support, but none was forthcoming.

"Of, course, Hazel," Stiffy acquiesced. "Your input is always welcomed."

The Switch Witch walked to the podium and said, "I had a boy in school once. He was a sweet boy, nice looking and well behaved when he entered high school. He came from a wealthy family in town, a family most of you would know, I'm sure. His father indulged him, giving the boy nice clothes, a fast car and anything he wanted. As a freshman, he played baseball and earned above-average grades, but by his sophomore year, he had quit the team and his grades started to slip. In his junior year, he was barely passing his classes and was beginning to get into trouble, first for minor things, but his conduct deteriorated and he progressed into committing more serious offenses. As his attitude and comportment continued to spiral down, his father used his money and influence to countermand the boy's improprieties. Additionally, the father sent him to counselors, paid for tutors and showered the boy with more and more expensive toys and appurtenances, but his son maintained on his pestilent course. Finally, the son was arrested for selling drugs and sentenced to prison, a fate even his father couldn't abrogate."

The Switch Witch paused and dabbed the corners of her mouth with an embroidered hanky as the crowd shifted in its seats.

"When the boy was being taken away in handcuffs, his father said, 'I gave you everything.'

"The boy turned back to face his father and said, 'But I didn't need everything.'"

The Switch Witch paused and looked up and down council.

After a few moments of silence, Stiffy asked, "And your point, Hazel?"

"You can't give them everything," the Switch Witch said. "But you can give them what they need," she finished and slowly walked back to her seat.

Fifth Beer

I have to hit the head. When I return, a fresh brewski is waiting for me because what difference does it make.

Thas a sweird schtory, *I articulate in beer-ese once I'm settled back in my seat.*

And that is by no means the end of it, either, *Monty replies in crisp articulation.*

Yous mean it ges sweirder?"

You have no idea, *Monty says, then resumed his story:*

It took That (insert appropriate adjective) Apate and his band of pirates over six months to get the language right in the application for the lottery. Within two weeks after they opened up the process, they had received more applications than the population of Junction.

Are you starting to see a pattern here?

I nod, choosing my words carefully.

It became a Herculean task to separate the pepper from the fly shit, if you'll pardon my French, and the town had to hire additional administrative staff to handle the paperwork. It was an unmitigated disaster. As the infrastructure of the borough sagged under the weight of that arduous burden, the excavating company went to work refitting the old golf course for residential living. One of their first objectives was to disassemble the dam that had been built at the north end of Elbow Creek in order to construct three ponds over the links ... and to ensure no golfer ever went home completely happy.

And this is where it gets fun, *Monty adds.*

I take a sip of beer in rapt anticipation. Monty has morphed into two people, and I can't decide which one to look at.

In order to accomplish that, they needed to dynamite the old structure. How did AC/DC put it? "Dynamite, I'm a power load. Dynamite, watch me explode."

Speaking of which, my head's about to explode, but Monty looks cool and collected. How's that work?

T.N.T., *I correct him.*

Huh? Well, explode it did, disintegrating the dreams and aspirations of the well-meaning yet grossly misdirected Stiffy, blowing up any hope of correcting antiquated transgressions.

Poor girl, I thought in perfect diction.

I don't know how familiar you are with Northeast Pennsylvania, but one of the things we're notorious for is our sinkholes. A sinkhole, if you don't know, is a geological anomaly that occurs, simply put, when rock formation below the soil is eroded away by water, which over time creates an underground cavern. The surface above the cavern is always unstable, but it can remain intact for very long periods of time until something happens to trigger a collapse, and that's what happened when they fired that first blast of dynamite. A huge sinkhole opened and swallowed the old clubhouse, which had yet to be demolished, but now was.

When it made the news, the Pennsylvania Department of Environmental Protection rushed in and shut down the entire operation. They spent a few months testing the area for other rogue formations and/or fissures and determined that some of the spots were potentially unstable and inappropriate for a housing development at that time.

Hugely disappointed but undeterred, Stiffy came up with a new plan, one most townsfolk liked, but not the two holdout-council members from the last regime. The Fart and Hiccups were up for reelection right about this time, and everybody figured they'd be voted out of office, but lo and behold, there was a shift in sea winds, as there invariably is in the ebb and flow of politics. They both retained their seats, much to the displeasure of Stiffy.

First Cup of Coffee

We order coffee for obvious reasons. I'm about one blast over the line, maybe two, but Monty looks as sober as a judge, like he could go all night.

Monty takes a tentative sip of the steaming hot brew and goes on:

Stiffy began the next town meeting with, "I think we should go back to the original wishes of the town's founder and put in a park, but not just any park, a park to rival the finest in the land. I propose we put in a small zoo, like the one in New York City, complete with a Delacorte Clock of our own. Like the one in Central Park, ours will have little bronze mine workers and train engineers as musicians playing polka tunes on the hour from dawn to dusk. We'll name it the Field-ershmidt Clock, since the Fieldershmidt family has generously offered to pay for it."

"Pillow talk, eh?" The Fart said. "Here come da judge!"

"You're disgusting," Stiffy seethed. I can assure you her pillow talk never included politics, *Monty confides.*

"I hope we're going to have hot dog vendors. I love those New York hot dogs," The Fart ridiculed.

"Excuse me," came from the timid voice of Tiny Titties sitting in the audience. "Does this mean I won't be getting a new house?"

"Yes, I'm afraid so. Sorry, Bosom of Hope," Stiffy said gently.

In a thunderous voice that seemed to come from heaven above, Tiny Titties erupted, "Another lie and abuse of my people!" she shouted and stomped out of the room.

"That electrical charge seems to be kicking in again," The Fart joked.

Stiffy ignored him and picked up where she'd left off. "Along that same theme, I'd like to see a colorful, brightly lit, state-of-the-art carousel in the middle of the park, our centerpiece, a place where visitors from all over—school trips, wedding parties—all sorts of people will come and ride the merry-go-round, take pictures, laugh and have fun," Stiffy gushed, her excitement reaching a fever pitch. "And an arboretum with sumptuous flowers and a bounty of flora and a peace garden for mediation and prayer and a two-and-a-half-mile nature walk around the circumference of the park and ..."

"Somebody hose her down, quickly," interrupted The Fart.

"And best of all," Stiffy continued, giving The Fart a dirty look out of the corners of her eyes, "a museum commemorating the good people who worked so hard—including up until present times—building Junction and the surrounding areas." She looked at the audience for a reaction and took a breath.

"And how are we going to pay for the finest park in the land?" The Fart asked with a disingenuous smile.

"Well," Stiffy said haughtily, "we can convert some of the grant money, sell corporate sponsorships and borrow against future revenue."

"Future revenue?" The Fart punctuated his stiletto-delivered words with a finger poking the air in front of him. "Where's that revenue coming from? More taxes? So, in other words, we're all going to pay for your mistake?"

"No, not at all," Stiffy responded enthusiastically. "We're going to charge admission. We'll build a fence covered by hedgerow around the park and sell day or season passes, just like other recreation areas and sites of interest do."

"If you build it, they will come, eh?" The Fart taunted.

"Exactly," Stiffy said, smiling.

The Fart pounded his fist on the table and challenged, "So, if we want to enjoy the park, we're going to have to pay for that privilege, is that it? You're going to make the innocent residents of Junction pay for your hole in the ground, after all."

"If you can prove who you are and your residency in Junction, you may purchase a season pass for a small processing fee, probably about the same cost as a day pass for a family of four," Stiffy clarified.

"If you can prove who you are and your residency in Junction? What a great idea," The Fart responded with tongue planted resolutely in cheek.

"May I say a few words, please?" the Switch Witch asked as she stood up and raised her hand.

"Well, it's not really … sure, go ahead," Stiffy said, cutting to the chase.

The Switch Witch stood at the podium scarcely peering over the top and began, "A farmer owned an old donkey, and one day the old donkey fell into a hole.

He was trapped because the hole was much too deep for him to climb out. The farmer was in a quandary as to how he was going to get his donkey out of the hole, and he spent a great deal of time trying to figure out how to solve the problem—time he couldn't afford to waste. Eventually, the farmer gave up and decided to bury his donkey in the hole. Some of the farmer's neighbors came by to help the farmer, and they all started shoveling dirt into the hole and onto the donkey."

The Switch Witch pulled from her black skirt pocket an embroidered hanky and dabbed the corners of her mouth. She slowly looked around the room, then continued. "The donkey had been shaking off the dirt that was being thrown on his back and every so often would take a step on the new pile of dirt. As the farmer and his friends watched in amazement, with each step the donkey was getting closer to the top of the hole. So, they started shoveling like mad until the donkey was able to walk out of the hole. The first thing the donkey did when he was free was to walk over to the farmer and bite him for trying to bury him alive. The farmer was so mad at his donkey that he bit him back."

The Switch Witch stood still, staring at Stiffy. After a respectful and well-practiced amount of time, Stiffy asked, "And your point, Hazel?"

"If you try to bury your problem, as sure as angels, it will come back and bite you in the ass."

The whole room went perfectly still. No one had ever heard the Switch Witch use profanity before, so it was a momentous occasion for the town of Junction. Or maybe she was simply referring to the donkey by its alternative appellation. It remains an enigma of great debate.

"Thank you, Hazel," Stiffy said. "Your thoughts are always appreciated."

The Switch Witch hadn't moved from the podium, so Stiffy finally asked, "Is there something else, Hazel?"

"I think you should name the new park Tent City," the Switch Witch said, then slowly made her way back to her seat.

Second Cup of Coffee

My bladder's exploding again while Monty, who apparently doesn't rent beer but buys it outright like he did his first-class ticket, looks at ease. When I get back to my seat, I chug the remains of my coffee and order another. Monty continues to sip his first cup as the cobwebs start to fade and he reconstructs into a single image.

Stiffy and her cohorts made elaborate plans for everything in the park, particularly for the museum, *Monty recommences.* They would highlight every ethnic group that had ever set foot in Junction, including indigenous peoples, Latinos, Middle Easterners, Indians, Asians—any contemporarily fashionable underrepresented identity they could think of. When the smoke cleared, they had included everyone except the obvious.

"So, you're going to honor the whole world ... except the people who actually built the railroads and this town?" The Fart asked defiantly.

"We believe the Fieldershmidt Clock will ... " Stiffy tried to explicate.

"We?" The Fart heckled. "What, do you have a mouse in your pocket?"

"Some of the members of council and I believe the Fieldershmidt Clock will recognize the people of your ilk," Stiffy misfired.

"Ilk!" The Fart screeched.

"H'ilk!" Hiccups echoed, sort of.

"Bad choice of words," Stiffy said. "Sorry. No offense intended. I should have said—"

"You should have said white people because that's exactly what you meant," The Fart seethed.

"Hic'solutely," hiccupped Hiccups.

I'm sure you can imagine how unpleasant that exchange was, and extremely disconcerting to the audience, which might not have been such a bad thing, except, as it turned out, it didn't really matter after all. They had started work on the park when ... what do you think happened? *Monty asked.*

I sit clueless.

When they set off that charge of dynamite, the blast must have shifted a whole lot of hollow ground that had been lying dormant, and with the added disruption of the new construction, three new sinkholes opened up. One of the holes ingested the half-built museum, another collapsed the almost-finished monkey cage, and the third swallowed what was to be the peace garden. That's when the DEP got involved and descended on the entire tract for research and study.

And thus ended the noble cause of Junction, Pennsylvania, to fix what wasn't broke ... except as an accelerant for power and money. In retrospect, I suppose Pimples's larceny and Stiffy's misguided crusade were just too much for the land to handle, and as the Earth always does to unpleasant interlopers, it shook them off like a dog shakes off fleas.

Third Cup of Coffee

I finish my last cup of coffee just as we're starting our approach into Philadelphia. Once on the ground, while re-

trieving our bags from the overhead compartment, I think to ask, Incidentally, Monty, do you have a nickname?

Well, you tell me," *he says.* My name is Montgomery Sledge Harding.

I think about the name for a moment, but Sledge commandeers my mental deliberation. And then, bam! It hits me: The Hammer, *I practically shout as we're making our way down the jet bridge.*

Monty gives me a big smile.

But never to your face, right?

He points a finger at me and winks.

I assume you're returning home, *I say.* Why were you in Chicago?

A judicial symposium titled "The Power of Justice vs. The Justice of Power," a real shillyshally dillydally if there ever was one, *he quips.*

My mind is churning like a cement mixer, and then it detonates. Wait a minute, *I practically shout.* Are you the judge?

I am *a judge, Monty says with a twinkle in his eye.*

Oh my God! *I exclaim before I can stop myself.*

We walk to the main concourse together while my head settles back down on my neck, and as we're about to part, I have one more question. By the way, *I say as casually as I can muster with AC/DC blasting away in my brain,* Whatever happened to the land?

Oh, PennDOT uses the holes to dump old, unrecyclable roadway. Actually, it's become quite a nuisance for Junction with intruders. You see, somebody put a sign where the main entrance to the Iron Horse Country Club used to be that reads, *Give me your tired, your poor, your huddled masses yearning to breathe free. Must bring your own tent.*

Holy hell, is the only thought I can manufacture in the agitating blender of my semi-debilitated semi-consciousness.

Thank God it's on the other side of the tracks, *Monty says as he disappears into the crowd.*

The Seagull

There were three of them on the beach, but there should have been four. The mother and the daughter sat in beach chairs. The seagull stood on the wet sand, nervously shuffling his webbed feet back and forth. He was watching the daughter, or more to the point, he was watching the tuna fish sandwich the daughter was holding, waiting for an opportune moment.

The daughter took a small bite of the sandwich while keeping her eyes on the gull. She'd had food pilfered out of her hand before by the aggressive predators the gulls had become—all those beachgoers and all that food, and the novice beachgoers barely pay attention.

How much of a novice is this girl? the gull calculated as he kept his eyes on the prize.

"I wish father was here," the daughter said to her mother without loosening her vigilance.

The mother was staring out to sea. "I know," she said.

The daughter watched the seagull as it watched her. "Shoo!" she shouted and took another nibble of her lunch. The daughter had come late to the mother and the father. They had tried for years and were about to give up hope when the mother became pregnant. The daughter was 10 years old, but people mistook her for much younger. That was because she was short for her age, but she possessed no shortage of certainty.

"I miss father already and it's only been about a week. He should be here," she said, petulantly defiant.

The mother didn't say anything. What was there to say?

Another bird landed a few feet from the girl but the seagull chased it off, protecting his territory.

"I hate seagulls," the daughter said. "I love to hear them and watch them soaring over the ocean, but I hate them."

"No, you don't," the mother said. "You don't like it when they take your food. Nobody likes it when somebody takes something away from them."

"Like father, you mean, don't you?"

The mother looked at her daughter.

"Why was father taken away?" the daughter asked her mother.

"He wasn't really taken away," the mother answered. "He's just not with us right now, is all."

The mother looked down the beach and saw a young boy—probably not much older than five or six—sitting in a low folding chair and eating a Creamsicle. A few gulls circled overhead. A portly man in baggy swim trunks stood by with a plastic Wiffle ball bat, and every time a gull came near, he would swing the bat and the bird would fly away.

How long can he protect his child like that? the mother pondered.

"I told father he should have an SOS meeting with Father, but I guess he didn't listen to me."

The comment jerked the mother out of her contemplative mood.

"When did you tell him that?" the mother asked, apprehensively.

"I don't know. Maybe a couple of weeks ago. He was upset about something, I don't remember what, but he was yelling at someone on the phone. I asked him what was wrong, and he said it was the capricious nature of being, that sometimes life is hard to figure out. That's when I told him to see Father for an SOS meeting."

Late in the just-ended school year, the daughter had completed a written science project that she stored on a thumb drive. The morning of the afternoon it was due, she realized she had forgotten to put the drive in her backpack. She panicked and decided to sneak out at lunchtime and run home to get it. She lived only a few blocks from her school, and if she crossed the park and cut through their backdoor neighbor's yard (a shortcut the daughter was forbidden to use), she could get home and back to school in about 15 minutes. She hoped she wouldn't be missed.

When she ran into her yard, she noticed that Father's bike was standing next to the back door. She didn't think much of it because Father had visited them before, for dinners or parties or other events. Father was a priest at Holy Redeemer, her family's church. He had been at Holy Redeemer for about 11 years, and he had become a popular fixture in the small town where he rode his bicycle everywhere he went. He liked to keep in shape and worked out regularly at the local gym. The daughter's father said Father worked out hard to compensate for being so short.

The daughter ran upstairs to grab her thumb drive. Coming out of her room, she saw her mother in the hall, looking around and adjusting her hair.

"I thought I heard something," the mother said. "What are you doing here?"

"I forgot my thumb drive and had to get it," the daughter said, out of breath. "Where's Father? I saw his bike out back."

"Does school know you left?"

"No, but I had to get my project—it's due this afternoon. Why's Father here?"

"Come on," the mother said. "I'll drive you back."

"No, that's okay. I can run back just as fast," the daughter said. "Why's Father here?"

The mother looked at the daughter for a moment. "He's here for an SOS meeting. Are you going to be in trouble?"

"No, not if I hurry. What's an SOS meeting?"

"It's a spiritual organizing session," the mother told her, a bit impatiently. "Father helps me stay spiritually connected. You better get going. If they say anything, you tell them I said it was all right."

The daughter had no idea what a spiritual organizing session was, or what it meant to be spiritually connected, but she knew her mother was happy after the visit from Father, and that's what she told her father—that he could be happy like mother was after an SOS meeting with Father.

The father worked for an insurance company in a nearby city, and he had a fixed schedule from which he never deviated. The mother could set her watch by the father's timetable, which she did, and was devastatingly surprised when he showed up unexpectedly in the middle of the day two weeks ago.

"He got mad at me when I explained about the SOS meeting," the daughter said. She turned her body toward her mother, spread her hands in a youthfully dramatic gesture of exasperation and said, "That wasn't like him at all. Sometimes I don't even know who my father is anymore."

The mother stared out to sea.

The seagull saw his chance. He swooped in on the daughter's outstretched hand and snatched the sandwich out of her grip.

The daughter screamed at the seagull as it took off, and the mother jumped up and ran after it—a futile effort, too little, too late.

The seagull alighted on a scarcely peopled section of the beach, dropped his treasure on the sand and began pecking at it. Rapidly, other seagulls descended upon him to fight over the half-eaten tuna fish sandwich, leaving the seagull with few spoils to show for his diligence.

And on it goes.

Uber

The Girl

The old man pulled his modest SUV next to the curb in front of the small medical center. The girl with an oversized purse and large hoop earrings dangling around her long box braids climbed into the backseat. It looked to the old man like she'd been crying.

"How are you today, Miss?" the old man asked the girl.

She mumbled an answer as the old man pushed a button on the screen and the address of her destination popped up.

"We're on our way. Should make it in about 15 minutes," the old man said.

The girl ignored him.

The old man looked in the rearview mirror and saw the girl dabbing her eyes with a tissue.

"Rough day?" he asked.

"Yeah," she said as her phone went off with some indistinguishable rap song.

"Uh-huh," she said into the phone. "Yeah, yeah, that's right," and her voice went up an octave on the word "right."

The old man could hear her crying.

"I don't know," she said. "I need to talk to him. I'm supposed to see him tonight. Not yet, no." And then she paused, apparently listening to whomever was on the other end of the conversation.

"No!" she yelled. "No way. Now look, after dinner I'll pack my stuff and sneak out when they go to bed. I'll text you when I'm leaving. Meet me at the laundromat."

She listened and then said, "No, the other one, the one that's open all night. On, um … oh, you know the street. I can't think right now."

The old man heard her sobbing.

"Okay," she said into her phone. "I'll see you later," and she paused again. "Thanks. I'll try," she said and disconnected the call.

They rode in silence for a bit.

"Are you okay, Miss?" the old man asked.

"Yeah, I'm just great," she said with a pronounced sarcastic undertone.

"Anything I can do to help?" he asked.

"Yeah, mind your own business," she said with absolutely no pronounced sarcastic undertone.

"I'm sorry," the old man said. "You're right. Please forgive me. I didn't mean to intrude."

"It's just such a mess," she sniveled. "I really messed up."

Trying to ease the tension, the old man asked, "Are you still in high school?"

"I graduated in June, and I'm supposed to start community college next month," she said, whimpering loudly.

"Whatever the problem, I don't think running away is the answer," the old man offered.

"What?" the girl said and bolted up straight. She looked at the old man for the first time and saw the thin graying hair on the back of his head. She looked in the rearview mirror and saw his eyes. They looked like they were … smiling. *Not twinkling or sparkling or any of that other hokey stuff,* she thought—they just looked like they were … well, smiling.

"How'd you know that?" she asked.

"I overheard your conversation and put two and two together, that's all," the old man said.

"Oh," the girl said. "Well, I can't face my father. He'll never understand. It's easier just to go away."

"Why do you say that?" the old man asked.

"He's very strict. He's Nazi strict. He's old school— real old school!"

"Do you have a boyfriend?" the old man asked.

"Yeah," the girl said.

"Can he help you with your problem?"

"I hope so."

"Is he a good guy?"

"Yeah, he's a really good guy," the girl said.

"It's my experience that good guys usually do the right thing," the old man said.

"I hope so," the girl said again.

"Well, keep a good thought."

"What?"

"Thomas Jefferson said, 'How much pain have costs us the evils which have never happened,'" the old man recited.

"Huh?"

"What he meant was, don't worry about things that might never happen. In other words, don't create your own problems."

"Is that what you think I'm doing?" the girl asked.

"Maybe," the old man said. "Take your father, is he usually supportive of you?"

"Oh, God, yes," the girl said. "Like when this teacher accused me of cheating on a test. I told my dad that I didn't cheat, and he believed me. He went to school with me and confronted the old witch. He made her show him my test and the guy's test I was supposedly cheating off of. I had two questions right that the other guy had wrong, and I had one wrong that he had right. My father asked her to grade the test, which she hadn't bothered to do because she just knew I was cheating and deserved an F, right? Ha! When she finished, I got a B and the other guy had a C. My father asked her why she thought I'd cheated, and she said we were sitting next to each other and I seemed to be looking his way."

"'If you look at these tests,' my father said, 'my daughter would have to be the greatest cheater in the history of cheaters because she got a better grade than the boy she cheated from. Obviously, you were mistaken.'"

"The teacher removed the cheating report from my record and gave me the B. On our way out, my father said to her, 'Judge people on what they do, not on what you think they do.'"

"Sounds like good advice," the old man said. "Maybe you should take it."

"Then there was last summer," the girl went on. "I really wanted to go to this party, but my father said absolutely not. It was at a boy's house who my father suspected ran with a gang, but he didn't, I swear. He liked to look tough and act tough, but he was afraid of his own shadow. Anyway, everybody was going but my dad wouldn't budge. So I snuck out and went and got caught. He grounded me for the rest of the summer— five freaking weeks! The man's a real nanderthol, or whatever that is."

The old man chuckled. "Your father sounds like he cares about you very much."

The girl sat sullen, crying again.

"You should give your father a chance," the old man said when they were stopped in front of her house. "Judge your dad on what he does, not on what you think he does."

"You think?" the girl said.

"I think," the old man said. "Sometimes problems have a way of turning into opportunities, and sometimes things that seem insurmountable turn out to be mole hills."

"Thank you," the girl said and got out of the car.

As the girl was walking toward her home, the old man rolled down his window. "You know," he said, "in my life, I've never been able to run away from problems. When I've tried, they followed me everywhere. And you know what? They only grew bigger. You can't outrun the boogeyman."

His eyes smiled at her, and she tried to smile back.

"Good luck," the old man said and pulled away.

When the girl walked into her house, her father and mother were sitting in the living room watching television. She went into the dining room and dropped her cumbersome bag with a thud on the old, scarred mahogany table. She took a deep breath and moved to the archway separating the two rooms in the old row house.

"Mama, Papa, I have something bad to tell you," she said through tears while her right hand played with a ring on her left hand. Her voice was shaking, but she tried to keep her composure, focusing on the far wall in the living room where a picture hung of Jesus surrounded by children.

Her parents looked at her and knew something terrible had happened. Her mother started to cry, crossed herself and sent a salutation to the deity. Her father sat frozen for a moment. Finally, he got up and walked to his daughter, put his arms around her and gave her a warm hug.

The Man

The man was waiting in front of a nice house in a nice neighborhood when the old man pulled up in front of him.

"How are you today?" the old man asked the man after he settled into the backseat, as they pulled away from the curb.

"Peachy keen," the man said, scrunching about in the backseat, trying to get comfortable.

"I can see from the destination on my screen that you're probably going to work," the old man probed.

"Exactamundo," the man replied.

"Do you like working second shift?" the old man continued.

"It beats being there when all the suits are in the building," the man said, snickering.

"Do they still wear suits?" the old man asked, incredulously.

"Nah. We just call 'em that because they're a bunch of freakin' butter-and-egg guys, real big-timers, if you know what I mean."

"I do, indeed," the old man said. "Do you always use Uber to go to work?"

"Car's in the shop. Needs a tire. Blew it out on my way home last night running over a pothole—blew out the whole side. Damn potholes. Can you believe it? Thank God the tire was under warranty. They can't get the one I need until tomorrow morning."

"What kind of tire is that?" the old man asked. "Must be a special order."

"It is," the man said. "A Michelin Pilot Sport 3 ZP. Costs about 500 bucks installed."

"My goodness, that's a lot for a tire."

"Not really. Hell, I could spend a thousand on it, if I were a big butter-and-egg guy," the man said and laughed.

"What kind of car do you drive?" the old man asked.

"A Vette, what else. Do I look like the kind of guy that'd drive a Toyota? Don't answer that," the man said and laughed again.

"No, sir," the old man rejoined. "You look exactly like the kind of guy who would drive a Corvette," and they laughed together.

"So, why do you hate your job?" the old man asked after they collected themselves.

"What? Where did that come from? What makes you think I hate my job?"

"Do you?"

"Well, yeah, but how'd you know?"

"I could sense it," the old man said. "It's in your demeanor and tone of voice."

"What are you, some kind of wizard? Yeah, I hate my job, every minute I'm there."

"What do you do?" the old man asked.

"It's a huge warehouse and I'm a floor supervisor. I'm kind of like a gasket: I keep the engine from seizing. I make sure the suits are happy and the migrants stay in line."

"Migrants?"

"I know, I know. It's a slur and probably racist and all that PC crapola."

"Why do you call them that?"

"Because a lot of them are Latino and they move around looking for work."

"Is that a bad thing?" the old man asked.

"Not really. I guess. You know, they got to feed their families," the man said.

"Are they good workers?"

"They're like everybody else. Some are good workers and some are bums. But that's true of all my workers, white, black, brown, male, female, whatever—loafing comes in all varieties. To be frank, the Latinos are probably my best workers. They're hungry, if you know what I mean."

"I think I do," the old man said.

"But really, they're good people. They bring me dishes from their native countries. And man, they're delicious. The food, not the workers," the man said and let out a resounding guffaw.

"Actually, it sounds to me like you're rather fond of them," the old man said.

"Maybe. I guess I am," the man said. "I just sort of lump them in with all the other nonsense."

"Like what?"

"Oh, we don't have time. Let me just say that it's a zoo and I'm the lion tamer."

"You're very colorful," the old man said. "Tell me something: Do they pay you to work there, or do you do it out of the kindness of your heart?"

The man laughed. "No, kindness of the heart is out of the question. Sure they pay me, and they pay me good. They better, for all the crap they throw at me."

"They must trust you a great deal if they're willing to give you all the crap that needs to be fixed."

"Yeah, they do, and for good reason. I'm good at fixing crap. I'm a real crap-master, the king of crap—ha, ha!"

"And are the facilities nice or is it just all full of crap?"

The man laughed again. "No, it's a real nice lay-out they have, very organized—clean and well lit, very modern. They keep it cool in the summer and warm in the winter—a good place to work."

"A place you hate," the old man chided.

"Yeah," the man said, quietly, like he was thinking about it.

"I guess you're running all over the building during your shift. Must get very tiring."

"Oh no. I have a nice office. I share it with the day- and night-shift floor supervisors, and I spend a good part of my day there working on a computer. If I need to go out in the warehouse, which I do several times a shift, I drive a golf cart."

"Tell me," the old man said, "do they make you work weekends and holidays? I know in this day and age, shipments of goods never stop."

"Some weekends and an occasional holiday, but it's usually at my choosing," the man responded. "I'm salaried, you know, but I get overtime for those extra hours—it's how I pay for expensive tires," he cracked wise.

"So, I'm guessing you don't get much time off."

"You're a piece of work, you know that," the man said to the old man. "I get plenty of time off: three weeks' vacation, five sick days, two floating holidays and one personal day. After all, I've been there almost 15 years. I've earned the time."

"Fifteen years!" the old man said and whistled. "You must really hate it to have stayed 15 years."

The man didn't say anything, just sat there mulling it over.

"What about benefits? Do they give you any real benefits, or do you have to pay through the nose for health care and retirement?"

"The health care is great. It's why I've stayed so long. I don't have to pay much every month for the coverage; the deductible is small and so are the co-pays. And they match everything I put into my 401(k)," the man said, and as he spoke, his voice became slower and lower.

"My, my," the old man said. "I can see why you hate that job—nice people to work with, bosses who trust you, good pay, overtime if you want it, a nice building to work in, your own office and a golf cart, terrific time off and fabulous benefits. I don't know how you endure it."

After a few moments, the man said, "I see, said the blind man," and he smiled. "You're a wise old man, aren't you?" he added as they stopped in front of his building.

The old man said to the man before he got out of the car and went into work, "All jobs are hard; that's why they call them jobs. Remember what Sir Francis Bacon wrote: 'In order for the light to shine so brightly, the darkness must be present.' In other words, take the good with the bad. Enjoy that Vette," the old man concluded and drove off.

After the man went through his emails and job reports, he pulled up his card statement online to check for the Uber charge. He was anal about his accounts (about everything, really) and always checked after he made a purchase.

Odd, he thought. There was no charge for the ride, which usually posted right away. "Must be a delay in the system today," he said out loud.

He spent the rest of his shift noticing people and things in a way that seemed different. He couldn't shake the feeling that something was peculiar, something disparate, but he couldn't put his finger on exactly what it was.

On his ride home, the Uber driver asked, "Shift over? How was your night?"

"Better than expected," he said. "Good. It was good." And that declarative answer caught him by surprise. "That's weird," the man said to himself. "Where'd that come from?"

When he got home, the first thing he did was check his statement for the Uber charges. The ride home already had posted, but still nothing from the ride into work. *Maybe that old man really is a wizard,* he mused as he poured himself a stiff drink.

The Little Boy

The old man pulled up in front of the veterinarian clinic. A woman and a boy came out of the building. The boy was carrying a small, oak box with a brass plate on the front. He was crying and the woman's eyes were red.

"Hello," the old man said to them once they were settled in their seats.

"Hi," the woman said, and then they rode in silence.

"Mommy, I don't want to bury him," the boy said to the woman after a few minutes. "Do we have to bury him? I want to keep him in my room."

"He was your dog, sweetie," she said, dabbing her eyes. "You may keep him anywhere you like."

"What was your dog's name?" the old man asked.

"Ralph," the boy said.

"I think Ralph is a fine name for a dog," the old man said. "And what kind of dog was Ralph?"

"Ralph was a good dog," the boy responded, sticking out his chin.

The old man chuckled. "I meant, what breed was he?"

"What do you mean?" the boy asked.

"He was a mixed breed," the woman offered.

After another brief pause, the boy started crying again and said, muffled through tears, "I didn't want Ralph to die."

The woman put her arm around the boy, and the old man asked, "Did I ever tell you about my dog?"

"I never knew you before," the boy said, sniffling and wiping his eyes with the back of his hand.

"You didn't? Are you sure? Well anyway, I had a dog who was a good dog, too."

"What was his name?"

"*Her.* Her name was Tink."

"Like Tinker Bell?" the boy asked with an uptick in his voice.

"Exactly! Tinker Bell was her full name, but I always called her Tink."

"Just like *Peter Pan*," the boy enthused. "That's my favorite movie."

"It is?" the old man asked. "Well, I'll be darned. Tink was a great dog. We'd run and play together all the time. Her favorite game was chasing sticks or balls I'd throw for her."

"Ralph, too!" the boy gushed. "I'd throw a stick and Ralph would chase it and chew it to smithereens."

"Wow, that's incredible because Tink loved to chew sticks to smithereens, too."

"What happened to Tink?" the boy asked.

"Well, unfortunately, like Ralph, she passed on."

"Were you sad?"

"I was heartbroken," the old man said. "It tore me apart, and I was in terrible pain."

"Me, too," the boy said.

"I was moping around and really feeling bad about everything, and then something happened."

"What?" the boy asked excitedly.

"Somebody, I don't remember who—it was so long ago—gave me a card with something written on it that changed everything. I was never again sad when I thought about Tink."

"What did it say?" the boy asked, bouncing in his seat.

"Why don't you read it for yourself. I just so happen to have one of those cards with me. Can you read?" the old man asked the boy as he reached into his shirt pocket and pulled out a card.

"Yes, I can read," the boy said and eagerly grabbed the card.

The card was decorated with colorful raised designs of a rainbow, a bridge and dogs running and playing. The boy studied the card, running his finger over the lithography, and said, "Wow, this is really cool."

"Go ahead and read it out loud," the old man encouraged.

The boy began to read: "Just this side of heaven is a place called Rain … bow Bridge. When an animal dies that has been es…, es…"

"Especially," the woman helped.

"Es…pechly," the boy continued, "close to someone here, that pet goes to Rain…bow Bridge. There are mmm…, mmm…"

"Meadows," she said slowly.

"…mead…dows and hills for all of our spe…, spe…"

"Sound it out," she said.

"…spe…"

"…sha," the woman coached.

"Here, Mommy," the boy said in frustration and handed the card to the woman. "You read it. It's too hard for me."

The woman took the card and read, "...meadows and hills for all our special friends so they can run and play together. The animals are happy and content, except for one small thing; they each miss someone very special to them, who had to be left behind. They all run and play together, but the day comes when one suddenly stops and looks into the distance. His bright eyes are intent. His eager body quivers. Suddenly he begins to run from the group, flying over the green grass, his legs carrying him faster and faster. You have been spotted, and when you and your..."

The woman stopped and thought for a moment.

"...when you and Ralph finally meet, you cling together in joyous reunion, never to be parted again. The happy kisses rain upon your face; your hands again caress the beloved head, and you look once more into the trusting eyes of your pet, so long gone from your life but never absent from your heart. Then you cross Rainbow Bridge together."

The woman was crying profusely by the time she finished reading.

"Is that true?" the boy asked.

"Only if you believe it," the old man said.

"What do you mean?"

"Do you believe in Santa Claus?" the old man asked the boy.

"Sure. Who doesn't believe in Santa Claus?"

"Well, hard as it may be to believe, there are people who don't. And do you know what they get from Santa? Zilch! Nada! Nothing! Not even coal in their stocking. You only get presents from Santa if you believe in Santa."

"I didn't know that," the boy said. "I believe the Rainbow Bridge is true and I want to go there now and see Ralph."

"Oh no, you can't go now," the old man said. "That would make Ralph very unhappy. You see, Ralph will be so excited to see you, but not for a long time. Ralph will be most happy if you live a long, long life first."

"Did you write it?" the boy asked.

"No," the old man said. "It's anonymous."

"Anon...a..."

"Anonymous," the old man repeated. "It means nobody knows who wrote it."

"Somebody had to write it," the boy said.

"Can you spell dog?" the old man asked the boy.

"Sure: d-o-g."

"Very good." Now spell it backward."

"G-o-d."

"What's that spell?" the old man asked.

The boy thought for a moment, then shouted, "God! You mean God wrote it?"

"I'm not saying that. I'm just saying that it's rather interesting, isn't it?" the old man asked.

"It sure is," the boy responded, then looked down to study the card some more.

When the old man stopped the car in front of an office building, the boy jumped over his mother and ran to a man standing in front of the building. The man swooped up the boy and gave him a hug. The boy was waving the card in front of the man's face, and the old man could see the boy's mouth going a mile a minute, his whole body animated with his head bobbing and weaving in excitement.

The woman leaned toward the front seat and said to the old man, "That was very kind of you. We've been trying desperately all week to cheer him up, to no avail.

But you, you were … well, unbelievable. Thank you so much."

She lowered her voice and added, "I couldn't say anything in front of my son, but we're meeting his father to go pick up a puppy. It's a surprise."

"That's wonderful," the old man said. "There's nothing in the world like a puppy to cure sorrow."

The woman got out of the car and walked over to join the man and the boy.

The kennel was an hour away, and as they drove up the long driveway into the farm, the boy could see lots of dogs running and playing in several big pens. They picked out an eight-week-old female golden retriever that the boy named Tinker Bell.

The Gambler

The old man drove through the huge parking lot in front of the car dealership and stopped next to the gambler who was looking around in confusion. The old man rolled down his window and asked, "Uber?"

"Oh, it's you," the gambler said. He got into the backseat and said, "I wasn't sure because nothing came up on my app about you or your vehicles. I didn't know what to look for."

"They seem to be having some problems with that," the old man offered. "How are you today?"

The gambler looked around the interior of the car and was less than impressed with its austerity. No indication that anybody owned the car, nothing other than drab gray. *But clean and well maintained,* he thought. *I'd have no trouble selling this one.*

"I'm good," the gambler said.

"Did you drop your car off?" the old man asked.

"No," the gambler responded, a bit indignantly. "I work here. I run the sales department for preowned cars."

"Oh, very good," the old man said. "I see you're going to the casino."

"Oh, yeah. Feeling lucky tonight!"

"What do you play?" the old man asked.

"Pontoon, baby," the gambler said.

"Huh?"

The gambler tittered. "Twenty-one, man. Blackjack, the game of fools," and he laughed again.

"You must be good at it."

"You know, some nights good, some not so good," the gambler said. "I try to play the percentages … in all things. That's why I Uber to the casino. No parking issues. You drop me off and pick me up at the front door, and I can have a few drinks and enjoy myself."

"You sound like an intelligent man," the old man said. "And lucky."

"That's me," the gambler said. "Lucky in war, lucky in love."

"Lucky in war?" the old man responded, bewildered. "Were you in the service?"

"Ha, ha! No. I was referring to war with my wife, where, actually, I have no luck at all. So, guess it's unlucky in war, unlucky in love."

"I'm sorry to hear that," the old man said.

"Don't worry about it," the gambler said. "I'm much luckier at blackjack, which is first and foremost on tonight's schedule."

"I thought the house always wins," the old man said.

"Usually they do," the gambler replied. "But you can lower those odds and even gain a little advantage—if you're smart."

"And you're smart?" the old man asked.

"Damn right. I always sit at third base and …"

"Third base?" the old man interrupted.

"That's the last seat to the right of the dealer, the last seat that gets dealt. If you sit there, you get to see what everybody else is doing before you have to make a decision. And if you're halfway astute, you can count the face cards and …"

"Face cards?" the old man interrupted again.

"Kings, queens, jacks. And tens, too, because they all count 10 points," the gambler explained. "If you count the face cards, which is relatively easy, even when they're using eight decks, you can figure fairly accurately your chances of busting."

"Busting?" the old man asked.

"Going over 21," the gambler said. "The idea is to have a higher point count than the dealer without going over 21."

"Sounds easy," the old man said.

"It is," the gambler said in a raised voice. "An easy way to lose all your money," and he laughed. "Really though, you don't have to lose all the time if you're careful. A good rule of thumb, sort of the golden rule of blackjack, is to hit on 16 and never hit on 17."

"I'll keep that in mind," the old man said. "Thanks."

"Don't mention it, but if I were you, I'd stick to the lottery. The odds stink, but you don't have to waste all your time doing it."

"Then why do you waste all your time doing it?" the old man asked.

"Because it beats the alternative," the gambler said.

"What's the alternative?"

"Being home with my wife. She ain't a happy camper these days."

"And why is that?" the old man probed.

"Well, let's just say we have a little problem."

"A little problem?"

"Yeah, only it isn't a little problem. It's a huge problem. And it isn't our problem. It's my problem."

"Oh?" the old man said. "In my experience, it generally takes two people to have a problem in a relationship."

"Right. There are definitely two people involved in the problem now, but I'm the one who started it all."

"How so?"

"I don't know why I'm talking to you about this. Are you some kind of psychologist or something?"

"Let's just say I'm something."

"You're a funny guy," the gambler said. "Look, it just happened. I don't even think I thought about it—it just happened."

"Stuff happens!" the old man inserted. "The battle cry of the self-inflicted."

"I am the self-inflicted, for sure," the gambler said, somewhat painfully. "I cheated on my wife. It was just a one-time thing and it didn't mean anything."

"It never seems to mean anything," the old man said. "But it always turns out to mean everything."

"You're very smart," the gambler said. "After it happened, the crazy bitch sent me a nude selfie. I didn't want it; I didn't ask for it. Hell, I was so consumed with guilt that I never wanted to see her again. But, as luck would have it—and I told you I have no luck in love— my wife saw the picture on my phone."

"Oh my. How did that happen?"

"I don't know. I thought I had it password protected, but I must have screwed it up."

"Hmmm, that's something to think about, isn't it?" the old man said.

"What do you mean? Do you think I let her see it on purpose?"

"I didn't say that."

"Yeah, but that's what you seemed to imply. Why would I do that?"

"Good question," the old man mused. "Why hadn't you deleted it?"

The gambler stared at the back of the old man's head. "Good question."

The old man looked in the rearview mirror and the gambler appeared pensive.

"It's all because of Bruce Springsteen," the gambler confided.

"How's that?"

"I love Springsteen's music, but my wife hates everything about him. Still, she buys me his albums all the time for my birthday and Christmas. Then, when I play them, she gets all pissy and makes my life miserable. Talk about self-inflicted behavior," the gambler said, nodding his head up and down.

"So, you cheated on your wife because she wouldn't let you listen to Bruce Springsteen?"

"Okay, that sounds stupid, but that's just one thing in our relationship. There were many other things, too."

"Did you two ever try counseling?"

"No. She wanted to, but I wouldn't do it."

"Why not?"

"Because I didn't want to sit around telling some stranger about our problems."

"And yet, here you are."

"Yeah, I know. Real irony at play here, wouldn't you say?"

"Yes, I would say," the old man responded whimsically. "Where's your relationship at now?"

"In the crapper," the gambler said dejectedly. "She's barely speaking to me, other than to tell me to get out and she's contacting a lawyer."

"Has she contacted a lawyer?"

"No, not yet, but she keeps threatening."

"And what do you say when she threatens that?"

"Nothing. I don't know what to say."

"Do you want to stay together?" the old man asked the gambler.

"Yes."

"It sounds to me like she does, too."

"Do you think?" the gambler asked the old man.

"Well, she hasn't called a lawyer yet."

"So what do I do? How do I fix this?"

"By overcoming your fear."

"My fear? What are you talking about? What am I afraid of?"

"Oh, I don't know. Getting hurt, maybe?"

"I'm already hurt. I hurt myself, and now she's turning the screw."

"And you're afraid to take a leap of faith and risk getting hurt some more, would be my guess," the old man said.

The gambler sat still with his head down as the old man drove up to the casino entrance.

Before the gambler got out of the car, the old man said, "A Chinese proverb says, 'Pearls don't lie on the seashore. If you want one, you must dive for it.' In other words, sometimes you have to hit on 17, my friend."

The gambler stood in front of the blackjack table trying to make up his mind. Eventually, the woman sitting at first base got up and left, and the gambler took her seat. He'd never sat on first base before. After a few hands, the gambler drew a 17. When the dealer asked him what he wanted to do, the gambler sat immobilized. When the dealer asked him again, the gambler looked up and said, "Hit me." Everyone at the table groaned, and the man sitting on third base mumbled under his breath, "Amateur night."

The dealer smiled at the gambler and slowly turned over the card. It was a four, giving the gambler 21. The gambler jumped up and raised his arms in the air, crying out a loud war yell. He danced a little jig, cashed in his chips and went home to try to hit on 17 again.

The Old Lady

The old man maneuvered his small SUV along the circular driveway in front of the hospital, stopping at the waiting area. The waiting area was empty this time of day, so his was the only car there. An orderly wheeled the old lady through the large revolving door and helped her into the backseat of the old man's car. The old lady looked frail and was crying.

"A pleasant good evening, madam," the old man said.

"Oh, yeah? What's pleasant about it?" the old lady responded and blew her nose.

"I suppose that's a matter of perspective," the old man said. "I didn't mean to be offensive."

"I'm sorry," the old lady said softly. "I'm afraid I'm not very good company tonight. I get like this whenever I find out I'm dying. Big joke, eh?"

"Your witticism belies your pain, I'm sure," the old man offered.

"Pain?" she said. "Oh yes, pain. I'm good at pain. Pain from the poison eating away my body. Pain from the poison they dump in my body to kill the poison that's eating away my body. It's a race between the two poisons to see which will kill me first. I'm betting on the cure."

"Are you going through this alone?" the old man asked.

"My son and one of my daughters are flying in over the next couple of days. All three of my children live in different states, so it's not easy for them to help. But they will be coming in and out over the next month to help pack up the house they grew up in and that I've lived in for 58 years. Then we'll sell it and I'll go into assisted living. Or straight to hospice, if I'm lucky."

"Why would that be lucky?"

"Because they give you lots of morphine in hospice, and boy, I do love morphine." The old lady giggled while wiping her eyes.

"In spite of it all," the old man said, "you seem to have a pretty good attitude."

"But I don't. I really don't. It's all subterfuge. I'm sad, so very, very sad. It's all so sad," the old lady lamented. "Death is a cold mistress."

"You sound literary," the old man probed.

"I taught high school English for more than 35 years," she said.

"Did you enjoy doing that?"

"I loved it," the old lady said, smiling. "I could have retired earlier, but I stayed until they kicked me out the door, right on my ass," and she giggled again, louder.

"Oh my, that must have hurt."

"It did, but nothing compared to this." She grew quiet and her demeanor changed—she seemed to physically withdraw into herself.

"Are you okay?" the old man asked.

"No, I'm not okay. I'm dying. I thought you may have picked up on that by now."

"I did. Please forgive me. You have every right to be sad. And depressed. And angry," the old man said. "Not that I'm the arbiter of how you should feel, but you're entitled to feel however you want to feel."

"It's my party and I'll die if I want to, die if I want to, die if I want to," the old lady sang, and she perked up a little.

"Exactly," the old man said. "Is your husband still with you?"

"No, he passed seven years ago." The old lady paused as if thinking about what she had just said. "Seven years is a long time to be alone, to be lonely, isn't it?"

"It certainly is, especially if you miss someone you cared about."

"Oh, I did. We did. We cared deeply for each other. We had a wonderful life together: three children who grew up to be good people, a slew of grandkids and even a couple of great-grandchildren. Don't misunderstand, our marriage wasn't all peaches and cream. Like all relationships, we had our ups and downs. But all in all, I think we did well—we were happy," and she smiled broadly.

"You seem to have wonderful memories," the old man said.

"I do. I do. I have wonderful memories. I had a good life."

"You *have* a good life," the old man corrected.

"I'm not so sure of that anymore," the old lady said. "May I tell you a secret?" she asked the old man.

"By all means," the old man replied.

"I'm scared to death. Oh, that's an amusing idiom for my situation, isn't it? Scared to death—that's almost funny. What I meant to say was that I'm scared *of* death—terrified!"

"Almost everybody is," the old man offered. "It's the unknown, and that can be petrifying."

"I don't want to die," the old lady said, sniffling again. "But at the same time, part of me is ready to move on—to what, though? That's what frightens me so."

"Let me ask you this," the old man said. "Do you believe in God?"

"Yes, I do, although I don't know who or what God is, to be honest. I look at the world and I think God must be schizophrenic or a sociopath."

"There is an ancient Greek philosophy that sees God as The Prime Mover, the mover of all life and the ultimate good. It's proffered in that philosophy that all mankind aspires to be like The Prime Mover; that is, aspires to move toward The Good. You can interpret that theory to mean there is no evil, only evil acts, and they are perpetrated in the pursuit of The Good. In other words, all people are always trying to move toward The Good, but some simply get lost along the way. You then might extrapolate that The Good is really what we think of as love—we all want love, and we spend our entire lives trying to find and keep love. People choose different methods to achieve that, some sublime and some grotesque, but we're all trying to get to the same place," the old man said, then hesitated.

"So, God is great, God is good, like we learned in Sunday school," the old lady said somewhat grimly.

"God is whatever you perceive Him, or Her, to be. It really doesn't matter how the Deity manifests itself; what matters is why you're here and where you're going."

"Why are we here then?" the old lady asked.

"That ancient Greek philosophy I spoke of would lead you to believe it's to do good—to love and to be loved. It seems so simple, but it's so very hard to do."

"It really is," the old lady agreed. "And now, where are we going? That's the $64,000 question."

"Please allow me to give you a quick lesson in science, Miss School Teacher," the old man teased.

"Be my guest, be my guest, be my guest. I'm all ears. And tears. Hey, I'm a poet and I don't know it," she said and giggled.

"The law of thermodynamics," the old man began, "states that the energy of a closed system must remain constant—it can neither increase nor decrease without interference from outside. The universe itself is a closed system, so the total amount of energy in existence has always been the same. The forms that energy takes, however, are constantly changing. One of those forms is the human ... what shall we call it? ... the human spirit, and since energy can neither be created nor destroyed, the real question is what happens to that energy once you 'shuffle off this mortal coil.'"

"Good question," the old lady said. "And what's the answer? I think you know, don't you? Please tell me," and she grew more serious.

"Hmmm," the old man sighed. "Here's what I can tell you: Whatever you believe happens to you is exactly what happens to you."

"How so?" she asked.

"Look, you have no way of knowing what happens after you die. It's something the brain isn't capable of knowing; it's beyond its corporeal capabilities. Mankind has wasted so much time and precious energy trying to figure out the unfigurable instead of doing good in the here and now. Ergo, since you have no way of knowing what's next, stop wasting time worrying about it—it's a poor use of your time. Believe what you believe and be at peace."

"That's not satisfying," the old lady said. "I want to know the truth."

"Do you remember what Glinda told Dorothy before she clicked the ruby slippers?" the old man asked the old lady.

"Yes. She said, 'You've always had the power, my dear.'"

"Dear lady," the old man said, "you've always had the power."

"I have?"

"Look into your heart. Look deep, past all the false prophets and noise, and there you will find your truth. But the journey begins with faith in yourself, and that's the biggest leap, and the hardest to do."

"You're a wise man, aren't you?" the old lady said when they pulled into her driveway. "Thank you for your kindness."

Before the old lady could get out of the car, the old man turned in his seat and looked at her. She was a bit surprised by his remarkably ordinary looks. His face was oval with the slightest outline of jowls and laugh lines around his eyes. His nose and ears were proportionate to his other features, and his eyebrows were gray and thick, but not bushy. The most notable thing about his countenance, she thought, was its total lack of any distinguishing characteristics. He looked exactly like everyman. It's not that she was disappointed, but she had expected to see a more sagacious, radiant appearance.

The old man smiled and said to her, "Have a good life."

"I'm going to try," she said and started to climb out. When she was halfway out of her seat, she turned and said to the old man, "Would you like to come in for a cup of tea?"

"I would like nothing more, madam," the old man said. "But there's one more waiting for me."

"You have another ride to pick up?"

"Yes, I do."

"Well then, thank you very much for the conversation. I think you may have helped me."

"You're more than welcome," the old man concluded as he put the car in gear.

The old woman went into her kitchen and put the kettle on the stove, and, while she waited for the water to boil, pulled up her Uber app because she wanted to give the old man a bigger tip. Unfortunately, she couldn't figure it out and castigated herself for being such a dinosaur. She called the Uber help line, and when a customer service representative came on, the old lady explained that she had just taken an Uber trip and would like to tip the driver. The rep gave her the obligatory and tedious salutations from a script and asked the old lady if she could hold while he looked up the trip. After a few minutes, he came back on the line and told the old lady that he couldn't find it, that Uber had no record of such a trip.

"Are you sure it was Uber?" the rep asked.

"I'm quite sure," the old lady said. "The only car service I use is Uber, so it had to be Uber. You must have a record of it."

"I'm sorry," the rep said, "but I've searched thoroughly and there was no trip. Must be a glitch in the system. Looks like you got a free one. Lucky you."

"Yes, lucky me," the old lady said and hung up. A smile radiated from her entire body.

The Drunk

The old man pulled in front of the stylish bistro and waited by the entrance. Eventually the drunk came bouncing out the door with a swagger and a stagger, threw himself into the backseat and yelled, "*Que pasa*, dude? How's it hangin'?"

"So much for sang-froid," the old man said, laughing.

The drunk was dressed sharply in pressed khaki slacks, blue sport coat, white shirt and tie.

"Looks like you're coming from a formal affair," the old man said.

"I don't know about the formal part, but I took my best shot at an affair," the drunk said.

"What do you mean?"

"I was talking to this really pretty woman and I thought I was doing okay, but all she wanted to talk about was motorcycles and how much she loves motorcycles and how much she loves guys who ride motorcycles and how much she loves riding on the back of a motorcycle with her legs wrapped around a guy driving a motorcycle. Now, if that's not a come-on, I don't know what is, legs wrapped around a guy and coming right out and saying it like that. A real come-on, right?"

"I'm not good at interpreting bar talk," the old man said.

"Well, take my word for it. I know all about bar talk and that was definitely a come-on. And then she asked if I have a motorcycle and I told her no, I don't have a motorcycle because I don't need a motorcycle. So, she said what do you mean, and I said I don't need a motorcycle because I'm perfectly happy with the size of my penis."

"Oh," the old man said. "I'm sure that worked well."

"Not so much," the drunk said. "She just walked away without saying a word. She didn't even ask to see it," and he laughed so hard he tilted to one side.

"You're in a jolly mood," the old man said.

"Definitely. I feel pretty good," the drunk said. "Was at a business networking event and met a couple of prospects, so it was a good night."

"Except for the motorcycle girl who wasn't interested in your manhood."

"Ha! You're pretty cool for an old guy," the drunk said. "But what's up with your name? No name or car description came up on my app. What's that about?"

"There appears to be some technical problems tonight."

"So what's your name?"

"What do you think my name is?" the old man asked the drunk.

"Fred! I think your name is Fred."

"Then I'm Fred."

"Okey-doke. Home, Fred," the drunk bellowed, quite pleased with himself.

"We're well on our way, sir."

After a short time, the old man asked the drunk, "Are you in sales?"

"Yepper," the drunk responded. "How'd you know?"

"You're dressed well, and you mentioned meeting prospects."

"I wear it well, eh? Yeah, I'm a salesman. Me and Willy Loman in the basement with the pipe."

"My goodness," the old man said, rather startled. "That's a dark image. Are you not happy with your position?"

"Nah, I love being a salesman. Can't you tell?"

"Not right off, no," the old man said. "What would you rather be doing?"

"I'd rather be rich and sailing all over the Caribbean on my yacht," the drunk said and snickered.

"I thought you were going to say you'd rather be a writer."

The drunk stopped laughing and sat up. He looked at the old man's eyes in the rearview mirror, but he could detect no malevolence.

"Why'd you say that?" he finally asked the old man.

"To be perfectly honest with you, no, you don't wear salesman well at all, but you do look like a writer," the old man said. "And you're very witty—good with words."

"You messing with me, old man?"

"By no means. I'm being honest with you."

Neither spoke for a while, and eventually the old man asked, "Why did you stop writing?"

The drunk shook his head back and forth. "Because I sucked. Pretty much everybody told me I sucked."

"I find that hard to believe," the old man soothed.

"Really? People used to line up to tell me how much I sucked. It was really quite unpleasant, quite painful," the drunk snorted. "I wrote a lot in college and submitted stories and poems to so many literary magazines that I lost count. I keep one of the rejections pinned to the wall over my desk. It was written in red ink on a scrap of paper and merely said, 'Sorry!'"

"That's callous. It must have hurt," the old man said.

"Oh yeah. I got real good at being hurt. Like when the writing award my senior year was given to someone else after I was pretty much assured it was mine to have. When I confronted the professor, he said I didn't need it—I had so much going for me and it would do the other person much more good."

"And did it do the other person much more good? What became of that person, do you know?"

"She went to Johannesburg and became a teacher. She didn't write, but she helped a lot of children who needed help. I, on the other hand, sold my soul and became a peddler, a pusher of shit."

"You're very hard on yourself," the old man said.

"And then my mother, my own mother!" The drunk paused with tears in his eyes.

"What happened with your mother?"

"I was in my last semester, a month or so before graduation, and my mother asked me what I wanted to do when I got out of college. I told her I wanted to be a writer, and she said, 'Oh no, not a writer. Everything's already been written.' You know, she never read anything I wrote, showed no interest at all," the drunk said as his voice trailed off.

"I'm sorry," the old man said.

"Why are you sorry? You didn't tell me I suck. Not yet, anyway," and the drunk laughed again through his tears.

"I'm sorry for the pain you suffered, both from rejections and from not writing. Not writing must be very painful for you."

"What are you, Fred? Some kind of clairvoyant or soothsayer?"

"I simply believe you're an interesting man with a lot to say that people want to hear, that's all."

"Well, you're the first then. Everybody else thinks I suck."

"Including you?"

"Oh, here we go. Jimmy Buffet's it's my own damn fault. Is that where this is going? Is that why you came into my life tonight, Fred? Well, you want to know something, Fred, since you find me so fucking interesting? It is my fault—it's my own damn fault!" and the drunk sat in the backseat crying like a newborn.

The old man waited, then said, "Good writing is hard. It very well may be the hardest thing in the world to do. You sit over a keyboard all by yourself and lay it out there for anybody to stomp all over. It's hard to trust yourself enough to share your heart. It's a huge risk to take after the arduous process of creating something out of whole cloth. Ernest Hemingway said, 'There is nothing to writing. All you do is sit down at a typewriter and bleed.'"

The drunk wiped his eyes and started to get out of the old man's car, now parked in front of the drunk's house.

"There's only one way to stop the pain," the old man said.

"Oh yeah? What's that?" the drunk asked the old man.

"What do you think?"

"I don't know," the drunk said, looking extremely tired. "I'll think about it later. Thanks for your interest. Seriously."

As the drunk slowly made his way up the walk, the old man rolled down his window and said to the drunk, through a smile, "Go, bleed."

The drunk caught the old man's smile like a shot of whiskey, feeling it spread through his body in a warm surge as the old man disappeared into the darkness.

The drunk brewed a pot of strong coffee and carried it into his home office. He sat in front of his computer drinking his first cup and staring at the blood-red letters printed on the scrap of paper pinned to the wall over his desk. "Sorry" reverberated through him like a blinding neon light, blinking its message deep and pervasive. He rubbed his eyes, put down the cup and bled:

She sat cross-legged on the floor in front of the anachronistic monstrosity trying to decide what to do. Should she open it and chance the release of who knows what dramas—what new sufferings—or let the auction company haul it away, unopened and safe, along with the other well-worn, barely salvageable furniture in her father's home office? The black, ponderous box with "Alpine Safe & Lock Co., Cincinnati, O. U.S.A." in gold, 19th-century script spread symmetrically around the door handle and dial, had been in the corner of the office since before she could remember, sitting like an inscrutable Buddha, collecting dust and lives.

What was it that Hal, her father's young law partner, had told her in one of their conversations about settling her father's affairs? "There are some things people aren't meant to see..."

Acknowledgments

Writing and publishing a book is no easy task, and it takes a cadre of talented folks to help push one over the finish line. Accordingly, I'd like to thank several individuals who are really good pushers:

To Brenda Lange, Kerry Boderman and Bill Kline, my editors who always make me look smarter than I am.

To Dina Hall, who designed the book cover thematically exact, as usual.

To Danielle Pizzino and Zachary Hartzell of Blank Creative for the great cover photo and my covertly deceptive head shot.

To John Hayes, my first reader and golf buddy. His criticisms are always spot on; his golf tips always cost me money.

To my publisher, Jennifer Bright, who has a knack for helping me see the light and whose cherry disposition is a light unto itself.

To Stephen King for giving me the idea for "Dick and Jane."

To the late literary agent Kae Tienstra, who helped me rediscover my passion and gave me the first push.

To Vincent Fazio, who introduced me to Kae Tienstra, and who generously pushed me along to finish this thing.

To my wife, Terry, for enduring the deranged, fire-breathing dragon of letters (as in, dragging out letters) within.

And, finally, to you holding this book. Thank you most of all.

About the Author

Richard Plinke graduated with high honors from Rutgers University, Camden College of Arts and Science with a Bachelor of Arts degree in English, which explains how he ended up in advertising sales for 40 years. Along the way, he founded and operated three media companies, trained countless salespeople and has been a motivational speaker. Mr. Plinke has published three critically acclaimed books on sales in the Dragon series and a collection of Facebook posts during the pandemic's lockdown, titled *COVID 19: House Arrest.* This is his first book of fiction. Mr. Plinke lives in the real Allentown, Pennsylvania, (not the fictitious one in the song) with his wife, Terry, and dog, Luna.